ASTRAY

A Fox Walker Novel

Indy Quillen

This is a work of fiction. All names, characters, places, and incidents are products of the author's imagination or are used fictitiously and are not to be construed as real. Any resemblance to actual events, locales, organizations, or persons, living or dead, is entirely coincidental.

ASTRAY

Copyright © 2022 by Indy Quillen

Cover design by James T. Egan of Bookfly Design
Formatting by Polgarus Studio

All Rights Reserved

For information address Treeline Press, 16212 Bothell Everett HWY Ste F #212, Mill Creek, WA 98012

Treeline Press, Mill Creek, WA

ISBN: 0997777789
ISBN: 9780997777789
Library of Congress Control Number: 2022904748

Printed in the United States

Treeline Press paperback edition / April 2022

eBook edition / April 2022

Praise for Astray: A Fox Walker Novel

"*Not everyone who goes missing is lost ... or wants to be found.* Wisdom from Fox Walker.
ASTRAY: A Fox Walker Novel. It's intense. It's compelling. And it's suspenseful story-telling at its finest. Author Indy Quillen has outdone herself with her latest offering in the Fox Walker book series."
—LAURA TAYLOR, 6-Time Romantic Times Award Winner

"*Astray* is Indy Quillen's finest novel to date—and her wildest, in every sense of the word. When Fox Walker and Nataya are forced out of their most treasured comfort zones, they must contend with both the unfamiliar wilderness of the Pacific Northwest and the intrusion of a third tracker into their team of two. On top of that, they are not the only ones following their quarry—a young woman who is doing everything she can to not be found."
—MARK A. CLEMENTS, Award Winning author of *The Land of Nod & Lorelei*

"Indy has a fantastic way of grabbing the authenticity of real life search and rescue, survival, mystery and suspense that puts you on the edge of the cliff, wondering what's next."
—CARL LACASSE, former Search and Rescue Team Captain

To the dedicated volunteers of Search and Rescue Teams serving throughout our country.

And as always, to Michael Q

Author's Note

The Fox Walker stories are based on real locations in and around the Rocky Mountains and San Juan Mountain Range in Colorado, as well as the North Cascades in the state of Washington, but please know that many of the names of places are as fictionalized as the characters who inhabit them. Also, although much research went into the understanding of the Ute nation and its culture, as well as their use of the Shoshone language, the Fox Walker character is a creation of my imagination and a work of fiction based on my life-long fascination with the Native American culture. Thus, I did take certain liberties in that creation and use of the language. As for the tracking and wilderness survival skills Walker possesses, these are based on real skills and knowledge many dedicated survivalists use and have shared with others.

A special thank you to Carl LaCasse for his time and his gracious offer to share his knowledge garnered from years of volunteering for search and rescue teams, and serving as a Search and Rescue Team Captain. His expertise was an invaluable asset in creating authenticity for this story, and I appreciate his willingness to allow me to share some of his experiences through my fictious character. While working with Carl, I gained insights and a great admiration for the dedicated individuals who serve in SAR teams all over our country.

CHAPTER ONE

Skagit River, Washington (Day One)

Amazing how quickly a perfect day could veer off course …

Dean McClure cast his fishing line and watched it lazily deliver his hand-tied fly to the exact location he desired, a deep pocket of still water. The ideal spot for steelhead to rest from the strong current of the rushing Skagit River.

Overhanging tree boughs along the shoreline offered shade, protection from predator birds and increased the chance fish lay beneath the surface. He smiled while working his rod and reel, the fly following the eddies of water. Indeed, Dean couldn't fathom a more perfect place to be than in his waders, knee deep in the surging stream of snow melt waters from the North Cascade Mountains of Washington, miles from civilization.

Sunlight warmed his back and danced upon the liquid crystal waters, creating a kaleidoscope of colored stars. With the white noise of the waters filling his senses, he had let his mind wander free of worldly concerns, and instead allowed a moment of bliss to settle around him.

But a persistent sound soon intruded and drew him from the

fog of contentment back to the present. Reluctantly, he turned his head toward the commotion, only to spot a man on the distant shoreline. A man wildly waving his arms over his head and shouting Dean's name.

Well, that can't be good.

Dean focused his full attention on not losing his footing on the slippery rocks as he worked his way across the strong current of the river.

The man waiting on shore had ceased his arm waving once he had Dean's attention. Instead, he paced back and forth along the edge of the raised bank and stopped often to check on Dean's progress, only to resume pacing. Deep shadows beneath the trees kept Dean from being able to clearly see the man's features, only the man's dress slacks and shirt.

Various scenarios ran through Dean's mind while he made as much haste as deemed safe under the circumstances. How had anyone even found him? And for what reason? He'd been retired from the Bureau for what seemed ages now. And his last consulting job had been a couple of years ago, when he'd worked with Fox Walker in Colorado to clear Matt Logan's name.

Dean mumbled under his breath in discontent while he navigated a particularly tricky spot in the river. Once he successfully cleared that section, he glanced up. Discontent dissolved into apprehension. Closer now, he recognized the man Steve Hicks, an FBI Agent from the Seattle Bureau. Dean stared a moment. He and Steve shared a history at the Bureau and had become fishing buddies after Dean's retirement. But the case in Colorado had cemented their friendship.

Dean lowered his head to again concentrate on crossing the water. Steve tracking him down at his favorite fishing spot didn't bode well, considering Steve wasn't dressed for fishing. What could this be about?

When he made it to the shoreline Steve reached out a strong hand. The younger man hauled Dean up the steep incline of the riverbank until they stood facing each other.

Before Dean could catch his breath, Steve spoke in a rush of words.

"I can't believe my luck—that you're really here! I mean, what are the odds? But I had to try, since I was nearby."

He watched Steve take a breath and calm himself before speaking again.

"I'm sorry to interrupt your fishing, Dean, I really am. You know I wouldn't bother you if it wasn't urgent."

Dean still tried to wrap his thoughts around why Steve would be nearby, and what could possibly be so urgent. But what tumbled out of his mouth was, "How'd you know I'd be at this particular location?"

"I didn't. But I remembered you liked to frequent that little fly-fishing shop near Lost Lake where I happened to be. I stopped in there and the owner confirmed you'd been in earlier. He said you mentioned heading out to this spot. I still can't believe my good fortune."

Dean inhaled another gulp of air and straightened up. It wasn't that he'd not kept in shape in retirement, but more that his body liked to remind him of his age. "What's this all about, Steve? You know I'm retired and enjoying it."

Steve shifted his stance. "This isn't a request from the Bureau. This is a request from me."

He watched Steve's eyes go dark with worry, but what concerned Dean more was the edge of panic he saw flickering along the edges. Not good. He waited.

"It's my daughter, Dean. Katie's gone missing."

CHAPTER TWO

Elk Meadow, Colorado (Day One)

Fox Walker put aside his knife and the piece of wood he had been carving, brushed away the shavings, and stood to stretch. He and Nataya were enjoying a well-deserved break following a busy season of courses for their Wilderness Survival School. After an early morning breakfast on the front porch they decided to extend the relaxing moment by working on some projects, while savoring the late summer weather … and the view.

He gazed out over the lake in front of the log cabin. Autumn would arrive soon enough. But for now, the waters reflected the intense blue Colorado sky as dark mountains reared up majestically from the surrounding meadows and woodlands. A scene he never grew tired of. And never took for granted.

Nataya looked up from her hand-sewing project and gave him a warm smile. The years had not dimmed the love he saw reflected in her eyes and felt in his own heart.

Hard to believe three years had passed since he'd discovered her living alone in the wilderness with no memory of her past and no desire for a rescue. He'd had to gain her trust first before he could save her from a serial killer. But his greatest reward had been when she regained her memories and decided to remain as Nataya. And to remain with him. She'd even managed to repay him by saving his life twice since they'd met.

He leaned over to study her work. "Looks as if you've finished."

"Yes, I just completed attaching the strap." She held up the shoulder satchel for him to examine.

His fingers brushed over the velvety soft, yet sturdy buckskin hide. "A work of art, yet functional. It's beautiful."

"Thanks. I'm pleased with how well it turned out." She stood, slipped the long strap over her head, and draped it across her torso, the satchel hanging at her left hip. "During our longer excursions into the wilds, I've often wished for something to store items in. Something smaller than a knapsack and less cumbersome than a carry basket. I think this will prove useful."

She removed the bag and held it to her face, inhaling the campfire aroma remaining in the hide from the smoking process. "My favorite part of working with buckskin is the wonderful smokey smell … well, that and working with the soft, pliable hide. Of course, there's also the hand sewing part." She grinned. "Okay, so I love all aspects of it equally."

Walker smiled and nodded. Then noticed she waited, watching him with an expectant look, so he added, "I'm thankful you enjoy it so much." She smiled, but still watched him in silence. He'd seen this hopeful expression more often lately during their conversations. It was something new, and he didn't quite know what she expected but found himself continuing the discussion. "You know, over the years I've made lots of functional pieces from the hides I tanned, but you bring an entirely new level of artistry to it." He slid his arm around her shoulders.

She looked up at him. "I know it's important to you, to not waste any part of an animal or bird that gives up its spirit that we might survive. Adding an element of beauty to the project is my gift of gratitude."

Walker turned into her arms, seeing her smile of contentment. He lifted her chin, gazing into those lovely cornflower blue eyes, and leaned in for a kiss. A moment later he heard the phone ring inside. "Never fails, does it?" He grimaced. "I better get it." They rarely received phone calls unless someone needed their help.

He opened the screen door and strode toward his corner desk. The ancient rotary dial phone had recently been replaced with a newer landline phone with voicemail and other fancy features. He hadn't really made peace with it yet. He noticed Nataya followed him in.

"Walker here."

"Walker, Dean McClure."

"Dean, it's great to hear your voice. It's been a while." He looked at Nataya, saw he had her attention.

"Yeah, too long. I hope you and Nataya are doing well? The Wilderness Survival School still keeping you busy?"

"Yes, and yes. Just finished our final summer course and have a break right now."

"Good to hear, on both accounts."

Walker waited for a heartbeat before he remarked, "Must be something pretty important that pulled you away from fishing?"

Dean chuckled, but it contained no humor. "You know me a little too well, and you have no idea how close to the mark you are with that comment. Yeah, I've got an urgent, time-sensitive request for you and Nataya."

"Sounds serious." He glanced at Nataya and switched to the speaker phone. "Fill me in."

"We've got a twenty-eight-year-old missing female as of early this morning here in Washington, the North Cascade Mountains. More specifically the Mt. Baker-Snoqualmie National Forest."

Walker grabbed a pen and paper and started to take notes.

Dean continued. "The missing woman's father is Steve Hicks, an FBI agent I know. In fact, you might remember him. He's the guy who brought in a team via helicopter to extract you, Nataya and Matt Logan from the wilderness."

"Yes, I remember him. He made sure Matt made it to the hospital to see his brother and his teammate."

"Yeah, that's the guy."

"So this is an FBI request?"

"No. It's a personal request. Steve's daughter, Katie, has been staying in a cottage on Lost Lake most of the summer. She was supposed to join her friends for a scheduled hike this morning at dawn. But when they arrived at her cottage, Katie didn't answer the door. Her Jeep was still parked beside the cottage. One of the gals called Steve. He told them where the spare key was, so they could get in and check on Katie. She was gone, as well as her backpack and hiking boots. Steve and I are here at the cottage now and the scene definitely points to her having left for the wilderness."

Walker paused in his note taking. "What's the chance that Katie simply decided to take off by herself and forgot to let anyone know?"

"None. Steve says he and Katie have been super tight ever since his wife passed when Katie was in high school. They have a pact—one she's never broken. Whenever she's going into the wilderness alone, she either signs in for the trail at a ranger station, or lets Steve or friends know where she's going. And her hiking buddies say she'd never take off like this without leaving them a note."

"But she did."

"Exactly. Steve is convinced something is seriously wrong. Katie's been exploring and hiking most of her life. She's never done anything like this."

"So I take it there are no signs of a struggle in the cabin, no reason to believe there was an abduction?"

"None. What I've seen coincides with what Steve believes. That Katie left on her own accord, everything neat and tidy … maybe even a little too neat. Like she plans on being away for a while. I did see subtle signs that she was in a rush this morning … a drawer not completely closed … things like that. Nothing nefarious."

"Okay." Walker paused. "Dean, time is ticking, why lose precious hours calling us in from out of state? Don't you have anyone close by to pick up her trail?"

"That's just it. There *is* no trail."

"What do you mean?"

"No prints leave the cottage. Nothing. It's like Katie walked out the door and simply vanished. You're the best person I know for finding a trail without prints to follow. We need you, Walker."

He looked at Nataya, saw her nod in the affirmative. "You've got us, Dean."

"Thanks, Walker. Means the world to Steve and me."

"So, now what?"

"A private jet is already en route to Montrose Airport. Probably be there waiting by the time you make the drive."

"Pretty sure we'd say yes to this, eh?"

"Had to take the chance, and as you stated, time is precious. Let's say I was prepared to take desperate measures to get you both here."

"It's no problem, Dean. I understand."

"Well at least with the time difference between Colorado and Washington, you'll gain an hour. And Walker, just a heads up. When I meet you at the airstrip here in Washington, there will be someone with me. A Search and Rescue guy named Carl. He'll be bringing all the gear and equipment the three of you might need while you're in this environment."

"The *three* of us?"

"I know you prefer to work alone or with Nataya, but this is out of my control. Steve set it up and insists on it."

Before Walker could speak, Dean rushed forward to explain.

"Please understand, this is day five on a homicide case Steve's been working. Took place on tribal land near Lost Lake. That's why he was near the cottage where Katie went missing. He can't leave the case and wants this SAR guy to take his place. But don't worry, the Search and Rescue Team Leader says Carl is the most experienced and knowledgeable guy for the region you'll be going into."

"Sounds like we have no choice."

"Sorry, Walker. At least you won't need to pack up much, just your usual. Carl will be providing equipment, shelter, and food. Everything except warm clothing. Steve mentioned you may end up in higher elevations, and you know snow is a possibility this time of year in the mountains."

"Got it."

"Any questions before I let you go?"

"None. But I do have a request."

"Sure."

"Ask Steve if he knows what brand and size of hiking boot Katie wears. Maybe one of her hiking friends knows. If so, I need a photo of the boot tread."

"Got it. Will do, Walker. Thanks again to you and Nataya. Steve and I appreciate this. See you at the airstrip in Washington in a few hours."

Walker hung up the phone receiver and turned to Nataya. "Guess we better hustle since the plane's already in the air and we have a drive ahead of us."

"So Dean isn't flying into Montrose to meet us."

"I think he hates flying as much as we do." Walker hadn't missed the fact Dean had twice mentioned they'd meet at an airstrip, not airport. Which probably meant they'd be transferring from the private jet to a small plane at some point. He decided not to call it to Nataya's attention. Only a year ago she had learned that the small plane crash which killed her parents had not been an accident. Indeed, he'd try not to dwell on that fact himself.

CHAPTER THREE

Skagit County, Washington (Day One)

Amped up with adrenaline, which always happened whenever he received "a call-out," seasoned Search and Rescue volunteer Carl Dubois stopped rushing about his small rental cabin. He knew better than to head into the wilderness without a double-check of his gear. He forced himself to stand still, and ran a hand through thick, unruly, chestnut brown hair. Hazel eyes focused on the equipment scattered across the wooden floor, he mentally ticked off each item from a list he knew by heart.

He decided to cut himself some slack for his higher than usual level of anticipation. After all, how often would he get the chance to spend time alongside a well-known tracker like Fox Walker. And Nataya would be with him. Carl could barely believe his good fortune.

Although Carl had never met them, months ago while doing some online research he'd stumbled onto a story about their Wilderness Survival School. The more he read, the more intrigued he became. So he read everything he could find online. The stories about how Fox Walker had been trained in the art of tracking and wilderness survival as a young boy. And his teacher, Grandfather, who had spent years showing him how to not just survive, but to thrive in the wilderness. And now Walker shared that knowledge with Nataya, and his students. Carl had even checked into signing up for one of their courses, but it was currently beyond his budget. This search with them could be the next best thing.

Which brought up the added stress part. Quickly extracting Walker and Nataya out of Colorado was critical to the search, so it fell to Carl to not only gather the standard SAR gear, but additional gear Walker and Nataya would need. And the last thing he planned to do was embarrass himself by forgetting some vital piece of equipment. He took a moment to relax and concentrate.

When completely satisfied everything was in order, Carl finally allowed himself a moment to revel in the knowledge he'd soon be working with the famous trackers. All the extra preparation angst would be worth it. He quickly donned his SAR Team uniform, an orange button-up shirt and olive-green pants. He then grabbed the heavier than the usual thirty-pound backpack, hauled it outside to his Jeep and stowed it in the back, alongside a Medic First Aid Kit and various tools that were permanent fixtures. He added two jugs of drinking water and headed back into the cabin for a final look around before locking up.

Aside from his volunteer work for the county sheriff's search and rescue team, Carl had spent six years building his own business as a licensed Wilderness and Fishing Guide. He now had a steady stream of clients throughout all four seasons. The moderate winters in Washington state made it easier to do than other locales. And when he did receive an urgent call-out from his SAR team, he knew plenty of qualified outdoors men and women, eager for the work, who could step in and take the client load for his business.

His line of work gave him enough income to pay rent for the small rustic cabin, plus cover vehicle and equipment expenses. Best of all, it afforded him a way of life he craved—year 'round full immersion in the natural world. Adventure. He couldn't imagine sitting in a cubicle all day … every day.

Carl kept his cabin neat and clean, but as he took in the "a bachelor lives here" décor of the cabin, he shook his head. His lifestyle choice also explained why, at thirty, he had no steady love interest in his life. Oh, he received plenty of attention from the opposite sex, until they saw where, and how he lived. He blew out a breath and let the thought flow with it. If it was going to happen, it would. It'd just take one helluva special gal, he guessed. He locked the door and headed to his Jeep.

A quick glance at his waterproof sportsman watch revealed he had just enough time to make the drive over to the private airstrip, where he would meet the plane bringing in Walker and Nataya.

He didn't even try to stop the grin as he hurried to his Jeep.

───◆───

Carl turned off the state highway onto a paved rural two-lane and began watching for the address he'd been given. Steve Hicks, the missing woman's father, had spoken to him to confirm the setup, and then quickly passed him over to a man named Dean McClure. Carl and Dean had been texting to coordinate the meet-up at the private airstrip.

Up ahead he spotted a silver-haired gentleman at the entrance to a private drive, so he slowed. The address on the mailbox matched. He pulled into the drive, stopped, and rolled down his window.

"I'm guessing you must be Dean McClure?"

"You'd be correct." He reached out a hand to shake Carl's. "And you must be Carl, our SAR guy?"

"Yes, sir."

"We've got permission to land. Thought I'd ride back to the airstrip with you. Steve needed to drop me off and go take care of work. He'll meet us later."

"Hop in."

Dean settled into the passenger seat. The large-framed man's head almost touched the top of Carl's Jeep, but he was fit and trim for his age. Carl began to follow the driveway, passing a residential house that sat back off the main road. He couldn't help but notice that Dean was dressed for fishing. Looked like the man's day wasn't panning out as intended. Carl understood.

Up ahead he spotted the runway stretched out in front of them. "Whoa, a grass strip? Why did Steve pick this?"

"Privacy, for one. It's also closest to where Katie went missing. He had a private jet pick them up and get them as close as possible. Then they switched to a puddle jumper for access to this landing strip."

"Okay, makes sense."

"You can pull over to the side, right there. They should be coming in soon."

Carl drove the Jeep to where Dean indicated, parked, and turned off the engine. Both men settled back into their seats to wait. "So Dean, I know Steve Hicks is the MP's father. How do you fit into the scenario?"

"I'm a friend of Steve's. Happened to be in the area."

Carl waited for more of an explanation.

"We used to work for the same agency," Dean said.

"Cool. What agency was that?"

Dean hesitated a moment before answering. "The FBI."

Carl's eyebrows arched upward, but he managed not to blurt out his surprise.

Dean continued, "Steve still works for the Bureau. I was a profiler and left years ago, but Steve and I have managed a few fishing trips together over the years. After I retired from the Bureau, I worked as a private consultant for a while, which is how I met Walker and Nataya. We worked a case together."

Carl struggled to absorb all the info at once. "So you personally know Walker?"

"Yeah, Steve does, too. That's why we both wanted him on this case."

"How does Steve know Walker?"

"Same case, different circumstances."

"Yeah?" Carl gave him his best "I'm really interested face."

Dean sighed. "It's a long tale. I ended up flying into Gunnison, Colorado and driving through a snowstorm to meet Walker. That's another story. But fortunately for everyone involved, Steve had also been in Denver. He was training recruits for the FBI Hostage Team Rescue program when the call came down the line. Steve led the HTR helicopter team in to extract Matt Logan, Fox Walker and Nataya from the wilderness, with a sniper on their trail."

Carl shook his head. "Wow. I can't imagine what kind of adventures you guys have had while in the Bureau."

Dean stared straight ahead. "It wasn't all as glamorous as you might imagine. Often it was more horrific than anything. But you know that, don't you, Carl?"

Carl watched Dean turn and study him. He sensed the man wouldn't entertain any bravado bullshit. He let his attention drift to the runway in front of him. "Yeah ... I do know."

"Let me guess, reality set in with the first search that didn't end in a rescue."

"Something like that. It was a suicide walk."

Dean grimaced. "That's a tough one."

"Yeah." Carl turned to face Dean. "I still sometimes have dreams of tracking his barefoot prints in the mud."

"Some cases stay with you like that." Dean rolled down his

window and laid his arm on the window frame.

Carl watched the man study the patches on his uniform sleeve. Patches for "Ground Search and Rescue," and "Mountain Rescue." He figured when they first shook hands the man had already noticed the Sheriff Department SAR patch on his other sleeve. The guy didn't seem to miss much.

Dean gave Carl a short nod. "Your SAR leader spoke highly of you. Says you'd be the best guy for our situation."

"Which is what, exactly?"

"Expert trackers coming into a vast wilderness environment they're not familiar with. And a missing woman who knows the area intimately." He turned toward Carl. "Walker likes to work alone, or alongside Nataya. He can be a bit … intimidating. Steve believes the tracker may have a need for your knowledge of this region. Don't be reluctant to speak up."

"Thanks, Dean. I appreciate that vote of confidence."

"No problem." Dean pointed to the sky where a small aircraft approached. "Time to greet our arrivals and get this show on the road."

Carl started the engine and wheeled the Jeep around so they could follow the runway, such as it was. He drove toward the end of the air strip while he kept watch on the plane as it touched down. They caught up as the small aircraft rolled to a stop.

Dean exited the Jeep. After he turned off the engine, Carl joined him, hanging back a bit to observe the reunion of the three.

Nataya was first to step off the plane, as if she couldn't wait to escape the thing. But a warmhearted smile lit up her face when she spotted Dean. She was more attractive than he expected, but in a natural, uncomplicated manner. A petite woman, but athletic just the same. Her long blonde hair flowed over her shoulders. She wore a leather belt draped low across her hips. Attached to it on the right was a knife sheath and small pouch. A shoulder satchel hung at her left hip.

Walker exited next. Compact but strong body, long black hair, stoic expression. Exactly as Carl expected. Walker wore a knife sheathed at his side, and a rucksack slung over his right shoulder. Carl took in the simple garb they both wore—old school, just as he had read—buckskin tunics, tall moccasin boots. With a closer study of them both, he noticed they each wore a beautifully crafted necklace. Walker's included a polished turquoise stone and the lynx claws Carl had read about. Nataya's necklace was understated with only beads, stones and small shells, yet beautiful in its simplicity.

Carl couldn't help but admire the obvious friendship the three shared as Nataya threw her arms around Dean's neck for an enthusiastic hug. While Walker's response was more reserved, there was a deep respect in his eyes as he shook Dean's hand. Carl held high hope that working with the two would allow him to become close with them, as well.

At that moment Dean turned toward him. "Walker, Nataya … this is Carl Dubois. He's extremely knowledgeable about the region and comes highly recommended. He has graciously offered his services to assist and is supplying any gear you two might need."

Nataya stepped forward and offered her hand to him. "Thank you for your generosity, Carl. It's nice to meet you."

Gone was the open friendliness he had witnessed with Dean, and in its place she offered a reserved smile. But he could detect a kindness in her eyes. He offered his best smile, dimples and all, but for once found himself tongue-tied.

Walker then shook Carl's hand, a strong, firm handshake that did not hint of any need to impress another male. He found it refreshingly honest. As for Walker's expression, he couldn't read it at all. At that moment he knew that none of the accolades from Dean meant anything to Walker. He'd have to prove his worth to the man. He squared his shoulders. He intended to do just that.

Dean then took charge, corralling everyone toward the waiting Jeep. "I'll give you directions as we go, Carl."

Carl pointed to the back of the Jeep. "Walker, there's room behind the seats for your pack, if you want."

Walker complied, then he and Nataya took the back seats. With Dean riding shotgun, Carl pulled out onto the driveway leading up to the paved road.

When they drew even with the house, Dean grabbed Carl's arm. "Stop a minute, son." Dean slid from his seat and slow jogged up toward the house.

Carl had to admire the older man's agility. Then he noticed a woman stood on the front porch, holding a brown grocery bag. His mind went directly to food, which made him recognize his hunger.

Dean returned with the bag in hand and a smile. He got in and started passing out sandwiches and water bottles. "Clare made us lunch. She thought we could use some nourishment to keep up our energy for our search."

"That was so thoughtful. How did she know?" Nataya asked as she took the offering.

"I had to get permission for the landing, it being a private airstrip. I mentioned the time-sensitive nature of our business in hopes she'd grant access."

Whatever Dean had told the lady, Carl was thankful it had resulted in food. He hungrily took a bite of his sandwich as he steered the vehicle out onto the paved road and took directions from Dean. He glanced in the rear-view mirror and met Walker's eyes, then focused back on the road, wondering what lay ahead for them.

CHAPTER FOUR

Skagit County, Washington (Day One)

Fox Walker leaned his head against the Jeep window for a better view of the mountains rising high above them while Carl navigated the road per Dean's directions. After departing the airstrip and heading east, they had briefly driven past open pastures and farms, dotted with patches of woodlands. But within minutes solemn peaks loomed high on either side of them as they followed the Skagit River, making its way amid the boulders of steep cliffs and sinuously winding its way through the valley.

The scenery changed yet again as they entered the densely forested slopes of the mountain range. Now he could only occasionally catch a glimpse of the craggy peaks above during brief openings in those impressively tall treetops. Walker glanced toward Nataya, noted her own immersion in the scenery. He leaned forward to catch Dean's attention. "Now I understand why you speak so highly about this part of the county."

Dean turned, as much as the seatbelt allowed, to look at Walker. "I was sure you'd see why I love it here. Glad you're enjoying the scenery."

"The views of the North Cascades from the plane were impressive, and much of the landscape reminded me of Colorado, but once on the ground I can see it's definitely quite different. For example, take those evergreens—towering high above everything else."

Nataya added, "They are so stately!"

Dean chuckled. "Yeah, no matter how long I live here, I never get over how crazy tall these trees grow." He turned toward the road. "Carl, turn onto that road coming up, please."

"Sure." Carl slowed the vehicle to make the turn from the state road to a narrow two-lane.

The road quickly took them deeper into the woods, the thick canopy of trees soon blocking out most of the sunlight. Walker sensed a difference in these forests from those he roamed in his home state. He studied them, searching for the reason.

The first thing to catch his eye was the lush ground cover, profuse with a variety of verdant ferns. Everywhere he looked, he saw green. When he peered closer into the deeper shadows, he better understood why. Most surfaces, including the ground, rocks, and tree trunks, were covered in plump layers of green moss. Looking higher into the trees, he noticed a variety of lichens clinging to the branches. Viewed together it gave the impression of a lush and damp environment. Which made sense when he considered what he'd heard about the amount of rain they received in this part of the country.

But he hadn't expected the woodlands to have such a mysterious vibe … maybe even a little foreboding. Perhaps the darkness beneath the impenetrably dense tree canopy overhead made his imagination run a bit wild. That and the fact some tree branches appeared to drip long strands of vegetative matter, giving them an eerie aspect. He wondered what they'd experience when they finally walked among these trees.

Nataya reached for his hand, even as she looked outside her

window. He wondered if she experienced the same mix of emotions.

Carl slowed the vehicle even more. Walker wondered if it was entirely due to the road conditions or if the young man also sensed a similar mystical aspect to the wilderness.

Walker rolled down his window to breathe in the fresh, crisp air, heavy with a pungent evergreen scent so familiar to him. But the fragrance also carried different notes of damp earth, and other scents that were new to him. He also noticed an abundance of giant cedar trees scattered throughout the forest.

Now that they drove slower, fully immersed in the forest, Walker could identify specific tree species, firs, spruce, pines and hemlock, as well as a variety of deciduous trees, like maples, oaks and alders. He recognized the familiar maidenhair and sword ferns. The diversity was amazing. And everywhere he looked, even along the roadsides, were brambles of berry bushes.

Dean gave Carl directions to turn onto the main street of a tiny community, then added. "After the second stop, turn right onto the gravel … well, mostly dirt, road."

Carl nodded. "Isn't that the way to Lost Lake?"

"Correct. I forgot you know this area."

"Yeah, I've been on quite a few search and rescue calls in the foothills, and also higher into the nearby mountain range. There's a trailhead at the lake that's popular with the tourists. Inexperienced hikers don't understand how quickly weather conditions can change when they rapidly gain elevation. It catches a lot of them unprepared." He made the first stop and took off again. "If Katie's cottage is at the lake, there's a good possibility she took that trail out of there."

"Maybe. Hoping you three can find prints, or something to confirm that." Dean pointed. "You probably know to turn right at the stop sign."

Carl gave a nod. "If I remember correctly, the road gets pretty gnarly from here."

"Yep. That's a good way to describe it. When I followed Steve here, he had me leave my Subaru over there in a parking lot." He gestured toward the motel on the corner. "There's not much room for parking at the cottage. I have to say, even though my vehicle would've done fine on the road, I'm glad I didn't have to put it through the paces."

"Wise decision."

Walker leaned forward while Carl navigated the deep furrows in the road. "Dean, do we have any idea how well Katie knows this area?"

"Steve said when Katie was in high school and college, she spent every summer at the cottage. She and a small group of friends took bushcraft classes from a mountain man, hermit-type guy who lived nearby. They spent entire months exploring the mountain slopes. Although Katie hadn't been to the cottage for a couple of years, one of her friends owns it and encouraged her to come spend the last couple of months before she begins a new job. She's been hanging out, fishing and relaxing … along with reconnecting with her friends and taking the usual hikes."

Carl maneuvered around a large pothole and over a gully then spoke. "Sounds like this gal is pretty experienced out in the wilderness."

"Extremely. But we all know that doesn't mean accidents can't happen."

"Yeah. And even experts get lost," Carl added grimly.

Until he heard what Steve had to say, Walker decided not to mention the other reason why Katie may have left—that she was running from something, or someone. He saw the lake come into view between the trees. Behind it, steep slopes led up to the craggy mountain tops, and in the distance a tall crown reigning over all.

Dean nodded toward the tallest peak. "That's Mount Baker."

Nataya leaned over to see the view through Walker's window. "What a lovely setting. I can understand why someone would want to spend the summer here."

"There's the cottage, Carl," Dean said. "The one with Katie's Jeep and the black SUV parked next to it. Looks like Steve's waiting for us."

Walker took another long look at the forest and mountain range beyond the lake ... the huge expanse of wilderness it encompassed. And he knew none of it.

CHAPTER FIVE

Lost Lake, Washington, (Day One)

Carl parked his Jeep beside the black SUV, his adrenaline naturally kicking in now that they were finally all gathered in one spot. For every hour that had ticked by since the initial call, his longing for action escalated. He turned off the engine, took the keys and exited before anyone else managed to leave their seats.

He hustled to the back of the vehicle to remove the gear, then noticed Walker make his way over to the edge of the gravel parking area. The man stood quietly with his back to everyone, surveying the land before him. How could the guy be so calm and nonchalant?

Carl pulled out Walker's rucksack as Nataya approached him. She gave him a polite smile as she reached for the bag. Something about the workmanship made him study it a moment longer. "This isn't store-bought. Waxed canvas with bark tanned leather pouches and trim?"

"Why yes, it is."

He noted the surprise in her voice, and when he handed the pack to her, an attentiveness in her eyes.

"We make a lot of our clothing and carrying bags from the hides we tan, like this shoulder satchel I'm carrying," she said and indicated the lovely bag at her hip.

"Wow. Buckskin, right?"

"Yes. That's correct." She gave him a genuine smile this time.

"Nice!" He wanted to ask all sorts of questions, but knew they needed to focus on the task before them. He grabbed his own large backpack and followed Nataya to where Walker stood.

Dean joined them. "This way. Steve's waiting." he said and ushered them toward the door of the cottage.

Carl fell in behind the group. A man held the door open for them. Although clean-cut, the guy had a rugged face and the tiniest hint of gray at the temples. He watched him greet Dean, Walker and Nataya, noticing his countenance showed both respect and gratitude.

He stepped up next, ready to introduce himself, but Steve spoke before he could.

"You must be Carl. I greatly appreciate your willingness to assist Walker and Nataya. It means a lot to me."

"No problem. It's an honor, sir." Surprised by his own response, Carl realized the man did give off serious "G-man" vibes.

Steve gave him a firm handshake and motioned for everyone to take a seat at the small kitchen table. Carl glanced around the cottage as he made his way toward a chair, noticed the open rafters of the ceiling, the tongue-and-groove walls. A typical lake cottage with one open room for the kitchen and living area. The kitchen window over the sink included a view of the lake. Bedrooms and bath were walled off with partitions. It was neat and clean, nothing fancy. But he did notice books scattered about the place and wished he could take the time to see what she'd been reading. Maybe get to know her.

Everyone took a seat while Steve remained standing. "I

cannot begin to express my appreciation that you were all willing to interrupt your lives and rush here to assist with this situation. That said, we've lost hours of time so I'll keep this brief and then answer any further questions you may have."

He began to pass out some photographs as he spoke. "This is a recent photo of Katie you can each keep with you. She's five foot six and weighs around one hundred twenty-five pounds." He glanced at Dean. "I take it you've given them the basics?"

"They know Katie left with her backpack and disappeared, leaving no obvious prints to follow. And that she's extremely familiar with the area surrounding the lake."

Steve looked to Walker. "You've probably noticed we had a heavy rain yesterday. But it quit before six in the evening, when Katie was last seen, and long before she disappeared this morning at predawn. She also didn't leave any note or inform anyone as to where she was headed. Something she has never done before."

Walker spoke. "I understand no one wants to say this out loud, but even with no signs of an abduction, there is a possibility she is running from someone, and hid her prints so they couldn't follow."

"That's my biggest concern," Steve said. "Which brings up another confusing issue. She purposefully left behind her cell phone—even hid it under the mattress. Makes me believe she didn't want anyone tracking her GPS coordinates. So even if she hid her prints to keep someone else from following, if she's in trouble why wouldn't she want at least me to have a way to find her?"

After a pause, Walker posed a possibility. "Unless having you follow her might put you in danger, as well?"

"That thought has crossed my mind."

Carl watched Steve's jaw tense and a quick flash of what looked almost like panic flash through the man's eyes. But then

Astray

the man wrestled back control and released a long sigh.

Dean spoke up. "You need to let Walker know what kind of gear she most likely has with her." He gave Steve a knowing look.

Steve gave a curt nod in response. "Yes. Of course." He looked at the trio. "Katie left behind her cell phone, but she didn't leave behind her conceal carry handgun. But we can't assume that means she feels threatened by anyone. You see, back when she started insisting on hiking alone, I convinced her to let me train her on how to shoot and properly handle a gun. And she made a promise to always carry when she's alone in the wilderness. And not just for protection from wildlife." He looked at each person. "I've seen the darker side of humanity, up close and personal. I had to make sure she knew how to protect herself."

Carl studied the FBI Agent. It made sense Steve would make that a priority for his daughter. He spoke up. "So, she may have taken it simply out of habit." He watched Steve nod in acknowledgement. "May I ask what she's carrying?"

"Sure. It's a 9mm M&P Shield. While it's still legal to open carry in the state of Washington, she'd wear it concealed at her waist." He gave each one of them a pointed look. "And yes, she's licensed for concealed carry. I want to assure you, she's not some inexperienced, nervous, hair-trigger shooter."

"Thank you for the heads up, though. It's important we know she's armed," Walker said.

Dean spoke up next. "After a search of the cottage—and based on what Steve knows about Katie's usual backpack kit—we believe she most likely also has bear spray with her, trekking poles, shelter, sleeping bag, water filter, food and a one-burner backpacking stove."

"In other words, she could stay out there in the wilderness a long while with no problem," Carl said.

Steve nodded. "But she'd normally let me, or someone, know if she was heading out for any kind of extended hike. She hid her cell phone and left without leaving any easy to find tracks. My instincts tell me something is wrong with this scenario."

Walker stood. "The sooner we start looking for a trail, the better our chances. Did you have an opportunity to get a photo of the boot tread?"

Steve reached down and picked up a pair of hiking boots. "I did one better. One of Katie's friends has the same brand of boots and wears just a half-size smaller. She let me borrow them for you to examine."

Walker took the boots and closely studied the tread and the boot size. "The wear pattern will be different, but this is a huge help, Steve. Thanks."

Then to Carl's surprise Walker handed the boots to him. He heard Steve give Walker a rundown of the expected weather conditions for the next few days for the region. Carl took advantage of the moment, grabbed his cell phone and took a quick photo of the boot tread. Then he reached for his pack, leaning against the table, and pulled the trekking pole loose. He held it next to the boot, located a rubber band wrapped around the pole, and moved it to match the length of the boot, marking the size for future reference.

The group had moved out to the front porch of the cottage when he joined them and sat his backpack next to Walker's rucksack. He noticed everyone, including Nataya, held back as Walker stepped out into the yard, which consisted of mostly dirt with clumps of moss and grass scattered about. Carl stepped closer to Nataya and listened as she explained Walker's methods to Steve. As she spoke, she nimbly wove her long hair into a single, thick braid.

"He's looking for what is missing. Or I guess a better way to put it would be, he's looking for what has been misplaced … not natural. If Katie deliberately brushed away her footprints, that action, in itself, leaves its own sign such as pebbles overturned, marks in the dirt, bits of nature missing from where they would normally lay. It can become as clear of a trail to follow as footprints." She draped the blonde braid over one shoulder.

"That makes sense," Steve said. "Still, it'd take a lot of experience to understand what you are seeing."

"Yes, and hours in nature to know what 'undisturbed land' looks like."

Eager to jump into action, as he always was for any search and rescue, Carl fought his impatience. He sensed a difference in this case. So far it appeared he'd been hired as more of a wilderness guide than as a SAR volunteer. He focused on Walker as he worked. The man made every move deliberate, watching the ground, occasionally kneeling, only to stand again and move farther away. Minutes ticked away. He had inched his way closer to the lakeshore when he stood from a crouched position and motioned for them to approach.

Carl forced himself not to sprint over to where Walker waited, but instead walked with the others. When they arrived, Walker knelt again and pointed to a place on the ground. Carl joined him, searching for what had caught the man's attention. He noticed the soil was moist and sandier down closer to the shoreline. He used his fingers to gently move aside some blades of grass and spotted a small indentation in the ground. How Walker had spotted it was beyond him. He studied the marking. "Looks like a partial heel print from a bare foot."

"Yes." Walker looked up at everyone gathered around them. "Katie didn't brush away any prints. The ground would've been too wet from the rains yesterday. So the only thing that made sense was that she wasn't wearing shoes. I suspected she walked away from the cottage barefoot, making sure to step onto the sparse vegetation. But the soil is still quite wet and held a few partial prints. The depth of the indentations I spotted indicate she was indeed wearing a pack."

"So, she carried the hiking boots and walked barefoot to keep from leaving clear boot prints," Nataya said, then turned to look at the lake. "She could've even walked along the shoreline in the shallow water, hoping to hide prints and not leave a scent trail."

"That's what I'd do," Walker said. "Now if we only knew which way, left or right, that she took along the shore." He looked both ways. "I guess we can split up and check each direction. See if we can pick up any sign."

Carl stared out over the water. "I think I might already know." He saw all heads turn his way. He pointed across the lake to the nearest shoreline, directly in front of them. "Straight across from here is where the road meets the trailhead. The popular one I mentioned earlier, which travels up into the mountain range."

"Good to know. We'll check to the left then." Walker motioned toward the lake. He turned to Steve and Dean. "Wouldn't hurt to have you two check the opposite direction for any obvious sign of human activity along the shore—just to be safe."

The three spread out and continued to the left of where they had been standing, moving closer and closer to the lake. When they reached the water's edge, Nataya spoke.

"I've got something."

Carl jogged over to join her and Walker. She'd not found any footprints but did find another muddy heel indent leading into the shallows. Most people would never have noticed it. All three of them studied the sandy bottom just beneath the softly lapping waves. He could see a barely visible depression the size of a woman's foot in the sand and pointed it out.

Walker agreed. "Right size for Katie's footprint. And the right amount of water erosion for the hours that have passed. The print shows she faced left, indicating she probably followed the shoreline."

The three of them followed the edge of the lake, spotting more and more shallow depressions. Walker stopped. "These are the right size and if Katie indeed was headed for the trailhead, they are going the correct direction. I'm good."

Carl saw Nataya nod in agreement. He spoke up. "I can grab our gear from the front porch while you two continue. I'll catch up."

"Good idea. Thanks." Walker returned to the task at hand.

Carl turned to leave and heard Walker call out.

"Hey Carl, in my pack you'll find a canteen. Could you fill it with water for us?"

Carl gave him a thumbs up, turned and sprinted toward the cottage, glad for the opportunity to expel some of his pent-up energy. He caught Dean and Steve's attention and waved them toward the cottage. They immediately hurried in that direction.

He easily beat the other two men to the cottage and grabbed Walker's rucksack. As he began to search through the bag for the canteen, he noticed Walker had heeded his advice to bring warm clothing. There were wool sweaters, soft leather boots with felt liners, and fleece parkas. All good news, because although he could supply their basic equipment and food needs, the weather might surprise them. And not in a pleasant way.

He discovered the canteen in an outside leather pouch as Steve and Dean arrived at the cottage. Carl filled them in on what had been discovered, and that they were ready to head out. He sent Steve to fill the canteen. Then he hefted the large backpack onto his shoulders, fastened the chest straps together and hooked the waist band. Dean handed him Walker's pack, which he shouldered on his left. Steve arrived with the canteen, which Carl slung onto his right shoulder.

Dean adjusted Carl's trekking pole into a strap on the backpack and chuckled. "You look like a pack mule, son."

Carl grinned. "I can handle it."

"Youth," snorted Dean.

Carl laughed and turned to see Steve holding out a beefy-looking phone. "Take this satellite phone with you. So we can stay in contact."

Dean shook his head. "Walker won't be keen about that."

"What do you mean?" Steve asked.

"Walker won't even carry a cell phone, let alone a SAT phone."

"Why not?"

"I've never asked him … but I've heard him mention not wanting the intrusion of technology interfering with his connection with nature … or something like that."

Carl looked back and forth between both men, then spoke up. "I thought that whole bit about him not carrying a cell phone was just some urban legend."

Steve didn't respond to Carl and instead stared at Dean. "You know how this whole 'staying behind thing' is ripping me apart. This is Katie we're talking about. I want full communication on what's happening out there, and I won't compromise on this. Besides, I'm not asking Walker to carry it, just Carl."

Dean gave a deep sigh of resignation and turned to Carl. "You okay with carrying the SAT phone?"

Carl looked at Dean and hoped the panic bubbling up in his gut didn't show on his face. The last thing he wanted to do was anger Walker. He wanted to gain the man's trust, not lose it. He looked at Steve. He was the one who had contacted Carl's SAR team captain and asked for someone to assist on the case. It was Steve who had essentially hired him—not Walker. And a big part of him understood the man's need to stay informed about his daughter.

He turned to Steve. "How 'bout this? Give me your cell number," he said as he pulled his cell from his pocket. "That way, as long as I have a signal we can secretly text back and forth.

I'll check my messages every night while in my tent. If or when we move into an area where I lose phone service, I'll have the SAT phone as backup. We can use the SMS text feature and Walker won't need to know our arrangement unless it's necessary." He secretly hoped that, if they did venture into the deeper wilderness and he lost his phone signal, by that time he would have gained Walker's trust and it wouldn't be an issue.

"I can do that," Steve said. "Thanks for understanding." He handed Carl the SAT phone and did a quick overview of its features.

Then Carl directed him to a pouch on the backpack where he could stow the phone for safe keeping.

Steve stood back and gave Carl a once over. "Make sure you check in with me daily, even if it's just a quick update."

"Will do. Okay, time to catch up with Walker and Nataya." He looked at Steve. "I'll be in touch."

Carl stepped off the porch and spotted Walker and Nataya near the opposite shore. They'd made great progress. He put some extra hustle into his pace. Even with the extra gear, it felt good to get into action. Finally.

CHAPTER SIX

Lost Lake, Washington (Day One)

Walker looked up from his kneeling position as Carl approached, carrying not only his backpack, but also Walker's rucksack and canteen. The heavy load didn't appear to affect his hurried gait. He murmured sideways to Nataya, "Looks like a damn astronaut heading out to explore Mars or something."

Nataya glanced up and gave Carl a wave then looked down to respond to Walker. "I suppose he's carrying the standard gear for Search and Rescue. But didn't Dean say he'd also have gear for us."

"Good point."

There was a beat of quiet before Nataya continued. "He does seem like a nice guy, though. And he did save us a lot of time by knowing the location of the trailhead."

"True," he admitted. But he still had concerns about how quickly Carl would be able to move through the thick forests if Katie's tracks took them off trail. Difficult to be agile with all that equipment. Carl joined them and Walker stood to take his pack and canteen from Carl. "Thanks for retrieving these so we could keep moving forward."

"No problem."

Walker studied Carl for a moment. "Now that we're ready to head out, why don't you let me share some of that load?"

"It's okay, I don't mind."

"Well, I do." Walker replied. "The faster we can all move, the better. And if we end up off trail and in the wilderness …"

"Yeah, I hear ya."

Walker studied Carl's setup. "What about those two sleeping bags you've got strapped to the outside of your backpack? Are those for Nataya and I?"

"Yeah."

"Well, let me take those. Everything in my rucksack is stuff we'll probably end up wearing soon, so I'll have room. For right now we can fasten them to the outside of my pack."

Carl removed the sleeping bags, helped Walker strap them to his pack, then studied his own backpack. "Yeah, that works better. Now everything fits inside. It's not near as bulky." He looked at Walker. "And the weight is fine for me. It's what I'm used to."

"Okay. It's a start for now."

Carl looked toward the lakeshore. "What did I miss?"

"Not much."

Nataya pointed ahead to a clump of saplings at the lake's edge. "We were discussing the fact those trees ahead would be a perfect place to exit the water without being spotted. Katie could've hidden there long enough to make sure no one followed."

"Sounds logical to me," Carl said.

Nataya looked at Walker. "You and Carl go on ahead. I'll catch up. I want to gather a few of these cattail leaves before we depart from the lake area."

Walker motioned for Carl to join him, and he continued to follow the barely visible impressions below the surface of the shallow water. Even though he was sure Katie had headed to that group of saplings, he moved slowly forward, making sure not to miss any sign that showed otherwise. By the time he and Carl reached the trees, Nataya had caught back up to them. He returned his attention back to the soil on the bank and a moment later spotted prints.

"There, someone stepped barefoot from the water onto the bank, entered the clump of trees."

Nataya moved in closer and peered between the grouping of tree trunks. "You can still see an impression where someone sat for a while. Maybe Katie did indeed wait and watch … to make sure no one followed her."

Carl leaned in through the branches. "I can see curved indentations in the ground, like the heel of hiking boots would make. Maybe she sat here and put on socks and boots while she waited."

"I would agree," Nataya said as she studied what Carl had pointed out.

"Good. Because over here's a boot print leaving the trees. It's too muddy to see any details, but looks close to the right size," Walker said. He waited for the other two to join him, then glanced up toward where he thought he could just make out the road.

Carl must have noticed and spoke up. "The road to the trailhead is ahead and to the right." He used his arm to give direction. "Katie could have gone straight to it from this angle. If that is where she was headed, that is."

"Excellent," Walker said. "Let's walk three abreast at the angle you've indicated and see if we can pick up any prints to confirm it." Walker picked out a landmark with the correct angle and moved forward, noting that Nataya and Carl were spaced out and keeping pace.

They made a slow progression through the knee-high grasses

and marshy soil, finding an occasional impression in the mud to keep them on course.

After a few minutes Carl engaged them in conversation about what they had found so far and wondering what their theory might be, what it might mean in the bigger picture. Walker preferred to work in quiet but reminded himself that he and Nataya had the benefit of years working together, thus had little need to talk. And since they weren't stalking anyone, at the moment, or needing to be silent, it really didn't hurt anything. But he still inwardly cringed when Carl started in again.

"I have to believe that when Katie hid in that clump of trees and put on her boots, she was convinced no one had followed. That she was safe."

"It's a good possibility," Nataya offered.

Carl continued. "That could mean that once she left the immediate lake area, she was no longer worried about someone following her ... which means maybe she didn't go to the trouble of trying to hide her tracks. Maybe speed was more important to her then and so we'll be able to easily follow her trail."

"Let's hope your theory is correct," Walker replied. They had left the marshy soil and were now on solid ground. "Here's our first clear boot print—tread and all." He watched Nataya and Carl hurry to where he knelt. "The tread matches." To his surprise, Carl pulled a cell phone from his pocket and held it up next to the track, showing a photo of the boot tread.

"Yeah, it does."

Walker gave him a long look. "So, without your cell phone to refer to, would you have the same confidence?"

Carl gave him a sheepish expression. "Nah, I guess not. I didn't think I had time to study and memorize the boot tread back at the cottage." He looked at Walker. "But obviously you were able to do it."

Walker liked Carl's honesty. "Yeah, well I've had years of

practice. But the more you make yourself do it, the easier it will be for you."

"Good point." Carl smiled, then gave a start as if suddenly remembering something. "You probably don't need this, but I'll share it, if that's okay." He pulled his trekking pole from his pack and handed it to Nataya, indicating the rubber band. "That marks the length of the boot that Steve showed us at the cottage."

Nataya knelt and laid the pole next to the print. "Considering the boot we studied was a half size smaller than Katie's size, I'd say we have her print. That's a clever idea." She handed the pole back to Carl.

Walker stood. "Okay, so the prints match Katie's boot tread. The depth of the impression matches her body weight, plus a pack." He looked forward at the prints ahead of them. "The length of her stride matches her height. Sign of her passage originated at the cottage and is heading toward the trailhead. I'm confident we've found Katie's trail." He glanced at each of them and saw they agreed. "We know Katie is at least eight hours ahead of us, probably more, but hopefully with such a clear and easy to follow trail we'll be able to make up for lost time."

They began to follow the boot prints in the mostly dirt road, the trailhead in sight. But within a few yards Katie's prints suddenly veered off the path, directly in front of a small General Store. All three halted and stared. Carl spoke first.

"What the heck?" He glanced around "Maybe she stopped for supplies?"

Walker considered it a moment. "Steve said when her friends stopped by at dawn, she was already gone. The store would've been closed, according to the sign in their window." He began to search the grass next to the road for any indications to which direction she had headed. He followed small signs of her passage to an outside mailbox, next to the store. Then they turned back toward the road.

Carl shook his head. "This gets weirder and weirder. She leaves in the wee hours… we believe she wanted to avoid being followed … and then she stops to mail something? What the heck?"

"I agree, but all we can do for now is follow the sign she left behind," Walker said, then turned to search the edges of the dirt road for where she might have entered it again. He quickly found prints.

"How can we be sure these are Katie's?" Carl gestured toward the road. "There are lots of prints around here from the store and going toward the trailhead. I'm sure there are other people with that same brand of boot. We could end up following the wrong person."

Nataya joined Walker as he replied to Carl. "Look at the length of her stride. It matches what we've been following. But I can show you more proof. When we found that first detailed boot print, I noticed a tiny pebble lodged into the tread, right here." He pointed to the spot in the boot print.

Carl knelt and studied it. "It's still there! I hadn't noticed that."

"That's why I'm so confident we've got Katie's trail again."

"Cool."

Walker looked at Nataya and saw her give him a grin. Well, at least the guy was open to learning without getting his feelings hurt. Now, if only he wasn't so talkative the rest of the time.

CHAPTER SEVEN

Lost Lake, Washington (Day One)

Dean sat on the edge of the concrete porch, staring out across the lake. Walker, Nataya and Carl were far beyond the shoreline and out of his view. So he listened as Steve fed him updates on their progress while following them with his binoculars. The trio's slow pace had to be torturous for the man.

Moments later Steve's voice held a note of excitement. "They must've found a clear path of prints. They're moving at a reasonably good pace, for tracking someone, that is."

"That's great news."

"Yeah, I can see the trailhead marker, and they're making excellent progress."

Dean sat up a bit straighter, watching the lake. "Hey, Steve. Do me a favor. Slowly bring your binoculars slightly down and to the right—don't be obvious—until you can see a rowboat, straight out from the cottage, opposite side of the inlet."

"Okay … got it."

"Describe what you see."

"Hmm … looks like one of those rental boats. Middle-aged

man is fishing. Well, kinda fishing. He's sitting there holding a rod and not moving. Not really dressed for it, either. I suppose he could be a tourist who decided to enjoy the nice day and rented a boat and tackle. It is strange, though." He turned toward Dean. "Why the interest?"

"Probably nothing, but I noticed him earlier. When all of us were busy watching Walker search for Katie's prints. The guy was fishing out front of the cottage next door."

"Oh, yeah. I do remember seeing him now. While you and I were walking the shore, looking for signs of any activity. So?"

"Not a good place to fish that time of day, but like you said, maybe he's just a tourist and doesn't know any better. But what struck me as odd was how nonchalant he was with all the activity we had going on here ... I mean, I would've been curious."

"Could be he didn't want to stare and appear nosey."

"Yeah, but I got a different vibe. More like he was hell bent on not doing anything that might draw attention to himself."

"Hmmm. I'll take a good look, and make sure I recognize him if he comes around again."

"Thanks, Steve. I'm probably being paranoid. Just a habit after all these years of reading people. Something doesn't sit right with the guy."

"Hey, if he got your attention, I'm glad you said something. That's your talent, man."

After a few moments he saw Steve shift his attention back to where he had watched Walker and gang. "How's our trio doing?"

"They're still following the marked trail and moving at a nice, steady pace. I'll lose them any second now in the tree line between them and us." He soon lowered the binoculars. "Well, now it's up to Carl to keep me updated. Hope he comes through for us." Steve sat down next to Dean. "I can't thank you enough for your assistance in getting Walker on board."

"No problem." He studied the man. "Must be tough staying behind like this."

"It's hell." Steve stared at the mountains beyond the lake, then turned to Dean. "I suppose it's a little too late to return you to your fishing spot?"

Dean grinned. "Yeah, just a bit." He let silence settle in for a moment. "So what is it about the homicide on tribal land that's keeping you from pursuing Katie on your own?"

Steve sighed. "One of the dead guys is believed to be a member of a black-market ring we've been trying to break up for a year now. They're stealing Native American artifacts and reselling them overseas. This is the closest we've come to getting a clue to their operation."

"Tell me about the homicide."

Steve leaned forward, elbows on his knees, hands clasped. "Lord knows I could use some advice from someone with your talents, unpleasant as the scenario is."

"Not my first rodeo, you know. But to balance it, I'm probably a bit rusty these days."

"I doubt that. And judging from what you just noticed with the guy and the rowboat, I'd say your gift for profiling is still there."

Dean gave a sad smile. "I could never decide if it was a gift or a curse." He put his hand on Steve's shoulder. "I wouldn't ask if I wasn't interested."

"Fair enough. But we do this on the condition I treat us to some burgers and beer in town. Then we'll talk."

"Deal."

Dean settled back into the cushioned seat of a booth and relaxed while the waiter brought their beers. He knew Steve well enough to know the man walked atop a thin ledge right now.

His professionalism seemed the only thing keeping him from panic mode in regards to his missing daughter. And he couldn't blame the guy. "So, give me the low down on this case." Dean hoped by engaging Steve in the details of the case, he'd get his mind off the fact Katie was out there in the wilderness somewhere, even if it was only a temporary distraction.

Steve took a long pull of beer from the bottle, then began. "Four days ago, the Bureau sent me in to talk to Tribal Police Chief, Daniel Night Hawk. He'd received a 'shots fired' call and went to check it out. Turned out to be at his friend's house. He found two dead. One was his long-time friend, Joseph Spirit Horse, an elder in the community. The second guy was a known felon the tribal police chief knew about and believed to be a part of the black-market ring."

Dean looked at Steve. "So one victim was a tribal member, in his own house."

"Yep."

"The other man, also found dead, was non-native and most likely hired from outside the rez."

"Correct."

Dean gave a heavy sigh. "Oh boy. I can guess the rest. The tribal police chief knows that because of the 1978 Supreme Court ruling, his hands are tied. He can't arrest or prosecute anyone who's non-native, even if they commit a crime on tribal land. Only a federally certified agent can do that. So, he can't go after whoever hired the non-native guy, most likely the black-market ringleader. He had no choice but to notify the Bureau."

"You got it. Night Hawk reluctantly called in and is less than enthusiastic about working with the Feds. This is day five and about all I've been able to learn so far is that he's as frustrated as we are with trying to break up this crime ring. Seems even if any of the tribes are able to track down an artifact that has been stolen, oversea museums are rarely interested in returning it."

"So other tribes are being targeted?"

"Yes, although lately, for some reason, the ring has concentrated all its attention on this particular reservation." Steve rubbed the back of his neck. "But the truly horrific aspect of this crime is the death of the elder. A peaceful man, a wisdom keeper, loved by his people." Steve paused and looked at Dean before continuing. "The old man had been tortured and horribly beaten … to the point he died before the tribal police chief arrived. Beating an old man to death!" He shook his head and remained quiet for a moment.

"Any idea why someone would torture him like that?"

"The only thing that comes to mind is that it had something to do with information the ring wanted. Still …."

Dean asked, "So who did in the two victims?"

"Well, that's where the story becomes stranger. "The felon found dead at the scene was the one who had done the beating, based on the condition of his knuckles."

"Any idea how he died?"

"Actually, yes. He was struck across his temple with a heavy wrench. We know that because we found it at the scene."

Dean's eyebrows arched. "With DNA that matched?"

"Yep. But here's where it gets even more bizarre. When we received the forensic report, there was also DNA from hair and tissue samples for someone else."

"The missing third person."

"Correct."

"Hair and tissue samples could indicate someone was hit in the back of the head. So maybe a guy was knocked out, then regained consciousness and got away?"

"Only thing that makes sense."

Dean nodded in agreement, then looked at Steve. "Wait a minute. What about the 'shots fired' call that sent the tribal police chief there in the first place?"

"No one on scene had been shot. But we did find a gun, close to the wrench, in the same general proximity as the elder's body. And, yeah, it had been fired. Dug four slugs out of the door frame and wall. Appears it was fired from across the room toward the front door."

"So maybe the third guy regained consciousness and got shot at as he fled the scene."

"Yeah, except who did the firing?"

"And who wielded the wrench?"

"Exactly."

Dean rotated his beer bottle in the moisture ring on the tabletop. "I'm sure you've already concluded that a fourth person—possibly an unexpected person—showed up at the scene."

Steve gave him a nod but waited.

"So, our elder is being questioned, refuses to give them what they want, is then beaten while another guy is probably standing guard, with a gun, to make sure no one interrupts them."

"That's my guess."

"But someone intervenes ... maybe someone who has access to a back entrance. He gets the drop on the guard with a blow to the back of the head, but the noise alerts the guy doing the beating. He turns in time to get the wrench upside of his temple—probably what killed him instead of simply knocking him out. Our 'hero' then goes to the aid of the elder. Maybe while our hero tends to the elder, the guard regains consciousness and manages to flee the scene." Dean noticed Steve was sitting up, alert, closely watching him. "This match your thinking?"

"Yeah, based on evidence at the scene. Question is, who uses a wrench to attack two hardened criminals, one with a gun, and then leaves behind all the evidence?"

Dean leaned forward. "You want me to profile the mystery hero?"

"Anything would be a help."

Dean took a drink of beer and ran scenarios through his mind, then looked up at Steve. "I believe our 'hero' was a friend of the elder, one hell of a friend, it would appear. Maybe he knew of the black-market ring … or at the least noticed something amiss at his friend's house. He sneaks in the back door, hears what's happening and grabs the nearest weapon."

"There was an open toolbox just inside the back door, on top of the dryer, in the laundry area."

Dean acknowledged. "Our 'hero' then sees what's happening to his friend. He had to move with efficiency and speed to achieve what he did. That brings me to believe that somewhere in his past he's had some military or civil service experience. But what he saw propelled him into an emotional response, with no thought to his own safety. The fact he left behind the wrench and gun … he's no criminal. His thought process didn't even follow that route."

"The gun and wrench handle had been hastily wiped of any clean prints—only smudges."

"You can thank TV for that. Everyone who's watched a crime show knows to wipe off prints. But again, he wasn't even very efficient with it … could be our hero heard sirens and panicked, hurriedly wiped the weapons, and left via the back door. After all, in his mind he had no reason to be tied to the elder's death. They were friends."

Dean sat up straighter. "Okay. That brings up another thought. What if our hero had no idea that the second felon he struck, the one who had been beating his friend, died at the scene? After all, the guard with the gun regained consciousness. Maybe our hero left because he simply didn't want to be involved … he didn't even think about the weapons being evidence in a murder."

"I would agree with that angle." Dean rotated the near empty beer bottle. "Your bigger problem is the guard, the man who escaped. He knows who your hero is. Maybe he can identify him to the black-market ringleader. But you have no idea who he is. Am I right?"

"Exactly. We don't have a clue at this point."

"I'd say you better make it a priority to figure out who he is and find him, before the other guys do."

CHAPTER EIGHT

Lost Lake, Washington (Day One)

He swore he could feel the sunlight warming his body to its core. The man closed his eyes and tilted his face to the source. He imagined the sun's energy soaking into his skin, stimulating his body to create healing elements, like Vitamin D. He visualized his diseased cells fighting to recover to their former healthy, robust state.

He wasn't an old man. Society considered him to be in his prime. He even still had thick, sandy blonde hair. Handsome good-looks and charisma meant he didn't lack for female companionship. And because of his immense wealth, he enjoyed the finer things in life.

Yet, none of those factors had changed the doctor's verdict. Nor a second opinion. Or a third.

The man opened his eyes, gazed out upon the sparkling waters of the lake, listened to the waves gently lapping against the boat and sucked in the fresh air. While one hand held a fishing rod, his free hand fingered the beaded necklace hanging around his neck. Bear claws hung on each side of a large piece of turquoise as the centerpiece. He clasped his hand around the turquoise, feeling the cold stone slowly take on his own body heat.

Science had failed him.

But he refused to give up on a cure. He shoved away any thoughts of failure. They weren't allowed to linger in his mind. He had plenty of resources and the money to make things happen. Now, if only he could slow time.

CHAPTER NINE

Lost Lake Trailhead, Washington (Day One)

Nataya savored the warmth of the sun on her back as they walked. She found pleasure in the fact the well-traveled trail they followed hadn't been carved out of the land and forced to follow a straight course. Instead, it meandered its way through the valley floor, following a natural path of least resistance. When she glanced back over her shoulder toward the lake, a stand of trees now blocked her view.

She returned her attention to the slopes of the mountain range ahead of them and Carl, leading the way. Once they'd found Katie's prints and confirmed they had her trail, Walker had asked Carl to take the lead. It gave the two of them the opportunity to study the surrounding land and acclimate to the new environment.

Nataya pointed out nearby nettle plants. "I'm excited to see so many familiar plants. It eases my mind to know there are resources for food and medicinal purposes available in this region."

"The abundance is astounding. I'm sure we'll see plenty of evidence of grazing animals, considering the plentiful grasses and the variety of berries." Walker glanced up ahead at Carl.

"Then again, with three of us moving quickly through the environment, we probably *won't* see much wildlife."

Nataya knew his remark partially referred to Carl and his large backpack. She decided to move the conversation back to the topic of nature. "I noticed blackberry and raspberry patches everywhere, even along the sides of the road as Carl drove us here. And many bushes still hold some berries, even this late in the summer. I've spotted blueberries, and there are also plenty of elderberries and Oregon grapes. Amazing."

She opened her shoulder satchel and removed the cattail leaves. "It's one of the reasons I wanted to collect these while we were at the lake."

Walker peered sideways and smiled. "You're going to make a container so you can collect some of those berries."

She grinned. "I can't resist."

They slowed their walking pace. With Walker's assistance, she quickly over-lapped the long cattail leaves, weaving them into a small flat mat. Then she pulled up the sides, wove in additional fronds and quickly created a small, square container. She held it up for Walker's inspection.

"Nicely done."

"I bet I have it full of berries before we make camp."

They both picked up their tempo to catch up with Carl, then Walker spoke again. "Your comment about making camp tonight leads me to believe you and I are thinking the same thing … that we don't believe this is going to be a quick search. And it certainly doesn't feel like a rescue. Yet."

"I have to wonder what would cause Katie to take such measures to keep her father from following her."

"Makes me wonder how long before she leaves this well-traveled trail for the wilderness."

Nataya brought her gaze up beyond the forests ahead, to the rocky slopes, rugged and wild, leading to the mountain peaks, rising high above, and thought about the lone woman.

Walker spoke in the quiet. "At least for now we've got an easy to follow trail of prints, and we're making good time—or we did."

Up ahead Carl had stopped and studied the ground in front of him, then to the right. He stepped off trail as Nataya and Walker caught up.

"Katie left the trail right here." He indicated where her prints veered off from the path.

Walker studied the sign. "I'll follow this. Carl, why don't you and Nataya move ahead on the trail and see if you pick up her prints again?" He slowly moved away from the path, searching the ground for signs of Katie's passage among the grasses and underbrush.

Nataya and Carl studied the prints and markings on the trail, watching for the now familiar boot print. They looked up when Walker called to them.

"Katie stayed behind these boulders for a short time before her tracks headed back toward you."

Carl had moved ahead and stopped. "Yeah, she returned right here. So maybe she hid out of view while some hikers passed by?"

"There are definitely other prints heading the opposite direction, back down the trail," Nataya said.

"She's never done that before," Carl said.

Walker joined them. "My guess is she didn't bother with it when we were closer to the trailhead and there were lots of hikers on the path. But now we rarely pass anyone. Maybe she doesn't want someone to remember seeing a lone woman hiker up here, in case someone asks."

"Or to be able to supply a description of her," Carl added.

"I agree with both points," Nataya said. "But also, as a woman up here alone, she may simply want to avoid meeting others—

strangers—while so far from the lake community. To play it safe."

Carl nodded. "True."

Walker indicated for Carl to take the lead again. "Let's be thankful for every mile she stays on the marked trail. We can take advantage and follow as far as the light allows."

"Which could be longer than you might believe," Carl said and smiled.

"What do you mean?"

"Up here so close to Canada, sunset isn't until late in the evening this time of the year. Even after that, twilight will give us enough light to set up camp."

Nataya glanced sideways at Walker. Evidently Carl believed as they did. That this search wouldn't be resolved before night.

Walker looked at Carl. "That's good news. Let's hope Katie stops earlier than we do, after all, she's been at this since before dawn. Maybe we can lessen the distance between us quite a bit."

Carl gave him a nod and resumed his position as lead, following Katie's prints and maintaining a good pace.

Nataya stayed at Walker's side while the path was wide enough to allow it. She waited until Carl had gained a good lead on them before she spoke.

"I know this arrangement isn't to your liking, but I'm glad you aren't taking out your frustration on Carl."

"Not his fault."

"True. He's only responding to a request for assistance."

"Yep."

"And he has actually been quite helpful to us so far."

"Yes, he has."

Nataya knew from his abbreviated answers it was not a topic he wanted to explore at the moment. She shifted her attention to the forests that loomed before them, the interior deep in shadows, and she couldn't help but wonder what would drive a young woman to this path, and where she might lead them.

CHAPTER TEN

Lost Lake Trail, Washington (Day One)

Walker had to admit Carl had been correct. Sunset didn't arrive until late into the evening, and even then, the sky remained remarkably light.

They took full advantage by pushing forward even as the trees grew thicker around them. Soon, the heavy shadows of the dense forest made it too easy to miss prints in the dirt trail. Concerned that Katie might, at any moment, leave the well-worn path, Walker called a halt for fear of losing her tracks.

Although he didn't expect hikers to be coming through this time of evening, he chose a small clearing far from view of the public trail. Carl reassured him they still traveled within the national forest, in an area where they could stay overnight without an issue.

Much to his pleasure, setting up the campsite went smoothly, the three of them working together seamlessly to put up the tube tents Carl supplied.

Carl put his hands on his hips and surveyed their work. "That was sure faster having your help." He then indicated that Walker and Nataya could use the larger of the two tube tents, since they would be sharing one. He grinned and gave Walker a wink when he said it. "Tell you what. I'll fix dinner for everyone." Then he chuckled. "Of course all I have is dehydrated meals, but I bet after hiking all day it will taste pretty darn good."

"Sounds good to me," Nataya said. "I think I'll do some foraging. Maybe find something to make us a hot tea, to go with your main course, Carl." She grinned.

Walker joined in. "I'll search out a water source. Need to refill our canteen."

"I can share water with you and Nataya."

"Thanks, Carl. But since you're using your water for our dinner, and Nataya wants to make tea, I'll try to resupply ours."

Carl nodded, then went about setting up his propane one-burner unit so he could heat water.

Walker and Nataya left camp, stepping quietly through the trees and underbrush. He knew she'd be collecting pine needles, different plants or herbs to create her tea. He would concentrate on looking for wild grape vine or a creek. He wasn't worried about finding a water source since they were in the foothills of mountains. There would be plenty of creeks and streams, created by snow and glacier melt, and rain.

Once they were out of sight of camp, and Nataya had wandered a distance from him, he took a moment to stop and simply savor his surroundings. He closed his eyes, inhaled the moist air, laden with a mixture of evergreens and damp soil, exhaled, let his shoulders drop and relax. Bird song had faded into silence as birds settled in to roost for the night, so the tree frogs had picked up the melody. He opened his eyes and let them slowly adjust to the gathering gloom of night.

The thick moss carpeting the soil, rocks and tree trunks lent a green hue even as dusk settled around them. He took a closer look at the various lichens that clung to the branches, sometimes draping in long strands. It gave the woods that mystical quality he had noticed earlier in the day when they'd driven through the thick forests. While he found it all fascinating, he couldn't stop the foreboding sensation that crept in with the otherworldliness of these woods.

A nearby Barred Owl gave its familiar "who cooks for you…who cooks for you all" call to break the spell, causing Walker to hasten his search for water. But it only took moments to spot a couple of thick grape vines, hanging from tree branches. He pulled his knife free and cut a diagonal notch into the lowest section of one of the vines, the beads of clear liquid instantly rising to the surface. Using a couple of large rocks, he propped up the canteen underneath to collect the steady drip of fluid, freeing him to search farther into the trees.

A few minutes later the sound of gurgling water came to his ears. He followed the sound, discovering a small stream below the hillside he stood upon. Good to know. They could refill their water in the morning before heading out.

He turned to head back, then stopped when he heard his name quietly spoken. He turned to see Nataya step from the nearby trees. She smiled and walked toward him.

"Did you have good luck with your foraging?"

"Very good. Such abundance of available foods, even in late summer."

"I'm looking forward to your tea. As for the dehydrated meal Carl is fixing, not so much."

"Let's hope we are pleasantly surprised."

They walked through the trees together in silence, stopped to collect the now full canteen, then headed into camp.

Carl greeted them with a wave and a smile. "Perfect timing, the water is boiling. Nataya, could I ask for your assistance?"

"Sure." She hurried over, held open the food pouch as Carl instructed so he could measure and pour in the hot water.

He sealed up the pouch again and checked his watch. "I'll stir it in five minutes. Then it will be ready in another ten minutes."

Nataya pointed to the water container. "May I use your cooking pot and water to make some tea for us?"

"Sure. Here, let me add more water." Carl filled the pot and adjusted the flame on the burner. "All yours."

"Thanks." Meanwhile, Nataya had found a flat stone to use as a place to process her plants. She unsheathed her knife and set to work.

Walker discovered a patch of dry conifer needles under a tree where he could sit, stretched out his legs and leaned back to relax. He had picked up an interesting piece of wood as he walked among the trees, pulled out a smaller knife from his ankle sheath and began to whittle at it. He'd always enjoyed making wooden tools, but lately had taken to carving objects simply for the pleasure of it. Seemed Nataya's artistic nature had influenced him.

He looked up when he noticed Carl giving Nataya sideways glances as she worked. After five minutes he gave the food a good stir, resealed the pouch, and then spoke up.

"Would it bother you if I watch … and ask questions?"

Nataya looked up. "Of course not. Come on over. Asking questions is how we learn ancestral skills. They certainly don't teach it in schools … although they should."

Carl nodded. "I wish they did."

Walker watched him sit down next to Nataya, much closer than he thought necessary. He continued to work on his carving but kept part of his attention tuned to her as she talked to Carl.

"The pine needles supply vitamin C and A and have many medicinal properties." She then indicated some rose hips she had gathered from a wild rose plant. "These contain antioxidants and boost our immune system." Next she pointed to some loose leaves she had gathered. "These are blackberry leaves. Besides enjoying the berries, we can use the leaves for our tea."

Carl studied the needles, hips and leaves as Nataya gathered them up to put in the steeping water. "For just drinking a tea, we'll sure be getting lots of good stuff."

"True. It's a great way to add nutrition to our daily food intake. And they can be used medicinally as well." She added the concoction to the boiling water.

"That already smells great!" Carl moved to stand up and noticed the small carton of berries. "Whoa—what a nice batch of berries. Is that our dessert if we eat all of our dinner?" he teased, dimples showing.

Nataya grinned.

Carl gingerly picked up the container and studied it. "You made this?"

"Yes, while we were hiking today. Earlier I had noticed the abundance of berries everywhere. So that's why I wanted to gather some of the cattail leaves at the lake."

"That is so cool. Could you teach me to do that?"

"Sure, I have extra materials."

Just then a buzzer went off, startling Walker until he realized it was Carl's watch. He grumbled about technology under his breath.

"Dinner's ready." Carl pulled out some bowls, utensils and cups that had been nested together in a pouch.

Everyone took turns spooning the food into their bowls. Nataya poured tea into the cups. Then each person found a place to sit … tree stump, fallen log or ground. Quiet prevailed as food became the priority until they satisfied their initial hunger pangs. After a few minutes, Walker spoke between mouthfuls. "This is really good, Carl."

"You sound surprised," Carl said then laughed. "Thanks, it's my preferred dehydrated meal. And believe me, I've tried a lot of different ones. Not all of them had favorable results. But I'm sure it helps that we've been hiking all day. Skunk would probably taste good at this point."

Walker caught himself grinning. "True."

Carl turned to Nataya. "By the way, this tea is really nice."

"Glad you like it. The best part is we can use what grows naturally around us. Make sure you can properly identify the plants, though. And harvest respectfully. Then you can experiment with whatever combinations you prefer."

"Makes me think of all the times I've spent out in the wilderness when a cup of hot tea sure would've been nice. I've learned to ID lots of plants in the area, but knowing what is edible, or could be used for teas or medicines, is beyond my confidence level. Guess I better start working on that aspect of my knowledge."

"I believe we should always be in the process of learning. I have so much more to learn, as well." Nataya filled everyone's cups with the remaining tea, so Carl could refill the pot and start water heating to wash up dishes later. She then sat the container of berries where everyone could enjoy them.

Walker watched Carl seat himself next to Nataya and begin to quiz her between bites of berries. It was good the guy was interested in learning more about the wilderness. It appeared the young man knew his way around the landscape, understood the environment, even knew a lot of the common trees and plants, but was missing the finer nuances of it all. Walker never took it for granted he'd had the opportunity to train with Grandfather from a young age. An opportunity very few ever received in their lifetime.

Carl pointed to Nataya's shoulder satchel. "I'd love to take a closer look at your buckskin satchel, now that we have the time." He did a quick glance at Walker. "Not that I don't admire the workmanship of your rucksack. But I'm sure you agree there's an artistry to Nataya's handiwork."

While Nataya thanked Carl for his compliment, Walker realized the two had previously discussed the handmade bags at some point. How many other conversations between them had he missed?

Nataya pulled the strap over her head and extended the bag to Carl.

Walker was relieved to see Carl wipe his berry-stained fingers on some nearby moss before taking the bag from Nataya. The young man studied it closely, running his hands over the hide and studying the seams and details.

"I like how you created a button from a slice of black walnut for the closure ... and the leaf pattern you added ... I'm guessing you used a darker shade of buckskin for that?"

"Yes. Hides all have different sorts of colors and shades depending on so many variables, like how long they are smoked, the hide quality and even type of hide."

Carl further examined the construction. "It looks like you used strips of leather to sew it together, instead of thread ... or I guess sinew?"

"Close. I cut long narrow strips from the buckskin hide to use in place of sinew or thread. It's quite durable. The process is called 'making thong.'"

Walker saw Carl's eyebrows arch quizzically. Then to his surprise, Nataya laughed.

"Not *that* kind of thong," she said and grinned.

Carl blushed, then chuckled as well, his dimples showing.

Walker watched the exchange in surprise. He'd never seen Nataya tease another man like that before. As Nataya went into detail about how she used an awl and the thong to sew all her buckskin projects, he rationalized that maybe she simply felt comfortable joking with such a young guy.

Then it struck him. Most likely Carl was closer to Nataya's age than he was. Being older than her had never been an issue, but it would make sense she'd feel comfortable being around someone her own age.

After the initial surprise of his revelation wore off, a new emotion slipped in. An unpleasant sense of being "left out." He scowled, reached for the piece of wood he'd been carving. He didn't like the feeling and wanted to distract his mind from it. But when he looked up again, he found Nataya watching him. Did she sense his emotions? She gave him a warm smile. One he knew was meant only for him. His brief brush with self-pity eased a bit. But just the same, when it came time to wash up the utensils from their dinner, he'd made sure to get involved with the other two. And a part of him knew he'd be watching Carl more closely.

The temperature had dropped with nightfall. Carl snuggled down into his sleeping bag, grateful for the opportunity to stretch out and relax. After a full day of hiking and a full belly, he welcomed sleep. He could hear Walker and Nataya settling into their tube tent and had a momentary wistful thought about being alone—but quickly brushed it away.

Someday.

As he relaxed, he took a moment to recount all they had accomplished during the day and decided to mark it as successful. After all, they'd found Katie's elusive tracks, even when she had attempted to hide her passage at the beginning. And they had managed to keep her trail the entire day.

He contemplated this "missing" woman they tracked. What would make her do the exact opposite of everything she'd ever done in her life? She had to know her father would be worried and desperate to find her. The fact she left behind her cell phone proved she was aware of that. It sounded like she and her father were exceptionally close.

Nothing made sense. Which is why he understood Steve Hick's insistence on the search. The man obviously sensed a "wrongness" to the whole scenario. He knew *he* sure did.

Every search he'd assisted on over the years had been different, and he'd been on some wild goose chases. But this one didn't fit anything he'd encountered before.

He longed to discuss it with Walker. But from the beginning he'd quickly noticed that any conversation he initiated had resulted in mostly silence from Walker. The man was reserved and apparently deep into his own thoughts. Which Carl understood. He was usually more introspective during active searches. But this assignment was different, and he wasn't quite sure of his role in this endeavor. He believed he'd been brought in to serve as more of a wilderness guide for Walker, in an area the man wasn't familiar with. Walker sure didn't need him as a tracker. In fact, given Walker's silence, Carl wasn't sure his opinion would even be appreciated. So after early efforts at conversation, he dropped his attempts.

His thoughts turned to Nataya. She was much more approachable. She even encouraged his questions. Maybe he could discuss it with her. He remembered her smile and attentiveness. Her beauty shone through in a natural way, but he was just as much in awe of her knowledge and ancestry skills. She looked to be close to his age, yet her connection with the natural world was far beyond his experience.

He'd spent years learning his way around the wilderness here in this region of the state. He knew the best fishing seasons and locations for rainbow trout, steelhead, salmon and others. He knew where to take the hunters for game. And yet today he had a glimpse into how much more there was to learn, on a deeper, intimate level. It came as a shock that he knew so little when viewed in the broader scheme of things.

He vowed to change that aspect of his life. And this opportunity to work with Walker and Nataya could be the beginning of that transformation. And maybe Nataya held the key.

Katie Hicks sat cross-legged on top of her sleeping bag, her headlamp illuminating the tiny interior of her one-person backpacking tent. She took a long cleansing breath in and exhaled, to release the tension from the day. And what a day it had been.

Leaving the cottage in the predawn hours, her heart pounding. The minutes had ticked by so fast as she slowly made her way through the shallows of the lake, so she wouldn't leave prints to be followed once it was light outside. Her father was busy with a case, and it'd be days before he realized she'd left for the wilderness. But when her hiking buddies arrived later, they might look for prints. It was important they didn't find any.

Then the minutes had dragged by like thick molasses while she'd hidden in the clump of trees by the edge of the lake, watching in the predawn darkness to make sure no one had witnessed her departure and tried to follow her.

Once she knew she'd left the cottage unseen, she'd not needed to hide her tracks. Speed became her top priority and she'd made remarkable progress, putting many miles between herself and the cottage. Better than she had anticipated, which made her smile. And she needed that smile.

The mindful breathing helped her calm her thoughts. She reflected on the fact the weather had cooperated with the usual late summer sunshine but not too hot temperatures. She knew not to take it for granted. She also understood that the distance she'd been able to hike was due, in large part, to the fact she could take advantage of the nearby well-maintained and often traveled trail. She knew exactly where it would take her, letting her concentrate on moving forward at a steady pace. One she could maintain for hours.

A check of her compass reading reminded her it wouldn't be much longer before her trek would force her to leave the trail and head into the wilderness. Soon she'd be constantly gaining elevation, which would slow her progress tremendously and her passage would be labor intensive.

But the important task to concentrate on for the moment would be to move forward as quickly as possible for every mile she still followed the trail. To give as much as her body could bear. And she could handle a lot.

A concern bubbled its way into her thoughts … that she had made her decision in haste, that she wouldn't remember the way, might even become lost. But when she re-examined her motive, she knew it to be right. She shoved the worry aside and reminded herself that although it had been a while, the trips had been numerous over the years. She'd remember. She had to.

She leaned over and pulled an envelope from a pouch in her backpack, took out the one-page hand-written letter. She carefully read it again, for the umpteenth time, yet the main message remained an enigma. But it contained one vague clue, written so only she could decipher it. And she was confident she had. Reading it again made her certain that her response was the correct action to take. Beyond that lay a riddle, and she had no answers to it, yet.

CHAPTER ELEVEN

Skagit County, Washington (Day Two)

Steve Hicks drove his vehicle past the now familiar scene, small houses and mobile home trailers stretched out alongside the narrow, paved road, the North Cascade Mountains as a backdrop. When a lone block building came into view, he pulled into the parking lot. The tribal police chief supposedly waited inside for him, just like the first five days. Five days of frustration, with only lab and autopsy reports to read, over and over. Each time hoping to find a previously missed clue. Each time hoping a fresh inspiration would surprise him.

He parked and sat quietly for a moment. Yesterday his daughter had gone missing. And the fact he had to be here today, instead of looking for Katie himself, was torturous. Knowing this was day six of an investigation going nowhere, meant Steve was in no mood for further games. He gave up trying to calm himself.

The door slammed a bit harder than he anticipated as he left his SUV and strode across the parking lot and into the building. He continued past a protesting receptionist, didn't wait for an invitation into the tribal police chief's office, and sat down in front of the man's desk.

Daniel Night Hawk glanced up long enough to see him, then calmly went back to whatever currently held his attention.

Steve gave it a couple of heartbeats before he spoke. "Look, I understand why you don't want me here. I mean, why would you want the FBI poking their nose into your business here on the rez? I get that. And yeah, you and I both know the law that puts me here sucks big time." He leaned forward, both hands on Daniel's desk. "But I'd hoped by now you'd have realized I'm not your typical Bureau guy."

He received a one-eyed glance before the tribal police chief went back to the work in front of him.

"The thing is, we both want to stop these guys, right? Bad enough they're non-native and you can't touch them without the federal government's blessings. But to add insult to injury, it's obvious they have no morals about stealing your cultural heritage and causing your tribe anguish."

That got Daniel's attention and Steve an eye-full of frustrated wrath.

Steve bowed his head a moment. "Okay, so it's not the first time you've fought that battle." He looked up again. "But this time the Feds want to catch the bad guys as much as you do. This crime ring is growing larger and bolder by the day." He locked eyes with Daniel. "Besides, I'm sure you're as determined as I am right now to find and prosecute whoever gave the order to torture Joseph Spirit Horse. Torture him to the point of death."

Daniel sat up straight, his face flushing with anger. This time, Steve saw the pain in his eyes, so he went on to plead his case.

"You know damn well you've got contacts I have no access to—people who will talk to you, but not to me. But I've got access to resources far beyond your capabilities. Resources that could shave hours, or even days, off this case time … maybe help us stop these guys before they do more harm." He paused to make sure Daniel watched him, then continued. "Think what we could accomplish if we cooperated and worked together as a team to get these guys."

"You done yet?"

"Not quite. Yeah, the Bureau wants this black-market ring stopped, but more importantly, *you and I* both believe that Joseph's death should not go unpunished."

Daniel dropped his head into his chest, closed his eyes for a moment. When he looked up Steve could see the defiance had dissolved, but a wariness remained.

"You're saying all this on the up and up?"

"Yes. I meant it earlier when I said I'm not your typical Bureau guy."

Daniel leaned back in his chair, quiet for a long moment. "It would bring us some peace, to accomplish something good from this tragedy." He sighed, then drew in a deep breath, as if collecting his determination as well as his thoughts. "I've spent the better part of the year trying to run down info on these guys ... hoping to get justice for what they have done to our tribe and others. But what they did to Joseph took everything to a new level."

"We've no knowledge of murder, until now. That match your intel?"

"Yeah, none that I know of. But torturing an old man ..." He looked away.

"We believe they might have a new leader, one with even less scruples than the previous. But I'm not fully convinced that's what pushed them to this level." Steve studied Daniel. "I'm hoping you have an idea what might have triggered this incident."

Daniel studied Steve for a long moment. "Possibly." Then he pulled a photo from a folder on his desk and slid it over toward Steve. "Could be this ... our most sacred artifact. Very ancient ... the Elders say it is very powerful."

Steve studied the photo. The hand carved piece indeed had the worn appearance of something created many decades ago, yet the intricate design was still easily discernible. He admired the workmanship and details of the wolf's head and elk head with antlers. Although the only added decorations were the gemstones used for the animal eyes, it was still breathtakingly beautiful in an almost mystical way. He looked up as Daniel spoke again.

"It's been stolen. All indications point to the black-market ring."

"I'm sorry to hear that."

"It's probably worth a few thousand dollars on the black market. But torture seems like a terribly desperate move for a couple thousand dollars. Makes me wonder if there's a particular collector who wants it—desperately."

"Yeah, I can see why you'd think that."

"But the relic is priceless to our tribe. And Joseph was deeply disturbed by the theft, as he felt it his responsibility to safeguard it. He took it as a personal affront and worked tirelessly to get information about the crime ring, which he shared with me. Joseph knew that, by government ruling, my hands were tied as to what I could legally do." Daniel clasped his hands together on the desktop. "Considering what happened to him, I can only surmise that there is the distinct possibility he went all vigilante—took matters into his own hands."

"You think he went after the artifact."

"I think he stole it back from them."

Steve sat back in his chair, contemplating what he'd just heard. "So, your theory is Joseph discovers and takes back the artifact. The bad guys figure it out and find him, then torture him to get the location."

"Except, Joseph would never give that information to the likes of them. He'd die first."

"Point proven." Steve studied the photo again. "That would explain the torture. But if the bad guys don't have it and the tribe doesn't have it …" He looked up at Daniel. "You think Joseph hid it for safekeeping?"

"That's my guess. It's missing. He's dead. We may never learn what happened to it."

Steve paused, then looked at Daniel. "Who would Joseph trust with that kind of information?"

Daniel didn't hesitate. "Richard Bright Star, another Elder. He and Joseph spent many years together. When it came to spiritual matters, Bright Star was Joseph's mentor."

"Will he talk to us?"

"Doubtful. When I told him about Joseph's death, silence was his only response."

Steve stood, and waited.

"Yeah, okay. We can give it another try." Daniel grabbed his keys. "But we better take my Bronco instead of your shiny new SUV. It won't sit well with Bright Star."

"Why? Because it's expensive?"

"No, because it reeks of government bureaucracy."

Twenty minutes later Steve found himself transported back in time and plopped into a foreign country. At least that was what his mind experienced. While crossing the front yard they had passed by an old well water hand pump, still in use it appeared. Then there was some sort of domed hut with animal hides draped over it. He could only guess it was a sweat lodge or something similar.

Daniel ushered him to the front porch of a century old wood-frame house with faded paint. That is, where you could find any paint on the wooden planks. But there were new boards patchworked with the old on the porch and steps leading up to it. The shade felt good after being in the sun, but it took a moment for his eyes to adjust and notice the old man seated in a rocking chair across from him. The man was as brown and wrinkled as a raisin left in the sun too long.

Daniel approached the man, and they began to speak in their native language, with much hand gesturing from Daniel and terse words from the old man. Steve got the distinct feeling he was the topic of the conversation. But a few more hand gestures and the topic appeared to be settled.

Daniel motioned for Steve to take a seat and he sat down next to him. "Richard Bright Star says it is too hot in the house for this conversation. We will speak freely on this topic out here in the open air."

Steve wondered if the old man referred to the actual temperature of the house, or if it was an excuse to keep a white lawman outside. But he nodded in agreement.

The old man shouted something in his language and a teenage girl with raven black hair appeared with a tray of semi-cold cans of soda. She passed them out, giving Steve a long look, then disappeared into the dark recesses of the house once more.

All three of them opened the cans of soda and took a drink while Daniel quietly explained that Mary Singing River was the old man's niece and helped take care of him, along with other family members. He turned to Steve. "Richard understands English, so you can ask him questions, but he doesn't speak it too well. So I will translate if needed."

Steve faced the old man, reached into his shirt pocket, and pulled out a Backwoods Cigar. In his peripheral vision he could see the surprise on Daniel's face. He walked to a table in front of the old man and laid down the tobacco offering.

Bright Star's expression never changed. Steve wondered if the man's deeply creased countenance was permanently sealed into its present state. But when Steve again sat across from him, the old man gave him a slight nod.

Steve leaned forward. "Thank you for seeing Daniel and me. I am deeply saddened by Joseph Spirit Horse's death."

"Murder."

Steve blinked. "Yes, his murder. I understand he was a good friend."

"A good friend. A good man."

Richard spoke in a subdued voice, yet Steve could sense an underlying power. "Yes, that's what I have heard. Daniel and I believe he gave his life to protect the artifact for his tribe."

"Joseph died a warrior's death."

"Yes. A warrior's death." Steve studied the man but couldn't read anything in his expression. He tried another angle. "Joseph died trying to save the tribe's sacred artifact from the black-market crime ring."

Richard Bright Star merely nodded.

Steve took a breath to stay calm. The old man either had firsthand knowledge about the artifact, or had come to the same conclusion as he and Daniel. He asked the question. "Richard, Joseph took back the relic from the men who stole it, didn't he?"

The old man began to speak in his native language, this time launching into a long narrative full of phrases, hand gestures, pauses and many nuances. When he finished, he leaned back in his chair with no change of expression.

Daniel turned to Steve. "He doesn't know." He stood to leave.

Steve grabbed his arm. "Hold on. He was reciting a novel just then. Tell me what he said."

Daniel gave an audible sigh, stayed standing a moment, then reluctantly sat back down. He looked away from Steve as he spoke. "He says the spirits tell him the sacred relic is safe, for now. That it is currently protected from the evil powers who seek it. But he does not know which side will win."

Steve noted the expression on Daniel's face, as if bracing for the coming ridicule. Steve instead turned to the old man. "Richard, Daniel and I want to find the relic and return it to the tribe."

Richard studied Steve for a long moment before he spoke again in his native language. When the old man finished, Steve turned to Daniel for the translation, and noticed a stunned expression on the tribal cop's face as he spoke.

"He says we must seek out a white man. A man who fishes salmon on the river. Joseph's friend. Richard says he only knows the name, 'Jake'."

Steve stared at Daniel, guessing he had the same astonished expression on his own face. Then he realized the old man had spoken again, in English this time.

"Go to the Dark Horse Tavern," he said, then leaned back in the rocker, closed his eyes, and started snoring.

CHAPTER TWELVE

Lost Lake Trail, Washington (Day Two)

They'd broken camp in the predawn hours, well before the sun rose above the horizon, or in this case, the mountains. The trail had narrowed considerably since then, weaving its way deeper into the thick forests and snaking its way up the mountain slopes.

The three took turns in the lead, the other two following in single file. It was currently Walker's turn in front. Katie's boot prints were especially easy to follow now that they were many miles away from the busy part of the trail. Indeed, most of the tourists and day-hikers they'd seen yesterday had turned back within hours, using the shortcut trails leading back to the lake.

He glanced up at the bright sunny sky peeking through the heavy canopy of towering evergreens. The warmth of the sun didn't reach them in the cover of trees, but hiking uphill kept them warm, for now. The temperature continued to drop as they gained elevation, meaning nightfall would be chillier than yesterday. In fact, it would be cold. Walker didn't need to live in this state to know that fact. He knew the mountains. Although, he had to admit he'd never hiked near a sleeping volcano with glacier fields adorning its crown. He gazed around him. The lush environment fascinated him. He could well understand why Washington was referred to as the Evergreen State.

Nataya and Carl's voices drifted up to him from behind.

"I can't believe it," Carl said. "Here's some more!"

"Good catch," Nataya replied. "I guess the rain two days ago, followed by sunny weather, brought all the mushrooms out. Chanterelles are one of my favorites. We'll have a feast tonight."

Walker let the conversation fade into the background. After last night, when Nataya had encouraged Carl to ask questions, Walker noticed that whenever he took the lead on the trail the young man took advantage of the situation. Carl and Nataya were often heard in conversation as they followed behind. The topics usually ranged around plants, how to identify them, what to use them for, and which ones were edible.

Walker couldn't blame the guy for using his time with them to further educate himself about the natural world. Which left him wondering why it bothered him?

He took a few more paces in thought. Maybe it was simply the murmur of voices in the background. He was accustomed to hearing only nature sounds. Yeah, that was probably it.

He glanced back at Nataya and Carl. They both knelt at the edge of the trail, gathering mushrooms and chatting excitedly. He looked straight ahead again with a frown. Okay, maybe it was time to admit something to himself… that part of his irritation stemmed from the fact he wasn't accustomed to seeing Nataya interacting so much with another man. And a younger man, closer to her own age. An athletic, good-looking guy. And Walker was sure most women found Carl's boyish, dimpled-smile disarming, but he saw it as an outright flirt. Annoyance bubbled up, and Walker mentally shook himself.

It was admirable that Carl wanted to learn. And Nataya had

made it clear she was willing to help. He'd never had any doubts as to where her loyalty lay. He wouldn't start now.

Then he heard her laughing behind him and grumbled to himself. It sure would help the situation if she didn't appear to be so obviously enjoying the attention.

A moment later he heard Nataya call to him, using his Shoshone name, *Waahni Mia*. She usually only said it in private, but today she had used it on occasion in front of Carl. Was it her way of showing him special affection? He stopped and turned to see her and Carl hurrying to catch up, all smiles.

"You've got to check this out," Carl said. "We've got berries and some wild apples. We also found some young tender curly dock and purslane. We decided it's time for a snack break."

Walker didn't miss the excitement in the young guy's voice, and soon found himself joining in with them as they shared the harvest. He knew the nutritional plants would give them all a boost of energy, while conserving the stash of protein bars and snacks Carl carried in his pack.

Carl eagerly showed him their foraged foods for dinner tonight, Chanterelle mushrooms, an assortment of greens and wild onions. Then they all had a long drink of water and prepared to resume their hike again. Carl volunteered to take the lead.

Nataya gave Walker's hand a squeeze as he moved to a position behind her. He let some distance fall between them as he craved some quiet time to think.

His earlier reaction to Carl and Nataya's friendliness still lay heavy on his mind. He wanted to move past it, so he concentrated instead on the odd scenario with Katie.

Walker could tell by the cadence of Katie's prints that, although she was steadily pushing herself physically, there were no indications that she was fleeing in panic, as if escaping from someone. And there was a confidence in her stride that spoke to her familiarity with her surroundings. She knew where she was going—at least, so far. According to Steve she had left well-prepared for her trek. After merely hours of trailing her, it was no wonder the three of them soon concluded this wouldn't be a quick search and rescue. At least not in the typical sense.

Taking Steve's viewpoint into consideration, that Katie's behavior was completely opposite of normal ... breaking promises she'd never broken before, convinced Walker that there were outside influences dictating Katie's out-of-the-norm behavior. What they might be, he had no clue.

What he did know was that Katie might be missing, but that didn't mean she was lost.

Walker continued his thoughts as he trailed behind Nataya, until his mind automatically tuned into some specific bird language happening around them. The fact that they were following a well-traveled path and moving briskly—definitely not in any kind of stalking mode—meant they frequently caused nearby birds to "alarm" both in chirps and activity. At the moment several chickadees were moving as a group, keeping just ahead of them and chirping their alarm to anyone in earshot. He knew they'd not see any animals for a while, since the birds were warning of their approach. In fact, their fast pace had kept their encounters with wildlife to a minimum.

Understanding bird language had been some of his first lessons from Grandfather. Knowing when a land predator disrupted the birds versus an airborne threat, such as an accipiter, often revealed what might be lurking nearby *him*, as well. Walker used this bird behavior to his advantage when trailing someone, or when hunting, or to figure out when someone followed him.

He'd been watching activity behind them since they'd entered the trailhead. At first there were many people on the trail close to the lake. But as they put miles between themselves and the casual hikers, it became easier to see how many remained on the trail, based on the many bird alarms they set into motion. Toward evening yesterday, Walker knew someone still followed behind them.

He'd been watching today to see if the person stayed on the trail or had turned back toward the lake. From the size of alarming and bird displacement behind them, he determined there was either a lone person hiking behind them, or a small group who knew how to move quietly through nature. Either way, anyone following was still hours behind them. Considering it was a public, well-maintained trail, and the weather had been perfect for hiking, having others on the trail didn't worry him. It simply was a natural thing for him to be aware of his surroundings, and who or what might be nearby.

Up ahead he saw Carl stop and then begin to search off trail. Nataya and he caught up with the young man as he pointed to the ground.

"Katie went off trail here."

Walker agreed. "Now to figure out if she was avoiding another hiker, preparing to camp for the night, or leaving the trail behind for good."

"Yeah, let's hope it's not that last option," Carl said.

"Exactly." Walker stared into the thick trees. "We haven't yet found where Katie camped last night. Maybe this will be it."

The three of them automatically began their now familiar routine. Walker followed sign of Katie's passage through the forest while the other two checked for prints farther up the trail.

Before Walker found Katie's end destination, he heard Carl shout from the trail. He stopped to listen as Nataya called to him. "Katie did return to the trail, but many hours later. These prints are fresh—from early this morning."

"Okay." Walker glanced upward at the sky. "The sun's already dropping below the treetops. I'll look for her campsite. We might want to make use of it tonight and pick up her trail again in the morning." He continued to follow signs of her movement through the landscape … moss scraped from a rock here, soil disturbed there. He soon discovered a large impression in the moss and plants where Katie had set up a tent for the night.

Carl and Nataya joined him and studied the area as well. Carl pointed to the ground. "I don't see any indication of a campfire, so she must be using a little backpacker burner like I have."

"Makes sense." Walker continued, "It's going to be cold this evening. The fact we just now found Katie's campsite from last night indicates she's almost a full day ahead of us. We've enough distance between her and us that I suggest we have a campfire for warmth."

"I second that," Carl said as he raised his hand.

The three of them made quick work of setting up the tube tents, then Carl and Walker began to gather firewood while Nataya began to dig out a slight depression and move rocks to create a border to contain the campfire. It pleased Walker to see that, after only one night, they had settled into a smooth routine. Of course, it would make sense that Carl was accustomed to functioning as a team, but it gave Walker some peace of mind to know they could work together.

Still, he didn't know if he'd ever get used to all the talking between Carl and Nataya. Then he grimaced as he thought about how old that made him sound.

Nataya prepared her tinder bundle, laid small kindling nearby, along with larger twigs and sticks. Carl joined her as she pulled a ferrocerium rod from her shoulder satchel, and her carbon steel knife from its sheath.

"Okay if I watch?"

"Of course." She smiled. With practiced efficiency she used the flat top edge of her knife and stroked down the ferro rod, creating a cluster of sparks. The sparks landed within the tinder and began to smolder, then catch fire. She quickly added more tinder, and as the flames grew larger, she began to add kindling.

"Wow, you made that look easy," Carl said with a grin.

"Practice can make any method look easy." She laid larger twigs on the flames. "When Walker found me living alone in the wilderness, before my memories had returned, I was using quartz and iron pyrite stones to create sparks and start a fire. Talk about taking practice." Surprised at where her conversation had gone, she looked at Carl. "Sorry. I don't usually talk about my past."

"Please don't stop. I want to hear about your experiences. That is, if you don't mind sharing them."

Nataya smiled at the man's eagerness. "Besides showing me how the ancient Ute people made fire, Walker told me about the trappers and mountain men in this country. They carried an iron striker and flint, often in a small metal container along with char cloth. Later, when my memories returned, I discovered that many of the survival skills I had used in the wilderness were things I had read about in the books my Grandfather had given me ... books about indigenous peoples and how they lived, books about our ancient ancestors ... about how they used quartz or flint and iron pyrite long before iron tools were first made. After living in the wilderness as I did, I became more curious about fire making. I decided to study different methods and I practice them when we're out in the woods." She noticed Carl stared at her, eyes wide in amazement. She picked up the large ferro rod. "I have to admit that I find this so easy to use that I sometimes feel I'm cheating a bit." She grinned, hoping to lighten the mood.

"I'm pretty good with my Bic lighter." Carl laughed. "Seriously though, I think it's smart to learn alternate ways to make fire. I should make more of an effort to practice when I'm out in the field. Getting the right components for the tinder seems to be my biggest challenge, especially with all the moisture and rain we have here."

"I bet. I've found it takes lots of practice and experimentation. Even the type of tinder I choose dictates how I will position my knife and ferro rod, or flint and steel. Every time I'm out in the wilderness I look for new elements to try, as well as different techniques and tools. Never know when my favorite tinder components, or tools, might not be available."

"What was it you used tonight? It worked great. And it looked familiar."

"The fuzz from a Cattail head and some birch bark shavings"

Carl grinned. "So, yesterday when you cut some cattail leaves—"

"I also cut and saved a cattail head. And I always carry a small amount of birch bark with me, since it lights so well. It's like my secret ingredient when all else might fail."

"Hah—smart."

Carl added a couple larger pieces of wood to the flames. "We're fortunate to have lots of cedar here in the Cascades. Burns easily, even in the damp climate. I've always thought I'd like to make a bow drill set and use cedar for the base."

"That would be an excellent choice."

Walker joined them and laid down an armload of firewood by the campfire. He slid off his pack and looked at Nataya as he reached inside. "Thought you might want your wool sweater."

"Yes, thanks. It's definitely getting colder tonight." She pulled the heavy loose-fitting cardigan over the top of her buckskin tunic, while Walker did the same. She noticed Carl had already added a fleece jacket. She glanced around them. "I can't get over how lush it is here."

"Yeah," Carl said. "But then we do get a lot of rain most of the year. Summer not so much. That's why we've been so fortunate to have sunny weather so far. We're still at the end of the summer season. But the rains will move in soon for fall and get serious come winter. Of course, as we move up in elevation, all bets are off as to what we might run into."

Nataya grew quiet in contemplation, wondering where this missing woman might lead them, and even more puzzling, why. But with the fire blazing nicely she began to set up her kitchen, such as it was. She arranged some rocks around the fire so the cookpot could sit over the hot coals when they were ready. Then she chose a large flat stone to serve as a place to prepare the plants and mushrooms they'd gathered throughout the day.

Carl began to rummage about in his backpack and brought out the cook pot.

Nataya glanced his way. "Carl, could I ask a favor?"

"Sure."

"Let's have a look at what food supplies you have. Maybe you and I can collaborate for dinner tonight."

"Awesome idea." He quickly pulled out packages of jerky, protein bars, and sealed pouches of dehydrated meals.

Nataya noticed Walker had also taken an interest in Carl's supplies. Then she spotted an item that got her attention. "Is that pemmican?"

"Yeah, I always carry some."

"Perfect!" She reached for the package. "I'd love to be able to cook the mushrooms and greens in some oil. I can melt the fat in the pemmican cake." She could already imagine how wonderful the food was going to taste.

"Cool." Carl smiled and held up another pouch of dehydrated food. "How about some powdered eggs to add to your mushrooms, wild onion and greens? We could create one heck of an omelet if I had a skillet. But hey, I'd settle for some scrambled eggs instead. What do ya think?"

"I think that sounds heavenly." Nataya unsheathed her knife and set to work preparing the mushrooms, cleaning and cutting up the onion and other greens. As she worked, she noticed that

Walker had started carving on a stout stick. He often created tools when out in the wilderness and because she'd been foraging so many plants, she guessed he had decided to make her a digging stick. She smiled to herself and went back to concentrating on the food before her.

Before long a delicious aroma filled the air as the ingredients simmered in the melted fat. Carl added water to the powdered eggs, mixed them thoroughly, and then poured the mixture into the sauteed ingredients, cooking them until done.

The three of them dipped the finished meal into their bowls and settled around the campfire to eat. A long moment passed before anyone spoke.

Walker was the first to get a full sentence out between bites. "You both outdid yourselves on this meal. It's delicious."

Nataya wanted to savor every bite but knew the cold evening air would soon cool the food. She noticed Carl and Walker also ate quickly. They scraped out every morsel from the cookpot before she cleaned it and filled it with water to make tea.

The three of them relaxed next to the warm campfire while waiting for the water to come to a boil. Carl reached over, picked up a small log and laid it on the fire. Nataya watched him glance Walker's way, start to speak, then stop himself. She understood how intimidating Walker could appear with his stoic demeanor. He wasn't an easy man to read or get to know, even in a casual way. She decided to help Carl out. She checked the water, then casually turned toward the young man. "So Carl, Steve said you know this area intimately. I'm curious as to what lies ahead of us on this trail." She saw relief flood the man's face.

"Yeah, we should talk about that." He glanced at Walker and then continued. "We're not far from the highest point this trail reaches before it makes a wide arc and starts heading back down the mountainside. It eventually returns to the lake, although it takes you to the north end of the lake—opposite from where we started."

Nataya noticed Carl had Walker's attention, then she spoke. "So the question would be, why would Katie hike all the way up this way only to return to the lake?"

"Unless she really is simply on a hike and didn't tell anyone …"

"But, if I'm understanding you correctly, the trail wouldn't even take her directly back to her cottage," Nataya said.

"Correct."

Walker shook his head. "Steve Hicks doesn't rattle easily. Even if this is about his own daughter. I have to agree with his take on this. Something is wrong."

Nataya watched Walker. "You think outside forces are dictating her actions, don't you?"

"Yeah, I do." Walker relayed what he had read from Katie's prints, her lack of panic, her confidence and familiarity of the trail.

"She sounds like a person on a mission," Nataya offered.

"That's an excellent way to describe it."

Carl spoke up. "Which brings us back to the trail situation. If we believe she's not planning to head back down to the lake, she only has one other option. To go off trail into the wilderness. And soon."

Nataya watched Walker contemplate the information before he spoke.

"So, how much farther does the trail go before it veers back downward to the lake?"

"Maybe three miles."

Nataya looked at Walker. "So if she camped here last night, then by early this morning she would've already gone off trail. If we are reading all this correctly."

"Yeah, I have to agree with that. Which means we need to get an extra early start in the morning. She'll most likely be forced to move slower once she gets off trail. Maybe we can make up at least those three miles by hitting it hard and fast before we also have to go off trail to follow her."

"Yeah, and since Katie took this trail to enter the wilderness, I'm guessing she'll be heading up. Otherwise, she would've stayed in the valley. The elevation gain has been nothing compared to what we'll experience from here. And that also means 'weather'. We've been lucky so far," Carl added.

Nataya noticed Carl stopped there, but she understood the implications and decided she'd be extra grateful for the warm fire tonight.

Carl lay on his side in his sleeping bag, snug in the small tent. Using the thick material of the bag to block any glow escaping from the face of his cell phone, he took it off airplane mode and quickly scanned through his text messages. His SAR team leader and Steve Hicks had both reached out to him for updates. He composed a quick text to each, deciding not to mention the possibility that Katie might've gone into the wilderness. Better to wait and know for sure. He hit send and noticed the texts took a long time to deliver, so he checked the signal strength. He was down to one bar now.

He knew from experience that if they did soon leave the trail and head up the mountainside, he'd lose his signal altogether. He counted himself fortunate it had lasted this long, figuring the pleasant weather had played in his favor. He plugged the phone into a small power pack he carried. He'd try to keep it charged for now. Well, at least until he had to change to the SAT phone Steve had insisted he carry. He planned to use the SMS text option of the SAT phone to do his updates. He flinched at the idea of Walker learning he had it and hoped it wouldn't come to that.

The warm sleeping bag tempted him toward slumber, but he rolled faceup, put his hands under the back of his head and stared at the top of the tent. He mentally ran through all his supplies still on hand. The foraging he and Nataya did had undeniably saved on his food stores. And it certainly made dinner more appetizing. Hopefully they could continue to harvest foods while Walker did the time-consuming part of tracking Katie's prints.

The conversation around the campfire came to mind. He knew Nataya had opened the door for him to speak his thoughts tonight and he appreciated it. Now that the topic had been broached and he'd seen Walker listen to his input, he wouldn't be so reluctant to share in the future.

In fact, now that he better understood the scenario that they had been dropped into, he needed to keep speaking up and give his opinion, and not let Walker intimidate him. In most search and rescue situations he was accustomed to working with a team, in a specified area to cover, with support waiting in the wings to supply them with food and water when they needed it. But this scenario was closer to what he did for his business, being a hunting or fishing guide. And that was something he knew he excelled at.

Searching for a missing woman who didn't want to be found was another matter.

CHAPTER THIRTEEN

Skagit County, Washington (Day Two)

Steve followed Daniel through the entrance of Dark Horse Tavern, watched the bartender glance up to give Daniel a nod and friendly smile. The moment the bartender caught sight of Steve, though, the friendliness slid from the man's face.

He and Daniel crossed the low-lit room toward the bar. Steve did his best to keep a neutral expression and not let on he knew by now everyone in the room had already pegged him as a government man.

Daniel stood at the bar. "Hey, Ed. How's it going?"

"Can't complain."

Steve saw the bartender give Daniel a glance as if to say, 'Why did you bring this guy in here?' but the man didn't voice his thoughts. Instead, he simply said, "What can I get you guys?" He swiped the bar with a rag.

"Thanks, Ed." Daniel said. "But we're on duty." He titled his head toward Steve. "This is Steve Hicks, FBI. We're working a case together." He said it all casual-like, as if giving the weather forecast.

Ed stared at him.

Daniel leaned forward on the bar, making direct eye contact with Ed. "The two of us plan to search for and bring in whoever ordered the torture and ultimate death of Joseph Spirit Horse."

"Yeah?"

Daniel nodded. Steve watched some of the hardness leave Ed's eyes.

Daniel continued. "Yeah, in fact we went to see Richard Bright Star."

"So."

"He talked to us."

The bartender stopped working. Daniel had the man's full attention now. A level of respect shown in Ed's eyes. "Richard talked to you?" He glanced at Steve when he said it.

"Yeah. In fact, he told us to come here."

Ed blinked in surprise. "Richard sent you?"

"Yes, he seems to believe you can help us."

Now it was Ed's turn to lean into the bar, intent on Daniels' words. "Really. What did Richard say?"

"He says we need to find a white man who fishes salmon on the river. Joseph's friend. Goes by the name of Jake."

Ed's face lit up. "Yeah, that would be Jake, alright. He and Joseph are—were—fishing buddies, for sure. Joseph always told anyone who'd listen that he and Jake thought the same way when it came to salmon … that a person has to understand 'em if they want to catch 'em. That salmon need to be willing to give up their spirit to you … stuff like that."

"So they came in here often?"

"Not really. Sometimes they'd stop in for a cold one at the end of a long day on the river. Joseph doesn—didn't drive—so Jake provided transportation for their fishing trips. But Joseph sometimes came in with others from the rez and loved to talk about his and Jake's fishing trips. Adventures he called 'em. So I've heard all the stories over the years."

"That's all really great information. Do you happen to know Jake's last name?"

Ed shook his head. "If I knew it at one time, I've forgotten it."

"What about his bar tab? Does he pay with a card?"

"Nope, always pays with cash. You have to understand … Jake's a grizzled ole mountain man. Well, actually, it's kinda hard to tell how old he is with that beard. But he has no use for today's technology. That much I can tell you."

Steve read the disappointment on Daniel's face. He spoke to Ed. "You say he always drove Joseph to their fishing trips. Maybe Jake lives near the rez?"

Ed rubbed his chin in thought. "Well, I always got that impression." He perked up. "You know, there's a guy who probably does know. A young guy. One of Jake's Disciples."

Daniel straightened. "What do you mean—Disciple?"

Ed laughed. "Oh, it doesn't have anything to do with a cult or religion. Jake's a loner—big time. But, according to Joseph, he has a soft spot in his heart about leaving behind some kinda legacy … his woodsman knowledge … to the younger generation. Jake says they're too disconnected from nature, from the real world. That they're lost and don't even know it and need to find themselves. Joseph said that over the years Jake has mentored a few select groups. Taught them what he knows of the woods. Joseph always called them 'Jake's Disciples' because they all look up to Jake as a teacher."

"So you think one of them can help us?" Steve attempted to bring the topic back to point.

"Yeah. Trying to remember the guy's name. For a bartender I have a terrible time with names. But I know what everyone will order for drinks." Ed chuckled, then snapped his fingers. "Kevin. That's it."

"And his last name?" Daniel asked.

"Don't know. But come back tomorrow morning when I open. He'll be here."

"Any way to contact him tonight?" Steve asked.

"Nope. He works the night shift somewhere. But he stops in here for a late breakfast after work, before he goes home to crash."

Steve tried to let the disappointment settle after getting his hopes up. He'd try to be content with the fact that at least they had a lead to follow.

Ed interrupted his thoughts. "Hey, guys, might as well kick off for the night and enjoy some of my burgers. My treat."

Steve glanced at Daniel, saw him smile.

"Ed does make one mean burger."

Steve's stomach reminded him he hadn't eaten since breakfast. "Sounds good to me."

He and Daniel settled onto a couple of bar stools and ordered beers, since it appeared they were now off duty. Steve hoped filling his empty belly would placate the frustration of having to wait until morning to pick up the trail again. He reminded himself that he'd work smarter with some food and a good night's sleep.

He pulled his cell phone from his pants pocket and checked it on the sly. Carl had responded to his text with an update, letting him know the signal on his phone would soon be gone and they'd have to switch to the SAT phone, but the good news was they were still on Katie's trail, and she seemed to be doing fine. Steve read the words again. It helped him push down that sense of panic always on the verge of rising out of control. He couldn't let that happen. He knew he needed to keep a clear head. He also knew that to others his concern probably appeared unwarranted, but his gut told him something was very wrong in Katie's world. And every hour that passed with her still gone made it more difficult.

CHAPTER FOURTEEN

Lost Lake Trail, Washington (Day Three)

Carl considered himself an early riser, at least when it came to camping or search and rescue work, but when he crawled from his tent long before sunrise in the gray of predawn, he found Walker and Nataya sitting next to a small campfire.

Nataya looked up and smiled. Walker gave him a friendly nod.

"Morning," Carl said as he pulled on his boots, then ambled over to join them.

Nataya pointed to the cooking pot filled with steaming water. "Thought you might want some water for your coffee before I make tea."

"Thanks. Yeah, I'd like that." Carl enjoyed Nataya's teas in the evenings, but first thing in the morning he craved a shot of caffeine. It made him smile to realize she had noticed that aspect about him.

He walked over to where he'd hung the food pack from a tree limb, high in the air, and released the rope holding it. They were most certainly within bear territory now. When he first started spending time in the wilderness, it had only taken one time of having a bear sniff his tent while he tried to sleep to make him a firm believer in keeping food far away at night.

Carl pulled out some instant coffee from the pack and returned to the fire. "Either of you want any coffee, I have plenty," he said, holding it up. When they declined, he dumped some into his cup and added some of the now boiling water. He stirred the coffee and nodded his head toward his little propane burner. "You're more than welcome to make use of my backpack stove anytime you want."

Nataya looked up. "Thanks, Carl. That's kind of you. I guess I'm so used to making a fire, I didn't even think of it. Besides, we should probably save your fuel whenever we can." She added some crushed pine needles and dried blackberry leaves to the rest of the boiling water.

Carl watched her work. He was continually amazed at how many items Nataya pulled from her shoulder satchel by the end of day. It could only mean that as they hiked, she managed to forage far beyond what he noticed when they sought out plants together. He equated it to her being on autopilot when it came to plants. She didn't even need to think about it. She'd see a plant she knew, mindfully harvest it, then move on. If only he had a small portion of the plant knowledge she possessed.

He sipped the coffee, savoring the aroma and warmth. The morning still held onto the cold of last night. He zipped up his fleece jacket. Walker and Nataya still wore their heavy wool sweaters. He knew everyone would be eager to get moving so he pulled out some jerky and protein bars for breakfast.

As he ate, Carl took a moment to enjoy the peaceful morning. Ironically, in his SAR team he was known as the jokester and storyteller. But mornings were different, maybe because the caffeine hadn't had time to sweep away the cobwebs of sleep. Walker and Nataya were also quiet, but then, they always were. He'd have to be blind to not notice how well they worked together, often completing tasks with little or no conversation. He figured they must know each other so well, talk often wasn't necessary.

He took another drink of coffee and glanced at Nataya. She was so much fun to talk to, and he caught himself occasionally lightly flirting with her. Perhaps because she appeared to genuinely enjoy talking with him, joking and laughing easily. Their conversations were such a contrast to what he had observed with her and Walker's relationship. More than once the thought crossed his mind that perhaps Nataya missed having conversations with others. The older man sure wasn't much of a talker. In fact, lately Carl had occasionally glimpsed a look of displeasure or an outright frown on Walker's face while he and Nataya were kidding around.

Then a thought struck him. Maybe Walker didn't like the fact Nataya so obviously enjoyed talking with him, a clearly younger guy. In fact, Carl guessed she was closer to his own age than Walker's. Maybe that was the reason the tracker acted so aloof. And it would explain the expressions of disapproval he'd witnessed lately.

Well, if he was correct, that sure would explain a lot. Carl felt a grin begin but quickly stifled it. If he wanted to learn from Walker, he'd be smart to not offend the man. Going forward he'd strive to be more professional and less flirty with Nataya.

He took a last gulp of his drink as Walker and Nataya began to clean up, then joined them in breaking camp. They headed back toward the trail, Walker leading the way.

Carl let Nataya fall in behind Walker, and he brought up the rear. He wanted to inconspicuously check his cell phone. He pulled it from his pocket and noticed it tenuously held onto that one bar. But he had no illusions. He would lose the signal today, if indeed Katie led them into the wilderness.

He grabbed the SAT phone from an easy-to-reach side pouch

on his backpack, slid it out and checked it. Full battery charge. Good. He returned it to the pouch just as Walker reached the trail, waiting while he and Nataya caught up.

Carl watched the tracker take a long look at the sky, slowly turning to view the entire horizon. So, he did the same. Big fluffy white clouds hung mid-level on the horizon, with lots of blue sky in between them. Appeared to Carl that they were going to luck out with another sunny day. Then he overheard Walker tell Nataya that rain would be moving in later.

Carl looked back up to the sky. What had Walker seen that he'd missed? He started to ask the man, but clamped his mouth shut instead. Even with his recent revelation that he should feel free to speak up, he hesitated. This felt more like questioning Walker's judgment. He didn't want to jeopardize the progress he'd made so far. He took one last glance up at the sky and then turned to follow the other two.

An hour later, Carl had the lead when he spotted where Katie left the trail, about three miles from where they had camped last night, as he had predicted. The three of them performed their practiced routine, checking for her return to the path farther ahead, to no avail. They had then followed the barely discernible dirt path far enough to determine Katie didn't plan to return to the main trail. A part of him rejoiced that his theory had been proven correct and maybe he'd gain some points with Walker. The other part of him recognized that following Katie's tracks would now become more of a physical challenge as they left the easy to follow dirt and gravel trail for the thick bramble of trees and ground cover.

Carl pulled out his compass to take a reading, lining it up with the direction Katie's path took through the trees. "She's heading in a northeasterly track."

Walker stood behind Carl and lined up with the angle Carl indicated with his arm, then looked past it to the surrounding landscape and beyond, the mountains. "Tell me about this part of your land."

Carl's heart leapt in excitement. Finally, a chance to contribute. "This entire region is a part of the Mt. Baker-Snoqualmie National Forest." His arm encompassed the area in front of them. "That means we'll be able to freely disperse camp, as we've been doing. And you should know that I have every pass and special use permit we might possibly need to legally fish or gather edibles."

Walker nodded in understanding.

Carl looked back to his compass. "If Katie stays on this trajectory, we'll most likely be traversing the mountain slopes, and at a steep incline. We're in the Northern Cascades, close to the border of Canada. That means this time of year the weather can be unpredictable as we go higher in elevation, maybe even get snow." As he said it, he couldn't help noticing that the fluffy clouds of an hour ago were slowly spreading out into a thin blanket of white. Maybe Walker was right about the rain.

Carl forced himself to focus. "You already know from the scat we've seen that we're in bear country, but other wildlife predators up here include cougar, wolverines, lynx, wolves and bobcat." He looked at Walker. "I also serve as a wilderness guide, so I can attest to the fact that, with the abundant food sources, there is a lot of wildlife. I know at one time Washington State had the second largest elk population." Carl paused and stared into the forest. "As for wildlife encounters … I always carry bear spray, but I've not had any issues." He looked back at Walker. "Of course, when I'm in rescue mode I'm making noise, not only to forewarn wildlife I'm quickly moving through, but yelling to let a person know someone is nearby to offer them help."

"Thanks, Carl. I appreciate the information." Walker turned to study the direction Katie had taken. "We were able to move quickly while on that open trail. Appears it's going to be slow going now, not only to make sure we don't lose Katie's prints, but just the act of moving through the thick trees and underbrush."

Carl noticed Walker had glanced at his large backpack, as if making a point. Then the man turned away, took a few steps from where they stood and studied the path behind them. He'd noticed Walker doing this maneuver often during the past hour. Confident with his newly acquired status, he spoke up when Walker returned to their group.

"You watching for something in particular?"

"Bird sign."

Carl figured his confusion must have shown in his expression because Walker went on to explain. "You can use bird behavior to know when something is disturbing them, such as a land predator or hawk ... or possibly other people."

"Oh, thought maybe you were watching for Sasquatch to appear." The moment the words slipped out of his mouth, he regretted them. It was something he would've said while joking with his SAR team. He felt his face turn red. Before he could apologize, he heard Nataya chuckle, and saw a smile in Walker's eyes, even if it didn't quite reach his lips. Thank goodness he hadn't insulted the guy. He relaxed.

Walker looked down at the ground then tilted his head slightly, glancing up at Carl. "It would be good to remember that most indigenous peoples' legends and myths have an element of truth behind them. They are often a story with a lesson." He glanced back behind them. "But someone or *something* is following us."

Carl would swear he saw Walker grin as he turned away to study Katie's prints and continue on the path. He looked at

Nataya, but she had already moved on as well, so he fell in line behind her. But he couldn't resist one last glance back through the trees behind them before he followed their lead.

CHAPTER FIFTEEN

Skagit County, Washington (Day Three)

Steve and Daniel followed Ed through the tavern toward a table tucked into a quiet corner, where a broad-shouldered young man was finishing breakfast. The guy sopped up the last of the gravy with a biscuit as they approached.

"Hey, Kevin," Ed said as they stopped at the table. "This is Daniel, the Tribal Police Chief, and Steve, from the FBI. The two guys I told you about."

Kevin stood and shook their hands.

Steve noticed he studied them as he did. But when he spoke his voice held a respectful tone.

"So you guys want to find the person who gave the order to torture Joseph, eh? Well, if there's anything I can do to further that cause, I'd be happy to help."

Daniel answered. "We appreciate it, Kevin. We have reason to believe Jake might be able to help us with this case, so we're hoping you can direct us to him."

"Really? If that's true I'm surprised he hasn't already come forward. I mean, he and Joseph were like blood brothers." He looked at Daniel. "No insult intended."

"None taken."

Steve watched the exchange, realizing he had missed that point altogether. Why *hadn't* Jake already come forward?

Daniel continued. "We're hoping you know where Jake lives?"

"Yeah, sure I do."

"Could we follow you there?"

"Like now?"

"Yeah, like right now."

"I just finished a double-shift." He sighed. "But if it helps find the bad guys …"

"It might."

Steve settled Kevin's bill, improving the man's attitude, and the three of them left the tavern. Daniel followed Kevin's truck as he drove through the small burg and out of town, then turned down a dead-end road. The man parked in front of a small cottage-style house. Daniel pulled in behind him, and they joined the young man.

Kevin gestured toward the cottage. "Just because Jake's Jeep isn't in the driveway, doesn't mean he isn't here. Most times he pulls it into the alley behind the house. Says he doesn't like people knowing when he's home, or not. He's kinda funny like that." He led the way to the front door and started to knock, but the door creaked open a few inches.

"Well, that's not good," Kevin said. "Jake always keeps the doors locked." He shouted Jake's name through the slightly open door, but there was no answer. He turned to Steve and Daniel. "Do we go in?"

Daniel looked at Steve. "We're in your jurisdiction. But it's open so it's not like we're breaking and entering."

"Yeah, just trespassing," Steve replied. But he nodded his assent. "I can always say we were concerned for his safety." Out of habit, he pulled his side arm and motioned Daniel and Kevin behind him. He noticed that Daniel drew his weapon as well. He pushed open the door and stepped into the living room.

The place looked like a war zone. Furniture tossed about, books and papers scattered everywhere. He gave a quick prayer they weren't too late. He nodded to the guys to stay put, then quickly checked and cleared the rooms—each one in the same state of disarray—but no sign of Jake. Relieved, he holstered the gun and returned to the living room where Daniel and Kevin waited.

Daniel gave him a look. "Well, someone was searching for something."

"Yeah, gotta wonder why," Kevin muttered.

Steve didn't want to talk about the missing relic in front of Kevin. He figured Daniel was thinking along the same lines as he. At this point they didn't know if Jake had been targeted simply because he was Joseph's friend, or because he was their missing "hero" who had tried to save his friend from the crime ring. One thing was certain. They couldn't trust anyone at this point. "Bigger question is, where's Jake?"

Daniel looked at Kevin. "You said he sometimes parks in the alley?"

"Yeah, I can show you."

They followed Kevin out the back door. Steve rested his hand on his holstered gun, just in case.

As they crossed the backyard Kevin pointed to a large bramble of blackberry bushes. "There's a shed behind the bushes, where Jake keeps his outdoor equipment. You want to check it out first?"

"Sure." Steve let Kevin lead the way and as the young man worked to get the door of the shed open, he looked back toward the cottage. There was no way to see the shed from the house. Maybe they'd be lucky and find it hadn't been searched.

Kevin swung the door open and used his phone as a

flashlight. Inside they were greeted by a well-organized array of outdoor tools and camping equipment. Kevin panned the light around the walls and pointed to an empty hook. "That's where Jake stores his largest backpack, for long excursions." He looked at Steve and Daniel. "Guess he decided to go out for some 'woods' time. Too bad someone messed up his place while he's gone. That sucks."

Steve didn't comment on Kevin's assumption. Instead, he glanced around. "Is it normal for him to go out like that, without letting anyone know?"

"Yep. Does it all the time."

"What if he gets lost or injured?"

Kevin laughed. "Jake lost? Would never happen, around these parts anyway. He's been exploring this region for years. And the part about getting hurt? Jake always says he's not afraid of dying in the wilderness … says that's the way he hopes he goes."

Steve asked Kevin to continue searching the shed, looking for any notes or clues, until he heard Daniel call his name from out in the yard. He stepped out of the shed to see the man standing at the back of the yard, pointing.

"Here's a Jeep."

Kevin sprinted over, with Steve jogging behind.

"Yep, that's Jake's Jeep."

Daniel looked in through the passenger window. "The keys are still in the ignition."

Steve put his hands on his belt and studied the scene. "Why take your backpack and leave without your vehicle?" The moment the words left his lips, he thought of Katie. He glanced back up toward the cottage.

Kevin turned to Steve, his face suddenly pale. "You think Jake found his place like that …" He nodded toward the cottage. "And took off for the wilderness."

Steve didn't answer but turned and started walking toward the cottage. "Let's check the house closer. Maybe we missed a note or something."

The three walked in silence for a few moments, then Steve turned to Kevin. "Hey, if you want to head home for some much-deserved sleep, I think we're good now."

"Do I have to?"

Steve noticed the man's face had grown taut with worry. Not the face of someone who was in on the crime. He felt certain of that now. "Of course, not. You can stay if you want."

"Thanks. I think I'll hang around. Now I'm really worried about Jake. Maybe we'll find something to ease my mind."

Steve nodded. "I hear ya. Yeah, I hope so, too."

The three of them each took a different room to look through. Steve chose a bedroom converted into an office. Seemed the room had the most "damage," papers strewn everywhere, desk drawers pulled out, even cushions thrown from furniture. He started sorting through all of it, not expecting to find the artifact but hoping to find something to lead them to Jake.

He picked up a piece of paper with Jake's name on it. Jake Cress. Well, at least he had the guy's full name now. For some reason it sounded vaguely familiar, but he brushed the thought aside. He glanced down at the desk, then away, then back to it again. While the rest of the room lay in chaos, the top of the desk held a neatly arranged line of framed photos across the top. Why hadn't he noticed it when he entered the room? He sat down at the desk and studied the photos.

They weren't arranged in a way someone would normally display them on a desk, more like they had been staged so they could be easily studied. So that's what he did. Each photo was of a group of young people, outdoors in the woods or in Jake's backyard. Jake's Disciples, he guessed. Then he looked closer at one of the photos and sat back in the desk chair, stunned. Katie!

It took a minute for his brain to comprehend what he was looking at. Then he began looking close at the rest of the photos. Katie was in more than a few of them. She must've spent a good deal of time studying with the group. Now he understood why Jake's name sounded familiar. Katie had surely mentioned it in passing, while telling him about her bushcraft classes years ago. Why hadn't he paid closer attention?

One frame lay face down, the back ripped off. He picked it up. The photo was missing. He looked around, then over the edge of the desk. A torn photo lay face down on the floor. He picked it up and studied it. The photo had clearly been of two people, but one side was torn away. The one remaining was Kevin.

Steve shouted for the young man, who came running into the room.

"This looks like a recent photo of you." Steve held up the torn photo.

Kevin grinned. "Sorta, it was taken a couple of years ago." Then he frowned. "Why is it torn like that?"

Steve ignored the question. "Kevin, do you remember who the other person in the photo was?"

"Of course. It was of a girl named Katie."

Steve blinked, then turned toward the desk. "The same Katie as in these other photos?"

"Yeah." Kevin looked puzzled. "Why would someone tear the photo like that?"

Steve's body went numb as he slumped back into the desk chair. "Because whoever was in here, took it for reference."

Kevin's face paled. "Are the people who did this…" He glanced around the room. "… are they looking for her?"

"It would seem so."

"Looking for who?"

Steve glanced up to see Daniel standing in the doorway.

"My daughter, Katie."

Kevin's mouth fell open. Daniel looked confused.

Steve quickly filled Daniel and Kevin in on Katie's disappearance and the search he had put into place. He looked at Daniel. "The fact that both Katie and Jake disappeared in the same fashion has to mean something."

"I would agree."

"I mean, I understand leaving the vehicles behind so they couldn't be easily followed."

"Or maybe they left them behind because where they were going, they don't need them?" Daniel looked at Steve. "Your tracker friends are still following Katie?"

"Yes."

"And she has gone into the wilderness?"

"Well, yes. But Katie feels safe there. She knows she can hide in the wilderness."

"And it would seem the same is true for Jake."

Steve let that thought settle in. He looked around at the tossed room. "I guess it's evident why Jake didn't feel safe staying around here. Was he targeted simply because he knew Joseph? Or was it because he's involved with the …" He paused, not wanting to mention the missing relic in front of Kevin.

Daniel picked up the thread. "I'm not sure, but if Katie indeed left because she felt in danger, we need to notify every one of the people in these photos." He looked at the framed pictures on the desk.

"I can help," Kevin offered. "I know all these people. I can give you their names and phone numbers."

"Thanks, Kevin. That would be a great place to start." Steve looked back at the torn photo he still held in his hand. "But why are they targeting Katie, out of all these people?" He indicated the photos lined up on the desktop.

Kevin slowly raised his hand over his head. "I think I might know."

Steve and Daniel looked at him.

"Me and the others always knew Katie and Jake were especially close. Nothing romantic or weird like that, just a special bond because of their mutual affinity for the outdoors."

Steve stared at Kevin, trying to comprehend what he'd just heard. How could that be? He and Katie had that special bond. As a father and daughter, they got along great. Then he thought of all the times he'd been away on assignments … absent for much of her younger years. True, he and Katie had become especially close after his wife passed, but there had been a time when Katie might have looked for a father figure who was more available. He realized Kevin was still talking, tuned back in.

"Whoever broke in here maybe didn't know about Katie and Jake being closer than the others in those photos, but they may have seen that." He pointed to a framed photo hanging on the wall.

Steve got up and walked over to the photo. It was an older picture of Katie, taken maybe five years ago, standing next to a bearded man. The man looked to be in his late fifties in the photo, but it was difficult to tell with the beard and messy hair. If Steve was guessing correctly then the guy would be in his early sixties now. Steve pointed to the man and looked at Kevin. "This is Jake Cress?"

Kevin gave an affirmative thumbs up.

To Steve it looked like one of those selfie photos the younger generation was so fond of taking. The two of them were standing in front of an ancient looking log cabin, built the old way, with mud chinking between the logs. He turned back toward Kevin. "So you believe she's being targeted because she was singled out from all the others in this photo?"

"Yeah, that and it has to mean a lot to Jake that he displayed it separate from the others on the desk. He rarely let anyone take his picture." Kevin pointed to the torn photo. "That one was the most recent photo of Katie. I bet that's why it was taken."

Daniel walked over and joined Steve in studying the framed photo. He pointed to the cabin in the background. "Looks like a historic building. Maybe we can figure out where it is."

Steve turned to Kevin. "You know this building? Maybe it's in a state or national park around here?"

"Nope. Never seen it before. And Jake never mentioned a cabin to me." He looked from the photo to Steve. "One thing is for certain, though."

"What's that?"

"Katie knows."

CHAPTER SIXTEEN

Skagit County, Washington (Day Three)

Steve's phone pinged. He looked up at Daniel as he pulled it from his pocket.

"Kevin?"

Steve checked his phone. "Yeah. He came through for us, just like he said he would. He's emailed a list of the names and phone numbers for each person in the photos at Jake's place."

"Good. Now what?"

"I'll forward them to my partner at the Bureau and ask him to contact each of them, see if anyone's been approached by strangers asking about Jake Cress."

"And warn them, if they haven't."

"Yeah, that too. But with them taking Katie's photo, I figure she's their first target. Although, when they don't find her at the cottage, they may try to approach some of the others." Steve forwarded the email then pocketed the phone and looked at Daniel. "You said you have maps?'

"Yeah." Daniel began to pull some folded maps from a desk drawer. "I've got topo maps and road maps. Between them we should be able to get a good lay of the land in question." He spread the topo map out on his desktop, then opened and laid the road map on top.

Steve leaned over the desk to study the road map, then pointed to a spot. "Katie's cottage sits on this end of Lost Lake." He moved his finger along the map, locating the marked trail. "The trailhead starts here and heads up into the mountain slopes."

Daniel began searching the map for the burg closest to Jake's place, not far from the reservation. He found it, then followed the road to where Jake's cottage sat. He stabbed his finger on the spot, then looked back to where Steve still marked the trailhead Katie had taken. He studied the map in silence.

"Helluva lot of land between these two points," Steve said.

"Yeah, more than I thought there would be." Daniel stared at the map a moment longer, then looked to Steve. "I'm guessing we've both been assuming that Katie and Jake are doing a rendezvous somewhere."

Steve nodded.

"But what if we're wrong?"

"What do you mean?"

"It could be as simple as they both headed into the nearest wilderness to avoid being found."

Steve looked at the map again, the distance between the two points. "You could be right. Maybe I'm reading too much into this." His shoulders slumped. "Guess I had high hopes we could figure out where the two of them would meet and find them that way."

"Yeah, I know." Daniel looked up. "But you still have the trackers following Katie."

"Right."

"So when they locate her, maybe she'll know how to find Jake. If anyone could, it sounds like it would be her."

"Maybe." He didn't voice his many concerns flitting around in his mind, like would Katie even allow someone to get that close to her, how might she react if they did? She was, after all, armed. And why would she trust them? He shoved the worries down and returned his attention to the map. "Let's look at the topo map. I want to get a feel for the kind of land Jake might be heading into, and also, where Katie might be."

"Sure." Daniel moved the road map out of the way after marking the same points onto the topo map. "There's only one road behind Jake's place, and then he could've slipped into a green belt that runs along the stream there." His finger followed the stream. "The green belt and stream run right into the wilderness of the mountain slopes."

Steve studied the map where Daniel indicated. "Yeah. He could've easily left his place and gotten away unseen. Okay, now for Katie's location."

Daniel studied the line indicating the marked trail on the map. "Wow, once the trail leaves the valley floor next to the lake, it sure gains in elevation quickly."

"Yeah, the mountains are right there, in clear view from the lake, but I have to agree. I didn't realize how quickly it turns steep." He didn't voice his concerns about what kind of weather Katie might be heading into this time of year. Unpredictable, for sure.

Daniel's finger continued to follow the marked trail on the map. "Hmmm. Interesting."

"What?"

"Right here the trail arcs and then heads back down the mountain slopes … back toward the lake." He looked up at Steve. "If Katie is indeed in the wilderness to hide, I doubt she'd be following the trail back to the lake."

"Yeah, you're right. Which means she'll probably head off into the wilderness."

Daniel studied the map. "It's national forest land all around the trail and beyond."

Steve leaned over the map to look closer. "Good to know.

Laws for national forests are dictated by the state, and here in Washington, national forests are open to dispersed camping."

"Dispersed camping?"

"Yeah, you can camp anywhere that isn't private property. In other words, you aren't restricted to commercial campgrounds."

"She can easily hide out in the vast forests without breaking any laws." Daniel looked up from the map and gave Steve a knowing look. "You being an FBI agent and she being a single woman alone in the wilderness, I'm assuming she knows how to defend herself, and has the means to do it."

"Yeah, she can defend herself, and yes she has the means to do it."

Daniel gave him a grim smile. "That's good. She's in bear and cougar country."

"Well, she's not a hunter, but her handgun could at least scare away a predator." He didn't want to dwell on the fact that it also meant if someone was indeed looking for her, he was also most likely armed. He pointed back to the map. "Can you think of anything in this area between Katie and Jake that would be a good meeting place? And yeah, I know I may be off track, but it's all I've got for now."

"No, I don't. But let's take a closer look." Daniel reached across the desk to grab the road map again and knocked a folder off the desk, photos sliding out onto the floor.

Steve leaned down to pick up the folder and began to slide the photos back inside when one of them caught his attention. He stood back up, still holding the folder in one hand, the photo in the other, and stared at it.

"What is it?" Daniel asked.

He flipped the photo around for Daniel to see. "Who's this guy?"

"I don't have a name yet. Possibility that he's new with the crime ring. Why?"

"For some odd reason he looks familiar." Steve turned the photo back around to study it closer ... honed-in on the man's features. Then it hit him, and he sensed the color drain from his face.

"What? Do you know him?"

Steve shook his head. "No, but I saw this guy the day Katie went missing. He was fishing—more like pretending to fish—out in front of the cottage." He looked at Daniel. "What if he was there for Katie?"

"If so, you got there first." Daniel smiled, but it then faded. "Wait a minute, if that's the case, in order to have time to figure out who Katie was and where to find her, they would've had to hit Jake's place a day or so after Joseph's murder."

"That means Jake may have left for the wilderness days before Katie." Steve worked his jaw. "I still think they are connected in some way."

"Yeah, I agree."

Steve slammed his fist down on the desk. "Well, damnit."

"What?"

Steve held up the guy's photo. "He was watching everything. He would've seen the trackers looking for and finding Katie's trail. He would've seen them take off on the trailhead."

Daniel's eyes went wide. "Do you think he's following them?"

"Don't know. I mean, the guy certainly wasn't dressed for heading into the wilderness for any length of time." He paused. "But that doesn't mean he didn't send in someone else."

"True. But still, that would take time. Your trackers would be many hours ahead."

"Yeah, except they did all the time-consuming and difficult part of finding Katie's prints and tracking her up the trail. It would be much easier to start at the trailhead and track three people following a well-marked trail. Three people not trying to hide their prints."

Daniel held his silence.

Steve looked at the photo again. "What makes you think he's with the crime ring?"

"Nothing concrete, just a gut instinct. Sorry, I know that isn't much help."

"Gut instinct has saved my life more than a few times. Tell me everything you can about this guy."

"Sure. He'd been seen around the rez, at our tourist shops and such. The good-looking guy got the attention of the younger women. But what got *my* attention was tribe members saying he was asking lots of questions ... questions considered off-limits to non-native people."

"Like what?"

"He wanted to know all about our old legends and creation stories ... especially ones that included some of our sacred artifacts."

"Like the missing one."

"Especially that one."

"Let me guess. At the time, it wasn't missing,"

"You got it."

Steve motioned for Daniel to continue.

"Something about the man was ... off. He made the Elders jumpy. On one hand he had a great deal of charisma. But the older ones could sense there was no sincerity in the man. He was driven. Like he was on a mission."

"So definitely not an order-taker, more a leader."

"Yeah."

Steve stared at the photo in his hands, then looked up to Daniel. "I'm going to send this photo to the Bureau, if you don't mind?" He knew he didn't need the tribal cop's permission, but it just felt right to ask.

"Sure. Go for it."

"If anyone can find info on this guy, they can. And we need

info fast if we want to get ahead of … whatever this is. We need to know if this is the guy giving orders." He knew Daniel would understand the implication, that it also might mean the man had ordered Joseph's torture and subsequent murder.

Daniel interrupted his thoughts. "You got a way to contact your trackers, warn them someone might be following them?"

"Yeah, I do. But if I know Walker like I think I do, he's already figured it out."

CHAPTER SEVENTEEN

Mt. Baker-Snoqualmie National Forest, Washington (Day Three)

Nataya ducked under a low hanging limb, then followed in Walker's steps as he made his way through the trees. The forest canopy hung dense overhead, but even in the low light they still had to deal with lots of thorny berry patches and thick mats of vegetation underfoot.

Earlier in the morning they had made up hours by taking advantage of Katie's easy to follow tracks, and almost jogging up the open trail. Until she left it to enter the wilderness.

What they now followed could barely be considered a trail. Progress was painfully slow as they followed a barely visible path winding through the trees. The undergrowth and hard-packed earth meant boot prints were rare to find. Even so, Walker had other signs to watch for, broken twigs, moss rubbed from surfaces, smashed vegetation still in the process of righting themselves. He knew how to look for a disturbed landscape.

Occasional heavy sighs from behind her hinted Carl also struggled with the frustration of moving so slow. And he had the added burden of maneuvering the large pack through the tight spaces. She decided to make the best of their situation by using the opportunity to scout out plants and gather them as they slowly moved through the forest.

Nataya and Carl stepped into a small clearing and caught up with Walker, who waited. He pointed to the forest floor.

"Finally, some clear boot prints. And they definitely match Katie's tracks. She stopped here where the path, if you can call it that, splits and goes two different directions. She headed that way." He pointed to the angle the prints indicated.

"Maybe she's using a compass," Carl said. He pulled out his compass and stood where Katie had, then stepped in the direction the prints indicated, watching the reading. "Yeah, she adjusted her direction to that northeasterly angle she's been taking."

"I think you've got something there, Carl," Walker said. "Wish we could just follow that course and speed up our passage, but we can't count on her not changing direction somewhere along the way."

"Yeah, you're right,"

"Still," Nataya added. "At least this stays true to what we've all three voiced, that maybe Katie has a specific destination in mind."

"She's definitely not wandering aimlessly around in the wilderness, that's for sure. Nor is she in a panic." Walker peered through the trees and then over to Carl. "Any idea where this angle of travel will take us—if she stays on this course?"

"We'll be heading up higher into the foothills, and there will be more of this thick underbrush to make it through before we gain enough elevation to lose some of the vegetation and begin to have mostly conifers for company. Then maybe we can get a clear view. Maybe even spot Katie ahead of us."

"Okay. Good to know. Her prints are much fresher than they were this morning when we started out. We've made up some good distance on her."

Nataya could tell Walker was happy with their progress. A waft of moisture touched her face and she looked up at the thin white blanket of clouds overhead, now hiding the sun. The air was so heavy with moisture, she could smell it. There was no doubt they'd be getting rain before nightfall. Her hand went to her shoulder satchel where she'd already stashed cedar bark and dry grasses to use later as fire tinder, when everything might be wet.

Walker caught her eye and looked up as well. He turned to Carl. "In Colorado, being in the mountains during a thunderstorm could be a death sentence, the lightning strikes are so numerous."

"I've heard about your infamous storms. Always wondered if they were true or exaggerated."

"Pretty much true." Walker glanced at the sky. "You know the storms here. What's your take on this one rolling that's in?"

"We rarely get heavy thunderstorms, except up here in the mountains. By the looks of the sky right now, we'll be getting our usual, which starts as a light misty rain that will probably settle into a steady straight down rain later … no lightning."

Nataya could tell Walker was weighing the information. He had something on his mind.

"Sounds like the type of rain that maybe we could easily hike through, especially under the heavy cover of trees, for a while anyway?"

"Yeah, definitely. Most people in Washington go about everyday stuff all the time in light rain. I've got ponchos for us. If there's not a strong wind they'll keep us dry, even in a heavier rain."

Walker thought for a moment longer, then looked at Carl. "You have some bank line or paracord with you?"

"Always."

"Okay then. I suggest we keep moving forward a while longer."

"I'm good with that," Carl said.

"Who knows," Nataya said. "Maybe Katie's watching the sky as well and has decided to stop and set up camp early, before the rains move in. We could possibly make up even more miles between her and us."

Carl slid his backpack off. "Since we're already stopped, I'll get the ponchos out for each of us, so we have them handy." He gave Nataya and Walker each a pouch containing a poncho and kept one for himself, sticking it into his jacket pocket.

Nataya watched Walker slip the rucksack off his shoulder and pull out the waterproof leather boots they had brought. He handed her a pair. They quickly changed out of the soft moccasin boots and stowed them in Walker's pack. She noticed Carl had hoisted the backpack up into position and stood ready to continue.

"Thanks, Carl," Walker said. "Now let's see how much distance we can put in before we have to stop for the night."

As Nataya fell in behind Walker she couldn't help but think about Katie out there, alone, traversing the same wilderness. She tried to understand what the young woman might be planning, what she hoped to accomplish. But shook her head in frustration.

———

Walker pushed his way through yet another thick stand of shrubs, grasses, and ferns. Just when he thought the forest underbrush couldn't get any more overgrown, it did. The exertion alone threatened to cause them all to get too warm, but at least they were moving so slowly the air around them had time to cool them. Carl had reassured him that he was doing okay wielding that large pack through the rugged landscape. Walker didn't want anyone working up a sweat this close to nightfall and colder temperatures. It'd be too easy for hypothermia to set in.

Nataya and Carl still talked quietly on occasion while gathering plants and mushrooms as they followed. He'd gotten a bit more used to it. But it helped that the two of them had ceased the joking and laughter that made it more difficult to listen to the forest around them. Now that they no longer traversed the public hiking trail, he wanted to stay vigilant for signs of someone, or something, being nearby. He knew Nataya realized that aspect and figured she had explained to Carl that they needed to keep noise to a minimum, which he appreciated.

He heard the rain overhead before it could make its way to them. He stopped to look up and could see that it was more of a heavy mist, slowly gathering into drops of moisture and dripping from the leaves and evergreen needles overhead. And it had a lot of tree canopy to go through before it'd reach them far below. But still, he didn't want any of them even getting damp in the cool air. He stopped and pulled out his rain poncho, saw Nataya and Carl do the same. He put his arms through the sleeves, made sure the waterproof material covered his pack, then flipped the hood up over his head. He noticed that Carl quickly added a waterproof cover to his backpack before he donned his poncho.

When all three were ready, Carl took up his backpack again. The mist had begun to make its way through the tree canopy overhead as the three began their trudge through the underbrush.

Nataya spoke up. "I certainly won't need to worry about getting cold with the poncho on over my clothes. It's really holding in my body heat."

"Good point," Walker said. He stopped and turned to face them. "If any of us start getting too warm, we've got to speak up. We'll stop and cool off. The last thing we want to do is stay dry from the rain but get sweaty in our clothes, especially right as the night temps begin to drop."

Carl gave him a thumbs up and Nataya nodded. They all three turned and resumed their trek, heads bowed in the misty rain, Walker in the lead.

Two hours passed before the forest opened and the thick undergrowth thinned as the three trudged through the trees and plants. Walker breathed a sigh of relief at the ease they could now travel. He had to admit though, as arduous as the hike had been, he had still been able to appreciate how much the rain transformed the environment around them. The forest had taken on an even more mystical quality with the on and off misty rain and subdued bird song. The already intense greens of leaves, plants and moss had grown even more dramatic with the addition of moisture.

He breathed in the clean, fresh scent of super-charged air and found it energizing. He spoke over his shoulder. "Carl, now I understand why the locals don't let the rain stop them from being outdoors. It's nice."

"Yeah, if we waited for sunshine all the time, we'd not get much done outside," he laughed. "I think having so much rain in the winter makes us deeply appreciate the summer months. We savor every single moment. But then, after the summer heat we're always ready for the rains to roll back in when Autumn arrives. Speaking of that, I think our mist is going to change over to a serious rain sooner rather than later."

"Okay, thanks, Carl. Now that we're seeing less dense ground cover, let's start watching for a place to set up camp for the night. Katie's prints are definitely much fresher now, and I'm pleased with how much distance we've made up between her and us."

Walker continued to follow Katie's trail as it wove a path between the trees until he came to a small patch of open ground, where he stopped. He peered up through the trees to a thick canopy of conifer branches, dense enough that it had kept the misty rain from reaching the ground. "This is the first dry spot we've seen since it started raining. I know the moisture will eventually get through, but at least we can set up the tents on dry ground before the rain gets serious."

Carl nodded in agreement. "And we don't have a lot of brush to clear, either."

Nataya looked around. "Plenty of still dry wood to gather for our fire, too."

They gathered in the small clearing. Carl slipped off his pack, began the process of getting the tents free.

Walker came over to help. "I've got a project I could use your help with that will give us a dry place to cook dinner and hang out when the rains move in."

Carl's face brightened. "Sure thing."

"So, I'd like to set up the tents with the openings facing each other, with about six feet in between. Since we have limited time, that cordage you brought will help us make quick work of it."

"Yeah, no problem."

Walker liked Carl's enthusiasm as he laid out his plan for building a quick lean-to type shelter between the two tents, which would protect the campfire from the rain and give them a place to sit and stay dry. He felt Nataya's attention, turned to see her smiling at him, even her eyes sparkled in happiness. He returned her smile and went back to helping Carl with the tents. He knew she already understood his plan and would be gathering wood and getting the materials she needed to build a campfire.

Then it struck him. Could this be what she'd been striving for from the beginning? Had she been interacting with Carl so much to inspire him to work alongside Carl—as an equal—

instead of like an encumbrance he'd been stuck with without his approval? He glanced her way again, but she had busied herself gathering wood.

Then an unpleasant thought took hold. Had she guessed that all the attention from Carl might bring him to the point where he'd take more time with the young man, simply so that he wasn't always with Nataya? A part of him wanted to be upset that she may have manipulated him like that.

He mentally chastised himself. He knew that wasn't her style. It was time to admit the truth to himself. He'd made it almost impossible for Carl to interact with him from the beginning. Nataya had simply been doing exactly what he should've been doing—would've normally been doing—if he hadn't felt put upon by the FBI guy. And if he hadn't let his self-esteem get bruised by Carl's attention to Nataya. He glanced at her as she worked. To be honest, he knew he needed to take on this role to allow the group to work efficiently, with no egos involved.

All the angst he'd been holding onto about the attention Nataya had been giving to the handsome, younger man, simply faded away. He returned his focus to the work at hand as the two of them began to gather the limbs and small branches they needed for the shelter. Then Carl set to work cutting them to the lengths they needed, using a folding saw that was a part of his equipment. Before today he'd have scoffed at Carl's choice of tools. But with his new perspective of the young guy, he had to admit the tool didn't take up much room in Carl's pack and had turned out to be quite efficient at the job.

Walker checked the direction of the slight breeze that had started up, then began to lay out the pieces for the main framing, so it would block the wind, if needed. That accomplished, he turned to Carl.

"Now we'll make use of that cordage you brought along."

Carl found the #36 bank line cordage and pulled it free from the backpack. "I often carry this instead of paracord when space in my pack is at a premium."

Walker nodded. "I actually prefer it for lashing items together ... speaking of which, I'm sure you know your knots?" He looked at the young man.

"Sure do."

"Good. Let's bind the frame for extra sturdiness. Then we'll lay in these smaller limbs and sticks to fill in the wall and the small roof area, to protect the fire."

Carl studiously followed his instructions. Walker found it pleasant to work with someone who, although still striving to learn, was no novice, unlike many of his students. The young man asked a few questions as they worked.

"So, I've done a lot of lean-to shelters, but not one that incorporates an extension at the top like this ... like a small porch roof. I like it. Gives us more room to sit back farther into the shelter with the campfire closer to the opening."

"Thanks. Since there are three of us and I didn't think we'd have time for a large-scale construction, I figured this would serve us well."

"So, what would you have done if I didn't have the bank line with me?"

"Well, for one thing, I would've suggested we stop hiking a long while back. We'd need more time to prepare the shelter, either by collecting materials to make some cordage, or taking the time to cut and notch pieces of wood for a tighter fit. Nataya and I have had enough practice at making cordage to be rather quick at it, but it still would've taken time away from what we wanted to accomplish today—of making up some distance. I based my decision to keep hiking on the fact I knew you had the cordage on hand."

"Cool. I wondered if that was part of your decision-making process." He laid in a couple sticks to the frame of the wall. "That brings up another question I have."

"Sure, what?"

"Around noon, when the clouds went all flat, like a thin blanket, and we could see a sun dog, I could guess that we'd get rain later today. But you knew first thing this morning. How could you tell?"

Walker stopped what he was doing for a moment and looked at Carl. "Well, first it was how the smoke reacted during our early morning campfire. Even though there wasn't any breeze, the smoke didn't rise straight up in a column, like it should've. It spread out flat, which can mean low pressure moving in." He saw Carl nod. "Then when we got out on the trail where I could get a good view of the sky, I noticed the fluffy white clouds were all taller than wide, spaced far apart, and hanging mid-level in the sky. Along with the low pressure, that usually means a storm could move in."

"That's cool to know. I like learning stuff about weather, and I've never considered watching the campfire smoke like that, but it makes sense." Carl reached for the cordage and helped Walker lash some poles together. "You know, I've tried making some cordage, had pretty good results, but I've never really known which plants are best to use."

"We can certainly point those out to you as we move through the landscape. Even right around this campsite we have some plants that could be used," he said, pointing to a stand of fireweed plants. "It's really amazing how strong your cordage can be, even using what seems like fragile materials. Once it's woven together it's a new substance. Sometimes I have my students use paper towels, torn into strips, as a practice method. It proves to them how strong even flimsy materials can be when processed correctly."

"That's cool." Carl continued to add limbs to the frame. "I hope those students know how fortunate they are to be taking classes from you."

It was a simple statement, but the sentiment behind it deeply touched Walker. He let it resonate in his heart and held on to it. He looked at Nataya. She had paused in her work to watch him. No doubt she knew how much those words meant to him. He smiled at her and saw his own pleasure reflected in her eyes.

The misty rain had begun to change into the real thing as they worked. The slight breeze hadn't picked up, so for now it was falling straight down. Walker hoped it stayed that way. He and Carl finished packing moss into open spaces between limbs, then hurriedly laid some large slabs of bark over the wooden structure.

Finished, the two removed their ponchos, quickly shook the water from them then slipped into the shelter and hung the rain gear up to dry. Nataya, who sat in the center, tended a small campfire she'd already started while they had finished the shelter. While they had worked, she'd gathered and stacked enough wood in the shelter to last them the evening and leave a bit for the next morning.

Walker watched Carl check out the setup.

"This is really cool for a quick shelter. We can get in and out of our tents without getting wet and we have a dry, warm spot to eat dinner. Nice!"

"Thanks for your help, Carl," Walker said. "It made the work go faster."

Walker warmed his hands over the small fire, then sat down cross-legged on one side of Nataya. Carl sat on the other side of her. They all three worked together preparing a quick meal using what had been gathered throughout the day as they hiked, along with some of the dehydrated food Carl supplied.

When they each had dished up the food and settled by the fire to eat, Nataya peered out at the drizzle of moisture beyond their shelter. "So Carl, is this typical of the type of rains you receive here in the Pacific Northwest?"

Carl nodded, his mouth full of food.

"Makes me wonder how the indigenous peoples kept dry and warm in this damp climate." She turned to him. "Do you know much about the history of the region?"

"I'm no expert. Far from it. There are so many different tribes throughout the state, I wouldn't trust my memory regarding what I've read over the years. But since I live and work here as a Wilderness Guide, I've more recently done research for this specific area. I like to be able to educate clients about the land we're traversing versus simply leading them around. And most of them seem to like learning more about what's around them."

"I think that's admirable," Walker said.

"Thanks." Carl finished his food and gave Walker and Nataya his full attention. "First, some background. We're currently in Skagit County. When we left the airstrip, you probably remember the road followed a wide river. It's called Skagit River, and that entire river valley, which runs west, clear to Puget Sound, was home to a variety of tribes known as the Coastal Samish. In fact, there are so many different tribes, it's easier to explain it this way ... although each tribe has its own language, they are derived from two main linguistic groups, the Straits and the Lushootseed. Here in this part of Skagit County I'll be referring to the Lushootseed speaking tribes, which includes Skagit, Snohomish, Snoqualmie, Swinomish and Upper Skagit."

Carl reached for a log and added it to the fire, sending sparks floating upwards, a few making it past the porch roof and meeting the rain. He looked at Nataya. "You remember our conversation about there being so many cedar trees here?" He saw her nod. "Well, the tribes created waterproof clothing and watertight baskets using cedar bark. I'd seen old historic photos of the capes and hats they wore, which inspired me to do more searching. I've watched videos showing bark being harvested from cedar trees, then the inner bark prepared for weaving. It's quite a process."

Nataya smiled. "How ingenious."

"Yeah, and I read that the women also used the cedar bark and wove it with mountain goat fur, bird down, fireweed fluff and even dog fur to make blankets. They spun their yarn by rolling it on their thighs, without a spindle."

"What about clothing for the colder weather?" Walker asked.

"From what I could find, fur robes or blankets were worn. For the extreme cold, fur hats, moccasins and mittens were made from bearskin, coonskin or deer. The wealthiest people wore sea otter blankets." Carl glanced at Nataya and Walker. "I wish I could remember more of what I've read."

"That was all interesting," Nataya said. "Thank you for sharing. I'm always fascinated with how different peoples survived the elements in the past."

The three of them cleaned utensils from their meal and Nataya began to heat water for tea, a ritual by now. Carl put all the food pouches in a waterproof bag, slipped on his poncho and walked out into the trees to find a place to secure it, high from a tree branch for the night. Then he returned, hung the poncho to dry and joined them as Nataya poured him a cup of tea.

The three of them sipped tea and relaxed around the warm fire. The shelter not only kept them dry but held in the heat around them. The rain soon turned into a steady downpour and the wind picked up a bit but didn't penetrate the wood wall between them and the elements. No one appeared ready to crawl into the tents yet.

Carl looked at his watch. "It's only seven o'clock. Seems so much later. I guess 'cause the rain clouds made it darker sooner than usual."

"That and we started out extra early this morning and have

pushed ourselves really hard today," Nataya said, grinning.

"Yeah, you're right. It's been a long day. I am tired, but not sleepy at all."

Walker leaned in to add wood to the fire and looked at Carl. "Well then, it's the perfect time to tell us about this Sasquatch that's following us." He grinned. "Seriously, I'd like to learn more about the legend. Seems as much a part of the Pacific Northwest as the Rockies are to Colorado." Listening to Carl had given Walker the impression the young man was the probably the official storyteller of his SAR group.

Carl happily launched into his tale of how the name Sasquatch came from the Salish people, who lived in western Washington and southwestern British Columbia. How the indigenous peoples all over the Pacific Northwest had many different names and descriptions for the creature, many still prevalent in present day. "The translations range from, Wild Man of the Woods, to Night People, to Stick Indians, and many more. I found it interesting that although the physical description stays pretty close to the same, some tribes believe them evil, and others believe them benign."

He leaned forward. "But it was a journalist named Andrew Genzoli, who wrote for the *Humbolt Times* in 1958 about the experience of a camp of loggers in Oregon, that started the whole Bigfoot name. The journalist said the loggers had coined the term because of the large footprints they were finding. The story got picked up by some major national newspapers, spreading the story across the county and making Bigfoot a household name."

"I never knew the origins of that name," Nataya replied. "I have to say, though, I prefer the name Sasquatch."

"Yeah, so do I," Carl said. "I guess every region has its own legends and myths, even into present day. People are still saying they've encountered Sasquatch or heard the infamous 'knocks' they supposedly use for communication. In fact, some people swear they've heard them use their own language. I think Sasquatch or Bigfoot is a pretty cool legend to have for where we live."

"I would agree," Walker said. "And after hiking through the dense, often otherworldly feeling wilderness and not being able to clearly see through the undergrowth for more than a few feet, I can understand why some would still believe the legends."

Carl glanced over to Walker. "What about where you live in Colorado? Are there any special myths or legends you know about?"

Walker opened his mouth to speak, but instead flinched in surprise at the sound of a loud electronic buzzing noise. He looked at Carl, who's eyes were wide, not from fear, more like he'd been caught with his hand in the cookie jar. Carl quickly recovered and scrambled to his tent, ducked his head in and came back out holding a hefty-looking cell phone. He spoke into it.

"Carl here … hi, Steve."

Walker saw Carl look his way with a guilt-ridden expression, then focused back to the phone.

"Yeah, lost cell service yesterday. Yeah, Walker and Nataya are right here. Okay, putting you on speaker right now."

With an apologetic look, Carl motioned to Walker to shift positions so he could sit down between him and Nataya.

Walker heard Steve's voice over the phone. "Walker, can you hear me okay?"

"Yeah, I hear you."

"Good. First things first. You need to know that I insisted Carl keep in contact with me, hence the satellite phone. It wasn't his idea, so if you're going to be pissed with anyone, it's me."

"Good to know." He glanced at Carl and saw his eyes wide and remorseful, but Walker wasn't ready to completely forgive and forget. "Don't you trust me, Steve?"

"Give me a break, Walker. You know that isn't the case. You wouldn't be here if I didn't have complete trust in you. But do I need to remind you that it's my daughter out there? And I'm stuck back here?"

Then Walker heard it, a layer of panic laying subtly beneath the anger in Steve's voice. He put himself in Steve's place, of not being in complete control, and decided to cut the man some slack.

At Walker's silence, Steve continued. "In fact, I'm calling to personally thank all three of you for your due diligence and hard work of keeping Katie's trail. Knowing you are following her, when I cannot, means the world to me."

Walker breathed out his earlier frustration. "I understand, Steve. I know I speak for all of us that we're glad to help."

"You three following Katie may be more relevant than we could ever guess, but before I get to that, I'd like to request an update."

Walker nodded to Carl to take the initiative. He wanted to calm his initial anger with Steve. But he wasn't sure how he felt about Carl hiding the communications.

"Hey, Steve," Carl said. "Katie left the public trail this morning at its highest point, before the trail turned to head back toward the lake where it started." He hurried forward, "But we've managed to keep tracking her and even made up a lot of distance between her and us by hiking through the rain all afternoon." He looked to Walker. "How far ahead do you think Katie is at this point?"

"Judging by the age of her prints, she's no more than two to three hours ahead."

Steve replied. "That's really great news. Walker, I'm betting you've gotten a good read on her mental state while tracking her?"

Walker replied. "Although she initially hid her tracks at the cottage, once she made it to the trail she hasn't tried to hide her passage. There are no signs of panic … or injury. She walks with confidence and purpose, like she knows where she's going and is determined to get there."

"You have no idea how much comfort that gives me, Walker. Thanks." There was quiet for a moment on Steve's end before he spoke again. "Until today I had no idea the case I'm currently working on for the Bureau would have anything to do with Katie missing. But things have changed."

"Sounds like we need an update, as well."

"Yeah, it's a bit complicated." Steve launched into all that he and Daniel Night Hawk had discovered in the last twenty-four hours about the missing relic, Joseph and his fishing buddy, Jake Cress. "The real kicker is that Jake is the woodsman Dean told you about … the older guy Katie has known for years. He's the one she took bushcraft classes from, along with others her age. They spent a lot of time together exploring these woods." Steve paused. "But we discovered that Jake's cottage has been searched and he's missing. His Jeep is still at his cottage, but his backpack is gone. Just like Katie."

Walker glanced at Carl, whose eyes were wide, then looked into Nataya's eyes full of concern, before he spoke. "So what are the chances the two of them are planning to meet somewhere?"

"That's what Daniel and I first thought, until we checked a map. When we look at where Katie caught the trailhead, and the forest nearby Jake's cottage, there's a whole lot of nothing but wilderness out there between the two of them. Plus, the time element is different. Jake may have left for the wilderness as many as four days earlier than Katie."

"Makes me wonder what made Katie leave when she did," Walker said.

"Exactly. But the fact you sense that Katie is hiking with a destination in mind makes me wonder if our original thoughts aren't valid after all. We'll keep researching on our end. Our big hope is that once you catch up with Katie, she'll know where we can find Jake."

"Got it."

"There's more. Whoever ransacked Jake's cottage also took a photo of Katie with them. We believe they want to find Katie."

"To find Jake."

"Yeah."

Walker knew he didn't need to voice the underlying concern that whoever gave the order to torture Joseph, probably wouldn't hesitate to do the same to Katie to get the information they wanted.

Steve interrupted his thoughts. "But that's not the worst of it. There was a guy nosing around the reservation, asking questions about the missing relic—before it went missing. I recognized his photo. I saw him out on the lake the day you three were tracking Katie to the trailhead. Could've been watching everything unfold."

Walker hung his head a moment in thought, before looking back up and speaking into the SAT phone. "So, we may have someone following us ... which, by the way, matches signs in nature I'm seeing."

"Yeah, there is that possibility. The guy I saw was in his early fifties, sandy blonde hair, medium build. But Walker, he wasn't dressed for the wilderness. So it's likely he called someone else in to follow your trail."

"So, we really don't have a reliable description ... and we're leading him straight to Katie."

⁕

Carl lay in his sleeping bag replaying the day over in his mind, a roller coaster of emotions. First, he had been super excited that he and Walker had fostered a breakthrough. The tracker including him on projects and even asking him for his opinion meant the world to him. And then there was the fact Walker had encouraged him to be himself, sharing his stories and such. It felt good to be himself around the two. He knew he had a long way to go to gain the man's trust but had deemed it a good start.

Then Steve ruined it all with that unexpected phone call. Carl felt embarrassed and betrayed. But when Steve explained the situation, he could understand why the man felt forced to open the lines of communication with Walker. Still ...

He shook his head to rid himself of the emotions. He mentally recounted the whole tracking in the wilderness experience, as well as the fact they had made fantastic progress during the day, coming within hours of Katie. It was a big deal. He knew it was.

But the news from Steve flowed back into his brain, highlighting the possibility of someone following them, hoping to get to Katie. His heart raced. He took a calming breath. They'd sat around the fire until late into the night, discussing a multitude of different options for losing their pursuer. He hadn't missed the wariness in Walker's eyes the few times the man had given him his attention. Carl again pushed down his disappointment and focused on the task at hand. If he had to start over to win the man's trust, then that's what he'd do. He refused to give up.

As for the strategies they'd discussed, he had been impressed with Walker and Nataya's ideas. But no matter what plans they came up with, each one involved a great deal of time. They would lose some of the hard-fought distance they had made up between themselves and Katie. A bitter pill to swallow.

In the end, they chose a few different options and accepted that they'd lose precious miles. They decided that, if it meant keeping some bad guy from finding Katie, it would be worth the trade-off.

Carl thought about what kind of person could give the order to beat an old, defenseless man to death. This once, he decided he'd rather hope it was Sasquatch following them through the woods, versus a human.

CHAPTER EIGHTEEN

Mt. Baker-Snoqualmie National Forest, Washington (Day Three)

Katie stirred restlessly in the small tent. She'd made herself stop hiking earlier in the day than she wanted to, but knew she'd be glad to have her camp set up well before the rains rolled in. She'd already eaten dinner and retired to the tent when the showers arrived. She rested, recouping her energy from pushing her body to its limits all day. But it was still too soon to retire. She'd wake up in the middle of the night if she went to sleep now.

She pulled her backpack closer, opened a flap and pulled out the letter. Each night she'd read it again, looking for more clues, or an insight that she'd somehow missed. All to no avail. But by now it had become a ritual that had to be completed before she could go to sleep.

She opened the one-page letter and read the spidery handwriting.

Katie — I've done a very bad thing. But it was the right thing to do.

Others will disagree, and because of that, some men may come to you, asking about me. These are bad men, Katie. They know you took classes from me so tell them that, but nothing else. It's imperative you act as if you barely know me. Your life may depend on it!

Don't let on that we are close. And do NOT mention anything about our many excursions into the wilds or why we went there.

Don't worry about me. I had to disappear, but I'll be fine.

Guess I'll take that early retirement after all!
Stay safe,
Jake

By now Katie knew the words by heart yet didn't understand what had prompted the letter any more than she did the first time she had read it, four days ago. She had spent that first night trying to decide what to do.

The fact he stated he had done a bad thing had stunned her. What could've possibly happened that made him believe he had to disappear. Was his life in danger? Or was he hiding from the law? That question alone meant she had to keep her father out of the equation. Her father *was* the law, down to his core. And although he knew of the courses she and her other friends had taken from Jake, she doubted he even remembered the older woodsman's name. She understood. Until her mom had passed five years ago, his work had taken precedence over everything else. They were closer now, but it certainly hadn't always been that way. And she doubted he'd understand her close bond with Jake, who'd been like a second father to her during the years when she desperately needed one.

So telling her father was out of the question, for now. Which made her wish she could talk to Jake's fishing buddy, Joseph. Maybe he knew what was going on. But she had no idea how to contact the man, nor the time to figure it out.

The only clue she believed she understood in the letter made her fairly confident she knew where Jake had gone. If she was correct, he wouldn't be reachable by phone. With those details in mind, she had debated with herself all that night. But a deep and driving need to find him had begun to imbue her very being, until in the end she decided to listen to her instincts and go to Jake.

Besides, she didn't like the idea of waiting around for bad guys to potentially show up at her door. To play it safe, she'd made sure not to leave a trail from the cottage for anyone to follow just in case those guys did stop by after she left. At least she didn't have to worry about her father dropping in. He was busy with a case.

A flash of guilt slid through her body. Any day now her dad would be reading *her* letter and wondering what it all meant, just as she did with Jake's letter. She had mailed it as she left for the trailhead, knowing it'd take some days to get picked up and routed to him. She knew he'd eventually discover she was missing from the cottage, and she had to let him know she was okay. He wasn't going to be happy with her, that was for sure, and it wasn't fair to him. But she had to protect Jake until she could get to him and learn the truth. Then she laughed, and not with humor. She didn't even know what she was protecting, or whom from what. She sighed. All she knew was she had to get to Jake and talk to him.

Steve Hicks grabbed the mail, opened his front door, and slipped inside. It had been a long week, a roller coaster of emotions and more questions than answers. But he couldn't move forward until he heard back from the Bureau as to an ID on the guy Daniel's people had seen nosing around the rez. Besides, he needed a break from the small motel and a good night's sleep in his own bed. He tossed the mail on the kitchen counter, hung his jacket on the back of a chair and loosened his tie. Then poured himself a Blanton's Bourbon—neat. Maybe he'd missed this even more than his bed.

He sat down at the kitchen table and sorted through the stack of mail. A small envelope caught his attention. He picked it up. Katie's handwriting!

He found himself staring at it a moment, almost afraid to open it. He checked the postmark and realized it'd been mailed the day she went missing. He tore it open and took out one piece of paper, then unfolded it to see her handwritten note.

Dear Dad—I know. I've broken our promise. It hurt my heart to do it. I swore I never would, and until now, I've always kept it. Which should tell you how important it is that I do this now. I'm writing to let you know I am safe. I have something I must do, and I can't involve you until I understand the scenario better. Then I promise to reach out to you, okay? I would tell you not to worry, but I know you better than that. Just please trust me on this one.

Love you,
Katie

Steve sat back into his chair with a thud and stared at the letter, then read it again. Two things jumped out at him. First, everything matched what Walker had read from her tracks. She wasn't in a panic. She seemed to be on a mission of some sort. That part was the good news.

Astray

Second, she evidently believed she'd thwarted anyone from following her when she left the cottage. Which meant she wouldn't be on any kind of alert. She'd be focused on her goal of getting to where she was going. His heart rate increased, then he reminded himself that Walker was between her and whoever might be following.

Then he pictured Walker, armed only with his knives. But the tracker knew the score and Steve had a lot of faith in the man's wisdom and skills. Seemed that would have to suffice for the time being.

CHAPTER NINETEEN

Mt. Baker-Snoqualmie National Forest, Washington (Day Four)

The rains had come and gone during the night, and by the time the three of them ate a quick breakfast, blue skies had reappeared.

Walker drew in a deep breath of fresh air, much relieved they wouldn't need to wear the rain gear. They'd be able to move much quicker unencumbered. And although the rains had poured at times, they hadn't been torrential. It gave him confidence that signs of Katie's passage would still be visible in the landscape, although he'd need to stay attuned to the small nuances of nature to spot them.

They broke camp quickly and efficiently. Walker recognized that his pensive mood directly stemmed from the reveal of Carl's secrecy about the phones. The whole incident still annoyed him.

He saw Nataya give him a look, meant to remind him of their conversation last night in the tent. She had privately pointed out to him that Steve had requested Carl for the search, not them. Carl probably felt he owed loyalty to Steve, even if the young man might not agree with what was asked of him. Walker tried to keep that thought in mind as he made his way over to where they had left Katie's trail yesterday. He soon picked up sign of her passage.

He motioned for Carl. "I'd like you to take a compass reading to see if we're still heading in a northeastern track."

Carl did a quick reading and looked up. "Yep. We're right on course."

"So you still believe we'll soon come to a stream, if Katie stays on this course?"

"Yeah, even though I haven't been on this exact trail, we're heading toward a multitude of snowmelt streams and creeks, if we keep heading uphill into the mountain slopes, that is."

"Okay, hopefully one of them will serve our purpose. We'll see when we get to one." Walker noticed Carl's mood matched his own. Although the young man had obviously been appreciative that Walker had asked for his advice, gone was the lighthearted joking and sense of teamwork they had earlier forged.

Walker took the lead, watching the ground and surrounding brush for indications of Katie's passage. Nataya and Carl fell in behind him. Even with the sunny skies, the temperature began to grow cooler with the gain in elevation. And as Carl had predicted, the landscape slowly changed during the next few miles. Fewer deciduous trees graced their way while more and more conifers became their company. The underbrush thinned, which made moving through the forest less demanding.

Although Nataya would find the change a challenge for harvesting as many edible plants as she had been at the lower elevations, it meant bears would face the same issue. Hopefully they would stay where the berries were, bulking up for their winter hibernation. Once they had left the public trail, Walker had seen plenty of bear scat.

He appreciated that they now traveled with less talking. He

could more easily listen to nature around them, but he didn't mind that moving through the heavy brush of the landscape made just enough of a disturbance that they hadn't surprised any wildlife during their travels. Walker wanted to keep it that way.

The sun had risen to the tops of the forest canopy when Walker heard water in the distance, but he stayed true to following Katie's sign, hoping it would bring them to the stream he could hear ahead. As they worked their way through the trees, they came to a crest and then headed downhill. The sound of flowing water grew louder as they descended. Seconds later he could smell it.

The mountain stream tumbled over boulders and fallen trees, creating white water as it rushed down the steep slopes to lower ground. Walker knew the water would be frigid from snowmelt, and dangerous to cross, unless they could find a low spot without such a strong current. He was curious to see what course of action Katie had taken.

He continued to follow sign of her passage down to the water's edge. He studied the markings in the shoreline. He started to point them out to Carl, but instead clamped his mouth shut. He wasn't ready yet to engage with Carl in any teaching moments.

He saw that Nataya watched him and waited. When he stayed silent, she did the same, showing him respect for his decision. But he knew by the sadness in her eyes that she didn't agree with him.

She crouched next to the small indentions and prints, studied them for a few minutes. "Looks like she knelt here, perhaps to collect some water." She pointed to another set of prints. "Then she turned and headed upstream. Maybe she's looking for a better place to cross the water." She looked up at Walker. "Or it could be her trek follows the stream for a while."

Walker nodded in agreement, then looked upstream from where they stood. After a moment of quiet, he turned to the other two. "Like we discussed last night, we could take advantage of this scenario. If anyone is still following our trail, we could possibly lose them. Maybe not completely, but at least delay them by hours."

"We'd not have to spend too much time to pull it off," Nataya said.

Carl stood tall and studied Walker. "I'm up for it."

"Good. Let's get to work. First, we'll get rid of Katie's prints leading to the water and instead make sure we leave clear prints heading downstream. We'll follow the water downhill and hope we can find a spot with a slower current and shallow water."

The three of them walked along the shoreline of the stream until they came to a place where the water looked to be about knee deep. "Okay, the current still looks pretty strong. It'd be a bit dicey to cross here, but not impossible. I think it will be believable to whoever is following, and it's probably our best bet, without spending too much more time on this endeavor."

Walker and Nataya had Carl wait and watch while they walked downstream. They stepped through a thick mat of ground cover, where their prints wouldn't easily show, then continued onward to the water's edge. There they paused a moment before they each took three steps into the water. Then they stopped, made sure they had their balance before slowly, carefully stepping backwards into their own boot prints. They did this all the way back to the thick mat of groundcover they had passed through. Once there, they carefully pulled off their leather boots and switched to their moccasin boots.

"Okay, Carl. Your turn. Since you've not practiced this before, it's important to walk with your usual stride. Don't worry about walking over some of our prints, which would be normal if you followed behind us. Our goal is to have it look natural, so whoever might be following will simply assume we crossed the stream and do the same."

Carl studiously followed what Walker and Nataya had shown him, doing an excellent imitation of their movements. He returned back to them.

"Now what? I don't have different boots to change into."

"It's no problem." Walker held up an evergreen branch. "I'm going to brush away our prints from here, anyway. Our moccasin prints are simply easier to erase. Follow Nataya back upstream and I'll walk behind, erasing our prints."

They moved slowly making their way back to where they had spotted Katie's prints close to the stream.

Nataya turned to Carl. "We'll follow Katie's path upstream while Walker brushes away sign, just in case someone checks upstream before following our trail across the water."

Carl nodded. "But what happens when they cross and get to the other side and there are no prints leading out?"

"Depends on the person or persons. If they have much experience tracking, they might guess we spent some time walking downstream or upstream before we came out of the water, to try and throw someone off the trail. They'll search along the shoreline looking for prints where we came out of the water. That will take them some time."

"And if they give up and come back over to this side, we've brushed away our tracks," Carl said.

"Yes," Nataya said. "But to an experienced tracker, the absence of any sign is also a trail."

Carl nodded. "Yeah. Like at Katie's cottage. I see what you mean."

"Either way, hopefully it will delay them far more than the time we've spent creating the diversion."

They continued to follow Katie's trail as it led them alongside the waters, heading upstream. Walker stayed behind them, brushing away prints until Nataya came to a halt.

"She stopped here," she said, and began searching the area around the partial prints she'd found. "Okay, looks like she stood here for a bit, maybe she was searching for something … maybe a landmark?"

"Like a notch cut into a tree?" Carl said, pointing to a tree just ahead and to the right of them.

"Good catch," Walker admitted, then walked over to it. The notch had been cut years ago and had weathered. Then he searched the woods around them.

Nataya remained where she had last spotted Katie's boot print. She used the tree as a guidepost, looking beyond it into the surrounding trees. "I think I've found it."

Walker and Carl joined her as she pointed down toward the stream below. Just visible between the trees was a section of water, and laying across it were two large logs, side by side, placed to form a bridge across the stream.

Walker looked where she indicated. "I believe you're right. She knew that bridge was there. It's why she'd been walking alongside the stream. She was watching for the notched tree."

Carl pointed in front of them. "Now that we know where to look, I can see where she walked down the hillside."

Walker studied the rushing waters below, then turned to Nataya. "Time to switch back to our leather boots." They both made the change. "You two follow her trail down," Walker said. "And I'll continue to get rid of our tracks. That way when we cross the water there won't be any clear indication any of us were ever here, including Katie. An experienced tracker could still follow the sign we leave in the vegetation, but it'll slow them down."

All three proceeded down the hillside to the water's edge and the log bridge. Carl approached it first.

"Hey, that's cool. Somebody strung a rope across to use as a handrail. Sure glad to see that 'cause the rains last night probably made the moss slipperier than snot—which is bad enough in dry weather." He made sure the backpack was secure and wouldn't shift during his trek across the log bridge, then stepped up on the logs. He then grabbed the rope and began his journey over.

Nataya went next, Walker staying behind to make sure they didn't leave any footprints. When he was satisfied, he also made his way across the logs to the other side of the stream where Carl and Nataya waited. Neither of them had moved from the end of the log bridge, knowing he'd want to look for Katie's prints or signs of passage.

Walker stopped at the end of the bridge, thankful for the rope as well. Carl had been right about the moss on the logs. He peered over the end of the log bridge to the surrounding ground and pointed. "Well, someone was here before us." He knelt on the logs and studied the markings. "These were made about the same time frame as the ones on the other side of the stream, where we followed Katie. Still, I'd like to get a clean boot print to know it's her for sure." He stepped down from the log bridge and walked carefully forward, watching the ground. After a yard or so he stopped. "There we go." He looked up. "The tread matches. I'd say we're back on her trail again."

Nataya looked over her shoulder to the other side of the stream, where they had started from. "And hopefully, no one will see that we came through here."

"Yeah, if someone is truly trying to follow us, to get to Katie, hopefully we've set up a time-consuming puzzle that will keep them busy for quite a while." Walker waited for a comment from Carl but got only silence... then found it ironic that it disappointed him.

Walker again led the way, keeping an eye on the ground for signs of Katie's passage. He worked his way through the trees noticing that she took the easiest route through the landscape, going for time efficiency versus trying to hide her tracks. She must truly believe that no one was following her. It gave them an edge.

Within a mile they came to a clearing under the trees with evidence Katie had set up camp there last night. Nataya pointed to a boot print.

"You were right. Looks like Katie did stop early in the evening, to prepare her camp before the rains moved in."

Walker said, "It's a good sign." He gave a nod back over his shoulder from where they'd come. "We've gained a lot of ground on her, even with the time it took to set up the fake crossing back there." He looked forward from where they stood. "Carl, could you take a reading on your compass for us?"

"Sure thing." Carl pulled out his compass and checked the reading. "She's almost back to that northeastern path again."

Nataya studied the surrounding forest. "She's being smart and following this open area while she can, to cover the most ground in the shortest time frame." She peered through the trees. "Looks like we're heading up into rugged country soon." She pointed. "I see rocky cliffs ahead."

Carl studied their surroundings. "Yep. She was smart to camp here, and not just because of the rain. The course ahead will be level for a while but has deep drop-offs on the one side. Not a place you'd want to pitch a tent for the night."

Walker turned to Carl. "So where do you think this course will take us?"

Carl was quiet for a moment. "This route makes me think Katie has someplace on the other side of this mountain that she wants to get to. Although it'll be rugged and the weather might be unpredictable, it may still be the straightest course from here to there." He looked at Walker. "Also, if she doesn't want to be seen, she'll go high versus the easier route down in the foothills, where there are numerous hiking paths and lots of people roaming around, fishing and camping on that stream we crossed."

"That makes sense," Walker said. "I really hate to stop so early in the evening when we're getting this close … but I have to believe we should follow Katie's wisdom and set up camp here for the night."

"I've been on a ridgeline like that before," Carl said. "And I agree with your thinking. We'll probably need most of the day to get across to the other side and off the ridge. I, for one, wouldn't look forward to spending the night on it."

Nataya smiled. "Let's get a good night's rest and start fresh tomorrow."

Walker picked up a long straight tree limb and pulled out his knife. "You two okay with setting up camp?" He saw them both nod in agreement but give him a quizzical look. He started carving on the branch while he spoke. "Since we have plenty of daylight left, I'm going to hike back to that stream and see if I can spear us something for dinner tonight." He looked up. "No offense to your cooking, Carl."

Carl's eyes widened, clearly surprised by Walker's sudden humor, then grinned. "None taken."

⁜

Nataya put her herbal blend of the day into the hot water and sat back to relax, waiting for it to boil and steep for their evening tea. Walker had brought back two large trout that had fed them well, to the point no one wanted to do much except relax their bellies and work on non-strenuous projects.

She glanced over at Walker, who leisurely carved on a long limb. He had decided that hiking staffs would make their trek along the rocky ridge a bit easier the next day.

Carl already had his store-bought trekking pole, so he decided to try his hand at using hot coals to create a depression in a short section of wood he'd found. The coals scorched the wood, making it easier to scrape it out and create a bowl. It was a time-consuming process, but a perfect one for relaxing around a campfire. Nataya was positive he longed to regale them with stories from his search and rescue escapades or comical situations during his wilderness guide trips. Instead, he remained quiet and thoughtful.

Nataya served everyone hot tea and watched both men. She knew Carl's quiet disposition stemmed from his uncertainty about where he stood with Walker after the phone debacle. She hadn't tried to address it with the young man, because she wasn't quite sure where Walker stood either, even after their brief talk last night. But Walker's one attempted lighthearted jab at Carl's cooking gave her hope his mood was softening. It was a start.

The fire blazed, warming her as the sun set behind the tops of the mountains. She had no doubt the other two welcomed an early end to their trek as much as she had. They'd been pushing themselves hard every hour of every day, trying to make up the distance between them and Katie.

They were within hours of catching up with the woman, which brought up a whole new set of concerns. Nataya often wondered how they would approach her. How would Katie react to three strangers? A worry deep within kept bubbling up to the surface ... that it wasn't going to be as easy as they were pretending it would be.

CHAPTER TWENTY

Skagit County, Washington (Day Five)

Steve turned the steering wheel, leaned into the curve, and forced himself to re-focus on his driving. He slowed his thoughts as he slowed the speeding vehicle. His mind had been buzzing on overload since the call from the Bureau. His team had come through for him regarding the man he'd seen at the lake, the same mysterious man Daniel said had been on the reservation asking questions about the now missing relic. Problem was the intel brought up more questions than answers.

The sign for the reservation loomed ahead, so he slowed and took the turn. He wanted to talk to Daniel Night Hawk in person. And during their quick phone call he got the impression Daniel wanted to share something with him as well. He could only hope something constructive would come from their meeting, because he wasn't getting anywhere on his own.

Minutes later he sat down in front of Daniel's desk. "Thanks for meeting with me."

"No problem," Daniel said as he took the chair behind his desk. "I appreciate you driving out here. Were you able to get in touch with your trackers?"

"Yes. Walker said he'd noticed signs of someone behind them. But with them being on a public, maintained trail it could've been nothing more than other hikers. Now that Katie has gone off the main trail and into the forest, he'll be watching closely for anyone who might continue to follow them."

"And they didn't lose Katie's prints in the forest?"

"No, Fox Walker is an exceptional tracker. He's still on her trail."

"Fox Walker? Native American?"

"Yeah. He's Ute, from Colorado. I've worked with him before. You'd like him."

"I hope I get the opportunity to meet him."

"I'll try to make that happen." Steve leaned back in his chair. "My team at the Bureau got back to me about our mystery guy."

"Yeah?"

"Well, we know his name now … or I should say the one he's currently using. He's got more aliases than I've got fingers to count. Currently he's going by Victor Blake." Steve sighed. "The man has quite a complicated and colorful history, so to save time I'll just give you the Cliff Notes version that relates to what we're investigating."

"Sounds good to me."

"As your people mentioned, he's a charismatic person. He used that talent to start out as a grifter, worked his way up to loan sharking, and then money laundering. He amassed enough wealth and was clever enough to start getting involved on Wall Street and has made a fortune there. The man appears to have unlimited funds, so why he'd be messing around with this black-market crime ring is beyond me. Except for one thing …"

"Yeah, what would that be?"

"Rumor has it that within the last six months he started seeking out all kinds of Native American artifacts from all over the west. At first he tried to purchase them—illegally, of course. When he was turned down the pieces often later went missing. But no evidence has been collected that connects him. So now it makes sense that he's inserted himself into this crime ring, maybe as their boss."

Daniel nodded in agreement. "He can make use of whatever inside information they have. And they can do the stealing while he keeps his hands clean."

"That's my guess. But why? I mean, he obviously doesn't need the money. And it'd be small potatoes compared to what he's done in the past. So why the sudden obsession with the artifacts?" Steve watched Daniel shift in his chair, then look down at his desk in thought, his brows furrowed. He waited a moment and when the man remained silent, he spoke. "What is it, Daniel?"

When the tribal cop looked up, Steve couldn't read the man's expression.

"I'm sorry, Steve."

"Sorry about what?"

"I haven't been completely open with you about the missing artifact."

Steve frowned but remained silent, waiting.

"It's not that I lied to you about anything, it's more that I didn't give you all the details." Daniel met his eyes. "It's an Indian thing. We don't like to openly discuss our sacred items or traditions with … outsiders. I told you what I thought you needed to know, and nothing more."

Steve leaned forward in his chair. "Honestly, I do understand." He paused. "Are you saying that with the new information from the Bureau, you need to fill me in about the artifact?"

"Yes, but I do so reluctantly. Often our ancient ways and beliefs are met with ridicule."

Steve put his hands on Daniel's desk and met the man's gaze.

"I promise that I will listen with the utmost respect to whatever you are willing to share with me."

Daniel studied him for a moment, must have seen what he wanted, and pulled out the photo he had shown Steve days ago. He laid it on the desk. "This isn't the true size of the piece. It's been enlarged in the photo, so the details are easier to see. It's much smaller, around three inches wide. It's made to be worn around the neck on a leather thong. That's because it's an amulet. It was worn by the spiritual leaders of our tribe, you might call them a shaman or holy man, and passed down from holy man to holy man over time. Very ancient. Very sacred to our tribe."

Steve leaned over the photo, studying it. "It's exquisite in detail for such a small carving."

"Yes, true craftsmanship. It's carved from elk antler." Daniel pointed to the center of the amulet. "See the animal body in the center? Notice how it is shared between the wolf head on the left side and the head of an elk on the right ... how the elk antlers go backwards over the body to form an opening for the leather thong to go through?"

"I'm sure this has meaning for your tribe."

"Yes, the wolf represents personal protection and unity of strength for the tribe. The elk gives physical strength and endurance. It is said the wolf can psychically heal and the elk heals physically. Together they are powerful healers and strong protectors."

Steve looked up at Daniel. "So, you believe Victor wants this piece for an interested collector?"

"I'm saying he wants to possess it and use its powers for himself."

Steve felt his jaw drop open before he could stop it. He sat up straighter in his chair and stared at Daniel. "Something tells me you've just jumped lightyears ahead of me with that conclusion. Explain ... please."

Daniel studied him. "A financially independent man suddenly takes a peculiar interest in collecting ancient totems and amulets, manages to insert himself into a black-marketing group, and starts collecting these pieces in any way possible, often against wishes of the tribes. For this man it's not big money. Why take the risk? That leads me to believe it's personal. It reeks of desperation. He thinks he needs them." Daniel pointed to the photo of the amulet. "This particular amulet is well known for its protective and healing powers. I bet if we look at the other missing pieces, they have similar powers."

Steve tried to wrap his mind around the idea. It wouldn't be the first time someone had become obsessed with an old artifact, believing it had supernatural powers. History had plenty of stories to choose from on that topic.

He looked at Daniel. "So, do you believe it has powers?"

Daniel gave him an enigmatic stare that belied no answer. "Doesn't matter what I believe. What matters is whether Victor believes it."

Steve stared at the photo. "So that's why Joseph was so upset about it being stolen? That someone else outside the tribe might try to use it?"

"That was a big part of it. But there was another aspect. Joseph refused to wear the amulet because he was still training with Richard Bright Star and didn't deem himself worthy, yet. But because he was the caretaker of the amulet, he believed it offered him certain personal protection. That the wolf and elk watched over him. When the amulet was stolen from his care, he believed he lost that protection."

"So, he became desperate to take it back."

"Sadly, yes."

Steve studied the image thoughtfully. "So Joseph managed to steal it back from the black market ring, but then he had to worry about the bad guys coming to get it—again."

"Yes. I believe Joseph decided to hide the amulet, to save it from them, even though it would mean that by doing so he might give up his personal protection."

"And then he was murdered." Steve shook his head. "I feel like I've been transplanted back into a scene from a couple of centuries ago."

Daniel gave a humorless laugh. "Yeah, welcome to my world. Every day I straddle two different realities ... one foot in the history and beliefs of our tribe, which we strive to keep and preserve, and the other foot in today's modern world of technology."

Steve sighed. "Part of me envies your position. Seems it would be a blessing to have such deep roots to draw strength from. A grounding, so to speak. I think I could benefit from something like that."

Daniel watched Steve with a thoughtful expression. "I will say, it does help me understand how someone might become desperate and obsessed with the idea of an item containing what they long for." His gaze hardened. "But the fact this Victor guy was willing to order evil deeds to obtain the amulet bodes ill. If he should gain possession, I can't see any good coming from it. Our focus must be to find Jake before Victor does."

A vision came into Steve's mind ... of Katie and Jake together in front of a cabin. Everything else faded away and a sense of panic bubbled up. He knew only a great desire to leave all behind and go find her.

As if sensing where Steve's thoughts rushed, Daniel said, "Your trackers will find Katie faster than you could at this point. They are close to her now, right?"

"Yes."

"Then we must move quickly to find Jake. And I may have some help for us."

"We could use some."

Daniel pulled out a map and began to unfold it on the desk

as he explained, "After we left Jake's place, I sent a member of my tribe over there." He looked at Steve. "Yeah, I know I didn't have jurisdiction. So sue me."

Steve smiled and motioned for him to proceed.

"Walter Black Crow is an excellent hunter, who knows how to track. I wanted to see if he could pick up Jake's trail from the house. I finally heard back from him last night."

"Tell me some good news."

Daniel gave him a nod. "Walter was able to follow Jake from the house to the greenbelt behind it. Once Jake made it into the trees, he stopped trying to hide his trail." Daniel studied the map, then pointed to a spot. "So here's where Jake started. He then stayed in the greenbelt and followed the creek until he reached the nearby forest. Here the creek joins a larger stream, which he continued to follow." Daniel traced the wavy line on the map. "When he made it into the foothills, Jake picked up a trail that my guy knows. It goes into a small village up in the mountains, called Marten's Pass." Daniel moved his finger to a small spot on the map. "So Walter headed back into cell tower range and gave me a call. If Jake is hiding up in the mountains somewhere nearby, I'm guessing he may come into that town occasionally for supplies."

Steve looked up. "That *is* good news. So maybe you and I should head into that little village and nose around a bit?"

Daniel folded the map as he stood. "Exactly what I'm thinking."

CHAPTER TWENTY-ONE

Skagit County, Washington (Day Five)

The man known as Victor Blake knelt on the soft moss and grasses. Spread out around him in a circle lay a variety of ancient relics, some were animal totems, hand-carved from turquoise, bone or antlers. Others were pieces of jewelry created with semi-precious stones, animal teeth and claws and even a necklace made from snake vertebrae. Each piece held great meaning and power based on what he had learned about them through studies and research. He had tried to purchase them, but his money had been turned down. The tribes had had their chance. They simply did not understand his desperation to obtain the relics.

An empty space in the circle stared back at him. The powerful wolf/elk amulet belonged in that spot, and he was running out of time.

As if on cue, the SAT phone rang, meaning his guy out in the forest had an update for him. Victor stood, pulled the phone from his pocket, and answered after the first ring.

"Tell me good news, Colt."

"I'm still on their trail."

"Awesome. After we hang up, send me an SMS text with your GPS coordinates."

"Will do."

"How far away do you estimate they are?"

"A day, at most. The woman you want is hours ahead of the three tracking her. But they've been closing the distance each day, as I have."

"Still no idea where she's leading everyone?"

"None. Any new intel on your end?"

"No. The few students of Jake's that I managed to track down were closed-mouthed about him. It's as if someone got to them first. Warned them off from talking."

"You could always 'entice' them to be more cooperative, if you know what I mean?"

"Oh yeah? And look at how well *that* turned out the last time."

Victor didn't even try to mask his irritation. He'd inherited Colt when he'd made sure the previous black-market ringleader had an unfortunate accident, so he could secure the position for himself. Every time he thought about how Colt had let Diego torture the Elder to his death, he fumed. So unproductive. The dead can't give up their secrets. When he learned that Diego had been killed, he was glad. Poetic justice. Might be Colt would get the same treatment, simply for the principle of the matter, but for now he needed the man out there in the forest.

He turned his attention back to the conversation. "Continue on their trail and report your locations as you can. I'm following along on a map, watching for anything that might give us a clue as to where everyone is headed. In the meantime, I'm working on some options to speed up this hunt."

CHAPTER TWENTY-TWO

Mt. Baker-Snoqualmie National Forest, Washington (Day Five)

Walker knelt beside the partial boot print, barely discernible in the dry gravelly dirt, then stood again. The path that lay before him was a stark contrast to the lush, dense understory and moist soil he'd grown accustomed to these past days.

Katie's trail now led them along a narrow ridge, cutting across the face of a mountainside. Only conifers and the most tenuous plants rambled alongside of them. Carl had guessed Katie knew this to be the shortest route to the other side of the foothills. But so far, the loose gravel, scattered rocks and shoulder-wide trail had forced them to slow their pace to make sure every footfall landed on solid ground. As a constant reminder to pay attention, they looked over a fifty-foot, sometimes more, sheer drop-off to their right, ending on the rocky slopes below. It didn't help they walked into a continual strong headwind, slowing progress, and sapping their strength.

Walker currently led the way, and even though there existed only one logical way to proceed on the path, he still watched for sign of Katie's passage, if for no other reason than to make sure she hadn't doubled-backed—or worse—fallen from the ledge.

He glanced over the side, past the boulder encrusted slopes to the forest below. He caught occasional glimpses of the serpentine river, making its way through the trees. They again followed the river, but going downstream, back toward where they first encountered the swift running waters. In fact, they should be getting close to where they had set up their fake-crossing diversion on the opposite shore.

They rounded a bend in the path. To Walker's relief, the narrow trail widened considerably, allowing them more room to maneuver. Hopefully they could pick up their pace. He estimated they were only a couple of hours behind Katie at this point, and he didn't want to lose any ground.

Since leaving their camp in the predawn hours, he'd paid particular attention to any sign that someone followed. He hadn't been able to determine if it was human or animal that occasionally rousted the birds into alarm. So, he stayed tuned into the sounds around them, alert for any changes.

That's when he heard the whistle. It wasn't a bird. Nor did it sound human. He stopped, noting that Carl and Nataya also paused. He heard it again.

Carl shouted, "That's an emergency whistle!" He pointed toward the trees below. "I'm sure of it."

Now that Carl had named it, Walker knew it made sense. He and Nataya joined Carl at the edge of the cliff as he slipped off the backpack. They knelt and peered over to the trees below.

Carl pulled out a pair of small binoculars from his pack and lay prone on the ledge. Another whistle, weaker in strength, and Walker saw Carl working to hone-in on the sound, difficult to do with it reverberating off the cliffs and being carried away by the non-stop wind.

Walker knew he and Nataya were at a disadvantage without binoculars, but at the next even fainter sounding whistle, Nataya pointed. He saw what had caught her attention as several crows erupted from a treetop. He had Carl scan that area.

"I've got something." Carl made a quick adjustment to his binoculars as he studied the forest below. "There. I can see someone on the riverbank ... blue jacket. It's a young woman. It's not Katie. This girl is younger and has red hair. Uh-oh. She's soaking wet." He continued to study the scene. "Looks like she pulled herself out of the river and made it to shore, but maybe she's injured and can't get up. And those are cold, snow-melt waters."

Nataya turned to Walker, concern on her face. "If she can't get out of those wet clothes and start a fire, it won't take long for her to become hypothermic in these cool temperatures."

Carl studied the scene. "Hard to tell how long she's been there. Her core temp might already be dropping."

"I haven't heard the whistle anymore," Walker said. "Is she moving at all?"

Carl watched in silence for a long moment, then exclaimed. "There! I saw her move. She's still with us."

To Walker's surprise, Carl handed him the binoculars and jumped to his feet. He looked up to see Carl pull a smaller pouch from his backpack and rapidly dump out equipment, items Walker didn't know the young man carried. Then Carl was slipping on a climbing harness and had a lightweight rope coiled at his feet, along with other pieces of gear Walker didn't know by name.

Carl looked at Walker. "If her core temperature has dropped, she may only have minutes. It'd take hours to go back the way we came to get to her." He nodded back upstream. "I'm going over."

It took Walker a stunned moment to realize Carl meant he was going over the cliff edge. Then a sense of relief flowed through him. They had a way to possibly assist this woman. He looked at Carl. "Tell us how we can help."

Carl faced Nataya. "I want to bring her up here in case she needs to be evacuated out. Could you—"

"Yes. I'll get a fire started to warm her." Then she rushed off to gather materials.

Carl turned to Walker, talking as he strapped a First Aid Kit around his chest. "Have you ever assisted something like this?"

"Unfortunately, no."

Carl studied the gear at his feet, talking out loud, either for Walker's benefit or to help him think. "I could set this up so I can rappel myself down … and I wouldn't need your assistance … but I want that woman brought up here, and something tells me she isn't going to be able to assist. I'm sure I'll need your help to get her up here. So, pulley system it is." Carl looked at Walker and grinned. "Looks like you get a crash course in rope handling." Then he turned serious, grabbed the rope, and was on the move.

"Wait," Walker said. "How is that thin rope going to hold your weight?"

Carl gave him a sly smile. "It's a specially heat-treated cord. Lightweight to carry and use, but super strong. Even alpine climbers use it. It'll hold."

Carl moved into action while Walker watched and assisted as instructed. The young man wrapped one end of the rope six times around a nearby large conifer tree trunk, explaining that it would serve as an anchor point. Then he did the same with a second tree, as a backup.

With that completed, Carl had Walker also don a harness and began to attach gear to the rope, explaining to Walker how he would assist from the top as Carl rappelled down the cliff face. He looked over the edge. "This is an excellent spot because I can use those two trees as anchors, and there aren't any large outcroppings of rock, or branches, or shrubs sticking out to get in my way during my descent. It's a good straight drop. It'll make it easier to bring the woman up, as well." Carl showed Walker how to clip into the tree anchor point, and to dig in for a good foothold, then tested all the knots.

Carl gave him a thumbs up, then added, "I'll be down before you know it. I'll return with the woman as quickly as possible. You understand what to do when I get back, right?"

"Yep." Walker gave his most confident sounding reply, but noticed his heart rate increase with the seriousness of the scenario, and the part he was to play. One look at Carl's face told him there was no other way. Whatever the young man had seen in the binoculars prompted his actions, determined to get the woman up to their location as quickly as possible.

He tightly gripped the rope, then watched Carl go over the edge and drop from view.

Using his feet to push his body out and away from the rocks with every release of rope, Carl began to work his way down the face of the cliff. The driving need for expediency pushed him, but he didn't allow it to go beyond what he knew would be safe. If he became reckless and injured himself, he'd not be any help to the woman.

Although his heart rate had jumped when he'd heard that first whistle, adrenaline kicking in immediately, countless hours of training and on-the-job experience had just as quickly taken over. In the seconds it took for him to lower his body down toward the rocky slope below, he reviewed what his options might be, depending on the woman's injuries and mental state.

Then he was down, unhooked the harness, and was running toward the trees. He hadn't heard any more whistles since he had left the ledge, so he yelled as he ran, and thought he heard a faint cry for help. He shifted his angle toward the sound and pushed his way through the undercover and between trees.

Moments later he spotted the blue of her jacket and yelled again, if for no other reason than to give her hope. He rounded a large tree and saw her ahead. She had managed to pull her body backwards enough to lean against a tree trunk. But her legs lay prone on the ground, giving him confirmation that she indeed had an injury that prevented her from standing.

Within seconds he knelt beside her. "I'm here to help you. It's going to be okay."

The young woman grabbed his hand, a sob escaped her trembling lips, tears in her eyes.

"My name is Carl. What's your name?" he asked, knowing whether she could speak or not would tell him much about what state of hypothermia she might be experiencing.

"M-monica," she answered. Her severe shivering prevented her from much conversation.

Nevertheless, the shivering gave him hope she was still in the initial stages of hypothermia. "Are you here alone?" He watched her nod her head yes, then asked, "Where are you injured?"

She pointed toward her right foot. "Mm-my an-kle."

"Okay. I'm going to examine your ankle and then do a quick check of your legs to make sure there aren't any other injuries, okay?"

She nodded.

He knelt, pulled out his pocketknife and slit the bottom part of her pant leg so he could clearly see her ankle. Definitely broken. Beyond the purple coloring and swollen appearance, he could see the fractured bone. How it had not punctured through the skin was a miracle, in his opinion. He checked her legs, and although he was sure there were bruises and maybe minor cuts under the pants material, everything appeared sound. He knew once the shock of the injury settled, excruciating pain would soon set in. But her pale skin, blue lips and shivering indicated that raising her core temperature had to take precedence.

He returned to her side and talked to her as he opened the First Aid Kit. "Before I stabilize your ankle, we need to get you warmed up." He gently pulled her wet fleece jacket from her, then wrapped a mylar foil emergency blanket around her shoulders, covering her head as well. She tried to hold it closed with her hands, but they shook so much she couldn't do it. Carl quickly pulled out two chemical heat packs. As he put one in each hand, he folded her fingers over the pack and then helped her place each hand under the opposite armpit, to hold her fingers closed over the packs. Her armpits would assist the heat packs to quickly warm her fingers, and having her arms crossed over her torso would help hold in body heat. Carl wrapped the emergency blanket around her again and used medical tape to keep it closed.

He made sure she was as comfortable as he could make her for the moment, then spoke calmly to her. "Monica, I'm going to immobilize your injured ankle now. It's going to initially hurt, but hang in there with me because it will feel much better once I get the splint on, alright?"

She gave him a nod.

He did a quick search around the area for two thick sticks that would serve as a splint. He removed his jacket long enough to slip off his vest, then donned the jacket again.

As gently as possible, he used the vest to cradle her ankle and protect her skin from the rough sticks. He calmly explained each step to her as he performed it, mostly to alleviate her fear and distract her from the pain. Using gauze from the First Aid Kit, he wrapped it around the stick splint until her ankle was immobilized. She only cried out once in pain, but he was soon done, thankful it hadn't turned into a compound fracture with the skin punctured and bleeding.

Carl returned to her side and before he could utter a word, she spoke.

"Th-that f-f-feels mmm-uch b-better." She even gave him a faint grin.

Carl gave her his best smile. "Awesome. Monica, I need to get you out of these trees and up to where my friends are waiting." He pointed between the trees to the cliffs. "There will be a warm fire waiting for you," Indeed he could already see the smoke being whipped away from the ridge by the stiff winds.

"O-kay."

He pulled three-inch webbing from his jacket pocket. "I'm going to create a harness for you. That way, I can keep you safely attached to me while my friends help us get up the cliffs, to where they are." He could see the trepidation in her eyes. He put his hands on her shoulders and held her gaze. "It's going to be okay. I know what I'm doing."

She studied him, then gave a brave nod.

He removed the emergency blanket and tucked it in his pocket, then worked as quickly as possible without causing any more pain than necessary to create a harness around her. He finished and knelt beside her. "Okay, I'm going to help you get upright, but don't put any pressure on your right foot at all. Just lean on me for support, got it?"

He leaned down, put his arms under her armpits and lifted her slowly, but steadily to an upright position. He was sure the movement was causing her all sorts of agony, but she only moaned once. She trembled violently, probably as much from shock as the cold, he guessed. He noticed tears on her cheeks, and she bit her blue-tinged lips, but otherwise remained silent. She was a tough cookie and that gave him hope. But he knew he needed to expedite the process.

He glanced between the trees to the barely visible cliffs, then at the petite woman. "I'm going to carry you, Monica. Keep your arms around my neck as best you can, alright?" He used one hand to pull the emergency blanket from his pocket and wrapped it around her torso, then he lifted her into his arms. She clung to him, and he could feel her body trembling against his chest.

His brain screamed to rush to the cliffs and the awaiting lifeline, but he knew he had to make sure he had solid footing for every single step. Walking through molasses would've been faster, but he dared not make a mistake.

When at last he neared the cliffs he saw Nataya at the top, watching his progress with the binoculars. But he also felt Monica's grasp weakening, so he began talking to her as he walked toward the rope. He had little expectation that she'd have much strength to hold onto him at that point. He'd guessed it might be the case. It was the reason he'd opted to go with the pulley-system and was now grateful he'd made that decision.

Carl removed the emergency blanket for fear it would snag on something and impede the process. He had Monica upright, facing him and clipped into his gear, ready to signal Walker. The position left his arms and legs free to maneuver the climb. He instructed her to put her arms around him, but her hold was weak. He looked down at her face, trembling both from fear and the cold, and lifted her chin. He stared into her wide eyes. "You're going to do this like a rock star, Monica."

She tried to grin through the shivering, then gave him a fierce nod of acknowledgement and tightened her grip a bit.

Carl shouted, "Belay up!" to Walker. He felt the tension tighten on the rope and began his climb up, Walker assisting from the top.

———◆———

Walker concentrated on everything Carl had told him to do. He kept a steady pressure on the rope and listened for instructions from Carl as to when to pull or hold. He could tell when Carl was climbing upward and kept tension from the top to assist. They worked together, quickly creating a synchronized rhythm of rest … pull … rest. He was reminded once again of the teamwork that had developed between them over the last few days and was especially grateful for it right at the moment. He could see Nataya, waiting at the cliff edge to assist when it came time, which was speeding by far too quickly.

He guessed at least thirty minutes had passed when he saw Carl's head at the top of the ridge. Walker stayed clipped in, heels dug in, and kept the rope taut, as Carl had instructed, while the young man brought the woman up over the cliff edge, Nataya assisting as she could. Then Carl was on solid ground again. He flashed Walker a huge smile and thumbs up. Gone was the quiet mood of earlier. And Walker realized it was because Carl was in his element. This was where he thrived. Walker unclipped his harness from the tree anchor and hurried over to help.

Carl had the woman unclipped from his harness and was removing the webbing he had used to support her. Walker saw him glance over toward the alcove, where only smoke was visible, then at him, worry in his eyes. One look at the woman's coloring and he understood Carl's concern. He glanced at Nataya, saw unease on her brow, but otherwise she kept a neutral expression. He knew she didn't want to telegraph anything to the woman.

Walker followed Carl's earlier lead and lifted the woman into his arms to carry her to the fire, leaving the young man free to get out of his harness and gather up the equipment. Nataya had found a small alcove in the cliff wall where the small blaze would be protected from the worst of the wind. He noticed she had removed a sleeping bag from their rucksack and had it ready. But she motioned for him to first place the woman so that she was sitting up against the cliff wall. Carl joined them, and Nataya looked at both men.

"I'm going to remove those wet clothes before I wrap her in the sleeping bag. Could you and Carl hold it up as a windbreak?"

He nodded, knowing that Nataya was also offering privacy for the young woman. He and Carl held the material up as Nataya worked to get the wet outer clothes pulled off. Moments later she spoke again.

"Okay, you can help me get her into that bag now." Nataya said.

Walker lowered the bag to see that Nataya had removed Monica's wet outer clothes and had laid them out on rocks or hung from shrubs near the fire to dry. She had also pulled their parkas from his rucksack. She had put her parka on Monica and had his parka draped over the woman's legs.

"Let's get her tucked into that sleeping bag."

Carl joined Walker in lifting the young woman up so Nataya could move the bag under her. Once they had Monica safely snug inside it, they placed her next to the fire, her back resting against the cliff wall, and away from the wind. But for added protection, the two men sat around the blaze, blocking the strong air current from entering the alcove. Nataya began to heat water for tea so they could get some warm fluids into the woman's body.

As they sat by the fire, Walker finally had a moment to reflect on the whole operation. He'd been amazed at how quickly Carl had descended the fifty plus feet down the side of the steep cliff. The guy clearly knew what he was doing. Once Carl had landed and unhooked from the rope, Walker remembered the binoculars and had Nataya watch and relay Carl's progress down below. He couldn't help but be impressed with the man's quick action and cool-headed response to the emergency. Carl had succeeded with his part. Now they had the responsibility of getting the woman warm again. Her shivering and skin color indicated her core temperature had clearly dropped to a dangerous level.

The alcove was doing a great job of holding in most of the warmth of the fire, especially with the three of them positioned to keep the cold breezes from entering. They worked calmly, but intently, determined to get the woman's core temperature to rise. Nataya continually helped her to drink the warm tea.

He saw Carl checking his watch and guessed it had been around a half hour when the woman's color began to return to more normal, along with the appearance of a pink tinge to her lips. Her shivering soon slowed, her breathing more regular, and they knew they'd made it through the most immediate danger. When the woman spoke, there was no chattering of teeth, no trembling lips.

"Thank you." It was all she said, but her eyes said the rest.

Carl shifted his position and asked if he could check to make sure the splint was still in place. With Monica's assent, he unzipped the sleeping bag to get a good look at the injury. After viewing her ankle, Walker watched as Carl slowly and gently removed her boot to examine her foot. His forehead furrowed in concern. Walker saw Nataya pull some leaves from her satchel and add them to the water and return it to the heat. He knew she was adding some plants or herbs that would help with the pain.

Carl motioned for him to follow as he left the fire, out of Monica's hearing.

"I believe we cheated death from hypothermia back there, but she's not out of danger yet."

Walker caught Carl's eye. "You're thinking she might go into shock from that injury?"

"Yeah, it's a really bad break and the pain will soon be excruciating. It's obvious she can't walk out of here. I figure Nataya is fixing her a tea that will take the edge off somewhat, but I have another concern. When I pinched her toenail to check for capillary refill, it's obvious her toes aren't getting good blood flow, most likely due to the swelling at the break. She's in danger of losing her toes. We need to get her to a hospital asap."

Walker waited, encouraging Carl to finish his thoughts.

Carl studied Walker a moment, then spoke. "I think you and I should scout the trail ahead. Hopefully there are some wider ledges where a helicopter could get close enough to drop someone in and evac Monica out of here. The sooner, the better."

Walker didn't hesitate. "You're the expert in this scenario. I trust your judgment." He watched Carl digest his words and the meaning behind them.

The young man briefly smiled before turning serious again. "Thanks, Walker." He turned into the wind. "I say we hustle up this trail and see what we can find."

Walker turned to see Nataya watching. She gave him a nod, evidently guessing what they were discussing. He and Carl took off jogging up the gravelly dirt path, keeping as close to the cliff wall as possible. They didn't need to rescue a second person. As they moved forward, he hoped they wouldn't run into any more of those narrow passages to slow them down.

Minutes later he sighed in relief as the trail grew wider. They hurried forward. They had jogged along for about ten minutes when they came to a wide expanse of trail and stopped. Carl studied it and the mountain rearing up above them.

"This should work." He pulled out the SAT Phone. "I'm going to call my Team Leader and relay our coordinates to him. He can organize the rescue. It will be quicker that way."

Walker watched, impressed with Carl's cool-under-pressure attitude as he gave his leader all the pertinent information, including the fact they were continually being buffeted by strong winds on the ridgeline. Then he admitted to himself it was a stroke of good fortune that Carl had the phone with him.

Carl disconnected the call and looked at Walker. "He'll get back to me shortly. I'd like to stay here and wait if that's okay with you? I know I have a decent signal here."

"Of course." Walker leaned into a stronger than usual blast of wind. "They can do an evacuation in these conditions?"

"Guess we'll find out." Carl looked at Walker, must have seen the worry in his expression because he added. "I've seen them do it successfully in worse conditions, honest."

Both men moved closer to the protection of the cliff wall, Walker's hope rising and falling like the waves of wind buffeting them.

Long minutes later, he heard the SAT phone. Carl answered immediately. A few minutes of conversation, and he disconnected. "They can get a rescue chopper here within thirty minutes. We need to move Monica to this location. It sometimes takes longer than they estimate, but we want to be ready when they arrive."

They hurried back along the path, finding it much easier with the wind to their backs. They arrived to see that Nataya had gotten Monica dressed again in her now-dry clothes and was helping her with the fleece jacket. She wrapped the sleeping bag back around the woman's head and shoulders as Walker and Carl joined her to warm themselves at the fire.

Walker saw Carl kneel beside Monica. She gave him a smile, but it was laced with pain, her eyes watery with unshed tears.

Carl spoke to her in calm reassurance. "Monica, help is on the way. We're going to move you to where a helicopter will be able to evacuate you out of here and take you to a hospital, where doctors can take care of your ankle. It will be better soon, I promise."

She reached out and grabbed his arm, tears finally spilling down her cheeks. Walker figured they were a mixture of gratitude and pain. But before she could reply, Carl had turned to him and Nataya. "Okay, we'd better get going."

Carl stood and looked at Monica, then at his backpack, then to Walker. "Are you okay with carrying Monica to the extraction point?"

Walker quickly realized Carl didn't want to burden him with the heavy pack, which would be especially awkward for him to carry in the wind they were experiencing. He started to say he could do it, but then acknowledged that Carl's plan made better sense, as it would allow everyone to make the best progress in the shortest time. "No problem," he said.

Carl nodded and started to shoulder the bag, then stopped. "You'll need to put that sleeping bag back into your pack for transport. It'd be too difficult to carry Monica wrapped in that slippery material.

"Good point." Walker and Nataya quickly removed the sleeping bag and packed it into Walker's rucksack.

Nataya pulled her parka over Monica's fleece jacket for more protection from the wind. Then she reached into Walker's pack, removed a wool knit hat and gently pulled it onto Monica's head. He watched her quickly scoop a few hot coals into some moss and a bark holder. Then she slung his pack over one shoulder, and her satchel on the other shoulder, gently picked up the bark holder with her hand.

Walker knelt and helped Monica to her feet, having her lean on him for support. She put her arms around his neck, and he lifted her up into his arms. He had her turn toward his chest, hoping his body heat would help keep her from getting too chilled in the wind.

The three of them turned and began their trek to the extraction point, heads down into the wind. Within a minute Walker could see that the two in front of him could move more quickly, as he made sure each step was solid before taking another. He told them to go on ahead and he would catch up.

Maybe it would give Nataya time to get a small fire going again before he arrived with Monica.

Long minutes later he rounded a curve to see the wide ledge before them. Nataya had once again found a small indentation in the cliff wall to shelter the fire, and them. Apparently, she'd put the hot coals to good use and already had a small blaze going. She looked up as he approached.

Carl stood with his back to them, watching the skies, but he turned at the sound of Walker's approach. He hurried over and assisted him with getting Monica seated near the fire where she could relax, her back against the cliff wall. Carl pulled his sleeping bag from his backpack, and they tucked her into it. All three seated themselves to block the wind and keep as much warmth as possible captured in the small area.

Monica no longer shivered from the cold, but the distress caused by her pain was clearly etched into her face.

Walker knew they needed to keep her mind distracted from her suffering as much as possible until the helicopter could arrive. He leaned forward. "Monica, can you tell us what happened back there at the river?"

She nodded. "Yeah, but I feel stupid telling you."

Everyone waited.

"I got lost."

Carl spoke up. "Even wilderness experts get lost. You shouldn't feel badly about that."

"I know. But I made some bad decisions, and then I panicked, and made it worse." She sighed. "It started with the decision not to take the main trailhead. I knew it'd be crowded with people, and I wanted seclusion in nature for my hike." She gave a forced laugh. "Imagine that." She grimaced in pain a moment, then continued. "I decided to take one of the trails leading off from the lake, sure that it would eventually join up with the well-used main trail. And it did start out going straight up into the foothills, as I expected. But soon it started winding around and joining other little trails. At first I thought I could keep track of all the twists and turns, but by the time I knew I was in trouble I was deep within the forest and could no longer see the lake or get any kind of bearing as to my location.

"I got really scared and kind of started rushing through the trees searching for the main trail, still sure I had to be close. When I stopped, out of breath and on the verge of tears, I forced myself to calm down. That's when I spotted some fresh boot prints on a narrow little path. I decided to follow them, because at least I knew there were some other people around and I wasn't completely alone. It gave me hope. I followed them all day yesterday."

Walker didn't look at Nataya or Carl, sure they had picked up on the point that Monica may have been following their tracks. Maybe it was her passage that caused the bird distress he'd been seeing behind them? He tuned back into her story.

"Then today the trail and tracks led me down to that river below. I could see where the prints went into the water. The rushing waters looked fast and scary to me, but it was obvious that people had crossed there."

Walker saw Carl give him an "Oh shit" look. Nataya's eyebrows arched in surprise. Had Monica tried to cross at their faked crossing diversion and injured herself? It was highly possible. She hadn't noticed their expressions and continued her story.

"I made it almost all the way across when my right boot slipped off a rock and got wedged between boulders. I lost my balance and fell. Everything happened at once then. It's difficult to sort it out ... the surprise of the fall ... the shock of the cold water rushing over me. I did instantly know something was terribly wrong though because of the pain and the fact I couldn't move my right foot. It was jammed between rocks.

"The current was so strong that each time I tried to sit up, my daypack kept pulling me back under the water. I thought I was going to drown, so I shrugged it off and tried to keep hold of one strap, but the current pulled it away from me. But at least then I could sit upright. I worked my boot free, even though it hurt like hell.

"It took all my strength to drag myself out of the water and up onto the bank of the river. I immediately became chilled and knew I was in big trouble. My pack was gone. I couldn't start a fire or even get up and exercise to get warmed up. All I had was this whistle on the cord around my neck. So I started blowing it. I didn't know what else to do." A few tears rolled down her cheeks. "I was losing my strength to blow it and thought I was going to die."

Nataya put her arm around the woman. "You were in a bad scenario. Letting the pack go probably saved your life, even though it had consequences later. And you were wise to wear the whistle where you could get to it easily. That was smart."

Walker could see Monica calming with Nataya's words. Then he noticed Carl indicating he wanted Walker to move away from the fire so they could talk.

Carl spoke as soon as Walker joined him. "Who knew our little diversion tactic would cause someone to get injured." He shook his head. "But that makes it even more important that you and Nataya stay hot on Katie's trail. We've only lost less than two hours so far. I want you to know I will gladly stay behind with Monica and wait for the chopper to come in, so you two can continue."

"That's decent of you, Carl, and we appreciate it."

"Now that we know it was Monica following us, you could leave trail markers for me, to help me move faster and catch up. In fact—" He hurried over to his pack and pulled out a roll of bright orange plastic tape. He returned to Walker and handed it to him. "Our SAR team uses this all the time to mark trails."

"Good. That'll work. I'll mark the path whenever it takes a turn or becomes overgrown and difficult to see. That should help you move through quickly." He looked up at Carl. "Thanks for offering to do this. It means a lot."

"It's what makes sense. And I'm glad to help."

Walker and Nataya made ready to move out, but not before Carl insisted that they take the tube tent and some of the provisions from his backpack. Even though Walker knew he and Nataya would be fine without them, he accepted the gesture, knowing it would give Carl some peace of mind.

He watched as Nataya told Monica goodbye, saw the woman insist on returning the knit hat and parka to Nataya. They spoke together quietly, and he saw Monica smile through her pain.

They left Carl and Monica sitting next to the small fire, once again picked up the trail and hurried forward.

Carl fed another stick to the small fire. The wind made it too dangerous to let the blaze get very big. Even though the rescue chopper had their GPS coordinates, he hoped the smoke would help them visually hone into their location faster. Besides, he wanted to keep Monica as warm as he could before they evacuated her out. He could tell the level of pain had increased, so he didn't try to entice any conversation from her. He sat beside her and put an arm around her encouraging her to lean against him, her head on his shoulder. He didn't want to be obvious, but he constantly checked his watch and the sky, and listened for anything besides the wind.

His adrenaline kicked in the moment he heard the faint *whomp whomp* of a helicopter. It was too far away to see yet.

Monica must've heard it as she raised her head, then laid her hand on his arm. "I can't say thank you enough, Carl."

"You're welcome," Carl said as he helped her sit up straighter, then rose and kicked dirt over the fire to stop smoke from interfering with the evacuation.

She looked up at him. "I'm so grateful there are good people like you in the world. It makes up for the ones who don't care."

"That's kind of you, but I can't imagine someone not helping you in your situation."

Carl was removing the sleeping bag from around her shoulders when she gave him a look, her lips pressed firm.

"Well, that's exactly what happened."

He tuned in to her words. "What do you mean?"

"The man at the river."

"What man at the river?" Carl's heart rate jumped.

"When I approached the river, I could see a man through the trees. He was crossing the river from the other side. Then he stopped and appeared to be studying the ground on my side of the river. When he looked up and saw me, I guess he was kinda startled, because he had a strange expression. I was so excited to see a real, live person that I started running toward him. I told him I was lost. But when he asked my name, and I told him, he looked disappointed and completely lost interest. He mumbled something about having a task to complete, and he turned to leave. I begged him to let me come with him and he said he couldn't allow that. He kept looking at the ground as if searching for something and ignored me. Then he turned to walk upstream, away from me and the tracks I had been following. I begged him not to leave me, but he never hesitated."

Carl could hear the helicopter approaching. He only had seconds before he'd have to jump into action, but he gave Monica his full attention as she continued.

"Since he obviously didn't want to help me, I had no choice but to keep following the tracks as I had been all along. They went into the water, and he had just come from there, so I began to cross the river. But I know for certain he was still within hearing when I fell and blew that whistle … over and over. He refused to come back and help me."

The helicopter was above them now, churning up the dust around them, the noise drowning out anything either of them said. Carl wanted to get the man's description, maybe even a name, but all he could do was gather Monica up into his arms and carry her to where a man was being lowered from the chopper. Moments later the man was on the ground. Carl assisted getting Monica into a harness and attached to the rescue guy. The man signaled the people above that he was ready and gave Carl a thumbs up. Monica mouthed the words 'thank you' and then they were being pulled up above him. He watched until they were both safely aboard the helicopter. He got a wave from someone in the open door, and then they were off.

Seconds later he was standing alone, with only the wind for company.

CHAPTER TWENTY-THREE

Mt. Baker-Snoqualmie National Forest, Washington (Day Five)

Carl watched the helicopter until it disappeared from view. Then the relief of Monica's rescue settled, and her words came back full force.

All indicators pointed to the possibility that someone else was following them, besides Monica. From what she had said, it appeared the man had followed the three of them to the river, crossed, then came back, having figured out their ruse. Monica said he headed upstream, as they had. If it turned out to be true, the man following them was no amateur at tracking.

Carl instinctively reached for the SAT phone, and just as quickly remembered he had no way to reach Walker. Damn.

Then he remembered the orange tape, and that Walker promised to clearly mark their passage, to make it easier for him to follow … making it easier for anyone to follow. Well, double damn.

He took a deep breath and blew it out to relieve his angst. He hoisted up his backpack and began to hustle forward. Whoever followed was clearly still behind him, so he stood between that guy and Walker and Nataya. He needed to stay ahead and remove those orange markers before the guy following them could catch up.

As he hiked, he thought about what kind of person could walk away from someone in distress, like the man had done to Monica. Carl walked a few more steps, thought again of the orange ties, then grinned. Yeah, well maybe he could try his hand at some payback, not only for them but for Monica as well.

◆———◆———◆

Walker used his knife to cut a length of the orange tape Carl had given him, sheathed his blade and tied the plastic around a tree. He had no idea how much farther they might go before Carl caught up with them, so he used it sparingly. But knowing the young man's youth and vigor, he probably wouldn't be too far behind.

Besides, he and Nataya had watched the helicopter arrive and then leave while they still traversed the mountainside trail. He hoped Monica's rescue went smoothly and Carl was well on his way toward them. They'd only recently left the dirt trail and become immersed once again in the dense trees, their path at times barely visible beneath the thick underbrush of ferns, brambles, and moss-covered rocks.

Nataya showed no sign of the frustration he was battling because of their slower pace. Probably because she was delighted with the diversity of edibles they once again traveled through. He had no such distraction.

He wondered about his mood. Moving slowly through nature didn't usually bother him, but knowing they had lost two hours of time on their trek towards catching up with Katie added unwanted pressure. Instincts told him speed was of the essence. But for now he was at a loss for how to do that. He'd be watching for any opportunities, though. At least they were sheltered from the wind they'd fought while up on the mountainside. He'd count that as a positive factor.

He glanced up at the sunlight peeking through the treetops. They'd need to stop and set up for camp earlier than usual, allowing Carl the time to catch up before nightfall. And while they were stopped and waiting for the young man, who knew how much farther Katie would be able to move ahead. He sighed. He needed to stop the negative thinking. It wasn't like him, and he found it unsettling.

His fingers touched the orange tape in his pocket, bringing back a flood of images of the injured woman and her subsequent rescue. There was no doubt in his mind that having Carl with them, plus all his equipment and rock-climbing experience, had saved Monica's life.

Walker sighed heavily. He knew stubbornness had always been one of his weaknesses. Grandfather had often made a point of it during lessons.

Okay, he could acknowledge his stubbornness was based on the fact he was comfortable with his routines and techniques. Confident about his knowledge. He didn't care for all the new technologies, and he didn't want to learn about them.

He stopped in his tracks with the revelation clear in his mind. And right then, he finally understood what bothered him.

Walker looked forward through the trees and admitted to himself that being with Carl forced him to acknowledge that maybe he needed to re-consider some of his hard-held beliefs. Part of his ego tried to revolt from the notion. But once he accepted it, a sense of relief flooded into his mind, and his energy level spiked.

He pushed his way through a tall stand of ferns and noticed Katie's boot prints ahead in the dirt. The tracks clearly indicated she had stepped from the path they'd been following for days, and instead moved into the dense forest.

Yet, something wasn't right about the scene. He could hear Grandfather's voice in his mind saying, "stop and see." As a youngster that phrase had frustrated him. He'd stomp and fume about, eager to move forward, knowing it'd do no good. Grandfather would calmly wait for him to settle down, stay still, and look around at the details he had missed in his haste to get somewhere.

He tuned into Grandfather's reminder, halted, and analyzed the details around them. He heard Nataya stop behind him. She remained quiet, most likely also studying their surroundings.

Something about Katie's tracks bothered him. They were perfect—that was it. Every detail of her boot tread was clear and distinct, as if she'd gone out of her way to leave behind a recognizable sign of her passage. He knelt beside the prints.

Nataya joined him and moved aside some leaves to study the prints. She looked at Walker. "After following this path for so many miles, why would she veer off into the wilderness now?"

"Good question. Maybe her destination is nearby?" Walker studied the entire scene. "Or maybe she headed off-trail because she feared someone was following her."

"The helicopter," Nataya said. "Even being hours ahead of us, she would've at least heard it coming in over the valley, even if she didn't see it. Maybe it spooked her—made her worry that people are trying to find her."

"Good point." Walker stared at the prints. "But if that's the case, and she's trying to lose anyone following her, why did she make it so obvious that she left the path?" He stood, stared down the path ahead of them.

"True. It's more like an invitation to follow her rather than a way to lose someone."

"Exactly." He studied the prints for a long moment, then turned to look at Nataya. "What if Katie needs to continue on this path … but is concerned someone is trying to find her. It'd be much easier to lose someone in the dense forest," he gestured, "Out there."

Nataya gave him a slow smile. "So she leads them into the forest, loses them and then secretly heads back to this path."

"It's the only thing that makes sense." He pointed ahead. "I bet if we scout ahead in the direction we've been going, we'll find where she joined the trail again."

Nataya weighed the information. "It's a gamble. If she really is heading cross-country, we'll have to back-track to here and pick up her trail again …. and lose valuable time."

Walker stared at the prints, deep in thought, when he felt Nataya gently touch his elbow. He looked up slowly, knowing she'd seen or heard something. Then he spotted what had caught her attention. Movement. Far ahead and to their left, he could see branches moving … but not from a wind. He'd swear they were moving from tree to tree. He blinked his eyes and looked again, then realized they was watching the huge antlers of a bull elk moving through the forest. He watched in awe, calculating the size the animal would have to be, in order to be seen from such a distance. When it moved to directly in front of them, the antlers swiveled to face them. The elk stared at them a long moment, then turned and slowly made its way out of sight. He turned to look at Nataya, who smiled broadly. He figured he looked just as pleased.

Without a word between them, they headed down the path they'd been following, moving as quietly as possible, and watching ahead for the elk.

They followed the path far longer than Walker thought it'd take them to come to where the elk had crossed. But when he spotted the hoof prints entering the path from the forest, he stopped and stared. Nataya joined him.

"The elk came in from the forest right there," Walker said, then pointed. "And so did Katie."

Nataya knelt to examine both sets of prints. "Definitely Katie's prints. So she did return to the original trail. We were guessing correctly." She looked up to Walker. "These prints are much older than the ones we were following back there. She must've spent hours out there in the wilderness, probably creating a false trail, to lose anyone who might follow her."

"Yep." Walker found himself smiling for the first time in a while. "It had to have slowed her progress today. In fact, I believe her detour helped us make up what time we lost helping to rescue Monica."

Nataya returned his smile. "That is good news." She then turned to study the section of forest that surrounded them. She pointed off to the side, where an opening in the forest appeared, not far from the trail.

"That's the best campsite option I've seen all day," she said. "And dusk is quickly coming. Now that we know we have Katie's trail again, I should start setting up our tent and get a fire going."

"Yeah, you're right." Walker looked back down the path, from where they had come. "I need to return to Katie's detour and clearly mark the path, so Carl knows we did spot Katie's tracks going off into the forest but made the deliberate decision to stay on this path."

"Yes. Maybe you can use that orange tape to reinforce that fact. I'll get camp set up and keep a watch for you and Carl."

◆───◆───◆

Nataya finished setting up the tube tent, then cleared a patch of ground for Carl's tent, so he could do a quick setup once he arrived. Using some nearby rocks, she created a fire ring for their campfire. She wanted to keep the fire small, mostly so they didn't reveal their location with a lot of smoke going up through the tree canopy above. In truth she only needed enough fire to heat some water, but a warm blaze would be welcome on this chilly evening.

She pulled her harvest from the shoulder satchel. When they

had left the mountainside and once again traversed the narrow, forested path, she gathered some fresh Chanterelle mushrooms and wild onion. She would use some already harvested arrowhead roots to create a starchy thickener. She planned to make mushroom soup for everyone.

With those chores finished she began to gather firewood, watching the sun set as she worked. Dusk settled in. Even though the sky would stay rather light for a while yet, deep beneath the trees it was getting quite dark, quickly. She looked up at a noise not far away and saw Walker step into view.

She rose from the fire and walked over to greet him with a hug. The two settled by the campfire and Nataya began to prepare the mushrooms and plants she'd collected. Now she was glad Carl had insisted they keep the metal pot with them. As she worked, Walker relayed that he'd used the orange tape to double-mark the trees just past the detour Katie had created. Then made sure his boot prints were easy to see heading forward down the path they wanted Carl to stay on.

Nataya balanced the cooking pot on some rocks, positioning it so it sat over the hot coals, then resumed her place next to Walker. She studied him.

"There's something on your mind."

He looked up, a faraway gaze in his eyes, then focused on her. "Yeah. That elk crossing the path like it did."

She waited for him to explain.

"I'm sure you noticed the elk left the woods and entered the path at exactly where Katie had entered it?"

Nataya nodded. "So maybe that path also serves as an animal run?"

"I'm sure animals make use of it. But …" He looked away.

"What is it?"

He turned toward her. "It's difficult to explain … I don't know … maybe the mystical quality of these forests has clouded my sense of reality."

Nataya felt the hair on her arms raise. She didn't know anyone as tuned into the natural world as Walker. It was often a deeply spiritual experience for him. "I'd like to hear what you're thinking."

He looked at Nataya. "If I didn't know better, I'd swear that elk was following Katie. And it made sure we saw it ... to guide us to the direction we should take to stay with her as well."

She could see the conflict in his eyes. He wasn't ready to accept his own statement, yet had sensed something out there that made no logical sense. She offered an explanation. "Perhaps Katie was following a deer run out there in the woods and used it to return to the main trail ... and so did the elk."

"Yeah. Maybe that's what happened. As simple as that."

Nataya could hear the doubt in his voice. But before she could reply she heard a noise and saw Walker react to it as well.

They both looked toward the path, but because her eyes were used to the bright firelight all she could see was a dark shadow of someone coming down the trail. She saw Walker's hand go to his knife. A second later she heard Carl's voice.

"Man, am I glad to see you two!" He stepped into the light of the campfire, a huge grin on his face. He pointed to the steaming broth cooking over the fire. "I swear I could smell that for the last five minutes. I knew I must be getting close."

Nataya laughed. "Well, it's about ready, so you better get your tent set up and then we can all catch up as we eat."

Moments later, they sat around the fire and enjoyed Nataya's mushroom soup while Carl assured them that Monica had been safely evacuated. His team leader had later contacted him to confirm she'd made it to the hospital and was doing well. Then he gave Walker and Nataya the sobering news the young woman had revealed, about the man following their tracks at the river.

Nataya looked at Walker. His furrowed brow said more than his words.

"So, at least we know for sure now," Walker said, then looked at Carl. "Damn. I put up all those orange ties."

"Don't worry," Carl said. "I took care of that. I purposely left a few of them at the beginning so that I could set up a diversion farther down the trail—which I did. Then I removed all the other markers as I went. I've tried to watch for any sign he was behind us but haven't seen anything. The fact he figured out our diversion at the river makes me believe this guy will also figure out my attempt at a diversion. I can hope I slowed him down. When I arrived at the spot where Katie left the trail, I moved all the nearby orange markers, so it looks like we followed her trail out into the woods. Then I walked off trail for a long way and removed the rest of markers leading to here. That's why it took me so long to catch up with you two. Hopefully it forces him to at least check out Katie's trail into the forest ... and slows him down again."

Nataya could see relief in Walker's face and hear it in his voice. "Good thinking, Carl. You've done all you could. If the guy is still on our trail, it's only because he's one helluva tracker."

"Thanks, Walker. But I've got to ask ... why *didn't* we follow Katie's trail out into the woods? Was it because it was too obvious?"

Walker grinned, "Good instincts." He then filled Carl in on why he and Nataya had decided to stay on the main trail. She noticed that when he told Carl about scouting ahead and finding where Katie had rejoined the trail, he didn't mention the elk.

"The best news," Walker said, "is that it appears Katie spent a lot of time out there creating her detour. When she rejoined the path, her prints were fresh, made within a couple of hours."

"Awesome," Carl said. "Wow, we saved a damsel in distress, outsmarted Katie's attempted detour, and made up for lost time. It's been a productive day." Then he held his cup up towards Nataya in a salute. "And we finished it all off with an epic meal."

She grinned at his compliment, glad to see his upbeat personality had returned. Then she glanced at Walker, who studied the young man. Gone was the short-lived annoyance caused by the SAT phone. His eyes held a new respect for Carl she hadn't seen before. Her grin grew into a full smile of happiness that the two men had mended any rifts.

Something told her their newfound sense of teamwork might come in handy. They still had no idea what situation this search might lead them into.

CHAPTER TWENTY-FOUR

Mt. Baker-Snoqualmie National Forest, Washington (Day Five)

Katie finished setting up her small backpacking tent, then laid out her sleeping bag inside. Exhaustion tugged at her body, and she longed to crawl into her tent and crash. But she needed nourishment to replenish the huge quantity of calories she'd burned through today, both from anxiety and physical exertion.

It started with the helicopter. Convinced someone was hunting for her, she'd let panic dictate her thoughts and decided she needed to make sure no one could follow. Creating a diversion from the trail into the dense woods had seemed like a great idea, at the time. But it had taken a huge toll on her.

Battling through the underbrush, everything snagging on her jacket and pack, tripping over the hidden roots … then the hard work of making her trail disappear … only to go through the same process to return to the main trail again. Maybe it had all been a mistake.

But at least she'd made a strong attempt at diverting anyone who might try to follow. Now she could once again concentrate on pushing forward as quickly as possible.

It was already dusk, with shadows getting deeper by the moment. She dug through her pack looking at what she had left to eat that would be quick and easy, found a protein bar and some jerky. It would do. She'd take the time in the morning to eat a hearty breakfast. Tonight, the priority would be some much-needed rest.

She forced herself to slowly chew her food and not gobble it down. To encourage herself to eat more slowly, she pulled Jake's note from her backpack. She still read it every night before retiring. And each time she tried to discern new meaning to his words. She read the first lines of the note.

I've done a very bad thing. But it was the right thing to do. But others will disagree. Because of that, some men may come to you, asking about me. These are bad men, Katie.

His words always made her heart leap in fear. She then read the ending.

And do NOT mention anything about our many excursions into the wilds or why we went there.

Don't worry about me. I had to disappear, but I'll be fine.

Guess I'll take that early retirement after all!

At least that part had given her the clue as to where Jake might have gone. She knew it would be quite a trek for her, but his words had triggered a resolve she couldn't ignore.

Something made her freeze. A sound? A movement? She held her breath and tried to look around without moving. Nothing.

She slowly swiveled her head toward the nearest trees and gasped. At the edge of the tree line stood a massive bull elk. His stately antlers branched up, blending with the nearby tree limbs. He looked majestic and … regal. That was the word she wanted.

Katie had no idea if she even breathed while watching him, until it dawned on her that he was watching her. The thought startled her, and at first frightened her, until she remembered he wasn't a predator, and she wasn't challenging him in any way.

The discomfort faded as she sat there in silence and watched him, allowing a peace and calm to wash over her. Was this what was meant by the phrase "being one with nature?" Whatever it was, she embraced it and savored every moment.

She had no idea how long she sat there, watching him, him watching her. Then with a soft snort he lowered his head, turned, and disappeared into the trees. And still she sat there, sensing that he remained among the trees, watching. But not in a scary way, in a protective way. She had no idea where that notion came from, but it gave her a sensation of comfort and she held onto it.

CHAPTER TWENTY-FIVE

Marten's Pass, Washington (Day Six)

Steve leaned forward, his hand on the dashboard as Daniel steered his truck through the tight curve hugging the mountain slope. Up ahead a one-street burg appeared, nestled in the foothills and surrounded by huge stands of evergreens. He studied it as they slowly drove through. "Marten's Pass?"

"Yep."

"Not much here."

"Nope. That's why we had to get you out of those official-looking FBI duds. Most people live this remotely for two reasons. They want nothing to do with modern day society—or the law."

Steve gave a sideways glance to see if Daniel was sharing one of his rare moments of sarcastic levity but saw no humor in his expression. He glanced at the few people out on the streets. "Sounds like I should let you do the talking, then."

"Good idea."

Twenty minutes later they managed to find a friendly soul. Mabel owned and operated the Mercantile store, and unlike the others they had met, she loved to talk. Steve guessed perhaps she didn't have anything to hide. Maybe she even lived there just because she liked the locale.

Daniel flashed her a charming smile that Steve didn't even know the man possessed, then encouraged her to keep talking about how she and her husband had moved there to "get away from it all" after their kids had grown up and moved on. They opened the store to have something for their retirement years. Her husband had since passed.

Mabel gave a sad smile. "We certainly enjoyed some good times up here, so I decided to stay on. Besides, where would I go—the old folks' home? I don't think so!" She laughed.

Daniel continued his banter with her as he studied a nearby display of apple butter, then asked her if it was homemade. She proudly admitted she made it and he picked up two jars to purchase.

Mabel happily obliged. She glanced at Steve. "You sure are a quiet one."

Steve gave her his most friendly smile, then reached over for a jar of black raspberry jelly and handed it to her. "My favorite," was all he said.

Daniel casually leaned on the counter, watching Mabel. "I bet you know everyone who lives here … and can spot a stranger in a wink."

She nodded enthusiastically. "Like you two."

Daniel acknowledged her perception, then pulled the photo of Jake and Katie out of his jacket pocket. "The young lady in this photo, Katie, is missing out there in the wilderness somewhere." He gestured towards the trees. "We're trying to find her."

Mabel's smile disappeared, but she politely took the photo and studied it. Then looked up at them. She studied Steve. "And who are you to this woman?"

Steve looked at Daniel, who shrugged and said, "Looks like we have to come clean." He looked Mabel in the eye. "Steve here is Katie's father. The man in the photo with Katie is a friend of hers, named Jake Cress. Jake is in serious trouble, and we think she's with him. We want to find them both. Before some very bad guys find them first."

Mabel appraised them. "That's quite a story. How do I know you two aren't the bad guys trying to find them?"

"That's a legitimate question," Daniel said, then pulled out his Tribal Police Chief badge, then had Steve show her his FBI badge.

Mabel's eyes grew wide. "Well, my oh my." She leaned forward conspiratorially. "The FBI, eh? You fellas were smart not to show up in town looking all official-like. No one would've talked to you." She looked at Daniel slyly. "But you knew that."

Daniel gave her another one of his rare smiles. "Hopefully you'll help us out?"

Mabel studied the photo as she thought out loud. "People are private around here, and I respect that. But since neither of these two are residents, I guess I can speak more freely." She looked at Daniel and Steve. "You say they are in danger?"

"Most definitely," Steve replied.

"I don't remember seeing the young lady around here, although she does resemble her father," she said, glancing at Steve. "But I recognize the man. Don't know him as Jake. Everyone here in town calls him 'the hermit' as it's a rare occasion when he comes into town for supplies … going on more than five years now. He's never given his name and pays cash for what he purchases. Only see him on occasion in the summertime, never in the winter."

"How does he get into town? Steve asked.

"He drives an ancient, beat-up looking Chevy pickup. But by the sound of the motor, it's got a newer engine in it. Doesn't look reliable, but I'm guessing it is. Around here it's best to not go sporting new stuff around town. Smart one, he is."

"So you have no idea where he goes from here?" Daniel asked.

"Sorry, fellas. No clue. There are hundreds of miles of old logging roads threading their way through this wilderness. He could be anywhere up there." She put her hand in her chin. "But I do remember in the beginning seeing his truck loaded up with lumber and such as he drove through town. We all just figured he had a cabin up in the woods somewhere. That's why we call him the hermit—and the fact he's always alone."

"Mabel," Daniel said, "you've been a huge help. We appreciate you talking to us. Thank you."

Steve handed her one of his cards. "Please, if you see him, or hear of anyone else asking questions in town, give me a call."

"Glad I could help out. You fellas be careful out there." She looked directly at Steve. "And I hope you find your daughter."

Steve and Daniel walked back to the truck in silence. Once they both got in and settled, Steve spoke. "Well, at least we do know he's probably up here fairly close by. That cabin in the photo must be where he's hiding out."

Daniel looked out the windshield, turned the key in the ignition, and the truck roared to life. "Yeah, but there's still a whole lot of wilderness out there, and we have no idea where to start."

Daniel's police radio broke the silence. Daniel picked up the receiver. "Daniel here."

"Chief, I've been trying to reach you."

"What is it?"

There was a moment of silence, then static and the voice again. "Richard Bright Star's niece came in. She brought a note from Richard for you. Said it was important."

Daniel glanced at Steve. "Okay, what does it say?"

"I'll read it to you … it says … 'The man who fishes salmon on the river is in danger. The coyotes are circling.'" A moment of silence followed. "Do you know what that means?"

Daniel looked at Steve as he answered. "Yeah, afraid I do."

CHAPTER TWENTY-SIX

Mt. Baker-Snoqualmie National Forest, Washington (Day Six)

Walker pushed his way through a large stand of ferns and thick brambles on either side of the narrow path they followed. He'd hardly consider it even an animal run at this point, it was so obscure. But he had spotted Katie's partial prints often enough to know they still followed her trail. In fact, as the forest had grown denser, he'd noticed small notches cut out of trees at key points where the trail veered around obstacles. He had to believe they were trail markers Katie knew about and followed. And he could understand why. The trail was overgrown and almost impossible to find in the thick trees and underbrush.

Whether Katie's pilgrimage had anything to do with the missing man named Jake, as Steve seemed to believe, he couldn't say for sure. But he did know her quest must be extremely important to her. It hadn't been easy. And she hadn't given up.

Walker stopped to straighten his back and stretch. He took the opportunity to check out what bit of sky he could see through the treetops. They had started the morning under a thin veil of gauzy whiteness. But as the hours marched by, the fine layer of moisture had thickened and bunched up into opaque masses blocking the sun. He glanced back at Nataya and Carl, who had stopped behind him and used the break to catch their breath. Both had determination etched into their expressions, but he could see the physical toll in their stances.

He thought back to earlier, after they broke camp that morning and started following Katie's trail. The path had been shoulder-width and vegetation not as dense. Carl had had no problem spotting the elk hoof prints that ran over the top of Katie's prints. The same ones Walker and Nataya had discovered. Carl was fascinated with them, but when Walker remained mute on the subject, he quickly dropped the conversation. Until, that is, they reached Katie's abandoned campsite from the previous night.

Walker agreed with Nataya and Carl that it had been a marvel to see how close the elk had ventured to Katie's campsite. The prints indicated it had even stood there for a while. Carl's enthusiasm on the discovery led Walker to reluctantly share his notion that the elk had been following Katie. Although, in his next breath he stated it held no logic.

Carl had studied him for a long moment, then spoke. "Yeah, maybe the elk sensed no danger from Katie and had merely been curious," he offered. The topic soon got dropped as they moved into the more challenging terrain, making conversation difficult.

Walker turned and bent to his task again. It took most of his energy and concentration to simply move forward, let alone search for prints in the underbrush. He knew Carl had it even worse, trying to shoulder his pack through as well. Even as slow as they moved, they were creating a lot of noise. At least they were giving any nearby animals plenty of warning of their presence. The deeper into the wilderness they roamed, the more wildlife they spotted … coyote, deer, grouse and even an elusive fisher, a member of the weasel family.

Walker soon recognized, by the sudden drop in temperature and the slow burn in his leg muscles, that they were ascending in elevation rather quickly. Thankfully the three of them were acclimated to higher altitudes, but that didn't mean it wasn't a challenge.

After a long hour, the path widened as they skirted the side of the mountain slope. The terrain opened-up and he was greeted by a panoramic view of a lush and densely forested valley below. He halted and gazed out over the miles upon miles of treetops, a verdant carpet of woodlands fingering its way up the slopes of the mountain range.

Walker checked the sky for the sun, a nebulous glow fighting its way through the milky white voluminous cloud bank gathering above them. Its position told him they had little time before dark and showed the promise of "weather" heading their way.

He waited at the vantage point to let Nataya and Carl catch up, then pointed out to the terrain below. "See anything you recognize, Carl?"

Carl moved up beside Walker to study the landscape below. "Yeah, I do." He pointed to a far-away break in the tree line, with a spattering of partially hidden rooftops and signs of chimney smoke. "If that's the small mountain village I believe it is, we've come a long way from Lost Lake." He looked back behind them, but the large body of water remained hidden from view by the mountain slope they were crossing. "Wow, I didn't realize how much ground we've covered, until now." He turned to Walker. "You don't suppose Katie is headed for that little settlement, do you?"

Walker studied the scene. "Seems she's gone to an awful lot of trouble to 'disappear,' to now show up around other people.

Maybe she knows Jake is out in the wilderness, somewhere close to that settlement."

"Could be," Carl said. "But for sure this path will lead us down into the valley … eventually."

Nataya pulled her heavy wool sweater higher up around her neck. "We don't have enough daylight to reach those lower elevations today, though."

"Agreed," Walker said. "While I watch for Katie's prints, hopefully you two can spot a place for us to set up camp for tonight."

"And the sooner the better," Carl said, eyeing the clouds overhead. As if on cue, a mist of precipitation began to fall. Within seconds, it changed to tiny flecks of snow. "Oh man, I jinxed us."

The three moved off the vantage point, followed the path around the bend and back under cover of the trees to continue their trek.

Walker didn't mind the snow for now and was grateful there were no frigid winds to go along with it. But the longer they traveled, the larger the snowflakes. He was relieved when Nataya spoke up.

"Over there." She pointed up ahead and to their left where a grouping of huge cedar trees created a dense canopy, blocking the snow from reaching the ground. "We've got enough room to set up the tents on dry ground, along with some protection from the elements."

Walker looked at Carl. "We could put together another small lean-to shelter for the fire, like we did during the rain."

"Great idea." He glanced around. "Think it's going to be a wet snow."

Nataya surveyed the location. "The ground is going to be especially cold tonight. Before we set up the tents, I'll cut and gather a batch of these ferns. Between them and the moss, we

Astray

can insulate the tent floors a bit from the cold ground."

All three set to work on their tasks with calm concentration, overlaid with a sense of urgency as they watched the snow continue to fall around them, beyond the canopy of trees above. Walker took a moment to admire the smoothness of their teamwork, grateful for their efficiency.

After Walker and Carl gathered enough wood for the lean-to structure, they stopped to help Nataya erect the tube tents on top of the layers of moss and fern leaves. That task completed, Carl spoke. "I'll get the cordage so we can lash this structure together. I'm working up an appetite," he grinned.

"Thanks, Carl." Walker noticed flakes of snow beginning to drift through the thick layers of branches. "Good thing we've done this before."

Working seamlessly together, they soon sat near a warm fire, sheltered from the snow. Their work done, all three donned their parkas for added warmth before eating a warm meal.

Walker laid a small log on the fire. "Carl, is snow up here typical for the time of year?"

"It's early, even for up here near the glaciers. But it should stay in the higher elevations. Hopefully, we'll hike out of it quickly tomorrow. But you know how unpredictable mountain weather can be."

"That I do." Walker glanced at Nataya, wondering if she was remembering a particular snow from their past, when she had been held captive by a killer.

Carl interrupted his thoughts. "Well, at least if that guy is still following us, the snow will cover our prints from today." He grinned. A second later his smile faded. "Damn, it'll also cover Katie's prints from today."

"Yes," Walker said. "But based on the few prints I found today we're really close now. Maybe we can use your compass readings and manage to stay on the path long enough to find her campsite from tonight. At that point, if the snow stops before morning, we'll have fresh tracks to follow. Tracking should be much easier and maybe we can even catch up with her."

Nataya spoke. "We still have no idea how she's going to react to us finding her. Or how we might initiate contact with her."

"Yeah, there's that …" Walker said.

"This is going to sound weird, I know," Carl said. "But even though I haven't met Katie, after tracking her for so many days … it's like I know her. I mean, that happens on occasion during a search and rescue. But this is different. I admire her confidence … and I have a deep sense of protectiveness that probably doesn't make sense."

Nataya exchanged a look with Walker. "No, it makes perfect sense. We feel the same way, Carl."

All three jumped at the sound of the SAT phone ringing.

Carl snatched up the phone and answered. "Carl here. Hey, Steve … yeah, Walker and Nataya are here with me. I'm putting you on speaker now."

Steve's voice came through remarkably clear. "Thank goodness I could reach you. I need to update you on what's been happening back here in civilization. I'll make it brief. Daniel and I believe that Jake is hiding out in the wilderness somewhere close to a small mountain village."

"Would that happen to be Marten's Pass?" Carl asked.

"Why, yes. How'd you know that?"

"Katie's leading us in that direction. So far, anyway. We're within sight of it, but we're high up in elevation for tonight."

"Okay, that could be good news. Based on a photo we found at Jake's place, we believe he may be staying in a very old cabin, built long ago. But Jake may have updated it … made it livable in recent years."

"Okay. Good to know."

"Also, we have good reason to believe that the man following you is not Victor, but someone he hired. He may be feeding Victor coordinates as he travels."

Walker spoke up. "Victor's friend is no novice at tracking. But Carl set up diversions that we hope threw the guy off our trail, even if only momentarily. Hopefully it slowed him down by hours, maybe even a day."

"Good to hear. So maybe Victor doesn't know your current location then. Which brings me to the next bit of info I want to share with you. We believe we know why Victor is so obsessed with this amulet."

Walker glanced at Nataya and Carl, saw that Steve had their full attention as he reported that the man had been on a search for all types of totems and amulets. "This particular missing amulet is believed to be very powerful for protection and healing by the tribe, and was worn by the holy men for generations," Steve explained. "That made us wonder if perhaps there's something medical behind all of this. So the Bureau used the Patriot Act to access the man's medical records. We discovered that Victor has an inoperable brain tumor."

Carl spoke up. "Inoperable, as in untreatable … terminal … deadly?"

"All those," Steve said. "Daniel and I believe Victor is convinced the amulet can cure him. And according to the man's medical records, he's living on borrowed time. Which makes him desperate and extremely dangerous."

Carl silently mouthed the words "holy crap" to Walker and Nataya as they contemplated the new information.

Then Nataya spoke up. "Out of curiosity, what does the amulet look like?"

When Steve gave her the description of the wolf and elk head sharing a common body, Walker saw her look at him, her brow arched. He knew she was thinking about that elk that had visited Katie's camp.

Steve paused, and when he spoke again his tone altered so each word carried power, charged with tension.

"Things have dramatically changed since I asked you three to find Katie for me. It's turned into a highly volatile scenario. I cannot stress that point enough." He paused, then continued. "So here's the deal. I'm requesting that once you can confirm Katie's location, do not engage. I'm going to repeat that. *Do not engage.* I want you to instead immediately contact me with the GPS coordinates and a description of the situation. I'm asking that you not take any risk at that point. Let me take on that responsibility."

Walker looked at Nataya, saw her staring at the ground, a frown furrowing her brow. He looked at Carl, saw his eyes narrow, a firmness settling into his jawline. After a long moment of silence, Steve spoke again.

"Walker, I need you to acknowledge that you understand the danger. I don't want the three of you taking any chances here, understood?"

Walker gave it another heartbeat, then spoke into the phone while looking at Nataya and Carl. "Message received and understood, Steve. We appreciate your warning."

Walker thought he heard a sigh on Steve's end, not a sigh of relief, but one of exasperation. He figured Steve knew him well enough to realize that Walker had cleverly avoided making any such promise as to not engage.

The three stayed up talking around the warm fire while the snowstorm continued, creating a blanket of cottony whiteness all around them. The usual night sounds were muted by the insulating layers of frozen moisture.

But now, as Carl curled up in his sleeping bag, he appreciated the extra layer of insulation under his tent. His thoughts roamed back to what Steve had revealed to them, and Victor's desperation to find the amulet. It wouldn't be the first time he'd faced a potentially dangerous situation. His team had searched for fugitives of the law, even escaped convicts. He knew from experience to consider the potential for violence and be prepared for it. And he *did* need to mentally prepare for it. Surprise would be his enemy.

Those thoughts made him think of Katie. The very fact she was comfortable traveling out here in the wilderness alone, told him much about her level of self-confidence, knowledge, and bushcraft skills. He found himself admiring her, and looked forward to finally meeting her.

He had been relieved to learn he wasn't alone in his protective feelings about this young woman. It helped to know that Walker and Nataya understood what he was experiencing. In fact, he sensed it was one reason Walker had been reluctant to make any promises to the FBI guy about stepping away once they'd found Katie. The tracker had had dealings with the FBI before. Maybe he was picturing a scenario where everyone came rushing in, guns blazing. Carl shuddered at the thought, and now was especially relieved that Walker held the same protective convictions.

As different as he and Walker were, at least they both agreed on that point.

CHAPTER TWENTY-SEVEN

Mt. Baker-Snoqualmie National Forest, Washington (Day Six)

With her tent set up nearby, Katie huddled under the thick branches of a fir tree to avoid the deluge of snowflakes. But it was only a matter of time before the snow laden boughs would shift and allow the white powder to cascade down to where she sheltered. She was cold and tired from the strenuous trek to get as many miles in as possible for the day.

All she could think about was a large warm campfire. She hadn't seen or heard the helicopter anymore, but to be cautious, she opted for a small fire instead. Really just enough to heat water for her meal and warm her hands. At least the light in the growing darkness brought her comfort.

She forced herself to eat slowly and savor every bite of her one hot meal of the day. It was a reward of sorts, for all the miles she put in each day. But tonight she looked forward to an early bedtime and a warm sleeping bag. Tomorrow she'd have fresh snow to battle through. Fortunately, she'd be heading down out of these higher elevations to the valley below. She would enter the last leg of her journey.

Many times during the beginning of her trek she had

doubted herself, worried that she'd not remember the way. But instead, each mile into the forest increased her confidence as she found the familiar landmarks. She had even wondered, at times, if maybe she had over-reacted to Jake's note by taking off as quickly as she had. But she couldn't shake that gut-wrenching need to find Jake and talk to him. Then she could contact her father, who must be frantic by now—or very pissed—or both. It might have been him in the helicopter she heard. She made a promise to herself that the moment she knew what was going on with Jake, she'd let her father know she was okay.

Katie finished her meal, cleaned up her dishes and then took a moment to marvel at the snowy wonderland being created all around her. Snowflakes had begun to sift their way through the branches to settle on the ground, while others still gathered in thick white clumps on the limbs and evergreen boughs. She closed her eyes to enjoy the quietness of the evening as the mantel of snow began to enshroud the forest around her.

A snap of a twig caused her eyelids to flick open. She slowly looked around. The falling ice crystals played tricks with her vision as they danced in front of the trees and branches surrounding her. She remembered the huge bull elk from the night before and calmed her breathing. She didn't sense any danger. Indeed, a feeling of protection settled over her.

She sat there for a long moment, hoping to see the elk again, but it didn't appear. Still, she felt it was there, in the trees, watching over her.

CHAPTER TWENTY-EIGHT

Mt. Baker-Snoqualmie National Forest, Washington (Day Seven)

Nataya awoke to silence, unusual for sunrise in the forest. She rolled to her back in the sleeping bag, noticing the tent walls sagging down toward her. She reached up and gently pushed on them, sending a thick layer of snow sliding down off the tent, the walls springing back up into the proper position.

Walker stirred next to her and opened one eye. "Let me guess. We got quite a bit of snow last night?"

"Appears so. I haven't looked outside yet."

They both began the process of putting on their layers of clothing and donning their parkas. Lastly came their boots.

Nataya opened the door of the tent and looked out. A wonderland of pure white greeted her. It coated everything in sight, including the giant evergreens above them. All of nature had hunkered down in silence as a thick cloak of whiteness dampened any noise. She embraced the serenity and sheer loveliness of it for a moment, knowing that Walker did the same.

Thankfully there had been no wind last night, so the snow had fallen straight down and not drifted in under their lean-to shelter. Nataya crawled from the tent into the dry area. She had banked the fire last night and quickly uncovered a few hot coals to start the fire blazing again.

Carl exited his tent then and gave a low whistle. "Whoa. Did not expect to get this much snow. Beautiful though, isn't it?"

"Sure is," Walker said as he studied the land around them. He stood next to the lean-to and stared out between the trees. "I think your compass is going to come in handy, Carl."

"You thinking we'll follow that northeast bearing Katie's been using?"

"Yeah, pretty much." Walker turned to look at Carl. "Hopefully we'll occasionally come across sheltered places where we can brush aside the snow, find some sign and make sure we're on the path. Otherwise, we'll be running blind, at least until we catch up to where Katie camped last night. Then we'll have fresh tracks to follow and hopefully be able to make up some lost time."

"Well, with us making up for our lost time last night, let's hope that means we don't have a lot of this to get through before we find her camp."

"Yeah."

Nataya leaned back from the flames, now burning brightly, and watched the two men. A sense of contentment warmed her heart to see them talking together like long-time teammates. She could clearly see the mutual respect between them that had evolved these last few days. Instinctively she knew it to be important. Beyond the search, they were facing an unknown scenario. Being able to work together could give them an essential edge in a challenging situation.

Carl traipsed off to get the food bag, hung high in a tree. Walker began creating a path in the snow to where he remembered leaving the trail yesterday.

Nataya had water heating when Carl returned with the food.

He sat down next to her, and they began to sort through the remaining provisions.

"Guess it's a good thing I've been hanging up the food every night," he said.

"Did we have a visitor?" Nataya asked and looked up at him.

"Yeah, a black bear came through. Guess he could smell the food, but when he couldn't get to it, he left. Probably has happened more than we know, times when prints didn't show as easily as they do in the snow."

"I'm sure you're right about that."

Walker returned to the shelter, brushed snow off his clothes and joined them at the fire. He looked at Carl. "Did you see bear prints by chance?"

"Yeah, out by where the food bag was hung up."

Walker nodded. "He crossed the trail we were on yesterday and went the opposite direction, so hopefully he kept going the other way."

Nataya offered water to Carl for his usual cup of coffee, then prepared tea for her and Walker. They ate a hurried breakfast. She sensed their eagerness to get on the trail and find where Katie had camped last night. The sooner they had visual prints again, the easier their quest.

Once everything was stowed back into the packs, they followed Walker's footprints through the snow to the trail. Carl spoke up.

"Since we aren't tracking Katie's prints right now, I volunteer to lead the way, since we'll be following my compass heading."

"Thanks, Carl," Nataya answered. She knew he was also volunteering to break through the snow and create a path for the two of them, since he had boots better suited for the task.

Walker gave him a thumbs up, which made the young guy grin.

Nataya fell in behind Carl, following in the path he created, and Walker followed behind her. She heard him stop often. She knew he was listening and watching behind them.

Walker admired Carl's fortitude as he blazed a trail through the knee-high snowbanks, while wearing his heavy pack and consistently checking their heading to his compass.

A half dozen times they'd been able to stop under dense coverage of trees where the snowpack was lighter. Walker would kneel and gently brush the snow away until they could see the ground. Two times they had been able to see a narrow path of dirt, which helped him believe they were indeed still on Katie's trail. That was, if she stayed true to the path.

An hour and a half after leaving camp Carl pointed ahead to a square of dry ground amid the snow, where a tent had been set up. The surrounding prints in the snow looked promising.

They arrived at the spot and Walker checked the tracks. They were Katie's boot prints. He signaled success, causing Carl to hiss a "yes" and shake his fist in the air with his trekking pole. Then the young man spun around the opposite direction, dropping his arm and staring out between the trees.

Walker heard what had caused Carl's reaction, saw Nataya responding as well. A helicopter was somewhere nearby, but it was difficult to pinpoint the location. The sound echoed off the mountainsides all around them.

His first thought was that Steve and his FBI guys were up there checking out what they could find. But another notion came to him, and he called out to Carl and Nataya to take cover under the tree nearest to them, staying close to the trunk. Seconds later a chopper sped by, going the opposite direction and just north of them. He couldn't get a good look at the aircraft through the tree canopy.

"Carl, could you tell if it was a rescue chopper?"

Carl shook his head but pulled out his SAT phone and made a quick text.

Walker saw Carl study the screen as he walked toward them, his countenance somber.

"I checked with Steve. It's not his guys up there. So he's checking for emergency responders in the area. Still, it could be a private chopper …" He looked at Walker with an "oh shit" expression and didn't finish his thought.

CHAPTER TWENTY-NINE

Mt. Baker-Snoqualmie National Forest, Washington (Day Seven)

Victor leaned to his right and gazed out the side window of the helicopter to the treetops below. That's all he could see for miles ... treetops. And now snow.

He'd given the pilot the most recent GPS coordinates his guy on the ground had texted to him that morning, and they were homing-in on the location. He glanced at the instrumentation. The chopper was equipped with all the latest state-of-the-art gadgetry, from night vision to thermal imaging.

Victor flinched at the reminder of how much this flight was costing him per minute. Then he gave a humorless laugh. Why the hell did he care? He couldn't spend his wealth if he was dead. And if he couldn't track down the girl, and consequently Jake, he'd never find the amulet. And without the ancient relic, that's what he'd be—dead.

The pilot indicated they had reached the coordinates he'd been given. "Once you make contact, I'll take this bird up higher to avoid setting off any avalanches in the snowpack."

Victor called his guy on the ground and heard him answer after one ring. "Colt, can you see us above you?"

"That's you?"

"Yeah, we followed the coordinates you texted this morning."

"What the hell are you trying to do? Let anyone out here know where I'm located?"

Victor hadn't thought of that, but he sure as hell wasn't going to admit it. "We're starting at your location and plan to scout out the area in front of you … maybe spot a structure … figure out where everyone's headed. Get there first."

"And in the meantime, you're probably spooking the woman you want. Now she'll be convinced someone is looking for her via the air."

Victor saw the chopper pilot motion he was going to take the chopper up higher while they hovered. "There are plenty of rescues done out here all the time. She probably knows that. So I'll take the chance. All I know is this search is taking far too long. And time is not a commodity I have a lot of." That silenced his guy on the ground. "How far ahead would you guess they are from you, time wise?"

"They set up a few diversions to try and throw me off the trail. That slowed me down."

"So they know they're being followed?"

"Maybe. Or they're simply playing it safe. But as you can see, I've now got almost two feet of snow to wade through. I'd say they're at least a full day ahead of me."

"Are they still on that Northeastern trek?"

"Yeah, so far. And hopefully they stay on that heading, because all I can do now is follow my compass and hope to find some tracks later today."

"Okay. We're going to use that Northeast angle and fly ahead of you … see if we spot anything that looks like a place where the girl and Jake might be meeting."

"Good luck with that." Then Colt mumbled, "Good thing you're not looking for people, 'cause they'll hear you coming from miles away."

CHAPTER THIRTY

Mt. Baker-Snoqualmie National Forest, Washington (Day Seven)

Katie tapped the toe of her boot on the ground, knocking off the remaining bit of snow, glad to be out of the higher elevations. Even though she'd made good progress trudging through the white powder, it had been physically taxing.

As for her mental state, she'd been doing fine until she heard yet another helicopter overhead. She tried to catch a glimpse of it through the trees as it flew over, just north of her and going the opposite direction, but there were too many obstructions for a clear view. She wondered if the recent heavier-than-usual-snow for this time of year had caught some hikers unaware and they needed a rescue.

Or it could be her father. Her note might have spurred him into action. She sighed. She knew he wouldn't give up easily, which gave her all kinds of guilt pangs about what she'd done.

She brought her concentration back to the present as a helicopter came flying in low from behind her. She instinctively crouched down under a tree, hugging the trunk. She peeked up through the boughs to see a dark shape pass over, but she couldn't see any details.

Damn. Was it the same chopper? Had it spotted her tracks up in the snow and followed them? Even so, she couldn't imagine that anyone that high in the air could see her under the heavy coverage of trees. But to play it safe she stayed still for long minutes, listening for the telltale sound of the whirling blades. Moments later she heard it making another pass, but farther west of her—as if it was crisscrossing the valley. So maybe they did have a missing person. Maybe it wasn't about her at all.

Maybe was a big word right now, but she'd learned that letting panic set in didn't help her situation. So unless she discovered proof someone was looking for her, speed would be her number one priority. In fact, the quicker she could get to Jake and talk to him, the sooner she could figure out her next move.

Hours later a heavy fog began to settle in between the trees, hugging the ground with the coming dusk. She cursed softly. As if the landscape wasn't eerie enough on its own.

She stopped at the first clearing she encountered. No use trying to forge ahead in these conditions. She knew it'd be far too easy to step into a depression and twist an ankle, or worse, slip off a steep slope she couldn't see in the fog.

After quickly setting up her camp, Katie decided a small campfire was in order. She wanted some brightness to counter the gloominess tonight. She quickly got a blaze going, ate some much-needed nutrition, and then forced herself to try and relax by the warm flames. She pretended the shroud of fog surrounding her was a protective cover, keeping her safe and unseen. She closed her eyes and breathed slowly. She could sense her muscles relax, her shoulders drop, and her heart rate slow.

The whisper of movement against leaves made her eyelids fly open. She looked around without moving, then slowly turned her head. At least she'd had her eyes closed long enough to not be too blinded by the bright flames of her little campfire as she searched the murky shadows surrounding her.

A dark sleek silhouette caught her eye as it slipped through the brush nearest her. She stared, afraid to blink as her heart raced.

With her heart thumping against her ribs, she fought the instinct to yell. She found her hand moving toward the can of bear spray on her belt.

Katie blinked multiple times, sure her imagination worked overtime … sure a tree stump in the gathering gloom had tricked her eyes. She had almost convinced herself of it when the shape melted into the shadows of trees and slid out of view.

It wasn't human. She was sure of that. The profile fit that of a cougar or coyote. Maybe it had smelled her food cooking, and curious, had checked it out. Which made her especially thankful she had decided on a campfire. It most likely kept the animal from coming any closer.

She took a deep breath, the after-effects of the adrenaline rush causing her to tremble. The experience hadn't been the same as the elk, which had inspired such peace and a oneness with nature.

Maybe it was the gloomy atmosphere, but between the appearance of the helicopter and this, she felt she'd been given a warning. But of what?

She thought about her plans for tomorrow. With a steady pace, she should make her goal of reaching Jake. Was there a possibility that others were watching the area close to where he was hiding? Watching for him … or watching for her, so they could follow her to him? Could that be the warning?

"That's it," she stated aloud. Decision made. She'd still proceed as quickly as possible to where she believed Jake was hiding. But she'd take a route that allowed her to cross over small streams and creeks multiple times, and hike through a rockier landscape, leaving fewer prints. She would be able to keep up her fast pace, but if anyone did happen to be following her, they'd have to slow considerably to track her passage. She'd stay hours ahead of them, or maybe lose them completely.

Since initiating this quest, one thing had propelled her forward with as much immediacy as her body could endure ... her instincts insisted that speed was of the essence.

Katie stared into the nearby trees, still feeling the presence of the animal. Maybe it was a blessing that it had shown itself. It had helped her decide how to proceed in the morning.

It was time to crawl into her tent for the night, even if she didn't think she'd get much sleep. She'd keep the bear spray handy, just in case.

CHAPTER THIRTY-ONE

Mt. Baker-Snoqualmie National Forest, Washington (Day Eight)

Yesterday had turned out to be especially productive. Early in the day they reached Katie's campsite from the night before, and they'd easily followed her fresh tracks in the snow. The three made up valuable time. Even when they'd made it out of the snow and into the lower elevation, her trail had remained distinct. So they made camp last night with the expectation that they'd catch up with Katie early today.

But after breaking camp at daybreak today, everything went downhill in a hurry. It didn't take long for Walker to realize something had changed about Katie's trek. Her prints took erratic turns and twists that made no sense, unless she hoped to confuse and lose anyone attempting to follow her. And when she came to a body of water, instead of simply crossing it, as before, she stepped in and randomly waded downstream or upstream before stepping out again on the opposite shore to take up her trek. It only took her minutes to perform the maneuver, but it meant they had to walk along the shoreline, upstream and downstream, until they could pick up her tracks again. She stepped on rocks and mosses to avoid a boot print being left behind. In fact, she did everything she could to avoid being easily followed.

There was no doubt in Walker's mind that her tactics hadn't slowed her progress by much. He could tell by her strides she moved at a brisk pace. But the three of them stopped often and backtracked to pick up her trail again, and again. By now they had lost all the valuable time they had gained the previous day. He struggled to keep the disappointment at bay.

Walker stopped and stood still. Hand raised to shield his eyes against the bright sunshine, he squinted at the land before them. Behind him and to his left rose the slopes of mountains, highlighted for the moment by the sun poised at high noon, ready to begin its descent toward evening.

Nataya walked up to stand beside him. Carl joined them seconds later. No one spoke, but Walker sensed they all had the same thought, so he said it out loud.

"That helicopter flying around yesterday must have spooked Katie."

"She's not the only one," Carl said.

Walker understood Carl's apprehension. Yesterday, the helicopter had made multiple runs through the valley they were heading into. Steve had told them it wasn't the FBI or a rescue unit that he could find, so who was it? The thought that it could be Victor put them all on edge.

Nataya looked out over the land in front of them. "Maybe …"

Walker turned to her, waiting.

"If indeed Katie is headed to wherever Jake is, and the helicopter has her worried someone is trying to follow her there. Makes me wonder if she might be getting close to her destination."

"Good point," Walker said. "It would explain why she's being evasive while still moving forward as rapidly as possible."

Carl nodded. "If that's the case, even though speed seems to be her goal, the closer she gets to her destination, the more careful and secretive she might become, which will make it even more difficult for us to follow her."

Steve shifted the four-wheel drive truck into a lower gear and eased it down into a gully and back up again. The dirt road he and Daniel traveled had become more rugged the farther they followed it. It was the third road they'd taken today that took off from the little mountain town of Marten's Pass. He was convinced that one of the many back roads around the town would lead them to wherever Jake was hiding out. Perhaps the cabin in the photo.

He glanced over at Daniel, his hand on the dash to steady himself, as they rose and fell over the ruts and gullies. It was getting late in the day, and he had no idea how much longer the road would wind through the trees. As he tried to decide whether to turn around or not, the road took them up a steep incline that abruptly ended at the top of a high summit. "Guess we're at the end of the road." At that moment both he and Daniel's phones pinged with messages.

Daniel looked at his cell. "Looks like we're high enough out of the forest to get a phone signal."

Steve put the truck in park so they could take a moment to check their messages. "I needed a break anyway."

Steve saw a voicemail from a number he didn't recognize and punched it. When he realized it was from Mabel in Marten's Pass, he put it on speaker so Daniel could listen as well.

"… thought you boys would want to know that a man was in town early this morning asking around about that guy, Jake, that you're looking for. The stranger didn't have any photos to show, just a name. And since nobody in town, 'cept me, knows 'the hermit' is Jake, I don't think the man got much information.

Besides, none of us knows where the hermit lives anyway." She went on to describe the man asking questions, and he fit Victor's description. "Well, that's it. I just thought it was curious, and then I remembered that business card you gave me. Hope it helps in some way. You boys be careful."

Steve looked at Daniel. "So, if that was Victor in the helicopter yesterday, he must've spotted the town and decided the same thing we did. That Jake is probably nearby somewhere."

"Yeah, but that gives me hope he hasn't pinpointed Jake's location yet."

"But neither have we …"

Daniel pushed the button to listen to his messages. He listened and shook his head. Then he put the message on speaker and replayed it for Steve. It was from his office. "Hey Chief, got another message from Richard Bright Star … it simply says, '"The vultures are circling. You must become the falcon.'"

Steve stared at Daniel. "Vultures … the helicopter Carl called us about."

"I would say so."

"So, we need to be the falcon?" Steve shook his head and stared out the windshield. What the hell had he gotten himself into anyway. All this business about the amulet and unconventional tribal beliefs had forced his mind into unfamiliar territory. And it hadn't been lost on him that, if he hadn't been called in on the homicide case, he wouldn't have been close by when Katie went missing, nor would he have been able to quickly track down Dean … who helped him get Walker onboard. All coincidence?

Daniel broke into his thoughts. "So what if Victor is the 'vulture'?"

"You mean, what if he's the one in the chopper?"

"We know now that he's been looking in the same places we have been. He could be searching the area via chopper.

Couldn't we do the same? Doesn't the FBI have a helicopter we could use?"

Steve turned away, stared out the side window before turning back to Daniel. "I've kept Katie's disappearance to myself for a reason. I don't want the Bureau involved in my personal matters. I had no idea, until recently, that her disappearance might be tied to Jake …"

"But now it is. And it appears the bad guys believe she's involved with Jake and may be targeting her. And the black-market ring *is* being investigated by the Bureau. Seems to me we'd have a good reason to ask for air support on this."

Steve stared out the windshield of the truck. "It's not like I can just commandeer an FBI helicopter for my own personal use. There'd be all sorts of bureaucratic hoops to jump through. Which means armed agents would most likely be involved." His hands gripped the steering wheel until his knuckles turned white, as he visualized all the ways bringing in a chopper, armed with FBI Agents, might go wrong. He turned to Daniel. "I'm not ready to go that route. I want to keep the Bureau out of this … if we can." But inside his head he heard the words, 'you must become the falcon' and felt the knots in his gut.

At first Nataya attempted to keep her attitude upbeat, but after hours of frustration she reluctantly gave in to her disheartened state of mind. Knowing they were so close to Katie at the start of the day, only to watch the miles between them grow and grow as the sun crossed the sky, had been difficult to accept. Each time Katie's tracks took them into another body of water, she inwardly groaned with exasperation. She knew they would spend long minutes checking both sides of the stream, looking for footprints where Katie had left the water and returned to land. Then the prints would go off the path and disappear into the forest undergrowth, forcing them to practically crawl through the brush to pick up any sign of her passage. Meanwhile the prints they found grew older as the hours dragged by. But Nataya hadn't been alone in her discouragement. Everyone's mood on the trail had been solemn.

She welcomed the growing dusk. Setting up camp, making some much needed food and getting warm around a fire finally put an end to the disappointing day. Even Carl, who usually entertained them with stories, had been sullen and unusually quiet.

The game plan they came up with while sitting around the fire, was to get to bed early and start out again at first light, before the sun rose over the mountains, in hopes they could make up some of their lost time.

She and Walker retired to the tent and snuggled down into the sleeping bag. She noticed he stared upward. "Something bothers you. Something beyond the frustration of the day?"

He didn't turn to look at her. "Yeah."

"Do you want to talk about it?"

He gave a soft laugh. "I really don't know what to say … because I just don't know what I believe."

She waited.

He sighed. "When we stopped at the campsite where Katie spent last night, I noticed a wolf print."

Nataya blinked in surprise but stayed silent.

Walker continued. "There was a clear print in the mud, right where she left the trail to set up camp." He paused briefly. "I know we've seen lots of sign of wildlife as we've gone deeper into the forest, but I believe it'd be odd for a lone wolf to come so close to her campsite." He turned to her then. "And yes, everything indicated the print was made about the same time as Katie's prints while she set up camp." He waited a moment. "I asked Carl to tell me more about the wolves here in the national forest, and he explained they were all gone as of 1930. But since the early 2000's the gray wolf has slowly started to return to Washington ... on their own. Man hasn't reintroduced them to the region. Research shows they are coming in from British Columbia, Idaho and Montana." He looked away. "Stranger still ... I saw a few more prints as we traveled today."

"You're thinking about the elk ... and the amulet?"

"Yeah. You know how I feel about our spiritual connectivity with the natural world. But this ..."

"As you've always taught me, sometimes there is no logical explanation."

He smiled at her. "I needed to hear that. Thank you." He took a deep breath and stared up at the top of the tent. "Since a year ago spring, with everything we went through at the uranium mine, dealing with such human greed ... such ugliness, there have been times I've felt out of balance with the natural world." He turned to her again. "Don't get me wrong. Teaching the wilderness classes and spending time in the woods with you has restored my inner strength. But coming to this new environment has opened a door I needed. There's something about this place ... something out there that reminds me it's all so much bigger than 'us.'"

Nataya smiled and snuggled closer to him. "I understand. I sense it as well. Even though intellectually I know we're not that far from the surrounding cities, I'd swear we're hundreds of miles away in a vast wilderness. Maybe we needed to be here, at this point in our life journey, to help us find balance again."

Walker considered her words. "I keep having dreams about that amulet, and of coyotes circling us with only our campfire keeping them at bay. Last night I dreamt of a dark shadow above us, shaped like a vulture ... maybe because of that damned helicopter ... I don't know." He turned to Nataya. "Steve may be right about this turning into a very dangerous scenario. Be honest. Tell me how you feel about continuing to follow Katie."

Nataya took her time replying and chose her words with care. "I think there is much more at play here then we understand, but it still feels right to me. That we're supposed to be here, trying to help Steve find his daughter."

Walker nodded. "Then we continue. But if at any point you want to stop. I will understand."

Nataya nodded, but in her heart, she sensed they were in far too deep to turn back now.

Katie stopped long enough to catch her breath and peer through the trees. She used no headlamp. Instead, she had allowed her eyes to adjust to the growing darkness. An almost full moon shone so brightly above, she could see shadows in the open sections of the woods.

She was close. In fact, she knew her way so well she could probably get there blindfolded. Which was why she had elected to continue hiking on into the darkness. If anyone really was trying to follow her, they would've already stopped to set up camp before dark. Meaning she could reach Jake tonight, long before anyone could catch up with her. What she'd do after that, she had no idea. But she shoved that thought from her mind.

Her body ached from the long hours of hiking. She had taken only shorts breaks to eat or drink enough to keep her energy level where she needed it. She longed to stop and rest, to sit down by a warm fire, to sleep. But not yet.

She took a deep breath and shoved off again, walking under the trees into the growing darkness of night.

CHAPTER THIRTY-TWO

Mt. Baker-Snoqualmie National Forest, Washington (Day Eight)

Katie leaned against the large fir tree, staying in the shadow of it as she studied the unpretentious log cabin before her. She checked the time on her watch. Seven-thirty. Behind the window coverings light glowed out into the surrounding trees. Although she couldn't see any smoke coming from the chimney, she could smell the wood burning. She smiled. No doubt about it, Jake had been busy these last few years since she'd been able to visit him.

She compared the cabin before her to the neglected building Jake had secretly revealed to her all those years ago. Indeed, the first time she saw it the forest seemed hellbent on reclaiming it. Curious, Katie had explored the building and its contents with Jake as he shared its history.

One of his ancestors had purchased forty acres of land and built the cabin back in 1900. When the surrounding wilderness was declared a national forest in 1907, his ancestor was allowed to keep it as private property. It had been passed down through the family over the years, and regularly used as a hunting cabin. Over the decades fewer and fewer family members hunted, and soon no one stayed there or did any upkeep, so it was forgotten. Until Jake learned about it.

He told Katie the foundation and main log structure was sound, and he intended to restore and improve the cabin. He asked her to promise to keep it their secret. In the years following, Jake spent time each summer working on it. Katie had helped the first few years between college and travel. Then her work had gotten in the way.

Seeing it now made her happy. Jake had not given up on his dream of bringing it back from its sad state. He had often joked with her that he would "fix it up and retire there" where no one could bother him. They laughed about it at the time. But that had been the one clue she understood in his note to her. The soft glow behind the curtains indicated she had guessed correctly.

Thinking of the note made her remember the rest of his words in his letter and her heart beat a bit faster. What if the bad men had found him first? She watched the window and saw one figure move past it. That boded well, but to be extra careful she stepped out of the woods and checked the ground closer to the building. She found only one set of prints, and the size matched those of her friend.

Now, how to approach Jake without scaring him half to death. After considering a few options she decided to start with a whistle they both had used while traveling in the woods, often to keep in range of each other, or sometimes to give a warning that they were coming into camp from the wilderness, so they wouldn't startle the other.

She moved up closer to the cabin, hoping to make it easier for him to hear her. She gave the familiar whistle. Seconds later she saw movement within the cabin and the light went out. Okay, he'd either decided to retire early, or had heard the sound and was being cautious. She took a deep breath and gave another whistle, as loud as she could. She waited.

Nothing.

She slowly approached the front door and stood at the threshold, ready to knock when a sound startled her. She turned to her left and spotted a figure at the corner of the cabin. Her eyes accustomed to the dark, and with the full moon above, she recognized him. He held a shotgun at his side and stood beside a tree that blocked him from view of anyone in the woods, where Katie had come from. A flashlight flicked on and caught her in its beam, momentarily blinding her. She instinctively raised her forearm to guard her eyes.

"Katie!"

Jake's voice. She lowered her arm as he lowered the light beam. "Yes. It's me." She waited, expecting him to rush to her. He didn't. Instead, he asked her a question.

"Are you alone?"

"Yes, of course." Now she understood. He must be concerned that she'd been taken against her will and forced to bring the men to his cabin. She answered, keeping her voice calm and steady. "I remember our promise made all those many years ago."

"Cross your heart?"

Now she knew what he wanted. "Cross my heart." She then crossed her hands at her wrists, making an x over her heart. She saw his shoulders relax, and he leaned the shotgun against the tree trunk. But still he didn't move. Instead, he motioned her to come to him, into the shadows.

When she reached where he stood, he grabbed her in a bear hug. "Damn it's good to see you, Katie. I've been so worried about you." he whispered.

She returned his hug, but before she could speak, he laid his finger against her lips and grabbed his gun, then motioned her to follow him. They eased around the side of the cabin, Jake watching the trees around them. She kept her hand on his shoulder and followed his steps. They rounded the next corner to the back of the cabin. She halted, stunned by the view, even in the dark.

Although three sides of the cabin were snuggled against the mountain slopes and surrounded by dense woods, Jake had clear cut all the trees from behind the cabin, right up to where the ground suddenly sheared away, dropping hundreds of feet into a canyon. The luminous moon and blanket of twinkling stars accented the dark silhouette of the North Cascades beyond, soaring up into the sky and marching north into Canada.

"Something, isn't it?" Jake said, then motioned her forward. "Let's get inside." He opened the back door and guided Katie inside, then locked and bolted the heavy door. Only then did he speak again. "Let me get us some light."

Katie watched as he pulled the corner of a curtain aside and peered out behind the cabin, staring for a long moment. He let the curtain drop and moved to a table to light a lantern. He took her jacket and hung it on a hook by the door, then swung his arm toward the wood stove. "Go get yourself warm, child."

She smiled. He used to call her that all the time, even though she was an adult. Guess it was because of their age difference. She walked to the wood stove to warm her hands.

"When did you last eat, Katie?"

"I ate some lunch while I hiked."

He gave a nod and bustled around in the little kitchen area while she studied the interior of the one-room cabin. One counter and some cabinets made up the kitchen, a square table for two sat next to it. A comfortable looking small sofa and large chair sat near the wood burning stove, along with a few end tables. Across the room a bed covered in quilts and blankets snuggled into one corner. She guessed the narrow door opened to a washroom. The log walls had a few pictures hanging on them, but mostly hooks and racks where he could hang clothes or tools. The open rafters gave the illusion of more space than there was in the small structure.

Jake brought her a sandwich made with thick slices of bread and ham. "Nothing fancy, but I bet it'll taste pretty good after hiking all day." He grinned.

She thanked him and took a seat while he settled himself into what appeared to be his favorite chair. She tried not to devour the food too quickly, and in between bites she told him how happy she was to see he'd managed to bring the old cabin back to life, how great everything looked. He watched her, nodding and smiling.

When her food was finished, she waited for him to begin the conversation she had waited all these days to hear. Maybe now she would finally find out what had caused him to send her a warning and then disappear. He must have sensed it and leaned forward, his arms resting on his thighs, hands loosely clasped. He looked up at her.

"Why did you come here, Katie?"

She hadn't expected the question, and her surprise must have shown on her face, but she tried to cover it by taking a deep breath before answering. "I don't know, really. I read your note many times before I made the decision. But two things stood out to me. First, I was sure you were in trouble. And all my instincts told me I needed to find you as quickly as possible … and help if I could. Second, I didn't want to wait around for some 'bad guys' to show up at my door."

"I'm glad you came, Katie, I really am." He gave her a sad smile. "But to be honest, I don't think there is anything you can do to help me."

The pain of his statement must have reflected in her eyes because he gave her a smile filled with kindness before he continued.

"Don't get me wrong. I'm beyond happy that you're here. I've been so worried about you. And it's a great boost to my morale. I sure have needed someone to talk to about—everything. Maybe that's why you felt you needed to be here. That's the help you can give me."

Katie leaned forward, held his gaze. "What happened, Jake?"

"So much, Katie … so much. I guess I should start at the beginning." He told her about his friend, Joseph Spirit Horse, from the reservation. How they went river fishing every chance they could. "I think you met him a couple of times, right?"

Katie nodded, but stayed silent.

"Aside from you, I'd say he was my best friend."

She took note he used the past tense when speaking of his friend, but she remained silent and waited.

"Over time Joseph told me many things about his life, and his spiritual training with Richard Bright Star. You see, Joseph was the keeper of a very important piece of tribal history, an artifact, I guess you could say." Jake explained that the piece was an amulet that had been passed down through the years to the holy men of the tribe and considered very powerful. "Joseph viewed himself as still in training, spiritually, and wouldn't yet wear the piece. But the entire tribe knew it was in his care. When the artifact was stolen from him by a black-market ring that'd been working the nearby reservations, he became distraught and talked at length about it. He knew the tribal police chief's hands were tied, since the thieves were not from the reservation, but he was determined to get it back."

Jake leaned back into his chair, as a sadness crept into his face. "I tried to reason with Joseph about how dangerous his plans were. But I could tell he didn't want to hear it. Just over two weeks ago, he came to me, and I was startled by the deep-seated sense of dread surrounding him. I'd never seen him like that. He swore me to secrecy and told me he had found and stolen back the artifact. But he feared he might have been caught on surveillance cameras and that the black-market guys would come looking for him. So he hid the amulet. He wouldn't even tell me where it was, 'in case they got to me,' because of our friendship, he said."

Jake leaned forward, his forearms resting on his thighs. "I could understand his fear of the black-market guys. But there was more to it. Joseph revealed that, although he hadn't worn the amulet, he believed it still gave him protection while it was in his care. Even when the men had stolen it from him, he hadn't been harmed. But Joseph said that hiding it away where the thieves would never find it made him feel vulnerable, that he no longer had the protection."

He looked at Katie. "I know this sounds all woo-woo, but after knowing Joseph for so long, I could understand why he held such strong beliefs about the piece. It has quite a history with the tribe." Jake sighed. "A few days passed, and nothing happened. I began to relax about the whole incident. I drove over to Joseph's place to pick him up for our usual fishing trip and spotted a black SUV parked in front of his house. The back of my neck prickled, and I went on alert. I drove by, not looking over at the house in case someone watched. I went farther down the street and parked where no one could see me. Then I started making my way back toward Joseph's place, on foot, through the neighboring backyards and trees to the house. I knew I could get in through the back door."

Jake clasped his hands on his knees, straightened and gave a heavy sigh. "I'm not sure you really want to hear this, Katie."

She looked at him for a long moment. "I'm here to listen, remember?"

He gave her a nod, then took a deep breath before beginning again. "I quietly entered through the back door and immediately heard a man's voice, one I didn't recognize. I could tell the man wanted Joseph to tell him something and was hurting him to get what he wanted. I forced myself to stay calm. Beside me sat a washer and dryer with an open toolbox on top. I looked over and picked up the biggest thing I could get ahold of without making any noise—a large wrench. I hefted it in my hand and slowly worked my way across the kitchen.

"When I peeked around the corner, I spotted a man with his back to me. He held a gun and was observing whatever was going on across the room, while also watching the front door. I took another step and could see Joseph tied to a chair, and a second man was hitting him. I couldn't believe what I was seeing. I could barely recognize my friend. It was obvious they had tortured and beaten him for some time. Something went off inside of me, Katie. A white-hot rage I've not experienced since being in the service, so many years ago."

He looked up at her. She nodded and waited.

"It's taken me a while to piece together what exactly took place after that, because it all happened so fast. I remember rushing the man with the gun from behind and hitting him in the back of the head with the wrench. He went down like a stone, the gun falling from his hand. I must've grabbed it up while going after the guy hurting Joseph. He heard the commotion and was turning toward me when I hit him upside of the head with the wrench, letting loose all my anger. He crumbled, and I rushed over to Joseph."

Katie saw pain and despair in his eyes as Jake looked up at her for a moment.

"Joseph was a mess. What kind of animals would beat and torture a peaceful old man like that?"

He held her gaze then, with unshed tears in his eyes. And she recognized something else, too. A deep-seated rage still burned.

He looked away until he gained control of his voice again. "I got him out of the chair he was tied to and lowered him to the floor, where I held him in my arms. He was trying to tell me something, but I was focused on telling him to hang in there while I looked around the room for a phone, to call for help. That's when I noticed the first man I'd hit starting to stir, so I grabbed up the gun that was on the floor beside me and pointed it at him, told the man to stay put. It wasn't my gun hand, but the guy didn't know that. Still, the moment I turned my attention back to Joseph the guy started scrambling for the front door. I shot multiple times from my position on the floor, but he got away. I don't think I even hit him.

"That's when I felt Joseph tug on my arm. He was desperate to tell me something. I leaned down. His voice was raw, but he clearly said, 'I did not tell them.' I knew he meant the location of the amulet. I must've been crying because I saw tears fall on Joseph's face. Then he begged me to listen, and he told me where he had hidden the artifact. I promised him I'd protect it. I couldn't believe it when he died in my arms."

Katie stood, approached Jake, and knelt beside him. She took his hands. "I'm so sorry, Jake."

"Thank you, Katie." He looked up at her. "And thank you for being here and listening to me. I've not told anyone about this. It's been such a torment holding it in."

"You didn't contact the sheriff or tribal police?"

"When Joseph passed, everything went black for a while, until sirens broke through my haze of grief. I realized someone must've called in about the gun shots. I panicked. I couldn't get delayed. I had to make sure the amulet stayed safe from those people. I guess I wasn't thinking too clearly. I laid Joseph down and stood to leave. I noticed the gun and wrench, half remembering I should wipe away my prints, then ran out the back door and snaked my way through the backyards to get to my truck. The next day I learned that the second man I hit with the wrench died at the scene. I had accidentally killed him."

Katie didn't even try to hide her surprise. Then the words in the note came back to her. "That's why you said you had done a terrible thing, but it was the right thing."

Jake nodded and was silent for a long moment. "If anyone deserved to die…. But when I left, I had no idea the unconscious man was dead." He looked at Katie. "To make matters worse, the man who got away clearly saw me. He must've figured out my identity and told the black-market leader because the very next day, when I was finally able to return to my house, I discovered someone had already been there. Every room in the place had been torn apart. It was clear they were looking for the artifact. I had no idea what to do. So I turned and walked out the door, grabbed my backpack from my shed and headed up here on foot."

He looked at Katie. "It was while I was hiking up through the forest and replaying everything in my head that I remembered seeing all the students' photos lined up on the desk, like someone had studied them. You're the only person who knows about the cabin, so I wasn't worried about the others saying anything about it. But I needed to warn you not to let anyone know. When I got close to Marten's Pass, I wrote you that little note. Then I hid my pack just outside of town, walked in and mailed it. I returned to the woods and retrieved my pack, then continued to the cabin."

As the pieces fell into place for Katie, a stab of fear sliced through her. "The men who were at your house. They're convinced you know where it is. The amulet."

"Evidently."

She noticed he didn't meet her eyes. "But you don't—do you?"

He met her gaze. "But I do."

Victor cradled his head in his hands, willing the pain to subside. His symptoms had gone into overdrive today. He sensed time slipping through his fingers like sand and he cursed. He needed to move things forward. Now.

He popped a couple of pills without water, gulped them down and looked over at the helicopter pilot, who watched him in silence. He forced himself to speak. "Okay, regarding that cleared area in the woods we found yesterday, the one that looked like there might be structure tucked away under the trees … you're saying we can use the GPS coordinates to pinpoint it again, fly over it tonight so no one can see us, and use thermal imaging to look for heat signatures?"

"Yeah, no problem."

"Okay, let's get on with it."

"You okay to fly?"

Victor glared at him, and the man raised his hand as if to say, 'fine'. The pilot went out to ready the chopper. By the time he returned, Victor's medicine had started to calm his symptoms. As they left the hangar and walked out to the chopper, he willed himself not to throw up on the tarmac.

As they both settled in and buckled up for the ride, Victor thought about what Colt had said … that flying around in the chopper could warn Jake and the woman that someone was looking for them. He turned to the pilot. "I need you to go to those coordinates but keep our altitude as high as you possibly can and still get the images we need."

The pilot merely nodded. He'd been hired not to question anything his client asked of him, and he was being paid well to remain silent. He glanced over at Victor. The guy's paleness didn't give him much confidence that he wouldn't be doing a cleanup after this flight. He sighed and reminded himself of the promised payoff.

Katie stared at Jake. A part of her celebrated that he had managed to retrieve the amulet so important to Joseph's tribe. But a bigger part of her was terribly frightened by the implications of his news. She reached out and laid her hand on his. "I'm really scared, Jake. I think I may have messed things up by coming here."

He looked at her, tilted his head. "In what way?"

She told him then about how she hadn't let her father know her destination, and she'd made sure no one had seen her leave her cottage, but as she neared his cabin she began to worry about being followed. "Maybe it was just the fact a helicopter had come through the area, as if searching for someone. It's made me jumpy, I guess."

"Yeah, I heard the chopper as well. Came right over the cabin yesterday. But then it moved on, and I heard it over other areas around the town of Marten's Pass. It appeared they had a missing person from the town or something. We do have a lot of rescues up here."

She nodded and tried to reassure herself. "To play it safe, as I drew closer, I made it as difficult as I could for someone to follow me here."

"I'm sure you did. Don't worry, Katie. We're pretty secluded up here. I'm sure no one knows about this cabin. I've been careful not to use my name when I do go into town for supplies, and I make sure no one follows me back up here. I've even kinda camouflaged the dirt road entrance to the cabin." He glanced toward the back of the cabin. "Although, I have to admit, when I clear cut the trees for that view out back, I wasn't thinking about someone being in the air … trying to find me."

She watched his brow wrinkle the slightest bit, in worry. It increased the feeling of dread that still sat in her gut.

He squeezed her hand. "I'm glad you came here. You know I can't abide cell phones, not that I could get a signal up here anyway, so I couldn't call and check on you. I've worried every day about you. The more I thought about it, the more I hoped you'd left, just in case those guys showed up." He looked away, his eyes losing focus for a moment. Then he blinked and was back with her. "How 'bout you help me bring in some firewood for the night. And then I have something I want to show you."

She gave him a quizzical look but followed him to the door. They slipped on their parkas, and he guided her in the dark to the stacked rows of split firewood.

They had both gathered up an armload and turned to head back to the cabin when he halted and looked upward. She heard it too then. A helicopter. It sounded very high, but directly over them. Something about it gave her shivers.

"Hurry." Jake nudged her forward and he stayed right beside her.

But she needed no encouragement to use all the speed she could muster while carrying the armful of wood.

Jake got a hand free long enough to yank the back door open and held it for her. They both hurried into the cabin as the chopper stayed overhead, but sounded as if it rose higher, farther away. They both stood still and caught their breath.

"I wanted us under the metal roof." His chin pointed up to the rafters overhead. Then he moved toward the wood stove, and she followed. After they unloaded their bundles of wood. He looked at her. "Maybe we're both a little jumpy, eh?"

She sensed he wanted her not to worry, but there was still a look of concern in his eyes that betrayed his true thoughts. She went along with him, more than anything to help calm herself. "I've never paid much attention to how often helicopters fly over around here, until I was trying to travel in secret."

"Yeah. When I was up here working in the summers, there were often planes and choppers at night." Jake still stood in the center of the cabin, head cocked, listening. "It's gone now." He studied her. "You know, it might be your father looking for you. I'm sure he's beside himself with worry."

"I know. I feel so guilty not letting him know about this. But I know him. He'd want to try and "fix" whatever was going on with you, but I didn't know yet what had happened. I wanted to talk with you first."

"I appreciate that." Jake gave her a long look. "And now that you know the story, what are you going to do?"

Katie stared at him. "I had planned to make sure you were okay and then let my father know I'm safe. But now I don't know what to do. I don't want you to go to jail because you defended Joseph."

"Yeah, I'd rather not have to do that either." He stared into space for a moment. "But maybe I can plead self-defense or something. Maybe it's what I need to do to keep you and the amulet safe …"

"No." Katie put her hands on her hips. "There's got to be another way."

Jake gave a sad smile, then walked over to the tiny kitchen area and opened a cabinet. He pulled out a can of baking powder, but instead of opening the lid he twisted off the bottom and something dropped into his hand. He held the can up for her to see. "Secret hiding spot, made to look like the real deal." He walked over, asked her to hold out her hand.

She did as he instructed and felt the weight of the object drop onto her palm before she recognized what it was. She stared up at Jake.

"Yes, that's the amulet."

She reverently touched it, moving the leather thong so she could see all the details of the carved piece. When she recognized the amulet consisted of a body shared with a wolf head and elk head with antlers, a shiver ran through her. She looked up at Jake. "This is so ironic."

"What do you mean?"

She proceeded to tell him about the night an elk had appeared at her camp. "I've been sensing his presence, even though I haven't seen him again." She noticed Jake's eyes were wide.

He asked the timeframe for the sightings.

"It was recent, as I neared your cabin." She thought back. "Four days ago."

He stared into space, nodding to himself. "Well, I'll be …."

"What?"

He looked at her. "For the last four nights, I've been especially worried about you. I got out that amulet and held it in my hands, thinking of you, asking it to protect you. At the time I felt silly doing it, but it made me feel better, like I was helping you in some way."

Katie didn't know what to say. Strange feelings flowed in and out of her, so many emotions tangled up together … fear … peace … friendship … danger.

The helicopter slowly followed the perimeter of the mountain slope, then veered away into the dark sky. Victor leaned back into his seat and spoke into his headset. "So tell me what we just saw."

The pilot pointed to a screen. "When we first approached the GPS coordinates and dropped to a lower altitude, we picked up a thermal signature—not a person, more like what a wood stove would put out from a chimney, not a campfire. I'd say there's definitely a cabin down there."

"Okay. That's good to know. What else?"

"For a brief moment I saw two distinct smaller heat signatures, like two warm bodies would make. They were away from the larger heat signature. Like outside the structure. When we were within hearing, they hurried toward the large heat signature. But then they disappeared."

"Disappeared?"

"I'm guessing maybe the structure has a metal roof and it blocked our thermal imaging. Lots of cabins and buildings up here have metal roofs."

"But you definitely saw two bodies?"

"Yeah, no doubt."

"Well done." Victor smiled. He'd already figured out that the clearing below them lined up with the Northeast heading the woman had been taking all along. So maybe she had finally reached her destination. And if so, wonder of wonders, she may have led him straight to Jake.

"I need you to be available tomorrow." He saw the pilot give him a nod of affirmation. His heart did a flip flop of excitement. He was close now. He was sure of it.

And none too soon.

CHAPTER THIRTY-THREE

Mt. Baker-Snoqualmie National Forest, Washington (Day Nine)

Carl awoke, startled out of a dream. Even as he desperately tried to cling to the vague images, they faded and disappeared as he became more aware of his surroundings.

The only thing he could recall was that Katie had been there in the dream. He shook his head to clear it. He found it amazing that he had such a strong protective feeling about someone he'd never personally met. But that sense of knowing her after following her trail so many days had only grown stronger. His admiration of her courage and skill set in their wilderness environment continued to build. Then, after the helicopter encounters, he'd sensed her wariness and perhaps hints of insecurity. Her actions proved she was at least concerned about being followed. He wished he could somehow let her know they were "the good guys" in this deal.

He sighed. No way would he be able to get back to sleep. He sat up in the sleeping bag and glanced at his watch, saw that dawn wasn't far off so he began to dress. He crawled out of the tent into the stillness of predawn. He had beaten Walker and Nataya out of their tent, a rare occurrence.

Carl dug through to the hot coals left from the campfire last night, found a few, added tinder and blew on it to ignite a flame. Once the fire blazed, he sat next to it, warmed his hands for a bit, then got water ready to heat.

He had finished pouring enough boiling water for his morning cup of coffee when Walker and Nataya exited their tent. They exchanged 'good mornings,' and Carl couldn't help but notice their more subdued than usual mood. Yesterday had been frustrating, and he wondered if they were as discouraged by it as he had been.

Nataya joined Carl by the fire and set about adding ingredients to the remaining water for her and Walker's morning tea. "You're up extra early. Couldn't sleep?"

"I slept fine, but a dream woke me, and I knew I'd not get back to sleep, so …" He shrugged.

She looked sideways at him. "A disturbing dream?"

"I don't know … Katie was in it, and it seemed I was trying to help her … so maybe it was a bad dream, but I can't remember any details now."

Nataya stared into the fire. "I think all three of us are having the same sense of protectiveness. As we get physically closer to Katie, we've also become more emotionally connected." She glanced at Walker, who stood apart from them, gazing into the trees. "He's been dreaming of coyotes circling us … and most recently he dreamt of a vulture wheeling in the sky above us."

Carl grinned. "Leave it to him to have such symbolic dreams." He saw her smile as well.

She called to Walker that their tea was ready and he joined them by the campfire. Carl tried to study him, without obviously staring. The man often had an unfocused gaze, as if he was viewing a different world, apart from what Carl was experiencing. He often wondered about it. But when Walker caught his gaze this time, it was laser sharp and focused. He gave Carl a grim smile.

"Tough day, wasn't it?"

Carl sighed in relief to know he wasn't alone in his frustration. "Yeah, a real ball-buster." Then he remembered Nataya sat next to him. She looked down at her tea, but he thought he could see a grin. He quickly added, "I'm just glad to know I'm not alone in feeling so discouraged."

"No, you're not alone," Walker said. "And hearing yet another helicopter late last night didn't help."

"Yeah, I checked the SAT phone and Steve hadn't sent a text or tried to call, so I'm guessing it wasn't him. Maybe we're reading more into it than there is … I mean, *we* had to call in a rescue chopper for Monica … hard to know."

A silence fell over them for a moment before Walker spoke. "We need to talk about something, Carl. Nataya and I have discussed the fact that Steve may be correct about the scenario facing us. There is a high possibility that it's turned into a dangerous one. I've given Nataya the option to say we step back, now. You should have that same option."

Carl stared at Walker, then looked to Nataya. He could tell they would accept whatever he decided and not hold it against him. He swallowed and took a breath before he spoke. "It wouldn't be the first time I've faced danger. And I understand the gravity of the situation. Things could go bad. But I just can't imagine not finishing what we've started."

Walker and Nataya stayed silent and closely watched him.

"Plus," Carl added. "I've come to believe that Katie is one hell of a special person. And I want to meet her and make sure she's safe." There. He'd voiced what he'd been secretly feeling for some time now. And it felt good to put it out there. He saw them both relax.

Walker spoke. "Yeah, we feel the same way. And I'm relieved that we all agree. Because we make a damn good team."

Carl couldn't stop the smile that came to his face. Walker had no idea how much it meant to hear that statement. But he forced himself to focus on Walker's words as the man's expression turned serious.

"But I'm leaving the option open. We have no idea what we'll be facing once we catch up with Katie. But for the present, I've been thinking a lot about how we even get to that point, and something occurred to me. Carl, when we finished our trek yesterday, did you by chance check our compass heading?"

"Yeah," he said. "In fact, I checked it on and off during the day. We wandered on and off course most of the day, but by the time we stopped for the night we were back on that same Northeast heading again."

Walker gave him a rare smile. "I thought so."

Carl sensed Nataya's focus on Walker, and he did as well.

"The fact Katie stopped following any path makes me believe she's close enough to her destination that she knows the way without a trail. That's why she could wander all around and make it difficult for us to follow. *But,* ultimately she's staying true to that Northeast heading."

Carl smiled. "I think I know where you're going with this." But he waited for Walker to confirm his guess.

Walker continued. "I'm suggesting we follow the compass heading today. We'll still watch for sign of Katie's passage as we travel, of course. But if we come to a stream or creek, we'll simply stay true to that heading and not worry about finding her prints. When she goes off trail, we'll stay to the compass heading. I'm guessing we'll still see prints every so often, because she most likely stayed true to her ultimate destination and didn't veer too far off course."

Carl's smile widened in response to Walker's thinking, and he could see Nataya was of like mind.

Walker continued. "Of course we're taking a risk. It means there's a chance we might lose her trail altogether. But I'm betting we won't."

"I agree," Carl said. "And I bet by taking a direct route, we'll have the chance to make up some of our lost time."

Nataya looked at both men. "I say we do it."

All three moved into action to break camp. Carl noticed the earlier gloom had lifted. A new energy filled the space around them.

Victor picked up the SAT phone, checked the SMS text message that Colt had sent that morning, and wrote down the GPS coordinates. He moved to his map, compared the man's location to the coordinates the pilot had given him. He called Colt and heard him answer on the second ring.

"What's up?'

"I'm going to give you some coordinates and I want you to hike to that location as quickly as possible. It's a clearing where the chopper will set down. We're picking you up."

"Why's that?"

"I think I know where Jake is hiding. And I believe Katie is already there."

Katie stood at the cabin's largest window and gazed at the massive mountain peaks in front of her as shafts of sunbeams burst forth from behind their dark profile. Minutes later the sun splashed the canyons below in vivid shades of gold and green.

Jake joined her, bringing her a cup of coffee. "Nice way to start the day, isn't it? When I saw those canyons and mountains for the first time, I knew I'd want to clear the area so I could enjoy it from the cabin. Besides, I want an open area where I can plant some gardens come springtime, since most of the ground around the cabin is covered in trees and shade."

"I think you did the right thing. It's inspirational." She noticed he stayed beside her and remained mute. She took the moment to savor the quiet and peacefulness. When she finally spoke, she avoided the bigger issue she knew they would eventually address. "So, you've accomplished most of your plans for the cabin since I was last here." She turned to him. "I'm so sorry I missed out on helping you with much of this."

He smiled. "No need to apologize. You did plenty. I took this project on without any expectations, and I appreciated whatever help you were able to give me. It's been a labor of love for me. I don't really know why. I guess it simply felt good to bring something so old and neglected back to life again."

"Well, you succeeded. It's cozy, yet also sturdy and durable. And I'm sure it'll be warm and comfy this winter."

Jake looked out the window for a moment, then back to her. "We have to talk about this, Katie."

"I know. I just wanted to enjoy this morning with you … you know, pretend I'm here on a pleasant visit … and nothing more."

"I hear ya. And it *has* been wonderful to see you again. Even under the current circumstances."

Katie turned to face him. "I've thought about it, and I see only one solution."

"What would that be?"

"Maybe tomorrow morning you could drive me into that little town nearby—where you buy supplies. I'll find a way to contact my father from there and let him know I'm safe and will be heading back down the mountain. That way, he'll stop worrying about me. But more important, if he's the one in the helicopter, he'll stop flying over this area. I don't want him to accidentally spot the cabin. Then I can take my time hiking back out of here. There's no reason for me to mention anything about seeing you. You and your cabin will remain a secret."

Jake studied her for a long moment. "Do you truly believe your father is going to accept your story about disappearing into the wilderness for over a week, without letting him know? You two have always been honest with each other."

Katie thought about the note she had sent to her father. She'd made it clear she had an agenda. He'd want some explanations. "Well, it'll take me a few days to hike back down out of the forest. That should give me plenty of time to come up with a story that he'll believe." It sounded lame, and she knew it. She looked at Jake. "Or maybe you and I can put our heads together and come up with something before I leave."

He gave her a cheerless smile. "Maybe."

Walker knelt to examine a partial heel print in the soft dirt, half hidden beneath a large fern. Up ahead, leading the way, Carl used his compass to find his heading, then picked out a landmark in front of him that would keep him on course. Once Carl reached the chosen landmark, he rechecked his compass and picked out the next point of reference. The process let him move forward through the landscape at a quick pace. The young man reminded Walker of an eager pup straining at his leash, which made him smile to himself.

Meanwhile, he and Nataya followed behind and off to each side of Carl's path, so they could casually keep watch for signs of Katie's passage.

They'd been at it all morning but had already made up most of the time they'd lost the day before. The best part being they were still finding sign of Katie's passage on occasion, as she often criss crossed over their more direct route. At least enough sign to know they still had her trail. Walker could tell by everyone's energy level that the mood had vastly improved from the day before. Based on the age of the most recent prints he and Nataya had found, they were close … very close.

Although Carl had been feeding their coordinates to Steve each day, the FBI guy hadn't shared any more info with them about his speculations regarding the hidden cabin he believed Jake might be using to hide. Maybe Steve didn't have any more of a clue than they did. So where and what they might soon face remained a mystery. What it all meant and how they would approach such a scenario remained a question that bothered Walker more than he wanted to admit.

CHAPTER THIRTY-FOUR

Mt. Baker-Snoqualmie National Forest, Washington (Day Nine)

Victor used one hand on the dashboard to steady himself, while the other one clasped the handle over the passenger window. He wasn't about to complain about Colt's breakneck pace on the deeply rutted dirt road. After all, he was the one insisting the guy drive as fast as possible, without dropping an axle.

It had taken hours to find a place to rent a truck suitable for the terrain, then additional hours to drive the mountain roads before they even reached the national forest. Panic sat heavily in his gut as the minutes ticked by.

Colt glanced sideways at him. "Tell me again why we couldn't just land that chopper down in that big clearing behind the cabin?"

Victor shot him a glare and ignored him. He knew his over-eager hired gun was already thinking about his promised fat payoff. Besides, Victor had already explained that he didn't want to give Jake that kind of a heads-up. Before the chopper pilot could set down, the man could easily escape into the woods, where they'd probably not find him … or at least not in time. No, the two of them would approach the cabin in stealth mode. Besides, he wasn't one hundred percent sure it was Jake in the cabin. He and Carl would need to observe the place to confirm that. Once they knew for sure, then they could capture Jake and call in the chopper to pick them up.

Victor checked their current GPS coordinates compared to the coordinates the chopper pilot had given him for the cabin. So far, so good—that is, if the two of them survived the beating they were taking on the poor excuse for a road.

Steve rolled the truck to a stop, put it in park and gave an audible sigh. Yet another dead end. He and Daniel were getting nowhere fast. Well, except there was nothing fast about taking these logging roads through the forest. He dreaded the return trip back over the same deeply rutted, boulder-infested dirt and mud track. Hours of wasted time. To make matters worse, he sensed Walker, Nataya and Carl were closing in on Katie's location, and he wanted to figure that out before they did.

It hadn't been lost on Steve that for the past two nights Carl had no longer given him any details, other than their location, when he sent texts via SMS on the SAT phone.

Until recently the young man's messages had been full of details about what they were seeing and their surroundings. Steve had no doubt it'd been a long trudge through the wilderness. He tried to give Carl the benefit of the doubt, that maybe that's all he had the energy for by the time they set up camp at night. But Steve didn't think that was the complete reason. Walker's reaction to their last phone conversation gave him an uneasy sense that the three of them were not going to listen to him about locating his daughter and then stepping away from the scene.

On one hand he understood their dedication to seeing the

search through. But damn it, this was his daughter's life they were dealing with. The thought of not having full control of the situation was maddening.

He shook his head. He wasn't being his usual self and that was a bad sign. Panic constantly threatened to bubble up through his defenses, and it took every bit of his willpower to subdue it, to simply function.

Lately he'd caught Daniel studying him, as he did now, and figured the man had a good sense of the torment he was experiencing. But true to his usual demeanor, the man had remained silent. Until now.

Daniel turned and looked straight ahead through the truck windshield and spoke quietly. "When are you going to listen to Richard Bright Star?"

"What do you mean?"

"He told us what we need to do."

"Which was what, exactly?"

"We must become the falcon."

Steve stared at Daniel.

The man looked at him, his expression completely serious.

Walker noticed Carl had knelt and was studying something on the ground. He walked forward and stopped beside the young man. "What is it?"

Carl cocked his head sideways to look up at Walker. "Katie's prints. They've been right in line with the northeast angle we're taking for a while now."

"Could be that we're close to her destination." Walker knelt and studied the prints with Carl as Nataya joined them. "These are still old, from last night."

Carl's excitement changed to a look of disappointment. "So maybe we're really not close at all?"

Walker looked over his shoulder to the sun's low position in the sky and then down to study the prints again. "Maybe we still are." He faced Carl. "Could be that Katie was close enough to her destination last night that she felt confident about continuing into the evening, maybe even after dark."

"Okay. That makes sense." He looked from Walker to Nataya. "If that's true. We may be only minutes away from … wherever it is that Katie has been leading us."

Nataya took a couple of steps forward, stopped and stared into the trees. "Steve seems to believe Jake is hiding in a cabin somewhere out here. If that's the case, Katie may already be there."

Walker stood and joined Nataya. "True." He didn't want to get that far ahead in his thinking. They still had to find her first. "I believe we should switch from using the compass to following her prints at this point. But Carl, keep an eye on the compass heading as well, okay?"

"Yeah, no problem."

CHAPTER THIRTY-FIVE

Mt. Baker-Snoqualmie National Forest, Washington (Day Nine)

For an hour they once again gained elevation at a rapid rate, causing Walker's leg muscles to burn with the exertion, then in the last few minutes the terrain had leveled out, letting him return his full concentration to following sign of Katie's passage. That and occasionally peering ahead through the dense cover of trees, only to see more trees.

Nataya followed behind, and Carl brought up the rear. Walker noticed the young man stopped on occasion to turn and look behind them, listening and watching. No doubt Carl worried Victor's man still followed, as did he.

He glanced up through the trees to find the sun's position in the sky above, directly above them. It was already noon, and because Katie's prints were clearly last night, not fresh from earlier today, he had no idea how far away they might be. Still, he believed they had to be getting close. So he stepped carefully and moved slowly through the landscape, so as to not startle the wildlife and set off an alarm that might be noticed by Katie—wherever she might be up ahead.

Walker leaned down to move fern fronds and get a better

look at a heel impression in the soft soil, then felt Nataya's hand rest gently on his shoulder. He slowly raised his head and looked up, knowing her signal meant she'd seen something ahead. It took only a moment before he spotted what had caught her eye. A roofline broke the horizon between trees. He sensed his heart rate jump and waited for Carl to catch up with him and Nataya.

Walker spoke quietly. "Definitely a man-made structure. Whether it's where Jake and Katie are, is another matter. But her prints head that direction." He looked at Nataya and Carl. "Since there are three of us, I suggest we stay hidden within the trees and fan out around the perimeter. We can check out the building and its surroundings, as well as watch for anyone moving around inside or outside. If we take our time and move carefully, we shouldn't be spotted from the building. We'll meet back here to compare notes."

"I'll take the center, if you like," Carl volunteered. "I know you two are much better at stealth and speed than I am."

Walker gave him a nod of acknowledgement, proud the man understood how best to serve the team. Nataya tipped her head to the right, indicating she'd head out that way and soon disappeared through the woods and understory. Before he angled off to the left, Walker saw Carl slip off his large backpack and lean it against a nearby tree, out of sight. Then both men slipped through the trees in different directions, making as little noise as possible.

Walker worked his way through the trees until he could get a clear view of the structure, a modest log cabin. The style reminded him of a bygone era, and although it had clearly been recently updated, it still maintained a historical appearance. He studied what he assumed to be the front entrance. There were a few small windows, but curtains covered them from the interior. He didn't see any movement from within, but the sun shined brightly outside, making it near impossible to see anyone inside. Walker continued to slip from one tree to another alongside the cabin until he could see behind it.

The completely different view surprised him. Here the land opened up into a wide expanse of grass and dirt that ran flat out away from the cabin until it dropped off into a canyon. Beyond the canyon, Walker faced a breathtaking view of the North Cascade Mountain range, rearing up dark against the midday sky. As he studied the peaks, he couldn't help but feel a bit homesick for the San Juan Mountains of his home in Colorado.

Reluctantly turning away from the scene, he studied the back of the cabin. Many cords of firewood sat stacked in rows, ready for the winter season. He could see a heat signature rising from the rock chimney, and smell burning wood. It also appeared the owner had begun preparation for next spring's garden with construction of wooden raised planter boxes. Wire fencing materials lay off to the side of the flat grassy stretch of yard. Everything indicated that someone had been working on the cabin and surrounding land.

He made his way back to where they had started. Carl already waited for him, and Nataya soon joined them. Walker gave his assessment of what he'd seen and his conclusions. Carl said he'd followed Katie's prints as close to the cabin as he dared, while staying hidden among the trees, but hadn't been able to see anyone moving around inside. But with the smell of smoke in the air, he agreed someone was in the cabin.

Nataya spoke next. "When I went to the right from here, I found a narrow dirt track cutting through the trees and leading up to the cabin. Closer to the structure someone had laid down some gravel. There's a three-sided carport built onto that side of the cabin," she said, pointing. "Parked inside is an ancient-looking pick-up truck. But it must run because there are tire tracks leading into the carport that look to be only days old.

Makes me further believe someone is inside the cabin."

Walker looked over his shoulder at the building. "I would agree. And since Katie's prints lead right to it, I believe we can safely presume Jake is inside."

"But what if Victor found Jake first? If Katie is in there, she could be a hostage for all we know," Nataya said.

He looked at Carl and then Nataya. "That's an important point and makes me believe it'd be premature to send our coordinates to Steve before we know the truth about what's happening in that cabin. We could endanger Katie's life." He saw them both nod in agreement. "I could use the ground cover to hide my movements by doing a belly crawl, follow Katie's prints to the cabin, and search for any other prints. But I'll have to move slowly …"

"In other words, it's going to take some time," Carl said.

"Unfortunately, yes."

"I see no other way, if we want to be one-hundred percent sure that Katie is in there alone with Jake. That they don't have company." Nataya sighed heavily.

Victor Blake popped two pills into his mouth and swallowed. The listing and rolling of the truck as it lurched through the ruts in the road and rose again reminded him of being in a boat on rough water. It wasn't helping his headache or the nausea in his belly. But he believed they were getting close to the cabin and that alone kept him hanging on.

Colt stopped the truck, leaned forward to look at the GPS coordinates they'd been following. "Something's wrong."

"What d'you mean?"

"According to the coordinates, we should be heading more west. It's like we missed a turn to the left somewhere. We've gone past our mark."

Victor slammed his fist on the dashboard. "Well, then turn around. We must've missed spotting it."

"I didn't miss seeing a road. I know that for sure. Unless …"

"Unless what?"

"Maybe the man you're searching for did something to disguise the entrance. That's what I'd do if I was trying to hide out up here."

Victor studied the man. "Yeah, well Jake has proved to be smart and wily. I think you've got something there. Get turned around and take it slow. We'll both watch for anything that looks wrong along the way."

A mile later, with Victor restlessly watching out the windows, Colt stopped the truck and stared at the side of the road. "Yeah, something's not quite right here."

"What do you mean?" Victor leaned forward. "I don't see anything odd."

Colt pointed. "The brush laying over that rotted fallen log is still green."

Victor stared at him, waiting.

"Like someone recently pulled some brush up over that log … trying to make it look as if that log's been there for a while."

"Check it out."

Colt opened his door and climbed out. When he got up close to the log, he looked back at Victor and said, "Yeah, this log has recently been dragged to this position, then the brush pulled up over it to hide the entrance to a one-lane dirt road." He pointed back behind him. "Would take us that direction."

"Can you move the log?"

Colt gave it a tug. "Yeah, it's big but rotted to hell. Lighter than it looks." He pulled on it until he cleared it from the road. He dusted off his hands and climbed back into the truck.

Moments later they bumped down the dirt trail and Colt gave Victor a sly smile. "Yeah, now we're back on track."

Nataya and Carl sat on the ground behind a stand of ferns and next to a large cedar tree, their silhouettes blending in with their surroundings. Walker had taken off his parka and wool sweater, leaving on his buckskin tunic so he could crawl through the vegetation without it snagging on his clothing. Within moments he disappeared into the ground cover. At first the two tracked Walker's movements through the brush toward the cabin, then switched to watching the door and windows of the cabin. And they talked quietly.

Carl looked up at Nataya. "So, now that we're finally here, what happens when we confirm Katie's in there? Are you going to ask me to contact Steve and give him the coordinates?"

Nataya looked away and remained quiet.

Carl spoke again. "If that's what you and Walker ask of me, I'll comply."

Nataya gave him her attention. "Is that what you want to do?"

He looked down and tugged at the edges of his jacket. "Honestly? No, I don't."

"Walker and I don't want to do that either."

He looked up at her and waited.

"At least not without trying to make contact first. We're here. Steve's not. Who knows how long before he could arrive once he receives the coordinates? What if Victor shows up before Steve can get here? If we can get Katie to safety before Steve arrives with … who knows what … that seems a better solution to us. What are your thoughts?"

Carl gave her a grin. "That's exactly what I was hoping to hear."

She smiled in relief to know the three of them were still of like mind. She had been worried that once they arrived at their destination, and it all became real, Carl might change his mind.

She glanced at the cabin. "I think Walker's heading back." She turned to Carl. "I've been thinking about how to approach the cabin. I've come up with a way this might work, and I want to run an idea past you ... see what you think."

Walker returned to where Nataya and Carl waited, more than ready to be done with crawling through the underbrush. The mossy ground might be soft, but it was also super moist, like crawling on sponges. The chilled air on his now damp clothes made him eager to take his sweater and parka from Nataya's outstretched hands. He quickly pulled them on, then they moved farther away from sight of the cabin, so they could safely talk.

They each found a dry log or stump to sit on, then Walker nodded toward the cabin. "I followed Katie's tracks straight toward the front door. When I ran out of ground cover to hide my progress I watched the windows for any movement, but with it being so light outside it made it impossible to see anything behind those curtains. So I crouched and made a dash for the side of the cabin. I stayed out of sight and checked for prints." He filled them in on how he saw only Katie's prints until she joined a man at the corner of the cabin and followed him to the back door, where they entered.

"So it didn't appear that she was being forced into the cabin?" Nataya asked.

"No signs of that. Appears she willingly followed him. I'm guessing it was Jake, and he was being super careful."

"That would make sense, even if he was expecting Katie," Carl said. He looked at Walker, then Nataya. "So we can safely assume Katie is inside with Jake?"

Walker nodded. "I believe so. To be sure, I checked at the back of the cabin and didn't find any other prints besides Jake and Katie." He then sighed. "Now we have to figure out how to approach them without causing them to bolt and take off."

"Or shoot us," Carl added.

"That, too."

Nataya held Walker's gaze. "Carl and I have been talking about a solution, while we were waiting."

"Oh yeah?"

"I know we all agree that they need to feel completely safe opening that door. At this point Katie has probably learned about Jake's place being searched, and that he's hiding from some bad guys. They'll both be suspicious of anyone coming to that door. There's one scenario we could think of that would allow us to gain access to the cabin and plead our case." She looked at Carl, then back to Walker. "They might open the door to a lone female hiker, looking lost and desperate for help."

Walker's heart skipped a beat. And he fought not to blurt out his dislike of the idea. But the expression on Nataya's face told him he had betrayed his initial reaction before he could conceal his surprise at the suggestion. All he said was, "It's too dangerous." But he knew it was a weak excuse.

Nataya leaned forward "Think about it, Walker. It makes sense. If either of you guys go to the door, they're going to assume Victor sent you. They might even be frightened enough to shoot first and ask questions later. With Katie in there, I think she would have sympathy for another woman hiker … alone and lost. She of all people knows what it's like to be on her own out here."

Walker turned to look at Carl and raised his eyebrows, waiting for him to weigh in.

Carl took a deep breath. "I understand your concern. This wasn't what I wanted as a solution either." He gave a sigh. "But

Nataya and I weighed out all the other options, and this one makes the most sense. I believe it will give us the best chance of success." When Walker didn't reply he continued. "Think about it. She can play on their sympathies, get them to let her into the cabin. Then she can explain why she's there and tell them about us. We can help them get out of here before that Victor guy shows up."

Walker knew they spoke the truth, but it wasn't what he wanted to hear. Potential peril existed. Yet he knew he'd also made a vow to never again leave her out of a situation because of the danger. His mind and his heart stood in opposition.

Nataya moved closer to him. She didn't need to remind him of his promise to her. He could see it in her eyes. She took his hand. "I believe it can work."

He lowered his head and accepted that it was the best option they had. When he looked up, he saw the same concern in Carl's eyes that he felt. He knew then this decision hadn't been easy for him either. It gave him some comfort. He held Nataya's gaze. "You're right. It is a good plan. The best plan."

The young man grabbed his backpack from where it rested against a tree. "I'll take the heavy equipment out of my pack and fit it to Nataya, so it looks like it belongs to her."

Carl spoke quietly, yet Walker sensed the urgency in his voice and realized how much time had slipped by as they had checked out the cabin and made certain Katie was inside. Who knew what was happening out there with Victor, or whoever followed them? He shoved the sense of panic down and focused on what they needed to accomplish.

Walker and Carl worked together to quickly outfit Nataya, making her look more like a traditional hiker. Nataya added some smudges of dirt to her face and hands, then unbraided her hair, to let it lay loose. Carl gave her hair a bit of a muss with his hand, then gave her a wink. The two men studied her and decided she looked ready to play her role.

CHAPTER THIRTY-SIX

Mt. Baker-Snoqualmie National Forest, Washington (Day Nine)

Since Katie didn't plan to leave until the next day, she had tried her best to spend the rest of the morning reminiscing and catching up with Jake. But he insisted on dragging out his maps and showing her the trails that would lead her away from the cabin, ultimately taking her into Marten's Pass. When he finished, they ate a light lunch. As they cleaned up the kitchen, she begged him to help her brainstorm a story she could give her father—a reason for her to have bolted into the wilderness. He reluctantly agreed.

Jake moved into his favorite chair in front of the woodstove. Katie took a spot next to the stove, sitting cross-legged on a rug so she could feed logs into the fire.

But before they began Katie looked up at Jake. "Thanks for letting me enjoy a bit of time with you this morning, before we talked about … you know. It's been far too long. That's on me—always being too busy. I regret that now."

"Don't have regrets, Katie. It is what it is. We were both wrapped up in our own worlds there for a while. You should know, though, that I've been proud of you for going out there and living the life you want. You needed to do that."

"Thanks, Jake. You gave me the confidence to accomplish it." She watched the flames through the open wood stove door for a moment, trying to decide how to proceed with what she wanted to say. Then decided to just dive in. "Let's talk about how I can help you clear up this situation you've found yourself in."

Jake turned his head and stared away from Katie. "I seriously don't think that's possible."

"There's got to be a way. Let's look at the facts. Only one man saw you at Joseph's house. And he was part of the black-market ring, right?"

Jake nodded.

"So, he's not going to go to the police."

"No, he would've told his boss what happened at Joseph's place. That's why they figured out who I am and where I lived. They came after me. As far as I know, they are still coming after me."

"But that's what I mean," Katie said. "I can leave here and have a story as to why I was up here in the mountains, something my father would believe. That way the bad guys would never tie me to you."

"If they came looking for you and found you gone, they might already believe you came to me. So I'm not sure they would buy your story." He turned to look at her. "I thought about this all night, Katie. And all I *do* know is that I don't want you involved in any way."

"Come on, Jake. I understand that you don't want to endanger me, I get that. But I'm sure we can figure out something … find a way to let you stay hiding out here, with no one the wiser."

He turned and held her gaze. "How long do you think that is really going to be possible? What if the black-market people track you down anyway, and decide to torture you to find out where I am?"

Katie could feel the blood drain from her face. But she wasn't ready to give up. "Maybe we get my father involved. Maybe the Bureau can give you some kind of protection if you make a deal to testify against the black-market ring?"

"Your father? The 'strictly by the law' man?" He gave her a look of doubt. "And if I do, what happens to the amulet ... when they discover it's part in all this mess? They'll take it away and stick it in some evidence box to gather dust. The tribe will never see it again."

He shook his head sadly. "Listen. When everything first happened, I panicked. The only thing I knew to do was to get away and hide so I could think and sort it all out. I've had the time to do that and the only solution I see, where I don't endanger others like you, is to turn myself in to the Tribal Police Chief for that man's accidental death. If I'm in jail the black-market people will stop searching for me or hurting my friends to find me. And at the least they won't be able to get to me."

Katie frowned. "You know that's not true. You've got something they want, and they could still do harm to your friends to force you to talk, even in jail. Besides, you know once they get what they want, they could still get to you, and silence you—even in jail. It's not the answer."

Jake stared into space for a long moment. "Yeah, you're right." He sighed heavily. "Truthfully the only way this stops, once and for all, and no one else gets hurt is if I'm dead."

Katie jumped to her feet. "You just stop it—right now!" She strode over to Jake, grabbed his shoulders. "That is not an option. Do you hear me?" Angry tears filled her eyes.

Jake gently grasped her wrists. "Okay. Okay"

"You do not get to give up this way. Do you hear me?"

"Yes, I hear you. I got it. We'll try to come up with a plan."

"One that doesn't involve your death or going to jail."

He gave her a melancholy smile. "I could always count on

you to stop me from feeling sorry for myself."

Then he surprised her with a laugh. "You always were so mule-headed, child. Looks like you've not outgrown that trait. And for once, I'm grateful."

Katie threw her arms around his shoulders and hugged him. "Thank you, Jake. I would never be able to forgive myself if I didn't try to help. Even if it's just to keep your secret."

"I understand that now. We'll think of something. I promise."

Katie jerked her head around at a soft rapping on the front door. Her eyes wide, she looked to Jake. He raised his hand to motion her to silence and to stay down. He rose and in one motion, moved to the side of the front door and picked up the shotgun that rested against the frame. But he didn't open the door.

A second knock, a little harder. Then a woman's voice. "Please, if anyone is in there, I need help. I'm lost."

Jake moved to the window and peeked around the edge of the curtain. Then he returned to Katie and whispered. "There's a woman hiker out there. She looks as if she's been out in the wilderness for a while. Could be she's really lost, spotted the cabin and came here hoping for help."

Katie stared at him. "Or it could be a set up."

Jake nodded. "Yep. Thought of that."

"But what if she's really lost and needs help? I couldn't live with myself if something happened to her because we didn't help her when we could."

"Yeah, I'm with you on this. You still got your sidearm?"

"Yeah, that's one promise to my father that I haven't broken yet."

"Good. Okay, we're going to open the door to her. I'll have my shotgun at the ready, but not on her. I don't want to scare her to death if she's legit. But I'm also not going to offer myself as a target to anyone out in the woods. I'll stay off to the side as much as I can. When I let her come in, I want you and your pistol ready for anything."

"You got it."

"Easier to apologize after the fact than to be ambushed because we trusted her."

"Agreed."

Nataya decided that being anxious and more than a bit nervous at this point played in her favor, so she didn't try to conceal it. It'd be authentic to sound scared and desperate to Katie and Jake. She could only imagine what was going on inside the cabin as she knocked a third time and called out for help. They'd certainly consider the possibility that she was involved in a trap.

When the door finally opened, she knew she'd guessed correctly. An older man with a gray beard and disheveled hair opened the door, but only wide enough to see her. He stayed partially hidden behind the door, and she could see that he held a shotgun at the ready. She was grateful it wasn't pointed at her, and sure Walker experienced the same relief, although she knew he'd be closely watching the man. The way the shotgun was being held also meant the man wasn't sure she was legit. She had to play upon that. She needed to gain his confidence and get inside.

She let relief show on her face. "Oh, thank goodness. I was praying someone was here."

The man she assumed was Jake studied her, then spoke.

"You said you're lost?"

She nodded.

"Where you trying to get to, missy?"

Nataya had anticipated the question. "I'm trying to get to a little mountain town by the name of Marten's Pass. I think it should be near here, but I've gotten so turned around in my directions, I'm not sure anymore. Do you know the town I'm talking about? Am I close?" All the while she talked, she hoped to see Katie inside, but didn't want to tip off Jake by obviously looking around.

Jake nodded. "Yeah, I know that town. It's not far as the crow flies. But to hike there, you've got quite a trek ahead of you."

Nataya let her shoulders sag at the news. "Oh, no."

Jake watched her closely. "How'd you get lost?"

She looked up at him and imitated Monica's tone to bring some authenticity to her story. "I'm embarrassed to admit it. I must've read my map wrong—took a bad turn. I'm supposed to meet some friends in that town. I thought I had it all figured out how to get there. I started getting worried last night when I didn't reach my destination, as I had planned. I've been scared all day today, and the longer I hiked, the more lost I felt."

Jake stared into her eyes. "Getting scared doesn't help you think straight. That's for sure."

She nodded and managed to squeeze one tear from her eye. It ran down her cheek, and she watched the man's expression shift. Her heart leaped. She'd scored a point.

Then she saw it. Jake glanced to his left for a mere second, as if looking at someone else, then turned to her again. He began to open the door a bit more. "Maybe I can help you chart a course on your map to reach town. You're welcome to come in and get warm. If you want to, that is. It's up to you."

Nataya forced herself to show an indecisiveness about going into a strange man's cabin, even as her heart leaped with excitement that she'd won him over. Her hesitation paid off.

The man motioned to someone and Nataya saw a young woman show herself, still off to the side of the door.

The woman spoke. "It's safe."

Nataya sighed in relief. She stepped up into the doorway and stopped. The young woman stood to the side, both hands holding a pistol, barrel pointed downward, but clearly ready if needed. It gave Nataya the moment she needed, a good excuse to pause and glance around the cabin, as if nervous about the guns. She used her right hand to grasp the doorframe, as if to steady herself, and held out two fingers against the wood trim. The sign the three behind her had agreed upon—to confirm that there were only two people in the cabin.

The woman motioned for her to come on in. "Sorry about the guns, but we have to be cautious out here."

Nataya stepped into the cabin, sure Walker and Carl were sighing in relief that only Jake and Katie were inside. But she also knew they would both be worried the moment the door closed behind her.

Once the door had been secured behind Nataya, Jake motioned her over to a small table with two chairs and gestured for her to sit down in one of them. He stayed off to the side, leaned against a kitchen counter and cradled the shotgun in his arms. Now that she could study him, the man looked to be younger than his scruffy beard and hair made him appear at first glance. She guessed him to be in his early sixties and quite fit for his age.

The young woman returned the pistol to a concealed holster at the small of her back and pulled her sweater over the top of it. Something about the movement gave Nataya the impression that, although smoothly done, it wasn't a part of the woman's daily routine. When she sat down in the opposite chair, Nataya studied her. She was definitely the same woman in the photo Steve had given them, a little older, close to her own age. But there was no broad smile, like in the photo.

The young woman spoke. "What's your name?"

"Jenny." Nataya decided to use her birth name, the one she'd known before her time of traumatic amnesia and her life alone in the wilderness, before regaining her memories, when she had chosen to stay as Nataya.

"I'm sorry if we frightened you, Jenny. We're out here all alone. You understand?"

Nataya nodded and noticed Katie hadn't offered her name or introduced Jake. She moved her hands to the tabletop and clasped them, where Katie and Jake could see them. She took a deep breath, exhaled and looked at Katie. "I'm actually very relieved to see that you and Jake are being extra cautious, Katie."

The young woman jumped back out of her chair as if she'd been struck by a blow, her eyes wide. As the chair crashed to the floor, she began to reach for her gun. Beside her Jake had started to raise the shotgun.

Nataya held up her empty hands. "I'm not your threat." She waited for them to stop their movements. "We were sent to find you and warn you. There are others looking for you who do mean you harm."

Katie leaned forward with an intensity that startled Nataya. "Who sent you?"

"Your father, Steve Hicks."

She threw up her hands and spun away. "Of course. I should've known." She turned back and looked at Jake. "I'm so sorry. I thought for sure I had kept him from following me."

But Jake was staring at Nataya. "You said 'we' were sent."

"Yes. Steve's involved with a homicide case on tribal land, so when Katie went missing, he asked for our help locating her." Nataya looked at Katie. "At the time your father had no idea it would turn out that you were connected to Jake and the homicide case. That all happened after the fact."

Jake spoke up. "Wait. What makes you think I'm connected to any homicide case?"

"Steve learned you were friends with Joseph, and that after he was murdered someone tore up your place looking for something. He thinks it's something that belonged to Joseph. Something you're trying to keep safe."

Jake looked at Katie then back to Nataya. "That's it?"

"Yes. But Steve believes there are people trying to find Katie, to get to you, and they are getting close. That they would kill to take back what they are looking for."

Jake nodded. "So who else is with you?"

"My partner, Fox Walker. My real name is Nataya. And there is a Search and Rescue guy with us, named Carl."

Jake's eyes narrowed. "I've heard of you and Walker. You're both pretty well-known in the tracking circles."

"Yes, I guess that could be true. Steve knows us from a case in Colorado, where we met."

Jake looked to Katie, who nodded and spoke.

"I remember my father mentioning those names." She looked at Jake, then back to Nataya. "That doesn't mean you are who you say you are. This could all be a ruse to get to Jake."

"What do you need from me to prove I'm speaking the truth?"

Katie thought about it for a moment. "Tell me how my father contacted you. Give me details."

"Sure. It was actually Dean McClure who contacted us for your father."

"You know Dean?"

Nataya smiled. "Yeah, we've known him longer than we've known your father." She continued. "A plane met us in Montrose, Colorado and flew us here. Dean and the SAR guy met us at a grass landing strip, near here. Then we were driven to Lost Lake where we met your father, at your cottage." Nataya waited. "Want me to describe your cottage?"

She nodded.

Nataya described what she could remember about the interior of the cabin. Then waited.

Katie stared at her. "Anyone might've gained access to my cabin." Katie stayed silent, in thought, then looked up. "So, tell me how you found my trail."

Nataya explained every detail of how Walker found her prints, and how they had followed them along the shoreline in the water, to the grouping of trees, even her side trek to the mailbox at the General Store and on to the trailhead.

Katie's eyes were wide. "I thought I was being pretty smart about making sure no one could follow me."

"You were. Not many would've figured it out, like Walker did. That's why your father wanted us for the search. He believed we could find your trail. He's been desperate to know you are okay, Katie." Nataya watched some of the tension leave the woman's body.

Katie took a deep breath and exhaled as if resolved to the situation. "So when is my father going to show up?"

Nataya held the woman's gaze. "We haven't given him your coordinates yet. He's waiting to hear from us."

Katie tilted her head, waiting.

"We wanted to confirm the bad guys hadn't gotten here before us, and see for ourselves that you were safe, Katie."

Katie gave Nataya a curt nod. "Thank you for that." She took a deep breath. "Don't get me wrong. My father's one of the good guys. And I know he's probably been going crazy with worry. But it was imperative for me to find out why Jake was in hiding before letting my father, and possibly the Bureau, get involved."

Nataya saw Jake gave Katie a look she couldn't read. She had questions as well but held them for now.

Jake said, "Katie, we need to hear about everything they know." He turned to Nataya. "Time to bring in the rest of your group. I suppose they are waiting outside?"

She nodded.

Jake shook his head in wonderment and motioned her to the door. Then he stopped her. "Wait. You say others might be following you—right now?"

"As far as we know."

"Then we don't stop being cautious. What's your signal?"

"I'm to go to that window," she pointed. "And flash a v for victory sign with my fingers. I can guarantee that while Carl's been waiting for my signal, Walker has been watching for sign of movement within the woods behind them."

"Good enough. Give them your signal."

Victor leaned against a large boulder, chest heaving with his struggle to suck in enough air to fill his lungs and slow his pounding heart. Meanwhile, Colt had quickly scaled the tall rocky outcropping above him to get a better look ahead.

Victor had insisted they leave the truck behind once they had gotten close to the GPS coordinates, so Jake wouldn't hear it and possibly take off. But he hadn't realized how much the elevation and hike would sap strength from his already depleted body. He gulped in air until he could once again breathe normally.

While Colt searched the woods with his binoculars, Victor calmed and tried to focus his thoughts. He found enough air to speak and called up to Colt. "You see anything yet?"

The man shushed him. Then a moment later he clambered back down the boulders and faced Victor. "What the hell? Why were you yelling up at me, after we just hiked through the forest so no one would hear the truck?" The man shook his head in frustration.

Victor realized the guy was right and for once, admitted it. "I'm sorry. I just wasn't thinking clearly. The stress of the hike kinda did me in. I'm okay now."

Colt studied him, then relaxed. "Yeah, I forgot about your condition. Apology accepted." He turned and pointed through the trees. "The cabin is in that direction. I've got a clear view of the front of it from here but we're far enough away that no one should see us through the trees. So I'm going to go back up on the boulder and watch for a little longer. Why don't you sit down and take a break?"

Victor decided that was a good idea. He found a log to sit on and leaned back against the rocks behind them. They were even warm from the sun heating them up. He closed his eyes and relaxed. What seemed only seconds later, Colt was shaking him.

"Victor, wake up."

He opened his eyes and focused on Colt, saw the way the man studied him, making sure he had his attention.

"A blonde woman went to the door of the cabin, talked to someone inside and then went in. I know I've been following three people, a female and two males. So if I'm correct and she's part of the group I've been following, I'm guessing the other two are waiting, hidden in the trees. Be very quiet now. I'm going back up and will watch for the other two."

Victor's heart beat hard against his chest wall. They were so close now.

Walker sensed Carl turn to him as he concentrated on the trees behind them. The woods had gone quiet in the distance.

Carl spoke quietly. "Nataya just gave us her signal that it's safe to approach the cabin."

Walker didn't even try to hide his sigh of relief. "Good." He looked behind them again. "Something is out there. Could be an animal. Not close enough for us to hear or see, but nature is reacting to it." He glanced toward the cabin. "I think we should stay within the trees, skirt the side of the cabin and go to the back door. Just in case someone is watching."

Carl checked over his shoulder, a worried expression on his face. "Sounds like a plan to me."

They both kept a good distance between them and made their way through the trees bordering the cabin. When they were even with the back of the structure, Walker stopped and waited for Carl. "Okay, from here we'll be in the open, but for only seconds as we sprint for the back door. Even if someone sees us from a distance, it shouldn't give them enough time to do anything about it."

He saw a determined set to Carl's jaw and the young man gave him a definitive nod that he was ready.

Walker took the lead and kept as close to the cabin as possible, moving quickly. He rounded the back of the cabin and rushed to the back door. Carl arrived a second later. To his surprise, Nataya opened the door and ushered them in, urging them to be quick.

Victor rested his body, recouping his strength while Colt watched the cabin with his binoculars. Miles away the chopper sat in a clearing, the pilot awaiting a call from him.

He looked up at the sound of Colt sliding down from the rock ledge. The man landed on solid ground, then joined Victor. He spoke with an intensity that belied his calm exterior.

"Okay, the other two just went to the cabin. They were being super cautious. I just barely caught sight of them as they left the woods and rushed toward the back. I'm presuming there's a rear door and that's where they entered. Now what?"

Victor massaged the back of his neck, trying to loosen up the muscles before his headache went full blast. "Assuming those are the three people you've been tracking—the ones following Katie—then it's plausible they just joined Katie and Jake in that cabin." He slid a pill bottle from his jacket pocket and popped two tablets into his mouth, swallowed and looked at Colt. "I had hoped Katie would lead us here and we could beat the three following her. But we can work this to our advantage. More people, more hostages. Now that we know everyone is inside the cabin, and we're alone out here, we can proceed."

Walker stood for a moment just inside the door, letting his eyes adjust to the dim light in the cabin. All the windows were covered with only a lantern lighting the interior. A young lady stood next to an older, gray bearded man. The woman matched the photo Steve had given them except she wore a guarded expression instead of a smile.

Walker's instincts screamed at him to jump into action, get everyone together, figure out what course of action they needed to take and make that move. But pushing the others into a state of panic would serve no purpose. Besides, he really had nothing concrete to substantiate his concerns, only his gut. Still, a part of his brain reminded him his instincts had served him well more times than not.

Nataya introduced everyone and Walker noticed Carl's attention riveted to Katie. The young woman also watched him with open curiosity.

Nataya turned to Walker. "I've explained to Katie and Jake about how Steve asked us to find Katie, but we haven't given him our most recent location. That we wanted to make sure Katie's safety hadn't been compromised before calling Steve on the SAT phone."

Jake's eyes widened. "You're carrying a SAT phone? They can trace that to here."

Carl held up the phone. "Not when I have it turned off. They can't ping it until I turn it on again. When we believed we were getting close, I turned it off. I haven't updated Steve since yesterday."

"Still, with him flying around here, even your coordinates from yesterday will give him enough to figure out we're here."

Walker spoke. "If you're referring to the helicopter that's been around here the last few days, that's not Steve. We asked him."

"Then who is it?" Jake asked. Then his face paled. "The black-market guys."

"Could be. The man searching for you is named Victor Blake. He wants the amulet Joseph was protecting. We believe Victor also has at least one other guy following us. To get to Katie—to get to you. We did everything we could to elude him, but he could still be out there in the woods, and still on our trail."

Jake looked to Katie, and back to the three. "Okay, we need to know everything you know so we can decide what to do from here."

"Agreed," Walker said. "But it's got to be brief. I'm not sure we have much time."

CHAPTER THIRTY-SEVEN

Mt. Baker-Snoqualmie National Forest, Washington (Day Nine)

Victor followed Colt as best he could, the pain in his head causing him to squint to keep out as much light as possible. They stayed on the one-lane dirt road to make the walking easier, until they caught a glimpse of a carport attached to a structure, an old truck parked inside. They slipped into the woods then, moving slowly to keep noise to a minimum. He could see the full structure through the trees now. A small log cabin, smoke curling from the chimney.

Colt stopped and turned to him. "Okay, this is the cabin where I saw the woman and two men enter. What's our game plan?" Then he took a longer look and asked, "You okay?"

Victor gave him a curt nod and studied the cabin. "You said that the two men entered at the back of the cabin?"

"Yeah, guess they didn't want to be seen out front, where someone behind them in the woods could spot them. They must be worried that someone might be on their trail and were playing it safe."

"Makes sense. So, that might be the likely place they will exit again. Let's make our way around to where we can see that back area. I know it's flat and wide open, so we'll have a good vantage point from the trees."

Colt nodded and began the trek through the trees, staying to the side of the cabin. To Victor the minutes dragged by like hours until they reached the edge of the open area. He leaned up against a tree and sucked in deep breaths to calm his breathing. He couldn't tell if his chest thumped in nervous fear or in the excitement of anticipation. So close to his quest.

Colt looked to him for direction. "You want to get closer? We could easily make our way to those rows of stacked firewood. I'll help ya. It'd be a perfect place to hide. And we'll be close to the back door when someone comes out of the cabin."

All Victor could muster was a nod. Hopefully once they got into place, he'd be able to rest and recuperate his energy. He refused to give up now.

"Any other questions?" Walker asked Jake and Katie as he, Nataya and Carl finished filling them in on what little they knew from Steve about Victor.

"So this … obsession … over the amulet is about Victor thinking he can use it to cure himself?" Jake asked.

"Whatever evidence Steve has in his possession has led him to that theory. We don't really know many details. Steve is convinced Victor believes you know where the amulet is hidden and will force you to reveal it to him."

Jake and Katie exchanged a look.

"Something you want to share?" Walker asked.

Jake shook his head. "Not really. But considering the circumstances, it's only fair you know what we know." He brought out the amulet from its hiding place and held it up for them to see.

Walker stared at it. "So no one knows you really have this?"

"Sounds like everyone believes it's still where Joseph hid it."

Walker studied the piece, noticed the carved wolf and elk head, glanced at Nataya, but remained silent.

Katie studied Walker, noting his lynx claw necklace. "When I was out in the wilderness, before I learned of the amulet, an elk came to my camp one night." She shook her head. "But maybe I imagined it … it was dark." Her expression was serious, yet hesitant, as if she expected to be mocked.

"We saw the tracks. You didn't imagine them," Walker said. "And two days later I spotted wolf prints near where you had camped."

Katie turned wide eyes to him but remained silent and thoughtful.

Jake spoke up. "I already know this man you call Victor will do anything to get possession of that amulet. Anything. But now I better understand the 'why.' It makes him even more dangerous."

Walker nodded in agreement. "And desperate. That's why we need to discuss what to do next. Victor may be homing-in on this cabin via his man who's been trailing us. Maybe it's time to call in Steve. Let him deal with both men."

He saw Katie and Jake exchange looks. The older man turned to her, reached up and put his hand on her shoulder. "This has gone far enough. Others are in danger now. We need to let your father handle this. We'll figure out the rest, I promise."

Walker couldn't see the man's expression, but after a moment Katie turned and gave Walker a reluctant nod. He didn't miss the unshed tears in her eyes and had to wonder what it all meant.

Carl pulled out the SAT phone and turned it on. But all he heard was static.

Jake pointed upwards. "It's the metal roof, son. You'll need to step outside to get a signal."

"Thanks," Carl said and walked toward the back door, then stopped. He looked at Walker, then the group. "Do I tell him anything beyond our coordinates?"

Jake spoke before Walker could. "Let Steve know Katie is safe … and that the four of you will all be leaving this area under cover of darkness tonight and heading for the nearest town, Marten's Pass."

Carl stared, confused.

"Tell him I'll be here at these coordinates. Waiting for Victor." Jake put his hand up to stop any arguments. "Who knows how long it will take Steve to get here? It's the best way to keep all of you safe."

Katie broke in. "You said—"

"That was before you and I knew all the facts, Katie. This whole deal is between me and Victor. And I don't want anyone else getting hurt because of it." He gave Walker and Carl a stern look. "I've made up my mind and time's awastin'."

Walker held Jake's gaze for a long moment, then turned to Carl and gave him a nod. He didn't like what Jake was doing, but he understood the man's motives.

Katie swiped at the tears running down her cheeks, but she remained silent.

Jake walked to the door and grabbed his shotgun before opening it. He stepped outside and scanned the trees lining his property. After a long moment, he gave Carl a nod. The young man slipped out the back door to make his call.

Jake walked back into the cabin with purpose, then pulled out a large topo map and opened it up on the table. He pointed to a spot on the map. "You'll be able to take the single-track road starting here at the cabin, and I'll show you on the map what to follow to get to the nearest little mountain town." He glanced up at them. "You'll be able to follow the track even in the dark, although it wouldn't hurt to have at least one headlamp." He looked to Katie. "You have one, right?" She only nodded, still weepy-eyed.

"Carl has one, as well," Walker said.

"Good. Gather 'round, and I'll show you a visual of what I'm talking about."

Carl stood on the back porch steps, a sudden sense of isolation made him scan the perimeter as Jake had done. He watched for any movement, anything that looked out of place among the trees. Nothing but quiet.

He switched on the SAT phone again. Still static. He looked up at the metal roofing on the cabin and decided he needed to move farther away. He began to walk out into the open area, all the while watching the display on the phone and changing the angle of the antenna until he had a decent signal. He stopped, called Steve's number and heard the man answer after the first ring.

"Carl—what the hell is going on out there?"

But when Carl opened his mouth to reply something crashed into the back of his head. Streaks of lightning bright white flashed across his vision. He sensed he was falling and then everything went black.

Nataya studied the map along with Walker as Jake pointed a finger to the course they would be following. He and Walker started to discuss how they could hide everyone's prints as they left the cabin, so if Victor's man followed them to the cabin, he wouldn't see that they'd already left. That's when it struck her that Carl had been gone for longer than it should take to call Steve with the coordinates and a short message.

She sensed a quick moment of panic, then reassured herself

that it was probably just a matter of Steve quizzing Carl on the situation—trying to draw more information out of the guy. They *had* been rather evasive with Steve lately.

She looked at the guys talking, Katie watching them, and waited a moment. But a sense of dread still sat in her chest. She slipped away from the group and walked over to the back door and slid outside, so as not to disturb the others. She'd feel better making sure all was well.

Nataya looked around the open area. No Carl. She suppressed a growing panic, her hand going to her sheathed knife, as she stepped away from the cabin and walked slowly, watching for any movement. She rounded a row of stacked firewood and spotted a boot. Carl!

She took a step to rush forward, then stopped, sensing a trap. She scanned the entire open area in front of her, the trees to the side, and saw nothing, heard nothing. Maybe she was being paranoid. She thought about all the detours that had been set for the man following them. There was just no way he could've caught up yet. She took a couple of steps, then ran, her heart pounding.

Carl's body lay prone on the ground. She didn't see any blood. A good sign. He was on his side, his wrists tied behind his back and his feet were bound. There'd be no reason to bind a dead body. But still her heart pounded as she tried to rouse him and pull him into a sitting position. She leaned him back against the woodpile and knelt before him, noticing a bandana gagged him from speaking.

Carl opened his eyes, then blinked rapidly, the light obviously causing him pain. He worked to focus in on her face. She put her fingers to her lips to keep him from making any sounds. "Did you see who did this?"

He shook his head no, then grimaced in agony from the movement.

Nataya slipped the small knife out from her ankle sheath. And whispered against his ear, "I'm going to cut you free." She carefully slid the knife behind him, ready to start cutting on the rope when she noticed his eyes suddenly go wide at something behind her, then flick closed as if still unconscious. She froze, a moment later felt the barrel of a gun against her head.

"Don't move and everyone lives through this, got it?"

She could feel Carl's hand against hers. She rapidly nodded her head 'yes' to the man behind her, as she laid the knife handle against Carl's hand and felt him grab it. She hoped the movement of her head had distracted the man as to what she did. Carl let his body go limp against the woodpile, freeing her arm.

The male voice behind her demanded she stand up. She pushed herself up, keeping her back to the man. Adrenaline rushed through her body from the imminent danger, but anger ran along with it. She'd been tricked and it didn't sit well with her. And it was her own damn fault.

"Put your hands up."

She did as told, then felt the man pull her knife free from the sheath at her waist.

"Okay, turn around."

She did so reluctantly. She perused the man in front of her. He didn't match the description of Victor, so maybe it was the man who had been tracking them? But how did he ever catch up so quickly? He should still be hours behind them. Something else was going on. Something she wasn't privy to. Her heart pounded so hard, she felt sure the man could hear it. She worked to slow her breathing, to calm herself. She needed to be clear headed to think.

A motion caused her to look to the other side of the woodpile, where a man had risen and stood watching her. Nataya studied him as he studied her. The man's sandy blonde hair and gray eyes matched Victor's description. But as for being in his early fifties, the man's pallor and strained expression aged him beyond his years.

"This isn't Katie." He looked at the man with the gun. "But she'll do. We need a hostage to force the others to show themselves."

The man with the gun said, "If you'd let me have my way, we'd be down to three against two right now."

"Yeah? And the gunshots would've alerted everyone, and we'd either ended up in a gun fight or the others would have escaped to the woods." The sickly man sighed. "Didn't you learn anything from that debacle on the reservation? I've got to have leverage to get the information I need. We need hostages, not dead bodies."

"Yeah, okay. I hear ya. But I've got a personal revenge I need to enact on that old man for what he did to Diego back on the reservation."

"You'll get your turn at the guy. But not until I have what I need in my hands."

CHAPTER THIRTY-EIGHT

Mt. Baker-Snoqualmie National Forest, Washington (Day Nine)

Walker studied the map in front of him, intent on the topography of the region they were going to traverse when something in the back of his mind made him look up. Where was Nataya? He glanced around the small cabin, noticed the narrow washroom door stood open. So Carl must still be outside. Maybe she'd joined him. But what could be taking them so long? A hollowness dropped into the pit of his stomach.

Before he could voice his concern, he heard a man's voice yelling from outside. In the cabin all three stared at each other for a second before Jake rushed to grab his shotgun by the door. They joined him as he stood to the side of the window and carefully peeked outside. He turned to Walker and Katie, the color draining from his face.

"They've got Nataya."

Walker's heart skipped a beat before he could respond. He took Jake's place at the window, his heart sinking at the sight of Nataya being held, a gun to her temple.

A rage coursed through him then, that someone would dare put her life in danger. Then guilt that it happened on his watch.

And where was Carl? What had they done to him? Had he even had a chance to call Steve? Pain made him gradually realize his fists were clenched so tight, his fingernails cut into his flesh. He forced himself to relax his hands, but when he spoke his voice betrayed him, shaking with still barely contained anger. "Jake, do you know those men?"

"One of them." Jake looked at Katie, then to Walker. "The one holding the gun on Nataya is from the black-market ring. The other man standing to the side, I don't know. Does he match the description for Victor?"

"From what Steve said, yes, I think so." His mind reeled with questions as to how these men had found Jake so quickly. Then he remembered the helicopter, and his sense that something had lurked out in the forest behind them.

The man holding Nataya yelled again, demanding they leave their weapons behind and exit the cabin, hands in the air. "I know there are three of you in there, so don't try any funny stuff."

Walker looked to Jake. "I don't think we have any choice." He knew a sadness along with his anger, that he had failed to keep them safe from these men. That they had somehow outsmarted him. Of course he wasn't infallible, but it'd been a long time since someone had bested him.

Jake's face held a hard look, and Walker knew the man was as angry as he was about the situation. A glance at Katie showed her in a state of shock, her face ashen. But before he could say anything Jake cracked open the window and yelled.

"Just hold your horses. We're coming out." Then Jake grabbed the amulet from his pocket and turned to Katie. "Here, put this on. If he decides to search the cabin, like they did my house, I don't want them finding it while we're being held at gunpoint." She slipped it over her head. Then zipped up the neckline of her sweater so it didn't show.

Jake held her shoulders. "Be strong, Joseph believed this would keep you safe. Now you need to believe it." He turned to Walker. "Listen to me. They only want me because they believe Joseph hid the amulet and I know where it is. Keep everyone else safe. You got that? It's me they want, and I don't want anyone else hurt."

Walker nodded, but he didn't like the options.

They lined up behind the door. Jake opened it and made a show of leaving his shotgun leaning against the doorframe. Katie went next, surprising Walker when she removed a concealed pistol from the small of her back and placed it on the floor of the cabin. Then Walker stepped up and removed the knife from the sheath on his hip, laid it down as well. He hoped by doing this no one would search them, because he had kept the smaller knife in his ankle sheath.

The three walked out to where the men waited. They stood side by side in a line, facing the two men and Nataya. Walker noticed she looked more mad than frightened. Then he noticed her indicating the wood pile with her eyes. Maybe that's where Carl was? And maybe he was still alive? He didn't dare let the men see him look that direction, so he kept his focus straight ahead, but also made sure the wood pile stayed in his peripheral vision. He looked down once, then back up, to let her know he'd seen her signal. It gave him hope that Carl might still be alive and figured Nataya wanted him to know it as well.

Walker studied the two men. The one holding Nataya clearly knew how to keep her subdued and in his control. Maybe a bodyguard, or former military man. And evidently one hell of a tracker.

Although the other man's physique gave the illusion of health, his complexion said otherwise. A gray paleness imbued his skin, which upon a closer look, also had a sheen of perspiration to it. He did not look healthy. He squinted as if the very light hurt his eyes. Walker wondered if the man could even see well enough to shoot the pistol he held. It had to be Victor. And he indeed looked desperate, running on pure adrenaline. Not good.

Jake called out, "What makes you so damn sure I know where Joseph hid the amulet, anyway?"

"Because you were there with him before he died," Victor yelled.

"He died before he could tell me."

"If that's true, why did you take off for the wilderness?"

"Ah gee now, let me think. Maybe because someone broke into my home. Maybe because I figured you'd give me the same treatment you gave Joseph?"

"I'm not stupid, Jake. Don't underestimate me. I know you and Joseph were buddies. The amulet wasn't at your home, meaning it's still hidden. Probably on that reservation somewhere. And you're going to take me to it."

Jake hung his head in false resignation, then looked up at Victor. "Let these others go. I'll cooperate and take you to where it's hidden only if you let everyone else leave here. Now."

Victor gave a humorless laugh. "I'm making the rules. Not you." He pointed and said, "Katie."

She jerked her head in his direction.

"Yeah," Victor said. "I thought that was you. Come here."

Jake grabbed her arm and yelled at Victor. "You don't need anyone else, only me."

Victor smiled. "You'll have to forgive me, but I don't agree. Katie, come here and I'll let the other woman go free. Otherwise, Colt shoots her. Right here, right now. And I will *still* take you hostage. That's the deal."

Katie looked to Jake, who was clearly distraught but trying not to show it. She squeezed his hand. He let his arm drop to his side, and she walked toward Victor.

Victor turned to the other man. "Colt, let the woman go free and take Katie."

The man frowned but did as told.

Nataya returned to Walker, holding his gaze before turning to stand beside him and Jake. He resisted the urge to pull her into his arms, feeling guilty about his relief, knowing Jake was in torment. His mind tried to rush forward as to how this would play out, but part of him didn't want to accept the possible consequences.

Victor studied Jake. "You see, Joseph's death taught me something. Joseph was willing to die to keep the amulet from me." His eyes narrowed even more. "And I bet you're cut from the same cloth. Threatening you most likely wouldn't give me the results I want." He walked over to Katie. "But what if it wasn't you who would suffer and then die if you don't give me what I want?"

Jake started to lunge toward Victor, but Walker stopped him.

"Don't let his words rattle you," Walker said quietly. "That's what he wants."

Victor pointed to Katie. "She's my guarantee that you're going to take me to where Joseph hid the amulet." He took the sleeve of his jacket and wiped his face of perspiration.

Walker could barely contain his own rage as he watched the man hold Katie as their hostage, gun against her temple. The days spent tracking her, the hope of finding her and keeping her safe … only to see this outcome felt like failure. And that alone infuriated him. He could well imagine the emotions working on Jake. Walker struggled to calm his anger, pulling from Grandfather's teaching. Anger would cloud his thinking and slow his reaction time. He couldn't let that happen.

Victor then pulled a SAT phone from his pocket with his free hand.

Walker wondered if it was Carl's phone, studied it and realized it wasn't. He tried to look around while Victor was occupied with the phone. Where *was* Carl?

Victor spoke into the phone. "It's all clear. We're ready." Then ended the call and he put the phone away, then brought the gun back up. "We're all going to walk away from the cabin now, nice and easy. No quick moves." He started backing toward the cliffs, everyone moved forward as he stepped back.

He talked as they moved farther from the cabin toward the canyon. "A helicopter is now on its way to this location." He motioned to the large open area in front of them. "We're making room for it to land here. Jake, you and Katie will be boarding with me."

Walker sensed Jake tense beside him, his own mind racing to figure a way out of the situation. For the moment, though, they held the advantage—Victor believed the amulet was hidden elsewhere. He had no idea Katie wore it. But how long before he discovered the truth. What would happen to Katie and Jake when he did? He felt certain Jake had come to the same conclusion and had no intention of getting on the helicopter when it arrived. Then his heart sank. So what would that mean for all of them?

Victor stopped when he reached the end of the stacked firewood, his back to the woods, the cliffs of the canyon to his right. He motioned to Colt. "Bring me Katie."

He wrapped his arm across her upper chest and shoulders, as Colt had done, and placed his gun against her head. "Now you, Jake. Stand over here where I can see you." He looked at Colt. "Take the others over to the far side of the lot where they can't interfere when the chopper lands and keep your gun on them the entire time. You just remember to do your part after the chopper leaves."

Colt gave a nod. "I take care of the rental truck … and extraneous baggage. Then we meet up later."

Victor's expression clearly showed his frustration that the

man had repeated it out loud, but it was done, so he simply gave a curt nod.

Walker had feared Victor might order them killed before the chopper arrived and took heart at the short delay of execution. Perhaps, because of his illness, the man had no stomach for it. But then again, if the hostages were alive when Victor and the chopper pilot left, they could honestly say they hadn't witnessed anything. And no doubt Victor would never leave loose ends—like Colt—alive, once he'd completed his job.

Options raced through Walker's mind. He still had the small knife in his ankle sheath. Did Nataya still have hers? Could they get to them without being seen? And if so, could they create an opportunity to use them?

The moment Victor took control of her, Katie noticed the weakness in his grip. The other man had held her with a firmness and solid stance that let her know she didn't have a chance at escaping. But Victor didn't have her tight against his chest, probably because he was shorter than the other guy and couldn't have seen over her head. He held her more against his side, leaving all sorts of open areas between his body and hers. She thought she might be able to maneuver a bit if given a chance.

For the first time since the nightmare began, she sensed opportunity. Her mind became more alert and raced with the possibilities. How many shows had she watched where victims were in this type of situation and got free? She remembered one scenario where the person let their legs go out from under them, their body weight dropping unexpectedly and pulling their captor off balance. Hell, as weak as Victor's grip felt, she might even be able to wrench free of his hold. Maybe knock the gun from his hand. But she'd need him to be distracted somehow. He would have to move the gun away from her head for just a split second.

That's when a movement beside her caught her eye. She held her breath to keep from letting out a gasp when she spotted Carl. He peeked out from behind the firewood, where he lay on the ground, his body hidden. When he noticed she had spotted him, he eased out a bit more, braced himself with his elbows, and showed her that he had a small knife.

She was sure her head currently blocked Victor's view of Carl, so she stayed as still as possible and watched him work his way closer to the end of the row of firewood. He crouched, his eyes intent upon her as he held her gaze, trying to communicate without speaking. She stared at him, watched his eyes look into hers then quickly fall to the ground at her feet. He did it three times. Her heart beating hard against her chest, she let the slightest smile grace her lips to show she understood. Somehow he knew what she'd been thinking.

◆───◆───◆

Walker grappled to keep control of his emotions, his focus on both armed men. The man guarding them had made them back up far enough away from the others that it'd be near impossible to rush to their rescue, even if he had the opportunity. He guessed that might be Victor's reasoning for his new positioning.

Walker glanced over at Victor, Katie, and Jake. Victor remained pale, but his face held a determined bearing. Jake watched Victor intently, looking wound tighter than a clock and ready to explode into action, which made Walker nervous.

Then he noticed Katie. Something remarkable had happened. Until Victor had taken over holding her hostage, she'd had the look of someone in shock. A frightened victim. But her face now held an alertness—and something else. Hope.

He saw her eyes flick to the rows of firewood and back again.

CHAPTER THIRTY-NINE

Mt. Baker-Snoqualmie National Forest, Washington (Day Nine)

Carl studied the group in front of him. Jake stood to the far side of Victor and couldn't see him, but Carl was sure he could count on his help if the opportunity arose.

Victor now alternated his attention between his guy guarding Walker and Nataya in front of him, and the sky above as he watched for the chopper. The man held Katie more to his side than right in front of him, probably because he wasn't much taller than her. As they stood now, Katie's head blocked Victor's view to the side where Carl hid among the stacks of firewood. He breathed slow and shallow, afraid any noise might cause Victor to turn his way. For the moment Katie was still the only person who could see him. Her eyes were wide. He could tell she was alert and thinking. And being super careful not to give away his presence.

Every muscle in his body tensed. He needed only a split second, but he'd have to react instantly, or the moment might be lost.

Walker ran various scenarios through his mind of what he might be able to do to stop the armed man once the helicopter picked up its cargo and left.

As if the guard sensed where Walker's mind roamed, and now out of range of Victor hearing him, Colt displayed his bravado. He pointed his weapon at Walker. "I'm sure you've figured out that I have orders to make sure there are no witnesses. But don't you worry." He gave Nataya a long look. "I'll take real good care of the lady here." He grinned at her, then looked back at Walker. "It'd be a downright shame not to take advantage of such a fortuitous opportunity. Just her and me, alone in these remote woods. No one to bother us. Hell, no one to *hear* us. Yeah, maybe we'll spend some time out here in that cabin over there."

With blood rushing into his head, Walker's jaw tightened, and his hands clenched into fists, even as he fought to suppress his rage.

The man had made a fatal error by tipping his hand. Walker already knew he and Nataya were in a life and death scenario, but this changed how he'd deal with Colt, given the opportunity.

Colt chuckled. Having had his moment of fun, he backed up so he could hold his gun on the two of them. After staring at Walker for a long moment, he ordered Walker and Nataya to step a few feet apart and then to sit down on the ground. Perhaps Colt worried he had riled Walker too much. That he might try to rush him, even at gunpoint.

Walker sat down with his knees raised, feet flat on the ground. He glanced sideways at Nataya to reassure her. He read her expression, aware she knew he'd be looking for an opportunity to retrieve his knife from its ankle sheath. It helped him get grounded again, and regain some control. Then a distant sound caught his ear … the noise only a machine would make. The chopper—heading their way, but still far off in the distance. The others hadn't noticed it yet. Walker took a deep breath, exhaled, and relaxed his muscles. He would need to act quickly.

At that moment, Colt tipped his head, listening, then frowned. Walker heard him mumble something about the chopper not sounding right. The man half turned, looking up into the sky. In that split second, Walker retrieved the knife from his ankle sheath. He kept it tight against his pant leg, holding it at the ready. Colt turned to face them again, still frowning.

Walker looked at Nataya and held her gaze. He knew she would divert Colt's attention.

A moment later, Nataya let out a loud gasp, brought one hand to her mouth while pointing with the other across the yard toward Victor.

Colt spun around to see what had happened. In one smooth motion, Walker immediately rocked forward onto his knees.

Victor yelled a warning, prompting Colt to turn back, his gun at the ready. Walker flicked the knife, watched it embed itself just below the man's sternum and between his ribs.

Colt dropped his gun. He stared down at Walker's knife in astonishment a heartbeat before he crumpled to the ground.

Walker's attention wheeled back to Victor, who moved the gun from Katie's head and pointed it toward he and Nataya. In his peripheral vision he glimpsed Nataya throwing herself from her sitting position to the ground as he dove forward from his knees, expecting a bullet any second. Instead, he watched Katie let her legs go out from under her, dropping her body and causing Victor to lose his hold on her. In that moment, in an explosive burst from the woodpile, he saw Carl launch his body forward in a flying tackle. He slammed into Victor, knocking the man off his feet. The gun flew from his hand.

Jake threw himself onto Victor. Carl took the opportunity to pull Katie free of the tangle of bodies. Jake yelled at Carl to protect her while he kept Victor occupied. But Carl already shielded her with his body. The other two men rolled and tumbled over the ground, each one fighting to attain dominance.

Walker scooped up the gun on the ground near Colt, then he and Nataya ran toward the jumble of arms and legs as the two men still scrambled on the ground. Walker could only surmise that the very ill Victor now functioned in a frenzy of desperation. Little else would keep him going. That and the fact he was fighting an older adversary. As the two rolled about, they shifted dangerously close to the cliffs at the edge of the canyon. Walker feared that Jake didn't realize it. And he doubted either man would hear his warning even if he yelled.

While he and Nataya rushed forward, Walker watched Jake finally gain control over Victor. Both men were on their knees. Jake crouched behind Victor, his arm around his captive's neck. And none too soon. The two men knelt at the edge of the cliffs.

But as Walker and Nataya closed in, he saw Victor grab a rock from the ground and slam it against Jake's head, knocking him to the ground.

Walker and Nataya arrived at the scene as Victor scrambled to his feet, head swiveling, searching frantically for his lost gun. Carl still shielded Katie with his body and now held Nataya's small knife out in a defensive stance.

That's when Walker remembered he held the guard's gun. He was a terrible shot from almost any distance, but maybe he could bluff Victor. He raised the weapon, but before he could speak, his ears picked up a deep growl, unlike any dog he'd ever heard.

In front of him, slipping from the trees close to Carl and Katie, a huge gray wolf lunged forward, snarling, teeth bared. He turned his attention to Victor.

Victor froze, his eyes wide with terror, then began to frantically search for his gun again and spotted it nearby in a clump of grass. He made a step toward it, but when he did, the wolf moved closer and growled again as it bared its teeth. Victor backed away from the wolf, still eyeing the gun on the ground. He glanced at Walker. "So shoot the damn thing!"

Walker lowered the gun he held. He watched as Victor backed ever closer to the edge of the cliffs. Behind him lay Jake's body. The wolf still advanced, a low growl rumbled from his throat, hackles raised on his back.

Victor shuffled backwards. He yelled at Walker. "For God's sake, shoot the beast."

Walker held his breath as the wolf advanced and Victor took yet another step backwards. The man stumbled over Jake's outstretched legs behind him. Victor tried frantically to regain his balance, feet rapidly taking a few more steps. Then as if in slow motion the man wavered, his arms wheeling in the air. He fell backwards, dropping out of view. Walker heard a short scream before it was cut off by the sound of a body hitting the rocks of the canyon walls. Then, silence.

Stunned, Walker looked to Nataya, who stared wide-eyed. He then turned toward Carl and Katie. The wolf stood quietly, staring at where Victor had been, then turned its head toward Katie before quietly loping back into the dense forest.

Long seconds passed in total silence. Carl broke the quiet, his voice taut, almost a whisper. "Please tell me I'm not the only one who just saw that."

But before anyone could answer they heard a moan from Jake. Katie gave a cry and rushed to where he lay. She knelt beside him, everyone joining around her.

Jake raised up on one elbow. "Man, what hit me? I've got one whopper of a headache. And my body feels like a semi-truck slammed into me."

Walker sighed in relief that the man still lived, even if a bit beaten up. He strode away from the others, knelt at the edge of the cliff, and stared below. He spotted Victor's crumpled body on the rocks. No way the man survived.

He turned back toward the group, then looked up. A strange whirling noise filled the air. Although he didn't see anything in the sky, he yelled, "Victor's chopper. Take cover!" He glanced back at the cabin. Too far away. He gestured towards the nearby trees of the forest.

Before they could move, a black helicopter rose out of the deep canyon in front of them like some horror movie specter. It hovered at eye level with them, long gun barrels jutting out from the side doors, looking as menacing as anything Walker had ever seen. Chills ran over his skin as the wind from the blades pummeled them all and sent them scurrying.

Walker and Carl helped Jake up and half-dragged, half-carried him away from the chopper. Katie and Nataya led the way into the woods.

As they scrambled forward, the helicopter began to move to the open area and hover. Walker dropped back, purposefully lagging behind to give them a target, hoping the others could reach the safety of the trees. He expected to hear gunshots at any moment, cutting him down as he ran for cover.

Instead, he heard a voice yelling through speakers on the chopper. It took a moment for his brain to register the words. Then, he recognized the voice.

He stopped, turned, and watched as the chopper hovered over the clearing.

CHAPTER FORTY

Mt. Baker-Snoqualmie National Forest, Washington (Day Nine)

Walker stood facing the chopper. As it rotated slightly to make the landing he could see open doors on the sides, but the armed men no longer pointed their weapons outward. It came to rest on the ground with a whirl of dust and debris. Walker sheltered his eyes until it settled, the whine of the engines gearing down.

The chopper blades had barely slowed when a tall, lean man exited the aircraft, dressed in full body armor. A shorter man in blue jeans and a jacket followed behind him, the contrast jarring. As they hustled forward, the taller man removed his helmet, eyes intent on Walker until the two men stopped in front of him.

"Walker."

"Steve."

Steve turned to the man standing beside him. "This is Daniel Night Hawk. Tribal Police Chief. Daniel, meet Fox Walker."

Walker extended his hand. They shook, both eyeing each other. He then returned his attention to Steve. "It's good to see you, Steve. Thought you were Victor's chopper coming in."

"*That* bird's been grounded, and the pilot is happily cooperating with the Bureau. Sorry about the stealth approach and weapons, but we didn't know what we might be walking into. As far as we knew, Victor was in control." Steve's steely eyes held Walker's attention. "I see you decided to ignore my request of not engaging."

"Circumstances changed. You would've done the same thing."

Walker saw Steve's gaze flick to the woods behind, so he turned and motioned for everyone to come out. Carl had Jake's arm over his shoulder to help support him, while Nataya and Katie came out of hiding among the trees. Everyone stopped and stared. Then Katie started to walk forward. Carl called out to her. She turned toward him. She must've said something to reassure him because he gave her a smile. She then continued forward, finally breaking into a run.

Steve studied Walker for a long moment, then gave him a nod of acknowledgment. "Thank you for keeping her safe, Walker."

"It was a team effort."

Then Katie was there, throwing her arms around Steve's neck, sobbing and hugging him. Steve held her.

Walker stepped aside to give them privacy, turned toward Carl and Nataya, who moved forward to assist Jake.

Daniel stepped closer to Walker. "Victor?"

"Dead. Fell over the cliffs."

He nodded his acknowledgement. "The amulet?"

"Safe." He glanced at Katie then back at Daniel.

Relief washed over the police chief's face. "Good."

Walker stared ahead. "The Amulet … it's an especially sacred piece to your tribe?"

"Yes."

"I can understand why."

Daniel turned to him. "What made you come to that conclusion?"

Walker hesitated, searching for the right words, then simply said, "We saw things."

Daniel stared straight ahead. "It took your friend, Steve, a long while to accept and act upon the wisdom of our elders."

"But he finally came around, I'm guessing?"

"Yes. But he doesn't yet realize it."

Walker grinned.

Then Nataya stood before him, and he pulled her into an embrace that could wait no longer.

Steve had sent the chopper away, calling for a forensic team to replace it. For the time being, he needed to start processing the crime scene before dusk settled over the terrain. He gathered everyone together and took notes as he had them walk him through what had occurred before his arrival.

Carl stood in the open area where he had called Steve on the SAT phone. "I vaguely remember being bashed in the head. Then waking up, bound and gagged, over there in the woodpile, which is where Nataya found me and slipped me her knife. I was able to free myself a bit later—after they'd taken Nataya hostage and had their attention elsewhere." He turned to Steve. "How did you find us? I don't remember giving you our coordinates before being knocked out."

"You didn't, but the line was left open. We could hear noises in the background and knew something had gone wrong, so I kept the call live. We had your previous location, and we had already discovered the grounded chopper, the pilot waiting for Victor's call. Once he knew the score, he was more than happy to play the part and let Victor think the chopper was on the way. We used your GPS coordinates on the SAT to find your exact location." Steve began to look around the immediate area. "Your SAT phone is probably still around here somewhere."

Everyone began to hunt around in the grass. Nataya held it up moments later.

"Damn sloppy of them. Guess they had no idea we were on to them," Steve said.

Nataya handed the phone to him. "Well, I made a similar mistake, thinking the man tracking us was farther away than he was."

As Nataya filled him in on finding Carl, Steve could tell she was still upset with herself for letting her guard down long enough that the men were able to take her hostage, thus forcing everyone in the cabin to come outside without their weapons. He doubted she would allow herself to ever be put in that kind of situation again.

Each person then relayed their version of the events as Steve followed them across the open expanse of land and to the scene of the final standoff.

He looked to his left, where the guard lay. "Shall we do this one first?"

"Sure," Walker answered.

Steve knelt and examined the body, turned and looked up at Walker. "Your knife?"

Walker answered in the affirmative. He then described the events leading up to the man's death, including Colt's promise to kill him … and much later, Nataya.

Steve shook his head. "Kinda laid his cards on the table, eh? He certainly didn't know who he was messing with." He checked the man for ID but found nothing. "Colt sounds like a nickname. Doesn't give us much to go on. Wonder how he was connected with Victor."

Jake spoke quietly. "He was with the black-market ring. The ones who came after Joseph."

Steve watched Katie grab Jake's arm. She looked frightened. No, terrified.

Jake gave her a look full of sorrow and put his hand on hers. "It's time to get this out in the open, Katie."

"No, Jake—please." Katie's eyes were wide and pleading.

Daniel cleared his throat, drawing everyone's attention to himself for the first time. Now, he stepped forward. He half turned his head to speak to Steve but remained facing Jake.

"The way I see it, Steve, I'm betting this dead guy here is the man who was guarding Joseph while he was being tortured. You know, the guy who got away when our mystery hero stepped in, tried to save Joseph's life and accidentally killed the man who had tortured Joseph."

Daniel shook his head sadly. "Guess we'll never know who our hero was ... there's absolutely no physical evidence at the scene to indicate anyone else was there besides the main players. And the only person who possibly saw our hero is ..." He glanced at the man on the ground. "Well, he's dead. There's no one to ID our hero guy, that's the truth."

Steve stared at Daniel, putting the pieces together and seeing where the man was going. A part of his brain screamed that he had to follow procedure. Had to follow the rule of law. Then he looked at Jake. A man whose eyes possessed such pain and deep remorse. A man who had tried to do right for his friend.

Memories of all the times Steve had watched bureaucracy stand in the way of true justice flooded his mind, and he closed his eyes against the despair of it all. When he opened them again, he said, "Yes, I have to agree with you, Daniel. I do believe you're correct."

Steve took a deep breath, his voice stronger now. "Shame we'll never get to meet our mystery hero, 'cause I know you feel the same way I do about him ... putting his life on the line trying to save Joseph. Hell of a guy." He turned to Daniel. "That's just the way it goes sometimes." He shrugged his shoulders. "Could even be we had it all wrong, and no one else was even there."

Jake's eyes grew misty, and he didn't appear able to speak. Steve simply put his hand on the man's shoulder and then turned away. When he did, he caught sight of Katie's expression. He did a double take. Her look told him that somehow, someway, he had managed to elevate himself in her eyes to the father he had always wanted to be for her.

Now, as he walked toward the other side of the open space, he found himself blinking back some extra moisture in his eyes.

Walker looked to Nataya as they followed behind the others toward the cliffs where Victor had met his fate. She had a thoughtful expression on her face. "What is it?" he whispered to her.

She waited a beat before answering, then whispered, "They were talking about Jake. He was the hero who tried to save Joseph."

"I was guessing that, but you know something, don't you?"

She nodded. "I overheard Colt tell Victor he wanted to kill Jake because of that incident. I didn't know what they were talking about, until now. But it makes sense. It's how Jake got mixed up in this whole thing … trying to save his friend. I can't imagine what he's been going through."

"Yeah, no wonder Katie holds him as such a dear friend."

The group gathered in a circle around the spot where the final struggle had taken place, but stayed far enough back to not disturb any evidence. Carl shared what he and Katie had done when the opportunity came, how Jake jumped in to help until Victor knocked him out. When it came time in the story for the appearance of the wolf, Carl faltered and stopped. He looked to Walker and Nataya.

Walker cleared his throat and spoke matter-of-factly. "At that time a wolf emerged from the nearby trees ..." He pointed toward the woods, noting that Jake's eyes widened in surprise.

"A wolf?" Steve asked, eyebrows raised.

"Yeah, it was enough to distract Victor, causing him to trip backwards over Jake's prone body. He lost his balance and fell off the cliff."

"A wolf ..."

Walker saw Steve glance at Daniel and receive a "See?" expression. Steve shook his head and turned toward the cliffs. Walker heard him mumbling about what a wacked out case it was and wondering how he'd wound up in the middle of it. Walker glanced at Daniel, who gave him a knowing look.

Carl gazed out the window at the eerie scene. The cold and dark of night had settled over the mountainside, except behind Jake's cabin. There, flood lights lit up the expanse of ground where the forensic team worked. The backdrop to the scene included the silhouette of a large chopper. And, of course, in true Washington fashion, the night had brought in a misty rain, so tarps had hurriedly been erected to protect the evidence. But unlike a yet unsolved crime, this one was a matter of collecting data and simply following procedures.

Jake stayed busy as he brewed coffee and supplied it to the crew outdoors, as well as to those relegated to the cabin. Walker and Nataya talked quietly together near the woodstove.

Carl turned to his right as Katie came to stand next to him and handed him a cup of coffee, which he gratefully accepted. She looked up at him and he lost himself for a moment in the intensity of those blue eyes. The photo of her didn't do them justice. He gazed deeper and saw a mix of emotions conflicting with each other. He figured he understood them all too well.

So much had happened in such a short span of time, and he still worked at processing it all himself.

Katie still held his gaze. "I haven't had the opportunity to thank you for saving my life."

Carl flushed but this time he didn't mind. "It was a team effort."

Katie raised her left hand and placed her palm on the center of his chest, over his heart. "It was more than that."

He smiled then, his best smile, and placed his free hand over hers. "You are most welcome."

He saw Katie grin, and when she lowered her hand Carl kept ahold of it. He noticed she didn't resist. They both turned to stare out the window, standing close together. After another moment of silence, he spoke. "I still can't get over how you knew exactly what I needed you to do and when."

She tilted her head. "Yeah, that was pretty cool, wasn't it? I was already picturing that scenario when you did your 'eye signal' thing. It was like you could read my mind, and it made the most sense to me, considering the situation." Then she smiled. "It helps that I've watched tons of shows with hostage scenes, I guess."

He grinned, then turned to look back outside. "I've been standing here thinking about this whole ordeal, how everything worked out. This could've turned out so different, different in a tragic way, if it hadn't been for your friendship with Jake."

"What do you mean?"

"Think about it. If you hadn't taken off to find Jake the way you did … well, Walker, Nataya and I wouldn't have been called in to find you. None of us would've been in the forest. Meaning none of us would have been at the cabin when Victor arrived. Jake would've been caught alone, with no knowledge Victor was coming for him. I don't want to think about how that might have ended."

Kate fell silent for a moment, staring outside. "It *was* a strange thing for me to do. Taking off like that. It went against everything I'd ever done in my life. Yet, it … felt right. Necessary, even. That's the only way I know how to describe it." She looked at him. "Do you understand what I mean?"

"Yeah, I do. I call it 'following my gut instinct'. But I'm sure there's probably a more scientific way to explain it."

She laughed. "I don't know. That's a pretty good explanation." She squeezed his hand, as her free hand went to where the amulet lay beneath her sweater. "There are still many mysteries in this world that we don't understand. And I find comfort in that."

CHAPTER FORTY-ONE

North Cascade Mountains, Washington (Day Ten)

Walker relaxed and soaked up the surrounding atmosphere as Carl drove his Jeep through the towering evergreens. The young man had volunteered to drive him and Nataya to a place that Steve had secured as lodging for them until he could get them on a plane back to Colorado. Walker had told Steve there was no rush, and he meant it. He and Nataya hoped for a few days of relaxation and then maybe some light exploring of the area. They were both still fascinated with the Pacific Northwest environment.

Carl turned the Jeep off the paved road onto a gravel drive, wove between trees and pulled up in front of a log cabin.

Walker turned in his seat. "This your place?"

Carl grinned and shook his head in the negative. "This is your lodging. It's yours for two weeks, secured and paid for by Steve Hicks and Dean McClure. It's stocked with everything you might need, firewood, food, drinks, and fishing equipment. Behind the cabin and down the hill is a river with a dock and rowboat. And I just happen to know someone who can point out all the best fishing spots." He laughed then.

A stunned Walker couldn't summon any words. He just stared.

"They wanted to do this as a thank you for all your time and effort. They both sincerely appreciate what you two did."

"Wow," Nataya managed to say. Then she looked at Carl. "But you were a part of our team. It wasn't just the two of us."

Carl's smile grew larger. "No worries. They found a way to thank me as well. Come on in and I'll show you around. My cabin is just down the way, so if you need anything, or a ride anywhere, you can just call me." He handed Walker the SAT phone. "I'll show you how to use it before I leave."

The three entered the small cabin and wandered around, checking everything out. Cozy and comfortable, Walker could tell Nataya adored it. The continual mental stress of the past hours made him yearn for rest. But more importantly, some much needed alone time with Nataya. He stared at the fireplace and found himself imagining a quiet evening with the two of them relaxing in front of a fire.

Carl showed Walker and Nataya how to use the SAT phone and then turned toward the door. "I'm going to leave you two to get settled."

"You're welcome to stay for some dinner, Carl," Nataya said.

"Thanks, but I want to get to my cabin, unload my gear, and get this trail dust washed off. Now that we're back in civilization, I'm feeling exceptionally grimy, to be honest." He laughed. Then he winked at Walker when Nataya wasn't looking.

Walker sat down in front of the fireplace, leaned back against the sofa, and stretched his legs out in front of him. He always had a difficult time leaving the wilderness, but the reward was the reminder of how wonderful a hot shower could be. This trip had been long, in terms of days, and the changes in weather and emotional stress had been intense, but the steamy water had washed away all the tension. And now the crackling of the fire encouraged his mind to unwind as well.

He glanced out the window to the gathering clouds, lit in shades of orange and pink by the setting sun. The colors were viewed in stripes as it was partitioned by tall tree trunks.

Nataya joined him then, her towel-dried hair left long and loose to finish drying by the fire. She had wrapped herself into a large fluffy robe she'd found hanging in the bath. "I feel like I'm in a movie, wearing something this luxurious."

Walker looked up at her and grinned. "You deserve to pamper yourself." He reached up and took her hand. She lowered her lithe body, curling up next to him with her feet tucked beneath the robe. He wrapped his arm around her, and she rested her head on his shoulder.

"Nice fire."

"Ummm. Thanks."

A moment of quiet passed, then she spoke. "I think Carl wants you to go fishing with him soon."

"Yeah, I got that impression as well."

She gave a soft laugh. "It would be a nice break for you both. And I wouldn't mind having some fresh trout to prepare." The fire hissed and popped for a few minutes before Nataya spoke again. "I think Carl and Katie will be a dynamic couple."

Walker turned to look at her, eyes wide. He couldn't decide if he was more surprised at the topic or the fact Nataya was engaging in this type of conversation. It wasn't like her at all. "You've already got them paired up as a couple?"

She leaned back to study him. "I think it's clear they're attracted to each other. Why else do you think Carl volunteered to go back up to the cabin in a few weeks to help Jake and Katie with their projects?"

"I don't know, maybe because he enjoys that type of work?"

Nataya smiled. "We'll see."

"You and Carl sure hit it off." It blurted out before he had a chance to censure it.

She looked at him with curiosity. "Because he and I talked together so much?"

"Yes, but more than that." Now that he'd opened the topic he reluctantly continued. "I guess I'd never seen you joke around and tease anyone like you did with him."

"Well, he is funny. Just seems to be who he is. I'll admit I did enjoy talking and sharing stories. It was ... different." She paused a moment before continuing, her tone softer. "When I was living alone in the wilderness, during my amnesia and before you found me, I learned to embrace the silence. Cherish it, even. And then you and I just picked up and continued from there, and it felt right. Being around Carl made me realize I sometimes miss those kinds of conversations, like Grandfather and I used to have ... discussions about our experiences and sharing stories. I guess I hadn't really thought about it much before."

Walker studied the flames dancing in the hearth. Did that mean Nataya wanted him to be more talkative? Scenes from their days on the trail flashed in and out of his mind ... new emotions to contend with ... new challenges he'd had to conquer. He started to speak, then stopped. He wasn't good at conversation, never had been.

Nataya shifted next to him. "There's something on your mind."

How did she read him so well? It was one of the qualities he loved about her. And one of the reasons they could communicate on so many levels without dialogue. But something new was happening here with their relationship. She seemed in the mood to speak her thoughts aloud. He took a deep breath and tried again. "There was a time, out on the trail, when I thought perhaps you were attracted to Carl."

She looked at him, eyes wide. "You did?"

He nodded.

Her face took on a thoughtful expression. "In hindsight I can see how all our conversations and joking must have looked to you." She studied Walker. "You never said anything."

"It took some getting used to … you being around another man, a younger man, one closer to your own age."

Nataya gave him a startled look. "I never thought about it that way." She paused, then asked, "Are you saying you were jealous?"

It was Walker's turn to be startled. He hesitated a moment, then decided maybe he should try sharing what had been troubling him. "I'll admit the thought crossed my mind." He was surprised at the weight that admission lifted from his heart when he uttered the words.

Nataya smiled. A soft, gentle, full of love smile. And her eyes held that gaze of deep devotion he'd always found so overwhelming.

She raised her arms to encircle his neck, the robe sliding off her shoulders, her lips close to his. "Well, then I believe I have some serious convincing to do … to prove that you are the only man for me."

As he pulled her into a kiss and lowered her to the rug, Walker decided that maybe this "having conversations" thing wasn't so bad after all.

CHAPTER FORTY-TWO

Skagit County, Washington (Day Twelve)

Steve Hicks kept his thoughts to himself as Daniel Night Hawk drove him through the reservation towards Richard Bright Star's place. He struggled to turn off the emotions that bombarded his brain.

Returning to the reservation brought back all the angst and frustration he'd battled during this case while dealing with the Bureau and the government's laws regarding the indigenous peoples here in Washington—or on any reservation in the country, for that matter. Sometimes it was mind-numbing in its absurdity.

Perhaps it was all the bureaucracy that had him fed up to the point where he had allowed himself to walk into that shadowy place of seeking justice versus following the strict rule of law. He shook his head to clear it. No. That was on him, and him alone.

He remembered then that for Dean McClure, one assignment in particular had been the turning point for the man. Maybe this case had been his big sign that it was time to reconsider his line of work.

Simply considering that option made him feel better, and he broke free of the angst. He decided to focus instead on the more positive outcomes of the case.

For one, Katie and Jake were staying on at the cabin to finish some much-needed work to fully winterize the place. He knew helping Jake and being out in nature would be the best healers for Katie. She was going to be fine. And although Carl had returned to his Wilderness Guide business, it was only for long enough to put things into order so he could join them in a few weeks.

Steve was sure Carl would be a big help to Jake with any labor-intensive chores. But he was sure Jake understood, as well as he did, that Katie was the bigger attraction. He knew his daughter well enough to see the young man had caught her attention. Steve had thought about it at some length and decided he couldn't think of a nicer guy for Katie to hang out with.

Daniel turned his vehicle into the familiar driveway, and Steve pulled his attention back into the moment. He glanced around Richard's property and noticed nothing had changed, that he could see, from when he first met Richard almost two weeks ago. Once again that same vibe washed over him. As if he'd stepped back in time. He closed his eyes for a moment and then opened them, only to find the same scene facing him.

Daniel parked his Bronco, turned off the engine and turned to Steve. "This is a good thing you're doing for the tribe. Bringing the amulet back to where it belongs."

"It's what Jake wants, and the Bureau doesn't need to know he had it all along, that it's not still missing. Besides, you and I promised Richard we'd do our best to return it." Steve looked down at the amulet, resting on a piece of soft buckskin. "I once asked you if you believed the amulet has powers, and you said it didn't matter what you thought, only what Victor thought."

Daniel remained quiet.

"But I'd like to know ... what you think."

Daniel stared out the windshield a moment before replying. "I stand by my first answer. It doesn't matter what I think. It's what you believe."

"Are you saying it only has power if I believe it has power?"

Daniel looked at him. "It's complicated."

Steve sighed out loud. "Somehow I knew you'd give me some abstruse answer." He smiled in resignation, wrapped the relic in the buckskin and put his hand on the door handle. "Let's do this."

Daniel led the way to the front porch where Richard waited in his rocker. A brightly colored wool handwoven blanket lay over his lap, covering his legs against the chill of the morning. He greeted them in his native language and Daniel answered.

Steve and Daniel each took a seat facing the old man.

Richard Bright Star surprised Steve by speaking in English. "You finally became the falcon. You and the hawk beat the coyotes."

"Yes, I guess we did."

"It took you long enough."

Steve smiled and gave a soft laugh. "Yeah, guess I'm a slow learner."

Richard's expression never changed, but he gave a guffaw that sounded like it could be a laugh. But when he spoke again his voice was somber. "Within the tribe you will be known as the 'falcon who hunts evil'."

A lump formed in Steve's throat, and he struggled to speak. "You honor me."

Daniel nudged him and he knew it must be time to hand the amulet back to the rightful owner. Richard would accept it on behalf of the tribe. Steve rose and gently handed the bundle to the old man, who took it and laid it on his lap.

Richard looked up at Steve and studied him for a long

moment. But Steve couldn't read the old man's eyes at all. How did he do that? Then Richard spoke in his native language, and behind him Steve heard Daniel translating.

He says, "Something has changed in your eyes, falcon who hunts evil. A fire still burns there, but it is now tempered."

Steve stared at the old man, stunned at the remark, but then answered. "Yeah, I guess that would be true. I'm seriously considering taking an early retirement from the Bureau."

The old man gave him a simple nod.

Steve returned to his seat next to Daniel. Richard began to speak again, with Daniel translating.

"He says he's glad that wrongs have been righted and justice done for Joseph Spirit Horse. And he is happy the 'man who fishes salmon' is safe. It is a good day."

Steve grinned at Richard and could swear that for one brief second, he thought he saw the hint of a smile on the old man's face.

EPILOGUE

Elk Meadows, Colorado

Walker leaned his elbows on the front porch railing of their Colorado log cabin and gazed out over the land before him. A scene he never tired of viewing. And never took for granted.

Nataya came out of the front door with a cup of coffee for each of them. Then she took up her position beside him and joined in his silent vigil.

The calm waters of the lake reflected the golds, scarlet, and orange of the surrounding woodlands, with a backdrop of the towering mountains beyond. He looked up to the clouds above the dark peaks, sunlit with vibrant streams of pink and purple as the sun began to dip to the mountain tops.

Walker lifted the cup to his lips, sipping at the steaming hot brew. "Thanks, it tastes especially good this evening."

She smiled. "Yes. I'd say Autumn has moved in to stay awhile."

They had returned home from the Pacific Northwest only a week ago, after spending two weeks at the cabin Steve and Dean had graciously reserved for them in the North Cascade Mountains. It had been a remarkable time filled with tranquility and the peacefulness often only found while secluded in nature. A time of exploration mixed with relaxation that had re-invigorated them. They were ready and eager for the Fall Survival Classes, which would resume later in the week.

Nataya broke the silence. "Carl called earlier, while you were down by the lake."

"Yeah? How's he doing?"

"Fine. He's still excited about the fact Steve and Dean gifted him with one of our wilderness courses as a thank you for his time and help. He wanted to know which course we would recommend as the best one for him. He wants to start planning for it well ahead of time, so he can line up people to cover for him with his clients. He sounded like a kid trying to wait for summer break from school."

Walker smiled and fingered the carved piece hanging from a leather thong at his neck. A trotting fox, carved from red jasper stone. And for the white tip of the tail, an inlay of howlite, or as his people sometimes referred to it, sacred buffalo or white turquoise. The piece had been gifted to him by Daniel Night Hawk as he and Nataya were leaving Washington to fly back to Colorado.

"Waahni Mia," Nataya whispered.

He turned to face her.

"Daniel went to considerable effort to honor our names."

"That he did," Walker replied. Daniel had also presented Nataya with a lovely miniature painting. It depicted a woman in a doeskin dress, dancing, especially appropriate since "Nataya" translated as "woman who dances."

Walker turned back to the scene in front of them, and they watched the sky change to a violet that expanded upward into indigo blue.

After a long moment, Nataya broke the silence with a soft voice. "You're still thinking about it, aren't you?"

Walker turned to her. "Thinking about what?"

"There."

Walker held her gaze, knowing all too well she referred to the wilderness they had so recently experienced while in the North Cascade Mountains of Washington. Indeed, he had found his dreams increasingly haunted by the memories. He simply nodded and turned to face the mountains again. But he heard her whisper.

"Me, too."

Acknowledgements

Readers are the lifeblood of writers. The Fox Walker Novels would go unread without your support. My sincere thanks and heartfelt gratitude to each of you.

Special acknowledgement to Carl LaCasse for sharing his experiences, expertise and knowledge of Search and Rescue operations, which add authenticity to this story.

Deepest gratitude and appreciation to Mark A. Clements as Content Editor. His feedback and suggestions were invaluable. Profound appreciation to Laura Taylor, my Editor for ASTRAY, for making sure readers enjoy a quality reading experience. And a big thank you to first readers, Carl LaCasse, and Andrew Helms.

Through all of the ups and downs of the writing life, one person is always there for me, encouraging and believing in me without fail. To Michael, my husband, I say, "To the moon and back, Babe."

Author Bio

Indy Quillen has always loved to write, but she took many side adventures along the path to publication, including raising a family while organic gardening and learning ancestry skills, owning and running a natural food store, training and competing in martial arts, and creating and selling nature-themed watercolors. She grew up in Indiana, lived in Colorado and in the San Diego area, and now resides with her husband in the Pacific Northwest. When she's not writing, or camping and practicing her bushcraft skills, she enjoys reading, gardening, traveling, hiking, bike riding and swimming.

Additional Books by the Author

TRACKER: A Fox Walker Novel

PURSUIT: A Fox Walker Novel

DUPLICITY: A Fox Walker Novel

REPUTATON: A Romantic Suspense Novel

From the Author

Thank you for reading ASTRAY: A Fox Walker Novel. If you enjoyed this story and I entertained you for a little while, I hope you'll consider giving it a rating or leave a review. Ratings and Reviews make it easier for other readers to find my books and enjoy them as well. Thank you for the consideration. I appreciate the kindness.

I enjoy connecting with my readers. Feel free to join me on Facebook (Indy Quillen) and Twitter (@IndyQuillen). Would you like to learn more about my ongoing quest to better my bushcraft and ancestral skills? Or maybe you'd like to be notified via email regarding upcoming sales and new book releases?

Use the info below to sign up for my Indy Quillen News & Updates Newsletter.

https://indyquillen.com/

Made in United States
North Haven, CT
28 October 2023

43310112R10183